M000047807

The
Tulip
Resistance

LYNNE LEATHAM ALLEN

An Imprint of Cedar Fort, Inc.
Springville, Utah

ISBN 13: 978-1-4621-1696-6

Published by Bonneville Books, an imprint of Cedar Fort, Inc.
2373 W. 700 S., Springville, UT 84663
Distributed by Cedar Fort, Inc., www.cedarfort.com

LIBRARY OF CONGRESS CATALOGING-IN-PUBLICATION DATA

Allen, Lynne, 1951-
The tulip resistance / Lynne Allen.
pages cm
ISBN 978-1-4621-1696-6 (perfect bound : acid-free paper)
1. World War, 1939-1945--Underground movements--Netherlands--Fiction. 2. Netherlands--History--German occupation, 1940-1945--Fiction. I. Title.
PS3601.L43254T85 2015
813'.6--dc23

2014045861

Cover design by Michelle May
Cover design © 2015 by Lyle Mortimer
Edited and typeset by Melissa J. Caldwell

Printed in the United States of America

10 9 8 7 6 5 4 3 2 1

Printed on acid-free paper

Dedicated to my friend Glenda,
for her hours of service and encouragement.

For Evil to flourish,
it only requires good men
to do nothing.

—Simon Wiesenthal

chapter ONE

April 1940

The two culprits crouched behind the splintered, weathered door, scheming against Bastiaan's know-it-all sister. Bastiaan chewed on his fingernails and spit them nervously into the air. His voice climbed to a high-pitched hysteria. "But she's my sister!"

"She'll forgive you. Sisters have to," Abram, Bastiaan's Jewish friend shot back. He peeked around the door again.

"Boy, getting up at four o'clock in the morning just to get even is downright spiteful!" Bastiaan scowled as he hunched over the chicken coop, half-scared of Abram's newest scheme.

"*Ja*, it gets you all fired up and the day seems a whole lot brighter already, doesn't it?" Abram said, peering up at Bastiaan.

"Ah, come on. You know how scared she is of that dumb cellar. We might give her a heart attack, even at her young age of fourteen."

"*Ja*," Abram retorted, his brown eyes gleaming.

"I don't know how I let you talk me into such things. Papa'll nail my hide to the wall and cuff your ears so hard they'll look like giant mushrooms on that cocky, pointed head of yours."

"Oh, he won't catch us. Besides your snitch of a sister needs some humbling. Maybe next time she won't humiliate us in front of the whole church social. Father Eisen wouldn't have known we put the alcohol in the punch if your sister hadn't tattled on us. I wouldn't trade it for the world though. The girls screaming with their tongues hanging out, and Jen Oberlson even puked!"

"Marieka can't help it. She's a girl," Bastiaan said, feeling an upsurge of guilt as his smile dissolved into a grimace.

"*Ja*, and flakey too. If she's stupid enough to mess with us older men of sixteen, then she should know we'd get even. Are you sure she milks at 4:00 a.m.? She's late!" Abram smirked, shaking his head.

"She'll be here. She has to. Papa gets her up if she isn't up by 3:30. Besides, she loves to milk Zippora." Bastiaan rolled his eyes and coughed. "But she's so superstitious about that cellar. It absolutely scares her, like it's haunted or something. I don't know if this is such a good idea."

"What's the story about it anyway? Why's she so terrified?" Abram asked.

Bastiaan frowned and stared at him thoughtfully. Then he replied, "Don't know. It means something to Papa, but he won't talk about it and gets mad if you ask him. So of course Marieka's imagination goes wild and thinks it's full of ghosts and demons out to get her."

"Who cares?" Abram shrugged again. "She's got it coming. Now get in there, or are you scared of it too?"

"No." Bastiaan flinched, trying to hold his voice steady, but looked away so Abram couldn't see his discomfort.

"She'll be here any minute. When I give you the signal, moan a bit and rattle the door. That'll teach her. She'll screech like old lady Carlson when the mouse ran across her feet during Father Eisen's sermon. I think he was talking about Paul's account of how women aren't supposed to be heard in church." Abram laughed. "I sure had a difficult time convincing the rabbi I hadn't converted to being a Christian. I told him I just like the social aspect, the girls. He didn't like it. He told me to stay away from your church and to always wear my kippa[1] and be proud I'm Jewish because 'Divine Presence' is always over my head." Abram liked rubbing in the "Divine Presence" part to Bastiaan. He was always reminding Bastiaan that Abram was one of the chosen people, as if he were higher up in God's eyes. But Bastiaan didn't mind. Abram had been his friend since they were three.

"You don't think it'll be too much?" Bastiaan asked with trepidation. Chestnut curls fell across his smooth, wide forehead as he ducked his six-foot frame through the chicken coop door. Dark lashes covered salient brown eyes looking down with anguish. His flawless bronze complexion sported the bashful smile of an awkward teenager about to dishonor his sister.

Abram was several inches shorter. His semetic-shaped nose, though

1. *Jewish skull cap*

slightly oversized for his oval shaped face added to his handsome Jewish features. His dark eyes were alive and sparkled with mischief. His mouth curled into an impish grin. "No, a little fear never hurt anybody. It makes them humble," he said, peering up at Bastiaan.

MARIEKA PULLED ONE strap of Bastiaan's hand-me-down overalls over her shoulder. She was tall and slender. She kept her mahogany-brown hair in one long braid that went to the small of her back. Her eyes were the same dark color of her father's, but her smile was the beautiful curvature and full lips of her mother's. She yawned in the dark and then headed for the barn. She flipped the single braid of her dark hair to the back and approached the pen where the old Jersey, Zippora, and her calf were. Her feet slid inside the worn oversized boots as she walked into the frost-covered coral. She felt like an elephant on the frozen mud. It took all her concentration to keep from doing the splits or landing on her backside while herding Zippora into the barn. Every time Marieka got two steps away from the cow, she would do a "Hans Brinker" and dodge her as skillfully as the old boy himself in a tight turn on ice. She could almost hear the rotten beast laugh.

"You know, Zippora, if I thought throwing a fit would take the miserable out of you, I would scream louder than Thor, the God of Thunder, in your ear. Maybe you wouldn't be so high and mighty then. So get into that barn before I do something you'll regret."

ABRAM CLAMPED A hand over his mouth to stifle his laughter as he watched Marieka through the splintered slats of the chicken coop. Bastiaan told him it would take her about twenty minutes to milk, and then she would head for the chicken coop where the old cellar neighbored the shed. According to the plan, she'd come out the side door, see the cellar door, and side step it as usual. That would be the signal for Bastiaan to groan and rattle the door, and wail and screech like the hounds of Hades had been let loose.

"Poor old Marieka won't have anywhere to run except in place," Abram snickered. "I can't wait to see the snooty tattletale's face turn several shades of pale. It serves you right."His voice turned to a whisper. "I'll teach you to mess with me."

At twenty past four, Marieka stepped over the plank at the bottom of the door. She slammed the bucket of milk onto the frozen ground, sloshing it over the side, and then headed for the hay. She found the pitchfork next to the fence, stabbed it roughly into the fodder, and threw it angrily over the fence.

"It looks like she's already mad enough to eat a bucket of nails and spit them out at the first poor misfit she sees," Abram whispered. "Maybe it's not such a good idea to mess with her right now." His voice rose as his eyes darted to Bastiaan and back to Marieka. "When it comes to a woman's temper, I'm out of here," Abram cringed.

Abram felt queasy as he watched her use the pitchfork as a weapon of anger.

His breathing quickened as he backed away from the now too revealing door. He stepped in a pile of chicken poop scattered throughout the coop. His formerly arrogant features had entwined with panic and disgust. He balanced on one foot while vigorously shaking the other to dislodge the slimy goo. In the process he twisted his ankle and did a balancing act that teetered on the edge of humiliation.

Abram tried to steady himself by putting his hand on the first thing he could find, which was the face of fat brown hen. It flew at the defenseless trespasser with the fury of a depraved harpy. He threw up his hands to deflect the bird but lost his balance and fell into the watering pan. He cried out as he tried to pull the enraged fowl from his face with one hand while the other he placed on the floor to steady himself, in yet another pile of chicken poop.

Upon hearing what he thought was the signal, Bastiaan wailed like an ailing banshee with a bellyache. His fingers curled around the edge of the decaying door and shook it with the ferocity of a rabid beast.

Marieka was standing in front of the cow's pen and jumped when she heard the unearthly commotion. She wondered what had possessed the chickens. Her breath caught in her throat; she feared the cellar had been opened somehow and had released the demons of hell onto the unsuspecting world. Then she heard a string of explicit swear words in a voice she recognized.

"What? What's going on?" she called.

Abram pushed the chicken coop door open and fell face-first onto the hideout's covering. His hair was strewn with straw, splotches of poop covered his clothes, a red streak was slashed across his cheek, and it looked as if he'd wet his pants.

Bastiaan started wailing, "Let me out of here!" as if he had been buried alive. He tried to move the decayed door, but it wouldn't budge. All the while, Abram was squealing like a baby pig with a possessed chicken attacking him.

Marieka cupped her hands over her nose and a hiccupped giggle escaped her throat. Tears rolled down her cheeks as she laughed breathlessly. She migrated toward the bumbling duo. Abram kicked the air and flailed his arms to get rid of the crazed bird while Bastiaan kept screaming to be let out of the dungeon.

"What are you two doing? Why are you out here at four o'clock in the morning?" Marieka asked, trying to control her laughter.

Abram clutched the chicken with both hands and finally propelled it through the air like a feathered cannon ball. He got on his hands and knees and crawled to the side of the barn where he stood with a puckish grin on his face. Bastiaan heaved the door, almost ripping it from its hinges, gasping for air as if he had been drowning. He climbed out of the old cellar and huddled together with Abram, with unabashed grin. Each pointing to the other, denying their own guilt.

When Marieka realized she was supposed to be the recipient of their foul play, her laughter turned to fury, and she shrieked a few select high-pitched words. She picked up a handful of rocks and threw them at the two delinquents.

"Oh, cut it out, Marieka! Can't you take a joke?" Bastiaan cried. "We were just going to teach you not to go blabbering to Father Eisen on us anymore."

"It's no joke to mess around with that old cellar," she shouted, grabbing another handful of rocks. "You half-brained nitwits. I hope you go where you will eat hot coals for eternity and your tongues thirst forever!" She threw the rocks at their hand-covered gaunt faces.

"Wow, Marieka. We were just kidding! Calm down!" Bastiaan wailed.

"What's going on here?" Hendrick Coevorden asked as he stepped onto the back porch, sipping a cup of tea.

"Am I ever glad to see you, Papa," Bastiaan said, crouched behind Abram. "Marieka has gone crazy on us! Tell her to calm down."

"Bastiaan and Abram thought it would be funny to scare the wits out of me, but they foiled their own plan, and I am just giving them what they deserve!" Marieka yelled. She bent down for another handful of dirt.

"Abram, you have business here?" Mr. Coevorden asked, looking sternly at him.

"Um, no, sir." Abram coughed and moved away from Bastiaan.

"Then I suggest you head for home if you don't want to be put to work." Hendrick set the cup of tea down on the wicker table by the door and walked toward the three kids.

"Uh, yes, sir, Mr. Coevorden. I'm out-a-here." Abram wasted no time heading down the road.

"Marieka, did you get the milking done?" Hendrick demanded with a stern look.

"Yes, Papa," Marieka said as she picked up the bucket of milk.

"Then get the eggs gathered and get to your delivering."

"Yes, Papa." Marieka headed for the house.

"Bastiaan, I'll deal with you later. Get the wood chopped. After breakfast, I want you to go into town and have Mr. Heingle fix the D-ring on the harness. It didn't fare the winter well. Now get to work."

Bastiaan turned away quickly so that Papa couldn't see the smile spread across his face. *If going to see Eilsa at Mr. Heingle's store is Papa's idea of punishment, I'll take it any time,* he thought.

Bastiaan looked into the grid glass window of the door in Heingle's store and scanned the room for Eilsa. His eyes dropped as he opened the door and the old bell rang, announcing his presence. He caught the familiar whiff of leather and soap, stirring the wistful memories of visits here with his papa when Bastiaan was a child. *Mr. Heingle's store never changes,* he thought as he looked at the tools above the counter. He remembered Mr. Heingle mussing his hair with his large calloused hands, then squatting down and looking him square in the eyes and asking, "Would you like to be the first to sample a piece of candy from my jars on the counter?"

Of course he did. Bastiaan smiled to himself remembering how his eyes would light up and he'd politely say, "Oh, yes, sir!" Then Mr. Heingle would let him choose any piece of candy he wanted. He always chose the red ones because they tasted like cherries.

Bastiaan approached the counter; his heart quickened when he saw Eilsa coming from the back. He looked past her at the new tools on the wall in an effort to hide his discomfort. He noticed an impish smile cross her face and disappear as she said, "Sir, what may I help you with today?

"Uh . . ." Bastiaan cleared his throat, took his hat off, and twisted it in his hands. "Is your father around? I have a harness that is in urgent need of fixing."

She smiled politely. "He's in the back. I'll get him."

She disappeared through the curtains and a moment later Mr. Heingle appeared.

"Ah, young Bastiaan. What can I do for you today?"

"Papa sent me to see if you could fix this harness, sir. He said it's awfully important."

"Well, young Bastiaan, I'll get right on it. Have a seat. I'll send Eilsa to get you a soda while you wait."

"Thanks. That's very kind of you, sir," Bastiaan said and took a seat at the only table. Two farmers, Mr. Husselman and Mr. Veltman, often used the little table for playing checkers. They were known to spend their afternoons here playing with half the village watching.

Bastiaan took off his hat just as Eilsa appeared through the curtains, tray in hand, with the soda. She set a glass and the open bottle in front of him. He squirmed as the rose fragrance of her hair reached him when she leaned over the table. He cleared his throat and coughed. "Uh, thanks." Eilsa smiled, suppressing a giggle, and skirted away.

Bastiaan sighed in frustration, berating himself for his awkwardness.

The bell on the door jingled; two old farmers wearing bib overalls and faded shirts entered. They were talking loudly and seemed to be arguing as they walked over to the little table where Bastiaan was sitting. Mr. Veltman cleared his throat and frowned. Bastiaan jumped up and offered them the table. The two nodded at him without a smile and sat down.

"Johan," Pieter Husselman said in his low, angry voice, "I hear tell that the Germans are invading other countries. I'm afraid we're going to see war."

"No, we won't. We're a neutral country."

"I tell you, we are not safe," Pieter argued.

"What makes you think so? I think you must be tipping the bottle too much or you're getting a little daft."

"Rumors of war are spreading. It has been reported in the newspapers. You ought to try reading them once in a while." Pieter's voice rose.

Bastiaan was listening so intently that he jumped when the bell jingled again and another couple of farmers entered.

"Agardas," Johan called, "Pieter here says we are about to be invaded by Germany. What do you think?"

"Have you not heard?" one farmer answered. "Germany invaded Norway and Denmark yesterday. Denmark surrendered that very day but the Norwegians are trying to hold out. Do you think we're next, Pieter? It would be a dark day for this country if such a thing were to happen."

Mr. Heingle startled Bastiaan when he came up behind him and said, "Your harness is done." He had been listening so intently to the conversation that he had forgotten why he was there.

"Let me know if you need any more help. Tell your Papa I'll get with him later on the bill."

"Oh thanks, Mr. Heingle," Bastiaan said as he picked up the harness. He dawdled toward the door, hesitant to leave and miss the farmers' conversation.

"Oh, Bastiaan, have a piece of candy for your journey home," Mr. Heingle said, jar in hand.

Bastiaan's face lit up and then he frowned. He wasn't a boy anymore; he didn't need candy. Besides, he didn't want Eilsa to think he was childish by taking a piece of candy like a little kid.

"Uh . . . no thanks, Mr. Heingle. Got to get home," he said, stealing a look in the direction of Eilsa.

Mr. Heingle glanced to where Bastiaan was looking and tried to hide a knowing smile behind his hand.

"Good-bye, Mr. Heingle."

Bastiaan walked home slowly, thinking about the old farmers' conversation. It disturbed him. They had to be wrong. It had to be stories of senile old men who had nothing better to do than spread gossip.

He decided they didn't know what they were talking about and hurried home with a lighter step. He didn't know whether to repeat the wild story to his father or to keep it to himself. His father may reprove him for listening in on others' conversations and then repeating the foolish rumors. Bastiaan decided it was best to keep such things to himself.

"Ah, Mr. Heingle did a fine piece of welding on this D-ring!" Papa said. "Let's hook up the team. I'm anxious to get to work. I hope the sun has melted the frost," Papa said as he and Bastiaan harnessed Nyes and Bet. As if on signal, the horses shook their manes simultaneously to adjust their collars.

Papa frowned. "Winter was too long this year. If we don't get this field plowed, we'll be late planting and risk the chance of a late harvest and an early frost."

ANNA COEVORDEN WAS in the kitchen preparing breakfast. "Marieka!" she called. "Get the cream separated and put it in the churn. You're running late this morning. Tell Mrs. Berg and Miss Remi you had a mishap again and are short of milk."

"Oh, Mama, they will think I'm a half-wit."

"Can't be helped. Just tell them they'll have more in a couple of days."

"Yes, Mama."

Marieka opened the lid on the container of cream and poured it in the churn. When the yellow curds of butter appeared, she shaped them into round balls, wrapped them in cheesecloth, and then stacked the butter in the basket behind the seat on her bicycle. She filled two one-gallon metal cans with the morning's milk, dividing it evenly between Mrs. Berg and Miss Remi, and loaded it into the basket along with two dozen eggs for Mr. Buskirk. She covered the basket with a small blanket and waved to her mama. "Be back soon."

The fields, green with the first whisperings of spring and the awakening tulips, were breathtaking as Marieka pulled away from her home. She could smell the scent of the Netherlands's famous blooms while lost in thought, peddling slowly along the canal's animating sedge.

Marieka's first stop was to a paint-chipped house encircled by a picket fence in need of repair and a whitewash.

"Aren't they beautiful!" Miss Remi, the middle-age spinster, said, walking up behind her. "I dig up the bulbs and sell them to Mr. Heingle, who in turn sells them for distribution throughout the world. Papa has been selling tulip bulbs for years, but with him being down with a stroke, I have been unable to harvest as he did, so I have had to turn to selling eggs and taking in mending to help out."

"Your tulips are the most beautiful in all of Holland. I love to ride by here in the spring. Their beauty is breathtaking," Marieka said, handing the can of milk to Miss Remi.

Miss Remi, a long-time Jewish friend and neighbor of the Coevordens, smiled, her blue eyes twinkling. She thanked Marieka and reached for the milk can.

"It feels light today."

"Yes, I had an accident this morning," Marieka said. "It's half the price."

"Oh dear, I will have to be careful using it then. Thank you, Marieka. I hope there will be more next time. See you in a couple of days."

Waving good-bye to Miss Remi, Marieka headed toward Ede to make the rest of her deliveries.

Marieka leaned her bike against Mrs. Berg's picket fence and hoped she would be as good-natured as Miss Remi was about the missing milk. She walked to the front door and rang the bell.

A medium-height woman with an ample figure answered the door. "Hello, ma'am," Marieka said. She started to explain about the lost milk as she handed the gallon can to Mrs. Berg.

"Oh, the can feels lighter today. Marieka, is there a problem?"

"No, ma'am. Just an accident while milking this morning. I am sorry there isn't as much milk today."

"Oh dear," Mrs. Berg said as she jerked the milk can out of Marieka's hand. "Please, Marieka, be more careful so such accidents don't happen."

"Yes, ma'am," Marieka said. "Mama said it is half today."

"As well it should be. I hope there will be more next time."

The rich fragrance of bread met Marieka's nose when she walked into the bakery. Mr. Buskirk, a short, fat older man with a ring of gray hair, reminded her of her plump, loving grandfather. She wondered if it was an unwritten law for all bakers to wear a white uniform, with aprons smeared with jam, cinnamon, and frosting. Mr. Buskirk was taking several round loaves of bread out of the oven with a large wooden paddle. "Ah, little Marieka." He smiled. "How nice to see you today. Have you some of your sweet butter for me?"

"Yes, and two dozen eggs."

"Good, good. Have a seat and enjoy one of my fresh pastries."

Marieka stared into the glass case displaying the delicious pastries.

"So many decisions," Mr. Buskirk said. "They all look so good, eh?"

"Oh, yes. Which one shall I choose?"

"May I suggest the banketletter. It's an almond pastry. I just took it out of the oven, and it's still warm. They melt in your mouth and your taste buds beg for more even while you are eating." Mr. Buskirk chortled.

"Oh, yes. That's what I want!"

Mr. Buskirk chuckled and handed a pastry to Marieka. She sat at a small table and ate it voraciously.

"Enjoy, my little Marieka. I could not have such delicious pastries without your wonderful butter."

"Then I will always bring my butter, if you will always make such delicious pastries."

"It's a deal." Mr. Buskirk chuckled again.

Just then, the door opened and Mrs. Eman came in, her hands and arms shaking.

"Ah, Mrs. Eman. How are you this fine morning?"

"Have you not heard the German's bombed the Norwegian ports and invaded Denmark yesterday?" she asked as she handed Mr. Buskirk twenty-five duits. "We will be next. We will, I just know it."

"Now, Mrs. Eman, calm down. You are listening to the tales of prattling gossips again. Why would the Germans want our little Netherlands? We have nothing to offer them. You worry yourself for no reason." Mr. Buskirk patted her hand.

"Do you really think so, Mr. Buskirk?" she said, wiping her tears with a handkerchief.

"Do not fear. Now would you like your usual today?"

"Yes, thank you. And thank you for your kind words. I will go home feeling better. You have a gentle way."

"Have a good day, Mrs. Eman, and stay away from the gossips," Mr. Buskirk clucked.

Marieka finished her last bite. "Good-bye, Mr. Buskirk," she said and hurried out the door. She wondered if it was true that Germany invaded those countries. *Would we be next? And was it true that the Netherlands had nothing to offer the Germans so they would not bother us? Why was Germany invading other countries?* Her mind spun as she hopped on her bike and headed home.

Marieka left her bike at the back door and hurried into the tiny kitchen. "Mama, did you hear? Germany invaded Denmark and the Norwegian ports yesterday. Is it true, Mama?"

"Where did you hear such things?"

"At Mr. Buskirk's bakery. Mrs. Eman came in upset and told Mr. Buskirk. But Mr. Buskirk said it was a tale of wagging tongues and not to believe it. Oh, what if it is true, Mama?"

"Marieka, you mustn't listen to gossip. It's the devil's work."

"But, Mama, I wasn't. There are so many who are scared and saying the same thing in the village."

"Marieka," her mother said, scolding. "Do not believe such tales. Now, put your bike away and get to your studies. They are waiting for you. You are late as usual."

"Yes, Mama."

Anna Coevorden stood in silence after Marieka left. There were stories of the Germans invading Poland. France and Great Britain had declared war on Germany, but the Dutch government issued a declaration of neutrality. Surely, the Germans would honor such a declaration. *I need to get busy and not worry about such things,* she thought.

The next week Marieka heard a broadcast on the radio while at Mr. Buskirk's bakery saying that Germany had invaded the Netherlands on May 10, 1940, without a declaration of war. The Netherlands had surrendered five days later. "We will all became subject to the invaders now with a new government and new imposed laws," Marieka said. Mr. Buskirk looked sad but didn't say any comforting words.

chapter TWO

July 1940

The rainbow-colored tulip fields lay dormant, their yellowed leaves expired, as if reflecting the oppressive spirit of Holland. The spirit, like the beauty of the fields, wilted with the onslaught of the German takeover.

All was quiet at Miss Remi's. The chickens and pig were gone from the yard. Marieka parked her bike next to the fence as Miss Remi opened the door holding a cloth to her cheek.

"Miss Remi, what happened? Where are your chickens and pig?"

Miss Remi pulled Marieka inside and shut the door. "The Germans came. They said they had a right to confiscate the pig and chickens to feed their army. I protested but one of them struck me."

"Oh, Miss Remi, how awful. And your father?"

"He is all right. They didn't search the house because they were more interested in the chickens and the pig." Miss Remi's hand shook as she took the milk can from Marieka.

"Do you have enough food?" Marieka asked.

"We have enough for a few days. I don't dare go into Ede to buy food. We are Jews you know."

"So?"

"The Germans hate Jews. I've heard rumors of the mistreatment of Jews in other countries."

Marieka's face darkened, "They are only rumors."

Marieka took Miss Remi to the kitchen, rinsed the cloth with cool water, and put it on her cheek.

"Miss Remi, my mama will be by tomorrow to check on you. She has been concerned about your papa and will be very upset with what happened here today."

"Thank you, Marieka. You are so kind. Maybe you shouldn't go to the village today." Miss Remi frowned.

"I have to deliver milk to Mrs. Berg and Mr. Buskirk's butter. I'll be okay."

"Be careful, Marieka. There are so many Germans around."

Yes, on the outside the village does appear to be the same as usual, with the exception of German soldiers everywhere. Marieka thought as she hurried to Mrs. Berg's and rang the bell. Mrs. Berg answered and seemed startled to see her. "Well, hello, Marieka. You are early today. Put the milk on the kitchen table," she ordered curtly.

Marieka sat the milk down and heard an unfamiliar male voice: "Griet, I am waiting."

Marieka turned around and looked wide-eyed at Mrs. Berg.

Mrs. Berg shoved her to the door and pushed her out. "It's none of your affair, missy."

"Yes, ma'am," Marieka said and left.

Delicious aromas met Marieka when she opened the door to the bakery. Four uniformed German soldiers were at the counter giving their breakfast orders to Mr. Buskirk. After giving Mr. Buskirk their orders, they sat down at the small table at the front.

Mr. Buskirk's hands shook as he set a teacup in front of each soldier and poured the steaming brew. The men spoke in German and ignored Mr. Buskirk as he finished and slipped quietly into the back.

Startled, Marieka stared at the soldiers for a moment and then tried to step past them. The tall, handsome blond soldier stood in front of her, blocking her path.

"Ah, what do we have here?" the handsome man said in Dutch looking down his nose at her. "A *Fräulein* has come to visit."

Marieka let out a gasp, clutched her blouse, and tried to step past him.

"What do you have, *Fräulein?* Are you bringing supplies for the German soldiers?" His voice dripped with sarcasm.

"Lieutenant Schmidt, leave the girl be," the older soldier barked in German.

The handsome soldier frowned and sat down, reluctant to follow the order. "You must forgive the rude behavior of my lieutenant," the older officer said in broken Dutch. "Do you have business here, Fräulein?"

"Yes, sir. I am delivering eggs and butter to Mr. Buskirk."

"Ah, that is good! So Mr. Buskirk can make more of these delicious pastries. Do not be afraid. You are free to go."

"Thank you, sir." Marieka headed toward the kitchen.

"Good morning, Mr. Buskirk," she said warily, setting the butter and eggs on the workbench. Mr. Buskirk looked up, his eyes questioning if she was okay.

Marieka didn't lift her face to his, fearing he would see the tears running down her cheeks. She didn't linger as usual but bade him a good morning and left. She trembled as she walked past the German soldiers again. They looked up at her but said nothing.

Outside, Marieka leaned against the side of the bakery and breathed a sigh of relief.

The lieutenant raised his brows, tilted his head toward the colonel, and grinned. "Ah, she is a pretty little Fräulein, huh?"

Colonel Heinrich Boere looked at him with a stern expression. "Lieutenant Schmidt, may I remind you of our orders? We are not to harass the Dutch people. We do not interfere in their affairs and terrorize them. Is that clear?"

Lieutenant Schmidt cleared his throat, his steely-blue eyes smoldering. "Yes, sir."

The soldiers asked for more tea and talked leisurely for half the morning. "Would you like anything else, sirs?" Mr. Buskirk asked, stammering.

Lieutenant Schmidt opened his mouth to harass the old baker but decided against it when he saw Colonel Boere's face.

Colonel Boere nodded to the old man and said, "You are dismissed."

A slight smile touched the corners of Mr. Buskirk's mouth. He let out an audible sigh and quickly disappeared into the back.

Colonel Boere leaned back, his hand curled around the teacup, and listened to Corporal Muller's story of getting tricked into milking a farm animal when he was a child. ". . . they didn't tell me it was a bull."

Colonel Boere laughed. "Don't you know the difference between a bull and a heifer?"

"Yes, in the daytime when I'm sober," he said and laughed.

The Germans had finished their breakfast when they heard gunfire coming from outside. They sprang to their feet, hands on their weapons, and ran out of the bakery. An eerie mood hung in the air; everyone stood immobilized. Two old women were across the street huddled together, whimpering like scared children. A middle-aged man was in the middle of the street with his supplies scattered in front of him, while a German soldier was shooting at his feet, saying, "Dance, you Jewish pig."

"Judging from the frightened faces, that private has succeeded in scaring half the town," Colonel Boere remarked. He stiffened as he watched the soldier and then barked, "Cease this behavior! Leave the Jew be. Get back to your duties. Now!"

The private placed his weapon on his shoulder, stood at attention, saluted, and turned on his heel, leaving the Jewish man alone in the street with his scattered food.

Colonel Boere yelled at the Jew, "Leave, or I will finish what my private started!" The Jew quickly picked up his spilled supplies and ran down the street. Lieutenant Schmidt drew his pistol and aimed it at the Jew's back. "Click," he said, sneering, and then laughed as he put the gun back in the holster. The other two soldiers joined in making fun of the Jew, but Colonel Boere did not. He failed to see the humor in another man's misery.

Bastiaan stood in front of the cracked mirror in the tiny bathroom and combed his thick curly hair. He dressed in his best shirt, which had seen better days, but thought he looked rather handsome in and hoped it would catch Eilsa's attention.

Marieka walked past the open door, leaned back and whistled, "Wow, look at you! Where are you going, Mr. Spiffy?"

Bastiaan shut the door. "Never mind, Miss Nosey!"

"Oh, you've got a date," Marieka said as she pushed the door back.

"I do not!"

"With Eilsa? Ooo."

"I don't either. If you must know, I'm going to the dance at Mr. Meijr's barn."

"Oh, *ja*, I remember it. Papa said I can't go because I have to milk so early. He said next time he would milk so I could go. Is Eilsa going to be there?" Marieka taunted.

"How would I know? Mind your own business!" Bastiaan snapped.

"Aha, I hit a raw nerve."

"You better get out of here before I cut off your braid," Bastiaan growled as he grabbed his papa's straight razor.

"Can't you take a little teasing? Boy, you sure are touchy when it comes to Eilsa."

Bastiaan headed toward Marieka with the razor. She stepped behind the door, slammed it on his hand, and ran off shrieking and giggling into the kitchen. Bastiaan ran after her.

Marieka ran behind Anna and yelled, "Mama, protect me!"

"Leave Marieka be," Anna said, her voice rigid. "I don't know, Bastiaan. I don't like it. You can get into a lot of trouble at night with the Germans around."

"Oh, Mama, you worry too much. The Germans have left us alone so far. Besides, I'm going with Abram so I won't be alone."

"Abram is a good boy, but he's Jewish. That's asking for trouble."

"Ah, Mama. We're just going to have fun."

"I still don't like it. I would rather you stay home where I know you are safe."

Bastiaan chuckled. "Don't worry. I'll be fine. Be home around eleven."

His feet flew over the dirt road faster than a lovesick bull. He could hear the music a mile away. Bastiaan imagined the couples doing the swing, with their legs stomping, skirts flying, and the old folks standing around complaining about how wicked the younger generation had become.

Outside the barn door, Bastiaan stopped to catch his breath. The Netherlands's Dance Band provided the music with a guitar, a saxophone, a bass, and drums. In the center, several couples were doing the swing. Bastiaan swept the line of girls and then the dance floor for Eilsa. He finally spotted her dancing with Larz Leigma. Larz was a year older and bigger than Bastiaan and always enjoyed making fun of him. Bastiaan's mood plummeted like the temperatures of an arctic breeze in the desert. He watched Eilsa's golden hair bob to the rhythm of the music, her face aglow. Her eyes didn't leave Larz's face.

Bastiaan's shoulders slumped. He turned to get lost in the crowd when his energetic friend came up behind him and poked him in the ribs. "Hey," Abram said. "I wasn't sure if you were going to make it, buddy."

Bastiaan turned, saw Abram wearing his Jewish kippa, and growled. "Hey, you promised no Jewish stuff tonight."

"Look around. Do you see any Germans?"

"Well, no, but that hat is bad news."

"Don't worry. I'll hide it if we run into any Germans." Abram laughed.

"No, get rid of it now!" Bastiaan grabbed for Abram's cap.

"Nah, it'll be fine," Abram said, adjusting his kippa. "I've worn it forever. I'd feel naked without it."

Bastiaan scowled. "I don't like it. It's asking for trouble. I just hope the Germans don't see it and sweep the floor with you in it."

"Oh, stop worrying. Let's have some fun. There's a line of girls over there that look like they're dying to dance. Let's go ask them."

"No, you go ahead. I'll just watch for a while."

"What's wrong with you?" Abram demanded and then saw Bastiaan's eyes following Eilsa on dance floor. "Oh, I get it. Larz stole your girl, huh?"

"She's not my girl!"

"And of all the boys to steal her!" Abram taunted.

"He didn't steal her. He can't steal what I don't have," Bastiaan murmured. "Besides, she looks happy."

"Ah, come on, Bastiaan. There are other girls. Don't blow our fun tonight mooning over Eilsa. Let's help those girls flip some skirts!"

Abram always had a smooth line in his hat and a smile in his pocket when it came to girls. He crossed the dance floor and approached the girls. They elbowed each other, pushing their way to the front, each wanting to be the first asked to dance.

Abram danced with every girl in the barn with the exception of Adrie Wasselman. Every time he tried to ask her to dance, she'd disappear behind the stack of straw or behind the refreshment table.

Abram shrugged. "Okay, if you don't want to dance with the most handsome guy in the place and the best dancer of the century, I'll just find a girl who will."

Finally, drained and out of breath, Abram searched for Bastiaan and found him sitting on a bale of straw, sulking.

"Are you going to sit here the whole night?" Abram asked. "Why don't you take a turn with the girls over there? They're pretty, ready, and willing. I'll bet they'd love to dance with a good-looking guy like you. I can't keep them all happy." Abram grinned.

Bastiaan looked at him out of the corner of his eye and grunted. "Leave me alone."

"Okay, but you'll have more fun if you'd just get over it and dance. Hey, let's have some refreshments," Abram said, spotting the punch bowl. He returned a few moments later with a glass of pink liquid and sat next to Bastiaan. His feet tapped annoyingly to the beat of the music.

"Darn it, Abram. You're bugging me."

Abram laughed and punched Bastiaan on the arm. "Can't let good music go to waste."

"Why don't you make yourself scarce? Go ask one of those willing girls to dance again," Bastiaan said and walked off.

Bastiaan headed toward the refreshment table but kept his eye on Eilsa. "She looks like she's sweet on that guy." He scowled, cranking his head toward the dance floor and not watching where he was going. He stepped on Adrie Wasselman's foot.

"Um . . . I'm sorry," Bastiaan said, looking into the bluest eyes he'd ever seen. "Adrie? Is that you?" he asked, unable to take his eyes away. Her long dark hair framed a delicate childlike face and fell in soft curls to her waist. She wore a pink cotton summer dress that warmed her creamy, flawless complexion. Bastiaan felt like he could melt when she smiled. He sucked in his breath. *She's beautiful,* he thought.

Adrie spun around to make a hasty retreat, but Bastiaan touched her hand. "Wait, don't go. You . . . you . . . you are so . . . what happened to you? Uh, I mean, you are all grown up . . ."

Adrie blushed and turned to leave.

"Wait, don't go."

Adrie ducked her head, hiding the blush that crept across her cheeks. "Oh, I shouldn't have come. I'd better go."

"Go? Go where?"

Adrie tried to slip behind the refreshment table, but Bastiaan blocked her retreat.

"Wait. I'm not having much fun either. Would you like to go outside and sit?"

"Um . . . I guess it wouldn't hurt."

Bastiaan awkwardly wound through the crowd with Adrie right behind. "Excuse me, may we get through?" What little confidence he had disappeared when he tripped on the bale of straw holding the door open. He could feel his ears turning red as he looked at Adrie. He brushed away an imaginary piece of straw from his shirt, trying to act audacious, and croaked, "Would you like to sit down?"

"Uh, *ja*, but where?"

Bastiaan pointed to the bales of straw that neatly lined the entrance on each side of the doors and said, "A throne for a queen." Adrie giggled softly and sat down under the lantern over the door.

Bastiaan sat next to her, fidgeting. Then he finally asked, "Where have you been? I haven't seen you since grade school."

"I haven't been to school for a long time," Adrie whispered.

"Oh? How come?"

"When Papa died, Mama needed my help with sewing orders, so she took me out of school to help. Mama says I need to get out and make friends. She thought coming to this dance would be an excellent opportunity for me."

Alfie Whittendom walked by, frowning, the smell of cigarette smoke lingering around him.

Adrie shrank and slid away from Bastiaan. She turned her head and continued, "She tried to teach me schooling at home. I didn't have hardly any contact with people, so I got scared to talk to anyone."

"You're here tonight. I think you are doing a great job talking," Bastiaan encouraged. "You're not hiding under the refreshment table."

"When Mama realized her mistake, she sent me to work part-time at Mrs. Digby's Boarding House," Adrie said shyly.

"Did you like that?"

"Sort of. After a while, I helped with cleaning and fixing meals, but serving the guests really scared me. Now Mama thinks I need to meet boys. I told her I didn't want to meet boys, but she kept insisting." Adrie's voice shook as she looked at Bastiaan out of the corner of her eye.

"What's wrong with boys? We're a heck of a lot of fun."

"She says boys make wonderful friends, but they only frighten me."

"Well, I think I'm a good friend . . . to Abram. We've been friends since we were three. Why don't you ask Abram if I'm a good friend?"

"Oh no, I couldn't do that. I believe you. Besides, Abram is a little too . . . uh . . . loud for me," Adrie said, cringing.

Bastiaan laughed. "That's a nice way of saying he is loud and obnoxious."

Adrie nodded and laughed softly.

"Would you like another drink of punch?" Bastiaan offered. "The bugs are getting too friendly out here."

"Oh, no thanks. I've had enough."

Bastiaan looked toward the sky. "I like a full moon. It's great when I have to sneak home at night," he said.

"Sneak home? What are you doing out so late that you have to sneak home?"

"It's nothing bad. I just go to the church to the youth meetings. Pastor Eisen is teaching us stuff, like loyalty to country, integrity, and faith in God. Sometimes we have a snack and visit afterward. I usually stay too long. I guess I shouldn't have used the word sneak, but I have to go in quietly so I don't wake Mama. With the Germans around these days, she gets worried."

"I would too. That's what a good mama does."

"*Ja,* she is a good mama," Bastiaan said thoughtfully.

Bastiaan cleared his throat and said, "I hate to break up our little talk, but would you like to dance?"

"Oh, I really don't know how to dance. That's why I hid every time Abram got close . . . well, one of the reasons anyway."

"It's easy. Just move your feet to the music. And if you step on a toe or two, it doesn't matter. It's all in fun."

Adrie hesitated but allowed Bastiaan to lead her onto the crowded dance floor. He took her right hand in his left and put his other hand gently on her back. Adrie stiffened when Bastiaan pulled her close but began to relax as he swayed to the music.

Bastiaan looked down and smiled at her about the same time she looked up at him. She turned away quickly, trying to hide her discomfort. Bastiaan bent over and whispered in her ear, "You're a natural."

Adrie murmured shyly, "Thank you. I think. I've never danced with a boy before."

Bastiaan laughed. "Then you really do have a natural ability for dancing."

They danced in silence. Bastiaan leaned his cheek on her soft hair and inhaled the sweet lilac fragrance that made his head spin. Adrie cautiously watched her feet so she wouldn't step on his toes, but she did.

"Uh . . . the music has stopped, Bastiaan," Adrie said as loud chatter filled the dance floor.

"Oh, has it? I hadn't noticed," Bastiaan said with a smile. "Would you like to dance the next one?"

"Yes, thank you. But when does the last dance end and the new one begin?" Adrie laughed.

The music began again to a faster beat. Bastiaan didn't pay attention to it as he held Adrie in his arms and moved slowly.

Abram bumped into Bastiaan. "Hey, I see you are finally dancing! That's great, and with a beautiful lady at that," he said. "May I have the next dance with her?"

"You may not. She is my dance partner. Go find your own."

Abram laughed. "You're a bit stingy, aren't you?"

"Yes, and I intend to stay that way."

Abram gave a big wink and walked away, his hands shoved into his pockets.

"That's my obnoxious buddy, Abram," Bastiaan said with his jaw set.

"Yes, I know."

"He thinks he's a lady's man."

"And he's a master of his trade," Adrie said, smiling.

Bastiaan laughed, pulled her close, and spun her around.

The music suddenly stopped, and the gaiety ceased as a lone German officer entered. Couples filtered off the dance floor as he approached. "Do not stop the dance for me," the handsome blond German said. "I have come to enjoy the festivities."

The crowd stood in stunned silence for a moment. "Play, play the music," Lieutenant Schmidt ordered. "Dance and have fun. I am not here on the affairs of the Third Reich."

The music started again. Couples stood rigid and refused to dance while he moved through them. Lieutenant Schmidt walked over to the refreshment table and helped himself to a cookie and a glass of punch. He turned to survey the room. A line of girls stood along the wall, but to his disappointment, the *fräulein* was not among them.

I'm setting myself up for harsh discipline by coming here if Colonel Boere finds out, the officer mused. *But I'm far from home and missing female companionship.*

Lieutenant Schmidt smiled as he watched the couples, and then he spotted the beautiful, young blonde girl in the center of the dance floor dancing with a pubescent boy. He gulped the remainder of his punch, set the glass down, and stepped through the crowd toward her. The crowd parted as if he were the plague. He tapped the gangly boy's shoulder and in a thick German accent asked, "May I cut in?"

A buzz of hushed whispers spread throughout the barn. The gossip would probably get back to his commander, but it was a small price to pay to dance with the beauty.

The boy nodded and coughed as he stepped back, his face twisted with anger. He walked off the dance floor, his shoulders hunched as if he had been defeated in a fight for dominance with a superior male.

The young girl looked into the handsome German's face, blushed, but didn't dare refuse.

The arrogant Lieutenant Schmidt took the girl in his arms and started to move with ease. He was polite and gentle as he spun her around the room. "What is your name, Fräulein?" he asked as he swayed to the music.

"My name is Eilsa," she said. The fear in her eyes began to subside with each turn of his easy manner.

When the music stopped, Lieutenant Schmidt held her hand and asked, "May I have the next dance?"

"Uh, yes," Eilsa rasped.

The music began with a lead guitar solo, joined by the bass and the other guitar playing in harmony, until all the instruments were playing a fast-paced jazz song. Lieutenant Schmidt boldly faced Eilsa, grabbed her hand, and turned her onto the floor. His fancy footwork was impressive to the onlookers as he moved her at his will.

Eilsa glanced over at Larz, his dark eyes smoldering. Eilsa knew that look and she wondered what was going through his head.

It seemed everyone got into the spirit of the music, especially Abram. Bastiaan watched as his friend, still wearing his Jewish skullcap, bounced around like an overeager aborigine and backed into the German. He held his breath when Lieutenant Schmidt turned around and saw the Jewish boy. Lieutenant Schmidt dropped Eilsa's hand and grabbed Abram by his shirt collar. "Jewish scum," he snarled. "Do you think you can touch a German officer? That is a death sentence in Germany!"

The music stopped, the silence heavy.

"Please, sir, I meant no harm. It was an accident," Abram apologized.

Lieutenant Schmidt's face twisted. His fist came up and hit Abram in the nose, knocking him to the floor.

"There are no accidents, Jew!" he shouted.

The hair on the back of Bastiaan's neck rose as he watched the commotion. Blood spurted from Abram's nose, and his eyes glazed over as he fell backward. Bastiaan's fists clenched into a ball as he pushed through the crowd, Adrie right behind him. His face tightened as angry tears threatened, but he didn't dare look at the officer in fear of bringing the officer's wrath on him also. He bent stiffly down and shoved a handkerchief onto Abram's nose.

"I suggest, Jew, you get out of my sight before I change my mind and shoot you."

Bastiaan lifted Abram's head and patted his cheeks. "Are you okay, Abram?"

Abram moaned, gasped, and coughed. His eyes had the far away, unfocused look of a drunk. He slurred, "*Ja,* but I think I should go home."

"Do you want me to go with you?" Bastiaan asked, lowering his voice to almost a whisper.

Abram's voice trembled and sounded a little too shrill. "No, I'll be okay. That's if there aren't any more German thugs out there. I think he came alone. I'll be fine," he said, shaking uncontrollably. "But thanks."

"Maybe we all better go home," Bastiaan said, looking around warily. "Adrie, may I walk you home? It isn't safe for you to be out alone."

Adrie held Bastiaan's hand in a viselike grip. Trembling, she whispered, "Thanks, Bastiaan, but I came with Mrs. Digby."

"Then I will walk you and Mrs. Digby home."

"That will not be necessary," she said, looking around nervously and then back to Bastiaan. "We will be safe. Her husband is with us. Maybe you ought to go with Abram. He needs your help more than I do."

Bastiaan said an anxious good-bye to Adrie and watched as she and Mr. and Mrs. Digby left the dance. It was early, about ten o'clock, but many began to leave. The officer ordered the band to play and bade Eilsa to dance again. Eilsa stepped back, but he stepped forward, grabbed her hand, and led her to the center of the dance floor.

"Come on, Abram. Let's get you home," Bastiaan said as he lifted Abram to his feet.

Abram moaned and made a series of obnoxious snorts and sniffs as they walked back to Ede. The blood soaked the hanky in a matter of minutes. Bastiaan took off his shirt and put it on Abram's nose.

"Boy, the swelling sure set in fast," Bastiaan said, looking at him in the moonlight. "You won't be able to see if your eyes keep swelling like that. You look like a boxer who didn't have the good sense to duck." Bastiaan chuckled.

"Not funny," Abram said through the cloth.

Abram's home was on the opposite side of the village. Bastiaan rang the bell, and Abram's mother answered. When she saw Abram, she screamed. "What happened? Abram, have you been fighting?

"No, Mama. Not exactly."

"Not exactly? What does that mean?"

"Uh . . . I sort of ran into a German officer. Literally."

"A German officer, where? Let me see your face."

"Mama, I'm okay. I just have a bloody nose. He only hit me once."

"Only once? Only once? Who did this? I'll file a complaint at the police department tomorrow!"

"Mama, that won't do any good. We're Jews, remember?"

"How did he know you were a Jew?"

"I sort of wore my kippa," Abram muttered sheepishly.

"I've told you, you're not to wear that in public! Not with so many Germans around."

"I know, Mama. Boy, do I know."

"I'll get some ice. Abram, you lie down." She began walking toward the kitchen but turned back to Bastiaan. "Thank you for bringing him home. Can I get you another shirt? Will you be okay walking home alone?"

"Thanks, Mrs. Berkovitz. *Ja,* I know a shortcut through the fields, so I won't be spotted by any Germans. I'll be safe. Good night, Mrs. Berkovitz."

LARZ BLUNDERED TO the edge of the dance floor. He'd looked forward to this dance for half the summer. He finally got up enough courage to ask Eilsa to the dance before that annoying Bastiaan Coevorden did and was quite proud of himself for doing so. He thought he had taken care of any and all competition for Eilsa, but then this German officer showed up. He sat down hard on a bench, his eyes smoldered like hot coals, leering at the couple on the dance floor. He propped his foot on a bucket, biting his nails and spitting them out as if they were daggers of hatred. He sat hunched while images flashed through his mind of ways he could take care of the German pig.

Finally Larz couldn't stand watching them any longer and left. He crept to the back of the barn and stumbled over a forgotten milk bucket that clattered across the ground as if to announce his murderous scheme. He hauled off and kicked the bucket across the barnyard as if daring someone to challenge him. He found a knife in the tool shed, stuffed it in his under his shirt, and hurried into the night. After a short walk, Larz came to a downhill slope beside the road surrounded by large bushes. He slid under the bushes to wait for the German officer.

Larz fidgeted and swatted at mosquitoes with a vengeance, cursing the lateness of the hour as the time ticked by excruciatingly slow. He acted out in his head a hundred times how he would slit the officer's throat and feel the triumph that would follow. Every time he imagined that German enjoying himself with his girl, rage pulsed through his blood. He had to constantly control the urge to shout out and charge back to the dance to kill him.

At last couples started to leave the dance. Some headed for farms, others headed for Ede. A lone straggler appeared. The moonlight bathed the earth in a soft blue hue, his uniform, his high collar, and the eagle swastika on his hat looked almost luminescent. Larz's insides churned as the audacity ignited, and he prepared to spring.

A gentle evening breeze lightly lifted an escaped curl on Lieutenant Schmidt's forehead as he languidly strolled down the road, smoking a cigarette. His thoughts were absorbed with the young Fräulein only to be interrupted by a sound behind him. He felt a chill go up his back to the nape of his neck. He spun around, instinctively throwing out his uniformed forearm, and deflected a knife, knocking it from the grasp as a dark form attacked him from behind. The assailant reached down to pick up the knife, and the lieutenant kicked him and sent him sprawling. He saw it was the boy from the dance and that his intent was obviously to take his life. The boy rolled over quickly and got to his feet, clutching the knife.

Lieutenant Schmidt laughed. "You foolish little boy. You think you can kill a German?"

Larz bellowed as he lunged at the officer again, this time slashing the blade across his hand. A low growl resonated in Lieutenant Schmidt's throat as he flashed his opponent an amused grin. He inhaled deeply, sidestepping another swipe and spun away from the blade. Larz came at him again. Lieutenant Schmidt anticipated the move and with catlike reflexes sunk a small stiletto, which had been hidden in his boot, into his stomach. Larz's eyes widened. He let out a moan, grabbed his stomach as blood dripped from his mouth, and then collapsed.

"Stupid boy," Lieutenant Schmidt said and kicked the body.

He took out his handkerchief and wrapped it around his hand. He strode back to his quarters, pondering his alibi.

The next day Lieutenant Schmidt was awakened by pounding on his door. He looked at the clock. It was still early for him to report to duty. He rubbed his eyes, yawned, and moaned as he got out of bed to go to the door. He opened it to a short, scared-looking private.

"Excuse me, sir, but the colonel has ordered you to his office. The town is in a frenzy. A boy was found murdered this morning and he needs you to restore order by finding out what happened."

"German pigs!" were the whispers throughout the village. The Dutch constable took the corpse to the funeral parlor. The director, Mr. Meir, looked over the pale body. "Do you know who has done this to the boy?"

"I don't know," Constable DeKeizer replied. "And it's best to leave it that way. If a German has done this, there is nothing anyone can do. An investigation will only cause further violence and death. Give his mother my condolences, and let this be the end of it."

"I will, but I'm afraid it will not be the end."

"If it is not, then there will be more bloodshed. I suggest you try to soothe it over with everyone and to let it be, for their sakes."

"Yes, sir," Mr. Meir said, shaking his head sadly.

"Those Germans are the ones who killed him!" Anna Coevorden made no effort to keep her voice down. "I told you it wasn't safe. That could have been you, Bastiaan! You are not to go out alone at night anymore. No, you are not going out of this house anymore, period!"

"Please, Mama. Be reasonable."

"I am. I'm your mama and that's as reasonable as I get!"

"Papa, talk to her! I can't be a prisoner in my own home."

Papa looked at Bastiaan. "I agree with your mama. You are not to go out at night anymore. And if there is a need to go to the village, we will go together."

"Oh, Papa, you too?"

"There's a war on, son. The Nazis don't care who they kill. We have to protect our family, our home, and ourselves."

The rosy hues of the sunrise shone through the tiny bathroom window as Lieutenant Schmidt readied for the day. Normally he would have taken a few minutes to enjoy a morning like, this but he snorted at its beauty when he looked at the gash on his hand. He jerked open the cupboard to get the disinfectant and gauze, letting out a string of swear words. He winced as he smeared the disinfectant across his hand and wrapped it in gauze, irritated that a mere boy could get the drop on him.

Inside the Dutch police station, he found a roomful of hysterical people. Ignoring them, he walked to Colonel Boere's office, rapped on the door, drew in a deep breath, and entered to report for duty.

Colonel Boere had already heard about the boy's death. He looked at Lieutenant Schmidt's bandaged hand suspiciously and asked, "What happened to your hand, Lieutenant?"

"It was cut in a fight, sir."

"What fight and when?"

"Last night, sir. I couldn't sleep and went for a walk."

"You were out alone at night?"

"Uh, yes, sir," Lieutenant Schmidt answered, staring directly at the colonel.

"Did you know that is grounds for discipline? It is dangerous, and I can't have one of my officers disobeying orders. That is not exemplary for the men."

"Yes, sir, but it was only for a short time."

"Cease your lies!" Colonel Boere shouted. "A boy from the village was killed last night. Do you know anything about that?"

"Yes, sir, I do. It was an accident. The boy attacked me and I had to defend myself."

"Why would a young Dutch boy attack a German officer?"

"I don't know, sir, but I was inclined to defend myself."

"If the villagers find out a German did this, there will be an uprising. Did you think of that?"

"Uh . . . no, sir. Not at the time."

"Well, maybe you should think!" yelled the commander. "You are an officer in the Third Reich. You are expected to think!"

"Yes, sir."

"There will be no discipline, and this will not be mentioned again. Do you understand?"

"Yes, sir.

"You hurt your hand cleaning your weapon, do you understand?"

"Yes, sir."

Colonel Boere got up and walked around his desk, facing the lieutenant. "Lieutenant Schmidt, I don't like you. You are arrogant, foolish, and undisciplined. I would just as soon send you to the front lines. If I find that you have stepped out of line again, I may shoot you myself. Is that clear?"

"Yes, sir."

"You are dismissed."

"Yes, sir. Heil Hitler," Lieutenant Schmidt said without emotion. He turned and left. "One day, Colonel, I will see to your demise," he said, sneering.

chapter THREE

August 1940

Colonel Boere's shoulders sagged as he read the dispatch from Hitler. Strands of his graying hair wisped across his balding head as he lowered it, staring at the unbelievable document. "How can I carry out such an order?"

Colonel Boere's gentle spirit didn't have the stomach for the Gestapo's and SS's ways. The rank of colonel came because of a heroic act on the battlefield: while wounded himself, he carried an officer to safety. His wounds prevented an assignment to another fighting unit, and his promotion allowed him to ask for a desirable position. He asked for a transfer to Holland, thinking it a subdued state with less war activity. The imposing of Hitler's harsh sanctions had not yet occurred in Holland because of their Germanic descent. Hitler assumed the Dutch people would be easy to convince to join the Nazi party so he didn't enforce the strict German sanctions as in other countries. Hence, Colonel Boere hoped he could sit out the war in Holland behind a desk in peace.

"This will cause an uprising," he said dejectedly, putting the dispatch down. "Rationing their food will only incite them."

A knock sounded at the door, and Colonel Boere reluctantly said, "Enter." Four men came into the room, saluted Heil Hitler, and stood at rigid attention.

"At ease," Colonel Boere said. "I have just received a dispatch from the Fatherland. Hereafter, we are to control and oversee the distribution of food and supplies to the Dutch people. Ration cards are to be distributed; if they want to eat, they will use them. If they do not have a ration card, they do not eat. Corporal Muller, you will go to the city office. There you will oversee the distribution of the ration cards. Lieutenant Schmidt, your assignment is to collect food and supplies at the bakery, Heingle's store, and the flour mill. They will be redistributed later with the use of the ration cards. Mr. Voygt, you will go with Corporal Muller to the city offices because you know the people, their circumstances, the members of their families, and their records. If they lie, their rations will be cut until the next week, and if they are Jews, they only receive half rations. You will also keep an accurate count of the cards distributed and to whom. If any cards are left, count them and return them to the city offices."

Colonel Boere looked directly at each man and said, "You will be firm, but I don't want bloodshed. Do you understand?"

Corporal Muller cleared his throat. "But what if trouble arises?"

"Arrest them! And be prepared," he said, looking directly into their eyes. "Until tomorrow, gentlemen."

"Heil Hitler," they said. Then they spun on their heels and left.

A SOILED HANDKERCHIEF always sat on Mr. Voygt's nose or in his hand. His constant snorting into the rag sounding like a Viking's call to battle. He had a habit of spitting on the sidewalk, which sickened those around him. His unstylish new clothes fit too snugly on his pear-shaped body, and his beady eyes bore into a person like he was a depraved murderer. Before the German occupation, Mr. Voygt lived in a rundown shack on the edge of Ede, often seen with undesirable companions.

When the Germans invaded the Netherlands, he saw an opportunity to take advantage of the situation. He went to the German authorities and offered his unique services. Previously he worked for a printing company, printing all public records for the area. He offered to spy on his neighbors and Jews for favors in return. The Germans rewarded him handsomely with the confiscated property of a Jewish home, an infinite amount of ration cards, and the freedom to take from others and go anywhere.[2]

---

2. Later the collaborators formed a party called the NSB, National Socialistiche Beweging: the only legal political party allowed in the Netherlands in 1941. Before then, they were Dutch collaborators who were actively involved with the German occupiers in capturing and arresting Jews.

Mr. Voygt licked his lips in anticipation. The record office was exhilarating, but he finished early so Colonel Boere ordered him to go with Lieutenant Schmidt to the flour mill.

Lieutenant Schmidt peered down his nose at the hypocrite sitting beside him and turned away in disgust. The truck halted abruptly in front of the flour mill as a cloud of dust engulfed it. Lieutenant Schmidt pushed open the truck's door almost tripping over himself in an effort to get away from the disgusting Judas.

"Break the door down, and load the wheat and flour into the trucks!" Lieutenant Schmidt yelled.

Mr. Dremsel, the owner, was working inside the mill, loading the hopper, when he heard the truck pull up. He ran out front and saw the soldiers loading his wheat and flour onto a truck. He faced the lieutenant and pled, "You can't take my wheat and flour. It provides bread to half of Holland."

Lieutenant Schmidt struck him. "Do you think you can defy the orders of the Führer? It is for the Fatherland and the army. Your precious citizens may have what is left. You are powerless to stop us, so if you want to live, I suggest you cease further objections."

Mr. Dremsel's son, Peter, came around the side of the building in time to see the lieutenant strike his father. Peter's eyes filled with tears as he helped his father to his feet. Mr. Dremsel's eyes moistened, and he grabbed fistfuls of his hair. He watched helplessly as the bags of wheat were loaded onto the truck. Then he saw Mr. Voygt standing there.

"You traitor!" Mr. Dremsel spat. "I helped to feed your hungry family while neighbors gave you clothing. This is how you repay our kindness? You are the lowest pariah of mankind, to betray your own people!"

"You high-minded people thought you were better than me, with your token gifts," Mr. Voygt said, sneering. "I saw the looks at church, your children scurrying away from mine. I'll have you shining my boots when you come crawling to me for food."

"That is all in your head, you ungrateful vermin. I would rather my stomach turn inside out with hunger than ask you for anything."

Mr. Voygt laughed, enjoying the power of the moment. "Well, we shall see. You won't be so haughty come winter when you are sick and bent. I will enjoy you groveling at my feet, Mr. Better-than-me."

As the last of the wheat was loaded, Lieutenant Schmidt lifted the tailgate and banged it shut. "Take this load to headquarters and wait for orders."

Peter watched the truck drive away with the last of their food and livelihood. His voice tightened as he said, "Don't worry, Papa. I'll fight the Germans with my last ounce of strength."

"No, Peter, it is too dangerous. You must stay away from them and stay at home."

Peter did not argue.

The breeze swept over the canals from the south, cooling the morning air. Marieka mounted her bike and headed for Ede, feeling invigorated as she lifted her chin into the breeze. Wispy strands escaped her neatly braided hair and playfully fluttered across her face. She closed her eyes and escaped into a wistful world of fantasy where there was no war.

Marieka worked her way through the village, ignoring the soldiers as she peddled toward Mr. Buskirk's bakery. A skinny German private stepped in front of her and yelled, "Halt! What do you have in your basket, Fräulein?"

Marieka put her foot down and steadied the bike. She jerked her head up and looked into his fuzz-covered face. "It's butter and milk for Mr. Buskirk's bakery, sir. I make deliveries there every day at this time."

"I must confiscate your delivery by the order of the Führer," the inexperienced soldier demanded.

Marieka paled and recoiled from the soldier, pushing her bike backward. He grabbed her, about to drag her off the bicycle when Colonel Boere walked up behind him and demanded, "What is going on here, soldier?"

The private's expression softened. "I am following orders, sir. Impounding milk and butter from this girl."

"You harass children, soldier? Leave her be!" Colonel Boere yelled. "She is a harmless farm girl."

The boy shrank under the colonel's authoritative stare, jerked a nervous salute, and hurried down the street.

"You may go now," Colonel Boere said gently to Marieka.

Marieka bit her lip and pushed past the colonel.

Marieka dropped her bike in front of Mr. Buskirk's bakery, staring straight ahead as she passed the guard on the porch. The bakery was full of her friends and neighbors, pushing and shoving each other to purchase a loaf of bread with strange slips of paper.

Mr. Buskirk's ring of gray hair looked like he'd fallen in a vat of starch and dried standing on end. He ran from the wheat, to the white bread, to the oven, and back to the customers as three armed German soldiers watched.

A young Jewish woman stood at the front of the line holding a baby with a toddler at her knee. "But I have little children to feed. This is not enough for my family for a week," she pled. The soldier pulled the pistol from his holster and pointed it at the toddler. "Then I will make it so you do not worry over such matters," he scoffed and cocked the gun.

"No!" she screamed. "I will make do. Please do not harm my child."

The soldier holstered the gun. "I thought you'd see things my way. Now get you and your Jewish brats out of my sight before I change my mind."

Tears filled the woman's eyes as she grabbed the loaf of bread, picked up the toddler, and ran from the bakery. The other customers stood by and watched.

Marieka's lips tightened into a colorless line as she edged past the soldier to the kitchen. Mr. Buskirk looked up at her anxiously. She nodded at him with a strained smile, sat the butter and eggs down, and then turned back through the anxious crowd. As she was leaving, a young man in front of her slipped a piece of paper into an older man's side pocket, neither looking at the other. The young man looked as if he were about sixteen, her brother's age. He walked out the door. The older man stayed in line, stared ahead, and didn't look to see what had been slipped in his pocket.

Marieka looked at the older gentleman for a moment. She was about to ask him if he noticed the young man had slipped something into his pocket when the German soldier stepped forward again. "What is the problem? Do you know this man? Is there something wrong?"

"No . . . no, sir. I just thought he reminded me of someone. I am sorry," she said and left.

Outside, the young man hurried down the street, turned into the alley, and disappeared. Marieka picked up her bike and waited at the side of the bakery. A few moments later the middle-aged man appeared with a loaf of bread tucked under his arm, his hat pulled low over his eyes, and he walked casually down the street in the opposite direction.

Marieka's eyes lowered when she noticed a guard staring at her. She hopped on her bike and headed down the street.

The man-made canals, built centuries earlier, were made for irrigation, excess water removal, and travel in the larger cities. Marieka usually rode along the canal, taking the twists and turns without care or thought. At the sight of her mother outside, Marieka dropped the bike and ran to her. "Oh, Mama," she said. "The Germans are everywhere and they have taken all the food. People have to purchase food with slips of paper."

Anna Coevorden jerked her head up and stared at her wide-eyed. Her voice shook as she said, "I was afraid they would take our freedom and instill harsh laws, but I never thought they would take our food. This is a way to control us. They think they can force Holland to join the Nazi party. We have enough food on our little farm. We must stay away from Ede and the Germans. You can't make deliveries anymore."

"Mama, I have to. Mrs. Berg needs milk for her twins, Mr. Buskirk needs eggs and butter, and Miss Remi needs to feed her father," Marieka said, following her mother around as she hung the laundry on the line.

"No, Marieka. It's too dangerous," her mother said through clenched teeth, a clothespin in her mouth.

"The Germans know that I deliver milk and butter. Four of them were in Mr. Buskirk's bakery a few weeks ago. The man in charge told his men to leave me alone and then again this morning. He likes Mr. Buskirk's pastries and wants me to continue making deliveries."

Anna gasped and stopped what she was doing. "You didn't tell me the Germans bothered you!"

Marieka stammered and turned away from her mother. "They didn't bother me."

Anna put one hand on her hip and pointed a finger at Marieka. "Oh, Marieka, you are in danger. Maybe I should have your father make the deliveries from now on."

"No, Mama. I'm safe as long as Colonel Boere is around."

"I do not like it. Men can do awful things to a young girl," Anna persisted.

"Mama, I have seen the German soldier's hit men Papa's age with their rifles. I will be safer then he would be," Marieka said, her voice rising.

"I don't like it," Anna Coevorden said, walking back and forth and wringing her hands. "I will let you go but only early in the morning before the Germans are awake." Anna stared Marieka directly in the eyes, and Marieka nodded her acquiescence.

chapter FOUR

A thin gray line appeared on the horizon as Marieka parked her bike in front of Mrs. Berg's home. She rang the bell and soon Mrs. Berg came out onto the porch, clasping her robe with one hand, her gray-blonde hair matted on the side of her head. "My goodness, Marieka! You scared the water out of me. What are you doing here so early in the morning? Don't you know people are asleep at this time? You should be horsewhipped."

"I have to make my deliveries early or Mama won't let me . . . because of the Germans," Marieka said timidly.

Mrs. Berg looked at her with cold eyes and sneered. "Put the milk on the table and leave. Get out of my sight before I take a broom to you, and tell your Mama I won't accept deliveries at this time of day."

"Yes, ma'am," Marieka stuttered and then ran out.

Crying, Marieka quietly entered the bakery, put the butter and eggs on the workbench, and left. Mr. Buskirk went to the door and called after her, "Marieka, are you okay?"

Marieka answered over her shoulder, trying to keep her voice steady, "*Ja*, got to get home."

THE SUMMER MORNING was warm and clear, free of wind or breeze. Lieutenant Schmidt arose, took a hot shower, and dressed in his tailored uniform he had purchased several months before when he was advanced to lieutenant. He buttoned the last button on the immaculate uniform, brushing away an imaginary piece of lint. He looked at his reflection in the mirror: the shined boots, shiny belt buckle, and the polished brass buttons, all proud symbols of his obedience to the Führer. He grabbed his hat, arranged it snuggly on his head, and went to breakfast as usual at Mr. Buskirk's bakery.

A couple weeks had gone by since he'd seen the beautiful Fräulein. He wondered why and asked Mr. Buskirk, "Are you still receiving butter and eggs from the young Fräulein?"

Mr. Buskirk sat the pastry in front of him, grunted, and turned to serve Colonel Boere without answering him.

The lieutenant asked again, more forcefully, "Does the Fräulein still deliver butter and eggs to you, sir?"

Mr. Buskirk cocked his head, looked at the lieutenant, snorted, and went to the back.

Lieutenant Schmidt's nostrils flared and his ears turned a bright crimson. He bristled at the man's attitude. He'd just as soon see him in a pillory or stocks[3] but he'd let it go for now. He knew if harm were to come to the old man, he would be the first person Colonel Boere would suspect.

Lieutenant Schmidt sneered. "She is coming early in the morning, isn't she?" he asked, watching Mr. Buskirk's face as he refilled the tea.

The baker's face drained of color. He wiped his hands on his apron, asked if there was anything else, nodded, and then went back to work in the kitchen without looking at Lieutenant Schmidt.

Lieutenant Schmidt tossed a coin on the table, crossed the room in a few quick strides, and slammed the door behind him.

Lieutenant Schmidt jumped as the alarm went off. He slammed his hand on it to shut the annoying thing off and knocked it onto the floor. He groaned, rolled over, sat on the edge of the bed, and put his feet into his brown felt slippers. He ran his hands through his thick tangled hair, yawned, and scratched his backside as he strolled across the bedroom. "Ugh, is there actually life this time of morning?" he groaned. He stumbled through the house to the door, stepped onto the porch, and watched across the street at Mr. Buskirk's bakery. Just as he suspected, Marieka appeared and turned down the alley at the side of the bakery. The officer could not keep the smile from his face. As Marieka disappeared into the bakery, Lieutenant Schmidt slipped back into his room to prepare for the day.

---

3. *A wooden device people put their head and hands through that was clamped shut.*

Marieka turned into the alley next to the bakery. She knocked lightly on the door, turned the doorknob, and poked her head in. "Good morning, Mr. Buskirk." Marieka inhaled deeply at the rich scent of baking bread and sweet pastries that greeted her.

"Little Marieka, it is not good for you to be out alone at this time of day," Mr. Buskirk said, winking.

"Mama thought it would be better because there are not so many Germans around. She says they're lazy and won't get up before the sun, so I am safe until then." She laughed.

"I wish that were true, but I fear the wolves do not sleep. They are always hunting for prey," Mr. Buskirk said, shaking his head slowly.

"Mama wants to lock me in the cellar until the war is over, but I convinced her you still need your butter." Marieka grinned.

"Please be careful, little Marieka, and peddle fast if one of those Nazi fiends comes your way!"

"Don't worry! I can peddle faster than they can run," she laughed.

"Good! Now you had better hurry home, little one. May God protect you." Mr. Buskirk held the door for her.

"And may He be with you also, my dear friend."

With the cumbersome load lightened, Marieka pushed the bike into the street and headed toward the road along the dike. The morning sun winked at her between the trees as she left the village. Suddenly a young man ran from a paint-chipped wooden house, as if the devil were chasing him and almost knocked her over.

"Hey!" she yelled, slamming on her brakes. She stopped, bawling him out for his rudeness, but he kept going. When the young man glanced back at her, she realized it was the same boy she'd seen in the bakery several weeks earlier. The terror on his face made her shiver. He crawled into the tall grass along the dike and slid into the cold, murky water.

Marieka saw two German soldiers out of the corner of her eye. They pointed their rifles at her. She screamed, gripped the bike white knuckled, and recoiled from the rifles.

One soldier poked the rifle into her side and asked in a heavy German accent, "Did you see a man run this way?"

Marieka stared at him.

He cocked the rifle and asked sharply, "Where is the man who came this way?"

Mutely Marieka shook her head.

"You lie!" he yelled.

The older soldier scouted around while the younger one continued to question the girl. He discovered the crushed grass along the dike and shouted, "He's gone into the water."

They turned to the canal and sprayed a volley of bullets up and down the dike. When they finished and were satisfied no one could have survived, they turned laughing, and walked past Marieka.

Marieka stood for what seemed like an eternity before she staggered to the dike and searched the water, hoping the young man had somehow escaped. Marieka felt queasy when she saw his lifeless body drifting in the canal. "You filthy Germans!" she screamed and then vomited in the grass.

Anna Coevorden paced back and forth on the front porch wringing her hands. "Oh, Lord, please protect her."

Marieka rolled her bike around the barn and into the yard, her face pale and her eyes bloodshot.

"Marieka!" Anna screamed. "What's happened?"

The girl let the bike fall and ran into her Mama's arms, sobbing.

"Marieka! What is it? What happened?"

"German soldiers," she said. "Killed a young man . . . right in front of me . . . in the water by the dike. He was running from them. They shot a volley into the water. I saw him floating in the canal. He was just a boy, no older than Bastiaan. Why, Mama? Why would they do such a thing? We have surrendered to the Nazis. Isn't that enough?"

Anna cried and hugged her. "I don't know, Marieka. They are evil men. They want all of Europe to join their Nazi party and destroy those who don't. You know I don't like you going to the village!"

"I know, Mama. It is frightening for me too, but our customers depend on our butter and eggs."

The troop train stopped in Ede at two thirty in the morning for supplies and water. During that time, a baggage handler entered the main car, put a briefcase behind the last seat, and quietly exited. He glanced over his shoulder as he briskly walked away, swallowed hard, and hoped he had gone unnoticed. He quickly ducked behind a nearby building as the sound of an explosion ripped through the air. He was thrown to the ground, and shrapnel pelted his back. The sound deafened him momentarily. He lifted up on one elbow and watched the intoxicating swirl of fire, smoke, and ruin as it spread through the main car to the others. The glare of the light blossomed into hues of red, yellow, and orange, swirling into a theatrical grandeur. His breath caught as he watched the fire devour the train car, licking every corner in its hunger to possess its quarry. Only half of the car remained, he watched as soldiers on fire jumped from it and limped away.

Soon a corporal was on the scene and began to take a tally of the soldiers that were on the train. He reported to Colonel Boere in the early morning hours at his home. "All forty soldiers are accounted for, wounded, dead, and alive, except one. I don't know if he took the full force of the blast, and there isn't anything left of him or if the blast blew him from the train."

"If he was blown away from the train, we should be able to find him. Search the area and put the word out to be on the lookout for a wounded soldier. Order a unit to clean up the debris and then report back to me," Colonel Boere said. Already unfastening his robe, he bade the corporal good-bye.

"Yes, sir!" The corporal saluted "Heil Hitler." He turned on his heel and left. Outside the headquarters, the corporal barked orders to the men to get the wreckage cleared away.

Colonel Boere entered headquarters ten minutes later and asked for a report of who was responsible for the train explosion but found that nobody knew anything and everyone was in a panic.

At nine o'clock that morning, Corporal Muller brought in a local farmer. He held his hat nervously in his hand and nodded a greeting to Colonel Boere as he stepped into his office.

"He says earlier this morning when he was herding cows, he saw a soldier hobbling along the edge of his field holding his shoulder."

"What did he look like?" Colonel Boere asked the farmer.

"I don't know. He was across the field. I just saw a man in a German uniform."

"Why didn't you contact us about this immediately?" Colonel Boere barked.

"Because it is none of my business what goes on in your German army," the old farmer said, looking into the colonel's eyes.

"I should have you arrested for such talk," Colonel Boere barked, his face reddening.

The old man stood erect and looked boldly at the colonel.

"Corporal, let him go. He has given us enough information. I doubt he knows anything else."

The corporal pushed the man and said, "You are free to go." The man stopped and stood for a moment looking into the corporal's eyes. The corporal swallowed, stepped back, and said politely, "Sir, you are free to go."

"Good day," the old farmer said. He put on his hat, nodded at Colonel Boere, and left.

Colonel Boere nodded to the man in respect.

"Conduct a search for the soldier. He couldn't have gone far," Colonel Boere ordered.

"Yes, sir. If we find him, do you want him alive?"

"Yes, he will have some questions to answer before I decide what to do with him."

chapter FIVE

The loud banging on the door awakened Lieutenant Schmidt. He opened it to a short, pimple-faced corporal. "Lieutenant, lieutenant," he said in shrill voice. "It is the train, sir, just outside of town. Someone has blown it up. No one got a good look at who did it. They disappeared into the dark like rats in light. There was gunfire, several of our men were wounded, and a couple were killed, but we managed to catch one of them. Colonel Boere has ordered your presence and expertise at the interrogation."

"Tell the colonel I will be there shortly," Lieutenant Schmidt said, shutting the door in the corporal's face. The anticipation of extracting information was energizing.

When Lieutenant Schmidt entered the police station, a trembling boy stood in front of the counter, his curly brown hair poking out of the cap stuffed low on his head. The boy's eyes were downcast. He didn't look up when Lieutenant Schmidt slammed the door. His skin was pasty white, a bloodstain was on his lower right pant leg, and his pants were covered with mud.

"You can go free and no harm will come to you if you tell us who is responsible for the bombing of the troop train." Colonel Boere's tone was as gentle as if he were soothing a small child.

The boy stood silent.

"Come now, you don't want us to use certain methods to get you to talk," Colonel Boere maintained a soft tone. "It is such a hardship for my men. You will suffer needlessly, and in the end, my men will obtain the information I seek anyway. You are too young to die. It is absurd to persist in remaining silent."

Lieutenant Schmidt stepped to the prisoner's side, his hands behind his back, rocking on the balls of his feet.

"What is your name?" Colonel Boere yelled, losing his patience. The boy looked up at Lieutenant Schmidt and whispered, "Dedriek."

"What is your last name?" the colonel demanded, but the boy remained silent. "While you are refusing to speak, my time is being wasted and your associates are getting away. I don't have time for such nonsense. Lieutenant Schmidt, take the boy to the back and see if you can convince him that his foolishness is futile."

Lieutenant Schmidt slapped the boy on the back of his head with a pair of gloves and ordered him to move toward the back door. "You know, young man, I'm not the one to be afraid of. It is the Gestapo at the prison of Fort Montluc in France you should fear."

The room was full of soldiers waiting for orders. Some had frightened looks on their faces while others looked determined to find and capture the men who did this. Dedriek had noticed that the tension seemed to escalate when the tall lieutenant entered. The two guards at the back were casually leaning against the door but stood alert. Lieutenant Schmidt shoved Dedriek toward the back door. The two guards hit him with the butts of their rifles. Dedriek fell against the splintered doorframe. He grabbed his leg and howled, while stashing a piece of splintered wood inside his shirtsleeve.

Anton, a man in his early twenties and the resistance leader, stood motionless as he watched the troops running around hysterically, shouting orders. The sun would be up soon, and he had to get in and out of the German headquarters, formerly the Dutch police station, before then. He peeked into the barred window, hoping to hear something of the prisoner who had just been brought in.

The Germans were unprepared for an explosion in the tiny village of Ede. It was unexpected and without any precedent. The resistance had been informed the week before of the troop train that would be passing through Ede from Düsseldorf, Germany, to Dunkirk, France, to the front lines. They had planned and prepared to blow it up.

Anton crept to the side of the building and watched as a tall, blond SS lieutenant marched up the steps of the Dutch police station. He knew the SS lieutenant had been summoned for the special assignment of retrieving information from an uncooperative prisoner. He also knew the prisoner was Dedriek, his younger brother.

Anton held the plastic explosive in his hand. He circled around to the back and heard shouting coming from inside but couldn't make out the words or hear his brother's voice.

He peeked in the small door window and saw two guards leading Dedriek to the cell in the back. The cell's small barred window had been boarded up and soundproofed so the sounds of the interrogations could not be heard in the small village. The most extreme tortures, however, were inflicted in the dungeons of Fort Montluc in France. Prisoners were roughed up here, but if Dedriek wouldn't talk, they would transport him to the prison in France. Few held their tongues in such a place.

Anton's plan was to blow the back door, shoot the guards, and pray his brother would be out of harm's way. He puttied the plastic explosive near the door handle and put a five-second fuse on it. He was about to light the fuse when he felt a hand on his shoulder. Anton spun around quickly lifting his rifle into the culprit's face.

"Hold on, Anton," the deep voice whispered. "Did you think you could take on the whole German army alone?"

"Trevier. I almost blew your head off!" he breathed. "You shouldn't sneak up on a fellow like that."

"The boys and I have come to offer some assistance."

"Thanks, Trevier. I was questioning my good sense doing this alone, but I didn't want to order the men to risk their lives for me.

"Nonsense, brother."

Anton lit the fuse and stepped around the corner. Trevier waved to the unseen men to get down as the blast exploded the door inward. Anton ran into the smoke-filled hall and shot the guards. He found Dedriek crouched by the wall. The tall officer quickly moved behind him, using Dedriek as a shield. He put a gun to the boy's head.

"Put down your weapons or the boy dies."

Anton hesitated but knew he had to react fast.

The arrogant German cocked his gun. "Now!"

Anton held up his left hand and with his right cautiously put the rifle on the floor.

"You stupid boy," the officer sneered.

Dedriek pulled the piece of splintered wood from his sleeve. It wasn't large or long enough to kill a man, but it would inflict a great deal of pain and divert his attention. Dedriek spun and jammed the sharp stick into the side of the lieutenant's neck. He screamed, and the gun went off. The boy quickly ducked as the shot hit the wall. The officer jumped and stepped behind the cell door. Several guards ran out the back. Trevier and his men picked them off as they came through the door.

Anton moved with the speed of an African cat, grabbed his brother by the scruff of his neck, and whisked him out the door. Trevier and his men turned and ran into the early morning darkness after Anton.

The guards couldn't pick up their trail in the dark.

When they were to safety, Anton yelled, "I should kick your butt, little brother! Next time I tell you to stay home, listen!"

"And miss the excitement? No way!" Dedriek smiled, looking innocently at Anton.

"I should take the hide off your back for scaring me to death and risking the lives of my men."

"Next time I won't forget to watch my back." Dedriek grinned.

"There will be no next time, little brother. You foolish teenage juvenile! You belong on the farm and out of danger."

The smile disappeared from Dedriek's face. "You're serious?"

"As serious as a Gestapo interrogator!" Anton said, looking down at him.

"But, Anton, you wouldn't be here if it wasn't for me!" Dedriek countered.

"That is utter nonsense, Dedriek. I can take care of myself, and Papa will take care of you . . . on the farm."

"But, Anton!"

"No! I have made up my mind. End of the discussion and end of your adventures in the resistance."

Anton turned toward Trevier. "We'll be wanted for what has happened this evening. We'll have to lay low for several weeks. Is the underground able to hide thirty or so men? Do we have enough provisions?"

"The last time I heard, there was a line of safe houses with provisions for Jews and British airmen."

"And for us?"

"It's a dangerous feat hosting the resistance."

The last time I visited the village was the night I took Abram home from the dance, Bastiaan thought wistfully, slapping Nye's rump with the reins. With the unrest, his father kept him busy on the farm and wouldn't let him near town. He yearned for the companionship of others his own age, but at the end of the day, his desire for a social life was swallowed up in exhaustion and sore muscles. His parents still let Marieka go to town, and as far as he could see, it wasn't safe for her either.

Papa had heard rumors that the Dutch were not cooperative with the Nazis. A passive resistance sprang up throughout Holland as the Nazis tried to implement harsher laws, such as food rationing. The resistance grew to a larger scale as the injustices escalated. The radio broadcasts consisted of Nazi propaganda replacing Dutch music, so the Dutch people listened to the BBC, until the Nazis learned of it and confiscated the radios. The newspaper had headlines of the Nazi's dismissing Jewish civil workers, such as the Chief Justice of the Supreme Court and forty-one Jewish professors at the universities. The Dutch students and fellow professors protested the action with no recompense. Then the decree was made to mandate the registration of all Jewish businesses, and then the registration of the individual Jew. Eventually the Jews were even transported out of Holland. Resistance groups were slow to form, but as the Nazi oppression took shape, so did the Dutch resistance. And, unfortunately, with it came Dutch traitors and collaborators.[4] Papa believed the rumors and refused to allow Bastiaan to go into Ede.

Bastiaan sighed, took a deep breath, and looked at the field of mown hay. He'd spent the afternoon raking it into large piles, and it was ready to pitch onto the wagon. He climbed down to get a drink from the water bucket tied to the wagon when he saw out of the corner of his eye a blur dive under a stack of hay.

Before he could find out what it was, he saw several German soldiers running toward the farm. He gulped and felt a paralyzing jolt go through him. He turned and croaked, "Papa, soldiers are coming!"

Hendrick turned to where Bastiaan was pointing and walked over to the side of the wagon. "Bastiaan," Papa whispered, "sit quietly on the wagon, and keep your back to them. I will do all the talking."

As the soldiers neared, the tall officer called out, "We are after a Jewish man who ran this way. Have you seen him?"

---

4. "Netherlands in World War II," Wikipedia, http://en.wikipedia.org/wiki/Netherlands_in_World_War_II.

Hendrick greeted him with a polite nod. "No, sir, I have not. I have been inside for lunch and just came back to finish my work."

"You lie," the lieutenant shouted.

"Sir, I do not lie," Hendrick said in a soft-spoken voice. "I stay on my farm with my family and do my work. I do not interfere in your affairs, and I hope you will not interfere with mine."

"Silence, you insolent fool! The German Army may interfere with whomever they see fit. If the Führer needs your harvest, we will take it."

Hendrick stepped back as the officer ranted. He clutched the side of the wagon, his heart slowing to a sluggish toddle when the officer ordered his men to search the house. Hendrick watched as the soldier's marched toward the house and pound on the door with the butts of their rifles.

Anna was at the window finishing breakfast dishes when she heard the commotion outside. She looked out and saw the soldiers approaching the house. She instinctively reached for Marieka and pulled her close as the soldiers broke down the door. A private aimed a pistol at the two women. "We are here by the orders of the Führer. Do not interfere with our search." They knocked over the chairs, tore dishes from the cupboards, and knocked cans from the open shelves.

Marieka sobbed against Anna's shoulder. Anna, though frightened, feigned courage and tightened her arms around Marieka, gently stroking her hair and whispering words of comfort as the soldiers left. "It's all right, Marieka. They are gone. They were searching for another man. They don't want us," Anna said softly.

"But will they do to him as they did to the other boy?" Marieka cried.

"I hope not. I hope they don't find him, so they can't make that choice," Anna gently whispered.

The officer scanned the field for signs of subterfuge. He kept a gun on Hendrick as he order the men to search every inch of the barn. They emptied the corn bin and bags of grain, climbed the loft, found a pitchfork, and stabbed it into the hay. The lieutenant grimaced bitterly as the corporal reported they had found nothing.

The lieutenant looked at Hendrick, his voice dripping with malice. "It would be unwise of you to hide a Jew. We do not let such offenses go unpunished. The prisons are full of good people like you who want to help their fellow men. They are tortured for their acts of kindness," he said, sneering. Turning to his men, he shouted, "Go on ahead! Search around the dike and the windmill."

Nyes shook her head, and saliva flew everywhere, speckling the officer as he walked by. It was as if she were saying good riddance to the nefarious intruder. Bastiaan wiped his hand across his forehead, hiding a smirk and choking down the laughter. His father climbed up on the wagon as Bastiaan motioned for Nyes to get moving.

"Papa," Bastiaan said as he slapped the horse's rump, directing her to the other side of the field, "there is a man hiding here." Bastiaan ducked his head when his father gave him a look. "He is under that pile of hay. I was too scared to tell the Germans, and then I was too scared of what they would do if I didn't. Papa, what should we do?"

Papa looked at the Germans disappearing into the rushes along the dike. "The hot sun will melt them in those heavy wool uniforms. They'll be back before long. Which pile of hay is he under?"

"That one," Bastiaan said, pointing to a tall stack.

"Then we will start at the other end of the field. They will come back. I don't think they will bother us again but keep your back to them."

"But what if they should find the man? Will they arrest us?"

"They will not find him."

The slow gait and red faces of the unit suggested possible heat stroke. The officer stopped and asked Hendrick for a drink from the water barrel.

Bastiaan was on the other side of the wagon, hunched over and slowly pitching hay. The soldiers guzzled the water as if they'd been scouting for the Jew in the Sahara desert. It pooled on their wool uniforms and they tugged at their collars for a cool wisp of air.

The officer let out a sigh and wiped the back of his hand across his mouth. "*Danke.*"

"*Bitte schon,*"[5] Papa said. "It is a little act of kindness that I show to my fellow men." Hendrick chuckled. "Sure is a different story when you are the one seeking human kindness." The lieutenant looked at him stiffly and stormed off.

The spent German unit disappeared wearily down the road toward Ede. When they were out of sight, Bastiaan ran to the pile of hay. "All right, you can come out now. If you think we are going to stick our necks out for the likes of you, you are mistaken. My family intends to ride

5. *You're welcome*

out the war on this farm and stay out of the affairs of both Jews and Germans."

The Jew crawled out from under the stack. He spit hay from his mouth, sneezed, and brushed it off his pants as he looked up at Bastiaan with a goofy smile. Bastiaan's eyes widened. "Abram? What are you doing here? And why are you running away?"

"Have you not heard the Germans are beginning to round up Jews and send them to Germany to work camps?" Abram said as he took a long piece of hay out of his hair. "They came in the night and yanked my family out of bed. My room is at the back near the cellar stairs, so I sneaked down the stairs and hid behind the wine shelves."

Bastiaan looked at him incredulously and didn't know whether to scold him for another one of his fantastic tales or listen without interruption, but he decided that Abram would not make something like this up.

"My father was making a tunnel in the wine cellar in case the German's came. I managed to slide the shelf out, crawl in, and pull it back. The Germans searched the cellar but when they saw the wine bottles, they took them and forgot about their search." Abram laughed. "The lushes. I stayed in the crawl space until I was sure it was safe and then ran here. I almost made it too, but one of the soldiers on the outskirts of town saw me. By the time he sounded the alarm, I was halfway across the fields, but they followed me," Abram said, looking at Mr. Coevorden. "I knew you would help me."

"Abram, you have put my family in danger!" Bastiaan shouted, his ears still ringing with the threats of the German officer.

Hendrick came up behind Bastiaan and put his hand on his shoulder. "Bastiaan, he is our friend. Would you see him sent to his death?"

"No, Papa," Bastiaan quietly murmured. "Abram, I am sorry. I let my fear take over my good sense. Please forgive me."

"There is nothing to forgive. I would have thought the same if I were in your shoes."

"What are we going to do with him, Papa? He can't stay here. If the Germans find him, it will mean prison for all of us."

"For now, we can give him a bed and something to eat. The Germans won't be back tonight."

chapter SIX

Marieka whirled around to look behind her as she rode along the canal. She struggled to keep the bike straight, but sometimes it veered dangerously close to the canal. Visions of Germans sneaking up behind her and poking their rifles in her back continued to plague her.

The next day, Marieka checked out the field where she had seen Bastiaan walk and discovered a hidden path bordering on Mr. Meijr's large potato field. Weeds grew over the path in some places and sometimes she had to get off and push the bike over the rough spots, but she felt safer on this path. *I wonder if the cream will turn to butter with all this bouncing,* she thought.

As Marieka came to a large mound of dirt, she was forced to get off her bike and push it over. She slipped and fell, spilling the contents of her basket. The lids on the gallon cans stayed snug, but the eggs flew out, half of them breaking, and the cheese cloth on the butter looked like a block of dirt.

"Oh, how utterly stupid of me!" She moaned, crawling on one knee to pick up the eggs and butter. "And I tore my dress and banged up my knee. Of all the dumb things to do," she said. Her knee was covered with blood and dirt and started to sting. She started to repack the basket on her bike, reached for another egg under a bush, and quickly jerked away as if she'd seen a snake. Underneath the bush was a dusty gray-green uniform.

"A German soldier out here?" she whispered. "Probably sleeping off a night of too much to drink." She quietly picked up the rest of her things and started to leave when she heard a moan. Marieka stepped closer and saw the leaves were spotted with blood.

"You're wounded?" she whispered. "I'm afraid to help a German soldier."

She picked up her bike and was about to leave when she heard, *Wasser*[6] one of the few German words she understood.

Marieka felt a tug at her heart. Could she walk away from someone in need? Someone injured? She had been taught to care for those in need. *You dumb German! What are you doing out here anyway? Why did I have to find you? Couldn't you just . . . die?*

Marieka knelt down, pushed back the branches, and gasped. He didn't look like the monster she imagined. He was but a helpless kid. His light hair was matted and streaked with debris; his slender eyebrows arched over his closed eyes and were darker than his flaxen hair. His square jaw was set, his teeth clenched as if he were biting on the pain, and his skin was bronzed as if he'd spent the summer outside, perhaps working on a farm.

Talking more to herself than to him, she asked, "How'd you get here anyway? I suppose I should report this to the German commander when I go to the village and have him come back for you."

"*Nein, nein,*" he said hoarsely.

"Hold on, German," Marieka said and gently put out her hand to push him back but hesitated. "Who are you? What if something awful happens? I've never touched a man before except Papa." She rocked back and forth on her heels for a moment wondering what she should do. "But he looks so pitiful lying there." She bent over, her hands trembling as she lifted the flap on the jacket and found an ugly wound on his shoulder. A piece of metal caked with dried blood was sticking out of his shoulder, fresh blood oozing under the shaft. In that instant all her fears crumbled. She saw a need to help him and also felt an overwhelming awareness of his vulnerability.

"If I pull the metal out, you'll really start bleeding," Marieka whispered. "You need a doctor. I should take you to the Germans."

"*Nein!*" he whispered again hoarsely. "I'm too far from my unit. They will consider me a deserter and shoot me," he said in very poor Dutch.

Marieka gasped. "But how did you get here anyway?"

"Please, Fräulein, do not take me there," he whispered weakly.

"Ahhhhh!" Marieka got up and paced back and forth, shaking her

6. *Water*

head and mumbling to herself. She looked down at the soldier again and wailed, "He's begging me not to take him to the Germans who can give him medical aid, but if I leave him here he'll die." She kicked at the dirt. "And I can't tell anyone. No one would understand helping a German soldier. They'd think I am nuts."

Marieka knelt on her good knee and prayed softly. "Oh, dear Lord, I need Thy help. Please tell me what to do. If I leave him here, he will die. If I take him to the Germans, he will be shot, and if I take him home, my parents will shoot me."

The soldier smiled at her words and passed out.

Marieka tore a piece of her slip and stuffed it around the wound. Retrieving her canteen from the handlebars, she lifted his head and poured a few drops of water onto his parched lips. Even though half conscious, he swallowed.

"I'll be back," she whispered and covered him with the bushes.

As she entered the village, Marieka hurried to Mrs. Berg's porch, rang the bell, but did not wait for her to come to the door. She put the milk in the cooler and ran out before a startled Mrs. Berg stepped into the kitchen. "What are you doing there, girl?" Mrs. Berg called after her, shaking her fist. "Insolent girl, she still needs that horsewhipping," she grumbled and then went back to bed.

Marieka climbed on the bike and hustled to Mr. Buskirk's bakery, swerving to avoid Mr. Smit delivering the mail. It scared him so bad, he dropped his pack of mail.

"Marieka, where are you going in such a hurry? You should be careful not to run over people," Mr. Smit said, picking up the mail.

"Sorry!" Marieka hollered over her shoulder but did not stop.

At the bakery, Marieka ran in, sat the butter and eggs on the workbench, and ran back to the door without saying anything.

"Marieka, you have hurt your knee!" Mr. Buskirk called after her.

"Oh, *ja*, I had a spill this morning. It's just a scrape, it looks worse than it is."

"You better stop by Doc Bijl's and have him look at it."

"Oh, it is just a scr . . . uh . . . *ja*, I'd better."

Mrs. Bijl opened the doctor's door wearing a patched pink flannel nightgown with a matching gathered nightcap. She untangled her wire rim glasses and put them on the end of her nose. It helped her eyes to uncross. She blinked. "Marieka, what are you doing here so early?"

"I came to see Dr. Bijl. I hurt my knee," she said, showing her.

"Oh, my child," Mrs. Bijl said as she turned toward the clinic. "I'll get Dr. Bijl."

Dr. Bijl appeared in a flannel nightshirt with a cap, and Marieka giggled.

Marieka followed him into a little room. A long, thin table was in the center with a round light above it. Cabinets that held bottles, bandages, and medical instruments lined the walls.

"Climb up on the table, Marieka, and let me have a look at your knee."

Marieka sat on the table facing him, her legs dangling over the side.

"Looks like you tore a patch of skin," Dr. Bijl said at first glance.

"*Ja*, I'm angry at how clumsy I was."

"Oh, Marieka, you are not clumsy. Accidents happen. Now this is going to sting a little." Dr. Bijl swabbed the loosened flap of skin with disinfectant and cleaned the dirt and debris out of the scrape. Marieka winced.

"It's just a scratch. It will heal quickly, but it's a good thing you came to me or it could have got ten infected." Dr. Bijl put a large gauze patch over it and then taped it. "Have your mama change the bandage in a day or so. Then leave the bandage off so it can dry out and scab over."

"Thank you, Dr. Bijl. You're so kind."

Dr. Bijl chuckled. "It's my pleasure."

"Uh . . . Dr. Bijl. Can I ask you a question? What would you do if you were to come upon a wounded enemy soldier? Would you help an enemy?"

"Oh, little Marieka. You do not understand the ways of a healer. I would help any man, whether he is an enemy, a Jew, black, brown, or white. I took an oath when I got my license to practice medicine to administer to all, and I took an oath to God long before that."

"What if I were to tell you I found a wounded enemy soldier?"

"Oh dear. It would be best to report him to the Germans."

"But I can't. He is too far from his unit. He says they will shoot him for being a deserter."

"Where is he? How did he get so far from his unit?"

"I don't know. He was not fully conscious. All he said was not to turn him over to the Germans. He has a piece of metal in his shoulder with blood oozing from it. I didn't dare pull it out. It looked like it needs a doctor's attention. Would you help him? I'm afraid if he doesn't get a doctor's help soon, he'll die."

"This is a very dangerous thing."

"But I can't just let him die."

"No, no, that is not the thing to do. I will get dressed and meet you . . . where?"

"At Mr. Meijr's barn. He is not far from there."

"I will meet you in half an hour."

"Thanks, Dr. Bijl."

chapter SEVEN

Marieka had ridden the path enough to know its turns and pitfalls. She also knew that riding too fast was an invitation for another spill. However, she was worried about the soldier and ignored her good sense. When she came to where she'd left the soldier, she dropped the bike and pushed it under another bush. She crouched beside the unconscious soldier. Marieka's eyes darted between the barn and the soldier, looking for Dr. Bijl.

Time seemed to pass excruciatingly slow. Finally, the familiar dark suit walked up the lane toward the barn. Marieka breathed a sigh of relief and ran across the open patch of weeds to meet him.

"Did they stop or follow you?"

"No, the Germans usually notice me and then go about their business. They know I am a doctor with many errands."

"Follow me," Marieka said. "He's in the bushes."

Dr. Bijl followed her through the patch of weeds and down a slope to a small cluster of wild bushes.

Marieka bent down and moved the branches aside as the doctor knelt and inspected the wound. "Did you put this cloth on his wound?" he asked.

"Yes, sir."

"That is good. We have to move him to a place where I can safely remove the shrapnel and stitch the wound closed. Let's get him to his feet and take him to Mr. Meijr's barn."

"Will he turn him in to the Germans?"

"It is a chance we'll have to take. What are you going to do with him once I patch him up?" Dr. Bijl asked.

"I don't know, but we can't give him back to the Germans."

Dr. Bijl took some smelling salts and waved it under the soldier's nose.

The German groaned and jerked away from the acid smell as he slowly opened his eyes. His eyebrows furrowed, and he looked through narrow slits in a dreamlike state, moaned, and then tried to move away.

"Hold on, young man. I'm a doctor. I've come to patch you up. What you do afterward is your affair. First, I must get you somewhere dry where we can lay you flat so I can operate on that shoulder."

Dr. Bijl put his arm around the soldier's side and told him to get to his feet when he lifted him. Marieka put her arm around his hip and lifted from his other side. The soldier slumped as he moved his feet haphazardly over the tall weeds, almost dragging Marieka and the doctor with him.

"Let's stop for a moment, Marieka. Can you support most of his weight while I rest?" Dr. Bijl huffed.

"Yes, I can hold him."

Dr. Bijl leaned the soldier against Marieka for only a moment and then said anxiously, "Let's go."

The soldier's legs buckled just before they reached the barn. "Come on, boy," Dr. Bijl coaxed. "You've got to help us."

Light flooded the dismal room as Marieka opened the barn door to her surprise, the tables and chairs from the dance a few months ago were still stacked against the wall.

She ran back to help Dr. Bijl. "Look, the tables from the dance. Would that be a suitable place to operate?"

"Excellent! You can help me lift him onto a table. Have you ever helped with a medical procedure?"

"No!" Marieka looked at him wide-eyed.

"Well, today you are going to learn a new thing."

"Oh no. I'm squeamish when it comes to blood."

"You'll have to put that nonsense aside because I am going to need your help."

Dr. Bijl instructed Marieka to lift the German when he counted to three.

After they got the soldier securely on the table, Dr. Bijl said, "Marieka, get a couple of lanterns and light them, but don't close the door. I'll need the sunlight."

Dr. Bijl slid the uniform from the good shoulder and cut it away from the wounded one. A small leather book fell out. "What do you think this is?" Marieka asked as she picked up the book. "I didn't know German soldiers were issued books to carry."

"Marieka, we have work to do. You can ask him later. This may hurt a little," Dr. Bijl said as he cut the shirt up the front and peeled it away from his shoulder. "You have lost a lot of blood, lad. You should be in a hospital."

"Or a morgue," the boy said sarcastically.

"I am going to put you out now. When you wake up, you'll be all fixed up." Dr. Bijl poured ether on a white cloth and placed it over the soldier's mouth and nose.

"Okay, Marieka, I'll need you to hand me the instruments when I ask for them. Can you handle that?"

"Uh, yes, I can do that," she stuttered.

"When I pull the shrapnel out, the wound is going to bleed profusely. I need you to put pressure on his shoulder and don't let go until I tell you. Hopefully it'll keep him from losing any more blood."

Marieka choked down the bile coming up in her throat and forced herself to take deep breaths.

Dr. Bijl took the forceps, clamped it on the shrapnel, and pulled, but it didn't move. "It must be embedded in the bone," he said. "Put your hand on the sharp point of the shrapnel and when I say so, pull." Marieka walked around to the front of the soldier, standing slightly to the side, grabbed the point, and waited for Dr. Bijl to tell her to pull.

"Ready . . . pull." The shrapnel moved imperceptibly.

"Stop!" Dr. Bijl ordered. He bent over and scraped around the shrapnel, removing tiny slivers of bone. "Okay, Marieka, let's try it again." The shrapnel moved slightly.

"Don't let go, Marieka. Keep the pressure on. It's coming." Dr. Bijl grabbed the shrapnel from a different angle and pulled. The shrapnel dislodged, sending Marieka reeling backward.

Blood spurted from the wound. Dr. Bijl quickly grabbed a sterilized cloth and stuffed it in the wound.

"The shoulder is broken," he said. "It looks like a clean break and can be set." He pulled the pieces of bone together and stitched the muscle inside. The doctor cleaned and disinfected the wound and stitched the outer layer, wrapping it in clean gauze.

Marieka let out a sigh of relief. "I didn't faint."

"Yes, young lady. Did you ever think about a medical career?"

"Oh no, I'm a farm girl."

"The boy is young and healthy. He will heal. My concern is the loss of blood and infection. Keep a close eye on him and push the liquids. If you have juices or even wine, it will help to build his blood. Watch for infection. If the wound emits an odor or has a strange color, then it is infected. Change the bandages twice a day and clean it with iodine. If there is any sign of infection, get in touch with me."

"Okay," Marieka said.

"Let's get him out of here before Mr. Meijr finds us," Dr. Bijl said as he cleaned up.

"How are we going to do that?"

"Get your bike. I'll think of something."

Marieka ran across the open field and pushed her bike to the barn. Dr. Bijl found two 1 x 10 wooden planks, tied them together, and attached a rope to the underside of the bicycle seat. Dr. Bijl and Marieka lifted him onto the planks.

Dr. Bijl found a tarp and wrapped it around him. "This will be a heavy load. You will probably have to push your bike home. I'll help you get him over the field."

"Thank you, Dr. Bijl."

Marieka groaned inwardly. "I didn't think this would be so hard." She dug in her heels and pushed the bike with all her strength, but the bike only moved an inch or two. Realizing she needed help, she whispered to the unconscious soldier, "I'll be right back." Then she covered the soldier with bushes again and ran toward her farm. *I hope one of the horses is in the barn,* she thought. Reaching the barn, Marieka ran in the side door. Bet was in the stall. She nickered as Marieka put the harness on her. "Oh, Bet, I need your help," Marieka whispered. "But you can't tell anyone." When she turned the corner, Papa stepped in front of her and Bet.

"You're late! And where do you think you're going with Bet?"

"Marieka looked down at her feet and stuttered, "I . . . oh . . . um."

"Marieka, you're not very good at making up stories, so I suggest you just tell the truth. Out with it."

Tears welled up in Marieka's eyes as she told Papa about the wounded soldier.

"Why didn't you report him to the Germans? They have medical facilities for their soldiers."

"He begged me not to. He said he was too far from his unit and would be shot as a deserter. I couldn't leave him there to die, and I couldn't report him. I tried to Papa, but I couldn't. Dr. Bijl built a sled and tied a rope to my bike, but it was too heavy for me to push."

"You did the right thing, Marieka. Where is he?"

"In the field next to Mr. Meijr's barn under some bushes."

Papa took hold of Bet's harness, and Marieka led him to where she'd left the soldier under the bushes. Hendrick attached the rope to the harness.

"What are we going to do with him, Papa? If the Germans search our house and barn again, they'll find him and we'll all be arrested."

"We'll figure out something to do with him."

"But what, Papa? Our wagon is our only transportation and the Germans are patrolling the road now."

"Don't worry, Marieka. We'll find a way."

Hendrick put Bet back in the stall and told Marieka to brush her down while he took care of the soldier. He pulled the soldier to the kitchen door and made such a commotion it alerted Anna.

"Hendrick, who is that? What are you going to do with him?" Anna Coevorden asked in a high-pitched shriek.

"He's a wounded German soldier."

"What? A what? What are you doing with a wounded German soldier?"

"Marieka found him."

"You bring a wounded German soldier home like a lost puppy?"

"No, Marieka does."

"Hendrick, be serious. Where did you find him? And why didn't you report him to the Germans? I don't like it. If the Germans search our house again, they will arrest us and we will be shot for not just one crime but two!"

"Anna, calm down. We can't turn our backs on people in need—it isn't Christian. We'll find a way to get him and Abram out of Holland. I'll need some help getting him upstairs, though. Where's Abram?"

"In the cellar staying out of sight like he's supposed to," Anna berated.

"Would you ask him to come up?" Hendrick said, unfastening the rope around the boy.

"Oh, we are signing our own death warrants." Anna wrung her hands, pacing back and forth.

"Calm down, Anna. Things will be all right."

"How?"

"With the Lord's help."

"It isn't His neck you're risking, it's ours!"

"He will help and protect us. Have faith, Anna."

Anna rolled her eyes and went to the top of the cellar stairs to call down for Abram.

Abram was sitting on a bucket of wheat trying to catch flies. He bounded up the stairs two at a time, almost slamming into Anna. "Thanks, Mrs. Coevorden. I was awfully bored down there."

"Don't get too excited. It's only for a moment, and then you're going right back," Anna said sternly.

"Oh, Mrs. Coevorden, you really know how to make a day a bummer," Abram said with a wink.

Anna looked at him with eyes dead as a carp, grunted, and abruptly walked away.

"Abram," Mr. Coevorden said, "will you help carry this young man upstairs to our bedroom?"

"Wow, Mr. Coevorden, who do you have here? Another Jew? Are you opening a home for outlaw Jews?"

"No, Abram. Take his legs."

Upon removing the dirt-crusted tarp, Abram noticed the filthy German uniform. "*Ziekers,*[7] Mr. Coevorden! A German soldier? You're bringing a German soldier here? Just hand me over."

"Abram, he's a fugitive just like you. The Germans will shoot him on sight if he's found. At least they'd let you live a couple weeks at a prison camp."

"Now that's comforting, Mr. Coevorden."

"Anna, burn this uniform and get one of Bastiaan's night shirts," Hendrick said, holding the dirty uniform out.

"Not before you give me his little book!" Marieka said as she shuffled in the back door.

"What book? What do you want his book for? You can't even read German," Anna said harshly.

"It looks like it is something special, and I bet he'll appreciate us not burning it. Besides, I want to know what it is."

---

7. Expression of surprise

Anna took the uniform between thumb and forefinger, threw it in the coals of the kitchen stove, and gruffly slammed the oven door.

Hendrick and Abram carried the soldier upstairs to his and Anna's room.

Hendrick pulled the blinds over the window. The soldier's face was as gray as a stonecutter's stone, and his breaths were short and quick. "Marieka," he said, "it is your responsibility to give him round the clock care. In a couple of days when he is stabilized, we'll move him. Let's just hope the Germans don't come back for another inspection for some time. This old sheet will have to do for redressing his wound. Make sure you burn the soiled bandages in the stove."

"Yes, Papa," Marieka said, fussing over him.

"Mama will sit with him in the mornings while you make deliveries. We can't change our routine. It'll cause suspicion. Abram," Hendrick ordered, "back to the cellar.

"Oh, do I have to, Mr. Coevorden? It's dark and lonely down there."

"It's better to be lonely than to be transported out of here with a hundred others, isn't it?

"*Ja, ja.*"

Papa carried the boards across the yard to the barn, set them next to Nye's stall, and then moved the large feeder, exposing a trap door.

He climbed down the ladder into the dark pit with the boards. A musty odor hung in the air like the heavy scent of garlic. He sat the boards on the dirt floor and then examined the contents of the shelf built in the wall. On the top shelf was a stack of threadbare blankets. A lantern, an old radio that probably didn't work, candles, matches, tin plates, and cups were crowded onto the second shelf. Mouse-eaten mattresses were stacked on four cots along the wall, and a warped wooden table with some broken chairs were in the middle of the room.

"This isn't clean enough for a wounded man," Hendrick mumbled. He grabbed the mattresses and piled them next to the ladder and then stacked the blankets on top of them. Then he grabbed the tin plates and cups. He was about to climb the ladder when Bastiaan stuck his head through the opening.

"Wow, Papa, what is this? I didn't know this was here." Bastiaan was so amazed that he leaned in too far and almost fell.

Hendrick dropped the tin plates, and the sound echoed like cymbals in a cave. He looked up at Bastiaan. "I thought you were still in the field. You about gave St. Peter another sinner to deal with."

"Oh, Papa, you're not a full-fledged sinner. I'm sure St. Peter could sneak you into heaven," Bastiaan teased.

"I hope you're right on that one, son," Hendrick said and laughed. "This is what you call a hideout."

"A hideout? For what?"

"Escaped prisoners were hidden here during World War I."

"Why? I thought the Netherlands was a neutral country. Why would they care if escaped soldiers hid here?" Bastiaan climbed down the ladder.

"In order for Holland to protect its neutral status, the Dutch government could give no favors to prisoners who sought refuge as a way of avoiding capture by the enemy. They couldn't be permitted to escape or return to active duty either, so they treated them harshly.[8] Many escaped from the Dutch internment camps, and my father helped them. The Dutch authorities looked very unfavorably on its neutral status being compromised." Hendrick's voice quivered. "They arrested my father."

"Bet that was hard for you, but isn't there already a shelter under the sunken door by the chicken coop?" Bastiaan asked seriously.

"That was a small shelter, or rather a decoy in case the place was ever searched by the Dutch authorities. If they found it, my father hoped it would satisfy them so they wouldn't keep searching. They were informed it was here. They arrested and executed my father without a trial. I was sixteen at the time. I swore I would never open this shelter and use it for such activities again, but here I am doing the same thing as my papa." Hendrick swiped at a tear, pretending something was irritating his eye.

"Are you going to put Abram down here?" Bastiaan asked, his eyebrows jutted upward as if he'd just received an epiphany.

"Yes, and the wounded soldier too," Hendrick said, handing a stack of items to Bastiaan.

"What wounded soldier?"

"I'll explain later," Hendrick said as he motioned for Bastiaan to go up the ladder. When they were at the top and standing outside the trap door, Hendrick said, "Go get the plywood we were going to build the new chicken coop with."

"What for, Papa?"

"We're going to repair this shelter for our guests."

---

8. *"Refugees in the Netherlands during the First World War 1914–1918," Menno Wielinga, http://www.wereldoorlog1418.nl/refugees/.*

The two worked tediously all the night. When they walked into the kitchen in the early morning, Anna glared at them. "Hendrick, what have you two been doing all night?"

"Bastiaan and I built a room for our guests."

"Guests? You call them guests?" Anna's voice rose, and her eyes narrowed. She looked at her husband as if he were a traitor.

Papa smiled. "How is our wounded guest? Has he awakened?"

"Only partially. He is delirious and thrashing about. Marieka sat up with him all night keeping a cool cloth on his head and giving him sips of water. He is going to be in a lot of pain when he wakes up."

"Then it would be a good idea if Marieka stops at Dr. Bijl's and picks up some pain medication."

Marieka came into the kitchen, stifling a yawn. "You need to get to your chores," Papa said. "No time for sleep now."

"But, Papa, I'm so tired."

"I'm sure you were a good nurse, but you still have chores to do."

"Yes, Papa," Marieka said, yawning, and headed out the door.

"Bastiaan, get some sleep for a couple hours. I'll do chores."

Bastiaan grinned and without hesitation ran up the stairs.

As Marieka pulled up to Miss Remi's house, she found the front door open. Marieka dropped her bike.

"Miss Remi?" she called. "Miss Remi, where are you?"

Marieka opened the screen door and poked her head in. The living room and kitchen were in shambles, the contents of the cupboards scattered on the floor, and the table and chairs overturned.

She walked to the back of the house to Miss Remi's white-haired father's room. His eyes were wide and glazed, his mouth open. He had a red hole in his forehead.

Marieka covered her mouth and screamed. She stumbled out of the house, grabbed her bike shakily, and pedaled home.

Anton's men kept off the main roads, traveling at night, while he took Dedriek home. The German patrols had doubled and seemed to pop up in the oddest places. Anton received a report that many innocent people in Ede were arrested and interrogated. He ranted, "I hate the evil injustices of the Germans! Why do they have to cause innocent people to suffer because of their desire for power. These people are my friends and neighbors. They don't know anything about the resistance."

Anton and his younger brother arrived home. "Papa, do not let this boy out of your sight," he ordered.

Dedriek kicked the ground and bit off a swear word. "There's no excitement on this farm. Dull, boring—that's what it is! I'll find you again, brother, and next time I'll make you so proud of me, you'll have to let me stay."

Anton gave his little brother a hug. "Mind Papa, and if any Germans come around, make yourself scarce." Anton kissed his papa, waved goodbye to Dedriek, and disappeared into the night.

"May God go with you, son. Come on, Dedriek, we've got to get up early."

"You know, Papa, I'd rather blow up a few bridges and communication networks. Feeding and milking cows just doesn't register high on my excitement list."

"You crazy, boy? You could get killed out there! And then where would my future grandchildren be?"

"Anton can have them."

"Well, I wouldn't count on those grandkids until they're hatched. Anton's life will be ashes if the Germans get a chance at him. You have a warm bed, good food, and the wonderful company of your mama and me. Anton is out there sleeping on the hard ground and eating a cold can of mash with nothing but those ugly, unshaven men to look at. Wouldn't you rather be here?"

"Well, Papa, you do have a point, but I'd still rather be out there where all the excitement is."

Dedriek's father put his hand on the back of his neck, smiled, and said, "Come on, son. Let's see if Mama has some bread and buttermilk. It's the perfect nightcap."

The gray arches loomed before Anton's men in the moonless night. The entrances on both sides of the bridge were guarded by four German soldiers and two German shepherds. A faint smell of cigarette smoke wafted through the air. Anton could hear the soldiers casually talking and laughing.

It seems a little bit too calm, Anton thought. *They seem too relaxed for being on alert. Something doesn't add up.*

Anton sat on his haunches. Trevier sat quietly next to him, knowing not to interrupt. The rendezvous with Rapier was to be on the north side of the river and they were on the southeast side with German guards in between. Anton looked at Trevier and instructed him to send a couple of men to scout the area.

"It may be a trap," Anton said. "We don't have much time until sun up. This place will be crawling with Germans, and it'll be impossible to cross the bridge then." The behavior of the guards grated on his nerves as he waited for his scouts to return.

"You were right, Anton," the scouts reported. "There's a squadron of German soldiers hidden on the north side of the bridge."

Anton frowned. "There are too many Germans to rush the bridge. We would lose too many men."

A tall, freckle-faced boy pushed his way to Anton's side and stuttered, "May I offer a suggestion?"

Anton saw the crooked grin of a young boy about the age of Dedriek.

"What if there is a ferry at a crossing down river? Would that help, sir?"

Anton looked up and grinned. "Sure would if there is one to be found."

"My name is Roch. I live in these parts. I was born and raised here."

"*Ja, ja,* we don't need to hear about your upbringing," Trevier interrupted.

"Shhh, let him talk," Anton whispered, annoyed.

"My papa and uncles ran sheep from the north pastures in the hills to the south pastures of the valley. The spring runoff causes the river to be too swift and dangerous to herd the sheep across it, so my papa and uncles made a ferry. It's on an old sheep trail, so I doubt the Germans know about it. We could use it to get across the river, but it's back a mile or so."

"Can you lead us there?"

"Sure, I know this area like my mama's face, but there are small bogs and marshes. You have to know where you are going to get through that stretch of the forest."

"Trevier, rouse the men. We'll follow Roch through the forest."

Roch headed for the thick boscage and circled wide to the east until he found the trail. "Go in single file," he whispered. "And try not to trample the brush, we don't want to leave an obvious trail for the Germans. And be quiet. Sound carries on the wind."

The men closely followed behind each other as branches constantly whipped their arms and faces. Roch hiked into the thick underbrush as if it was an open door.

Although the ferry was a little over a mile away, it took half the day to get through the wetlands. The men's arms, hands, and faces were covered with red, angry bites and cuts. They looked like they'd ran into an electric fan.

At midday, Roch stepped into a small, secluded cove. His father's ferry was tied to four large trees so the rising spring water wouldn't beat it against the brink. The large logs were girded with strong cable. The dark swollen logs were soaked but buoyant and reeked of sheep droppings.

"It doesn't look like much, but it is sound. I suggest we wait until dark before we cross. If a German scout plane should fly over, we'd be like sitting ducks."

The men made camp in the thick underbrush. Trevier grumbled as he shifted in the infernal undergrowth to find a comfortable spot. "I give up," he growled. He took his knife and cut off the offending branches and settled against the trunk of a white birch.

Anton assigned the men a two-hour watch and then fell asleep. When the sun was setting Roch woke him. "It will be dark soon. We'll cross the river and then get something to eat."

chapter EIGHT

The ebony tentacles pulled him deeper into the inky blackness. He struggled against it, but a powerful force pulled him back into the depths of oblivion. A light beckoned him, but the lurid gloom was engulfing. His strength was sapped, pulled like a sinking ship into the inexorable deep. An audible sound stirred his senses, a voice calling to him, a soft voice, a voice of comfort. He struggled toward it, but the gloom held him captive, pulling him back into a whirlpool of angry darkness.

The stirrings from the bed next to her awakened her. Marieka jumped and then noticed the droplets on the soldier's flushed brow. She put her hand on his forehead. "You have a fever, my German soldier. It is the infection Dr. Bijl warned me about." Marieka unwrapped the bandage to inspect his shoulder. The incision was swollen and bright red. She wrapped it, put a cool cloth on his forehead, covered him with a light sheet, and slipped from the room.

Marieka parked her bike next to Mr. Buskirk's bakery in the alley. Although she was late, she quietly stepped through the back door and put his order on the table. The baker was at the oven, taking out Danish pastries and pastries for the four German soldiers waiting for their breakfast. The tall blond soldier looked up when she entered. He leered at her, and she looked away. His eyes made her skin crawl.

Mr. Buskirk nodded his usual greeting. She smiled and slipped out the door with another task on her mind. Marieka left her bike in the alley and headed down the street to Dr. Bijl's office. Mrs. Bijl opened the door. "Why, Marieka, I wasn't expecting to see you so soon."

"I came to see Dr. Bijl. The scrape on my knee has become infected."

"Oh dear. Sit here. The doctor is in the next room. I'll get him."

Marieka fidgeted as the minutes ticked by. She tiptoed to the door and was about to reach for the handle when Dr. Bijl opened it. His white medical coat was splattered with blood in an outline where an apron had been. His rosy pink hands looked as if they just had a good scrub down. His eyes were bloodshot, and he frowned grimly.

"Marieka, Mama told me you were here. Something about an infected knee?"

"Well, more like an infected shoulder. I've come to get some medicine for the soldier. He's been unconscious and delirious for three days now. I'm worried the infection will kill him."

"Marieka, it's very dangerous for you to be here. The Germans have been looking for a deserter. You must get him out of your home. You and your family are in danger."

"Papa made a place to hide him, but he is too sick to move. Do you have some medicine for the infection?"

"Yes," he said and paused. "You will have to give him an injection."

"I don't know how to do that!"

"He's not conscious to swallow pills, so you'll have to give it in a shot. Clean the area on his hip with alcohol, fill the syringe with the medicine, stick it in, and empty it. Do this every day for three days. Keep the wound clean and sprinkle it with this powder. When he wakes, give him two pills a day until they are all gone."

"Where can I put this stuff so that the Germans won't notice it? It's too bulky."

Dr. Bijl put the syringe, bottle of medicine, and pills in a drawstring cloth bag. "Tie this around your waist under your dress."

"Thank you, Dr. Bijl. I must go before the German officers are done with their breakfast."

The doctor nervously coughed as she hurried to the door. He cleared his throat and called after her.

"Uh . . . I'm doing this against my better judgment, but I need help. It could put your life in grave danger."

"What is it, Dr. Bijl?"

"There is a young man in the other room who came in the night with a terrible wound. I tried to save him, but his wounds were too severe. Before he died, he asked me to deliver a note to Mr. Fiske. He said it was very important that the resistance receive it before the twentieth, which is tomorrow. Do you know Mr. Fiske? They don't live far from your place. He said Mr. Fiske would send it on to the resistance. Can you see to it that he receives this note?"

"I will, Dr. Bijl. The Germans are used to seeing me come and go. They will not suspect me."

"That's it! You should make another delivery, although I doubt milk and eggs would be a viable cover. I don't like asking a young girl with a lifetime ahead of her, but I am too old with many duties. If you do not feel this is something you are able to do, then I will have to think of another way or go myself. But I won't be able to get away until late tonight and by then it will be too late."

"Of course I will go. It isn't any more dangerous than hiding a deserter and a Jew." Marieka stopped and her eyes widened. "I shouldn't have told you about the Jew."

"It's all right, Marieka. Your secret is safe with me."

Dr. Bijl left the room for a moment while Marieka tied the pouch around her waist.

"You shouldn't place the note in the sack. You cannot be arrested for hiding medicine, but a note for the Resistance would not be so good."

"Where shall I put it?"

"Unbraid your hair, fold the note into a long strip, and weave it underneath."

Marieka beamed. "I would never think of looking in someone's hair."

She quickly untied the braid and wove the note near the top where her hair was the thickest and secured it with a pin. She turned her back to him and asked, "Can you see it, Dr. Bijl?"

"No. You have done an excellent job."

"I'd better go. The Germans will be finished with breakfast soon."

"Wait!" Dr. Bijl said. "Let's put a fresh bandage on your knee so there won't be any question why you came here." When Dr. Bijl finished, Marieka gave him a quick kiss on his leathery cheek and hurried out the back. She peeked out to see if any Germans were in sight. As she stepped from behind the doctor's office, she walked into the tall, handsome German officer.

"Fräulein, where have you been? I noticed you left your bicycle at the bakery. It is not like you to go off and leave your bicycle."

"Uh . . . I had to see Dr. Bijl for some medicine for my knee. It has become infected. He treated it and put a new bandage on it." She lifted her skirt to show him.

Lieutenant Schmidt looked at the clean bandage and nodded. "Little Fräulein, your knee looks as if it could use a rest. May I give you and your bike a ride back to your farm?"

"No, thank you. My knee is well enough, and I have another delivery. Dr. Bijl asked if I would deliver a loaf of bread to an elderly couple and inquire about how they are feeling. He said he wasn't able to get away and asked if I would go instead."

"I could help you deliver the bread, Fräulein." The officer smiled. He put his hand on Marieka's elbow to guide her across the street. Marieka pulled away and cried out, "No! I am fine. I must go."

He tipped his hat to her and said, "Have a good day, Fräulein," and he walked the other way to the headquarters.

Shaken, Marieka walked across the street and knocked quietly on the bakery door. Mr. Buskirk opened it.

"Marieka, what are you doing here? I thought you left an hour ago. The village will be swarming with Germans soon. You must leave."

"Mr. Buskirk, I have an unusual request. I told the blond German officer that I had a delivery of bread to make to an elderly couple. Dr. Bijl asked if I would make a special delivery," Marieka said and turned away in an effort to hide the rest of the story on her reddened face.

"Oh, my little Marieka, what have you gotten yourself into?"

"Mr. Buskirk, I was asked by Dr. Bijl to help an elderly couple. That is all."

"Little Marieka, do not lie to me. You are not so good at it, eh?"

"Mr. Buskirk, I cannot tell you why, just that I need some bread to deliver or the German officer will become suspicious, and that won't be good for you or me. I will pay you for the bread in a couple of days."

"That is not necessary. You know I will help you. I would not enjoy being questioned by the Germans or watch you questioned by them either. What is their name? I have to know where my deliveries are sent and write an order."

"I cannot tell you. It's best you do not know."

"Then we will have to come up with an imaginary name, say Mr. and Mrs. Dekker."

"Thank you, Mr. Buskirk. You are a dear."

Mr. Buskirk put two loaves of bread in a brown paper bag and taped the end.

Marieka noticed the blond officer watching her as she left.

Everything was a blur. Deeply gulping in the fresh morning air, Marieka rode as fast as she could along the dike. In her hurry to put as much distance as possible between her and the German, she failed to notice the lieutenant following behind. He stopped behind a lone tree and watched her go into the house. Then moments later she reappeared and biked up the road with the bread toward the old windmill.

"Have you ever felt such peace?" Marieka asked herself as she walked through the tall sedge next to the cottage. Her breath caught as she looked at the majestic windmill that seemed to be immortalized by time. It stood like a patriarch over the cottage, protecting it and the lowlands from the ever invading waters. The arms of the mill were still on the hot, windless day. Marieka felt the tranquility as she approached the porch as if she too were protected by the power of the dominant giant.

Marieka smiled and knocked on a weathered wooden door. An elderly woman with a gray braid wound on the top of her head answered. She was wearing a plain gray dress with a lace shawl draped over bony shoulders despite the heat. Her eyes twinkled in her soft, wrinkled face as she said hello.

"I have a delivery for Mr. Fiske. Is he at home?"

"*Ja*. Please come in."

As Marieka stepped into the cool, dimly lit cottage, she felt as if she'd walked into the past. The gray interior, the antique chairs, the embroidered towels, and the crocheted doilies reminded her of a painted portrait of Van Gogh.

Mr. Fiske entered from the back. He was thin, bow-legged, and hunched over with an overly large nose on a long, whiskerless face. His blue eyes sparkled as he smiled, and two elongated dimples appeared in the slender cracks of his cheeks.

"Marieka, so nice to see you. What brings you to our home today?"

"I have a very special delivery for you," she said, pronouncing her words slowly as she stared into his eyes.

Mr. Fisk watched her face for a few moments in bewilderment. Finally his eyes widened with understanding.

"You're making a delivery?" he asked slowly.

"Uh, yes, sir." Marieka nodded, glancing over at Mrs. Fiske.

"And who is this delivery from?" Mr. Fiske asked, raising one eyebrow.

"From Dr. Bijl. Well, sort of. He said it was from a wounded man that came to him last night."

"May this man's name have been Jully?"

"I think so, sir, but I do not know for sure."

"And where is Jully?" he asked in a grim tone.

"He is dead, sir."

Mr. Fiske's eyes moistened. A tear dropped onto his leathery cheek. "Won't you please be seated?" he mumbled, turning away from her. "Nena, will you take the bread into the kitchen please?" His wife took the bread, nodded her thanks, and shuffled through the same door Mr. Fiske had come through earlier.

Marieka's fingers disappeared into the top of her hair. She retrieved the long slip of paper as Mr. Fiske watched, puzzled.

"It was the only safe place we could think of."

He smiled and took the note. A grim shadow crossed his face as he read it and folded it again. "This is most important. Thank you for delivering this and also for your gift of bread."

"You're welcome. I'll be on my way now. Is there anything else I can do for you?"

"No. You have been of great service."

Mr. Fiske immediately left the cottage and put the sails on the arms of the windmill.

Within an hour, an unkempt-looking young man of eighteen appeared at back of the barn. Mr. Fiske opened the check-valve on the gate and began digging sediment from the bottom of the ditch. He glanced up and saw the boy crouched by the fence next to the barn.

"Peter, you must get this message to Rapier immediately," he said as he lifted another shovelful of mud from the ditch. "Tomorrow's attack on the communications network has been compromised. It seems there is a spy in the underground. If Rapier proceeds, it will be a massacre." Mr. Fiske stood and wiped his brow. "It cost Jully his life to get this message through," he whispered.

Peter sat quietly for a moment and wiped away a tear with his thumb. "This cursed war. It spares no one."

Mr. Fiske bent over and tugged at a large weed, dropping the message in the grass, and then moved further down the ditch. Peter waited for a few moments before reaching for the note. He quietly shrank behind the barn and disappeared.

Lieutenant Schmidt followed Marieka to the windmill. He watched as she entered the little cottage and again as she left a few moments later. The old woman wrapped in a shawl stood on the step and waved good-bye. He waited and watched as the elderly man put the sails on the arms of the windmill as the wind had picked up. For almost an hour he watched, but nothing seemed amiss so he left.

Anna Coevorden pushed open the swinging door, carrying a basket of wet laundry into the kitchen. Marieka ran into her, and Anna and the laundry fell in a heap onto the floor. "Heavens, Marieka. Don't sneak up on me like that! You'll make my hair as white as Sinkerklaas."

Marieka's tired eyes danced as she tried to control her laughter. Her mama was sitting in a pile of wet laundry with a sock hanging over her face. "Goodness, Mama . . ." She choked on a giggle. "I didn't purposely knock you over. I was in a hurry to check on the German soldier."

"I just came from him. His fever hasn't broken, nor has he awakened."

Marieka sidestepped the laundry, bounded up the stairs two at a time, and entered the darkened room, noisy as an armored division. She sat down next to the soldier and stared into his face. "Who are you, my handsome German soldier? I would like to put a name to your face so I don't have to call you 'German soldier' all the time." She wiped the sheen of sweat from his face as she continued talking to him. "It puzzles me why you deserted. I thought all Germans believed Hitler to be the one and only ruler of the world, a God of sorts in your eyes," she stated. "But there is only one God, and He is a God of love, a God in heaven, not a God of misery and hatred."

Marieka turned away from the soldier as she loosened the drawstring of the bag around her waist. "Dr. Bijl says I have to give you an injection." Marieka cringed and her hands shook as she took the bottle of medicine out of the bag and filled the syringe. Then she lowered the band on the borrowed pajama bottoms and swabbed his hip with alcohol. Holding the hated instrument in her hands, she looked away as she stabbed the needle into the upper part of his hip.

"You didn't even flinch!" She smiled and sighed deeply, looking upward, thankful the ordeal was over. "Of course, you are unconscious and can't feel anything," she said, covering him again with the light blanket. "Come on, German soldier. You're young. Fight this infection." She sat next to the bed and fell asleep.

Low guttural moans and thrashing awakened her. She jumped to see the soldier staring at her with half-lidded, fevered eyes.

"At last you are awake!" Marieka cried.

"*Wo ess Ich?*"[9] he slurred in German.

Marieka looked at him and shook her head. "*Ich versteche nicht.*"[10] Marieka had learned a few words of German in the last couple of months but was far from being fluent. She continued to talk to him even though she knew he did not understand her. "You are safe for the time being, in our home. *Ikh hie-ssuh*[11] Marieka Coevorden. I found you three days ago in a field, wounded and unconscious," she said, keeping her eyes averted from his. "You were conscious enough, however, to ask me not to take you back to your army. You said they would shoot you as a deserter." She gently tucked the blanket around his feet without looking up. "So I asked Dr. Bijl to fix you up, and then Papa and I brought you here," Marieka said, reaching for another blanket. "If we were to take you back to them now, they would know we helped you escape. I doubt they would treat you or us kindly."

The soldier tried to sit up and said in Dutch, "I must go. I have put you and your family in danger."

Marieka stopped in midstride. "I knew you could speak a few words of Dutch, but I didn't realize you are so fluent." Looking sternly into his face, she said, "You are in no condition to go anywhere, and besides, just where do you think you would go? Back to the Germans? The Gestapo would love to get their hands on you," she said, circling the bed. "You better get well first, and then we will talk about you leaving! What is your name? I've been referring to you as the German soldier all this time."

Making a vain attempt at a smile, the boy said, "My name is Jorg Bauer. I am eighteen years old. The Germans drafted me into the army a few weeks ago, or rather, I was forced into it."

Marieka sat next to the bed as he continued, "I do not hold with the

---

9. *Where am I?*

10. *I do not understand you.*

11. *My name is . . .*

beliefs of the Nazi party or Hitler. I was loaded on a troop train headed for the front lines in France. We were all new conscripts, forty or so of us that didn't know each other. All of us had the same scared look on our faces and were afraid to talk," he said, taking in ragged breaths. "We were taught a few basics, such as marching, loading a rifle, and how to salute. Then they threw us on a train and told us that we were heading into action." He clenched his teeth and his fist tightened into a ball. "I do not want to fight a war I do not believe in. When the blast blew me away from the train, I saw an opportunity to escape. I must get back to Germany to my family."

"Hold on. You are a long way from Germany. It would be a death sentence for you to go back," Marieka scolded.

Jorg attempted to lift up on his elbow but fell back on the pillow. Marieka gently wiped his face with a cool cloth and held a cup of water to his lips. "Dr. Bijl said you must take a pill for the infection and drink lots of water. You lost a lot of blood. Water will help to rebuild it. Do as I say or I shall spoon feed it to you, which I'm sure wouldn't be pleasant for either of us. Both of us may end up drenched."

Jorg sipped the water slowly. "Are there any Mormon elders around? I need a priesthood blessing," he said, his eyes drooping. He fell asleep before Marieka could figure out what he was talking about. She settled on his delirium as an explanation.

Marieka heard a knock. The broad smile of Abram poked in. "How's our nefarious German patient? You know you have to get us both out of here eventually. The Germans are constantly doing house-to-house searches for Jews, contraband, and criminals. It's only a matter of time before they search here again."

"Don't say such things, Abram!"

"It's true. You've got to get rid of us."

"You make it sound like it is as simple as getting rid of a puppy." Marieka put her head in her hands, sighed, and then turned to look at him. "Aren't you frightened, Abram?"

He stood transfixed for a moment, his shoulders drooping as he walked over and sat on the foot of the bed. "Of course I'm scared! I've heard what they are doing to Jews. But I don't want your family to suffer because of me."

"There is a way to get you to safety. It's through the Dutch underground."

"Sounds dangerous to me. Maybe I could be your adopted, dark-skinned, big-nosed brother. Do you think I could pass?"

"Ummmm, no," she said and smiled.

"Is he going to make it?" Abram nodded at the young soldier.

"He's strong. He'll be fine. We have to get both of you out of Holland. However, I imagine that the underground will not be too keen on the idea of helping a German deserter. I think they'd just as soon shoot him."

"He doesn't look much like a Nazi monster to me, and he doesn't look like he's much older than I am."

"He's not." Marieka studied the German for a moment and turned back to Abram. "Shouldn't you be hiding?"

"I'm taking a break. It's so boring down there. There's nothing to do and no one to talk to. I thought I would venture up and brighten your day," he said, grinning like a Cheshire cat.

"Well, your time is up. Get back to the cellar in case a snoopy neighbor or German shows up."

"Oh, all right. Could I borrow a book or something? The boredom is awful. It is worse than being strung up by my thumbs." He grabbed at his chest and feigned pain.

"Abram, you shouldn't say such things," Marieka scolded. "Now get back in the cellar. I'll bring you a book later . . . that's if you're good and stay there."

chapter NINE

Roch led Anton and his men through the forested hills and lowlands. Anton sent scouts ahead to rendezvous with Rapier. He suspected Rapier had probably heard of the bombing of the transport train and would tighten security accordingly.

The hideout of the one code-named Rapier was a secluded cave hidden in a hill on the north side of the river. The entrance was a fissure about the size of a small vehicle and camouflaged by juniper bushes. It opened into a large chamber and narrowed deeper into the mountain. An old desk a few feet inside the entrance was Rapier's so-called office. The desk was piled with junk. Behind it on the cave wall hung a large map of the Netherlands with red, blue, and yellow pins. They marked the communication networks, train stations, army headquarters, and German outposts. Airfields were marked with the yellow pins with the approximate number of Luftwaffe personnel and airplanes. The airfields were in the outlying areas of the Netherlands and extremely well-fortified. Next to the map was a large calendar with several dates circled in red: scheduled attacks. If the Germans were to discover the hideout, the men had a standing order to destroy the calendar and map first.

Several bedrolls were scattered around the cave floor and in the center was a cold, large blackened fire pit.

One of Rapier's men, Josiah, sat on his haunches, rolling a cigarette. He licked it and stuck it in his mouth, and then he noticed a movement on the outskirts of camp. Creeping to where he had seen the movement, he saw two men approaching. He sprang at the one nearest him and put a knife to his throat.

"Before I slit your throat, I would like a few answers," he whispered dangerously. The companion started toward the attacker. "If you don't want to see your friend's blood splattered all over you, I suggest you stay put and keep quiet. Now, who are you and how did you find this hideout?"

The man with the knife at his throat spoke up. "We are Anton's men. He sent us with a message for Rapier."

"Oh yeah? We shall see." Josiah ordered the shorter of the two to go in front toward the camp, and then he sent one of his men to get Rapier.

Rapier, with two men at his side, made his way through camp toward the intruders. The one in front was shorter and more slender than the two men at his side. The two on the outside were shaggy and unshaven, with hair hanging over their collars and in their eyes. The man in front had a trimmed beard and seemed to be more conscious of hygiene.

"Who are you and what do you want? You have thirty seconds to tell me before I blow your heads off."

"We are Anton's men and we have come to give you a message," the skinny man answered.

"How many men are in Anton's group?" the slender leader asked.

"About thirty, sir."

"Have you seen Germans following you?"

"No, not that we have been able to detect."

Rapier's eyes flashed. "Not that you are able to detect?" His voice rose. "You had better be darn sure that there are no Germans on your tails before turning up here!"

"Yes, sir," the one scout stuttered, shuffling his feet. "I'm pretty sure we were not tailed."

"Where are your men now?" Rapier demanded.

"In the forest. Ten miles to the south."

"Bring them within three miles of here and have Anton come in alone. Be sure no Germans are following you, do you understand?"

They nodded their heads with their mouths open, scared stupid.

Rapier looked behind the two scouts and saw a tall, slender, sandy-haired man running breathlessly into camp. He pulled the gun at his side, crouched, and aimed it at the man's chest. He slowly started to squeeze the trigger when one of his men yelled, "It's Peter!" Rapier lowered the gun.

Peter ran into camp but couldn't catch his breath as he handed Rapier a small white piece of paper.

"A spy?" Rapier yelled. "You mean someone has divulged information about our attack on the communications network tomorrow night? How did Jully find out?"

"I don't know," Peter wheezed. "But he lost his life trying to get the information to you before you walked into a trap."

Rapier crushed the paper. "A spy! I will find him and kill him with my own hands, for Jully." Rapier turned to the two scouts. "Plans have changed. Tell Anton to go west to the village of DeHoven. On the outskirts of town at the north end is a large old white manor. A widow lives there; her name is Madam Prinns. Tell him to give her the code name 'Jigsaw.' She will know I have sent you.'

The scouts backtracked the ten miles to their camp, but the place seemed deserted. Then Twig put his finger to his lips. "Shhh, listen. Someone's speaking German."

"How'd they . . . ?" Daan whispered.

"Shhh," Twig said. "Come." They cautiously crawled up the hill, lay on their stomachs, and watched the Germans search their former camp. "Traitor," Daan mouthed. Twig nodded.

"He's a part of our group. I wonder how Jully knew that?" Twig whispered.

Daan and Twig inched backward until they could no longer see the Germans. They got up and ran ahead, hoping to pick up Anton's trail. "One, maybe two, of our friends whom we've known all our lives is a traitor. Why would he do such a despicable thing?" Twig asked disgusted.

The smell of ham frying in the kitchen aroused Marieka's hunger. With an empty stomach as her coach, she bounded into the kitchen.

"Marieka! Why are you in such a hurry?" Anna asked, turning from the stove. "You scared me. I about burned my hand."

"It smells good. Where's Papa and Bastiaan? I'm anxious for breakfast."

"They'll be in shortly," Anna said, bending over to take the biscuits out of the oven. "While you're waiting, take the German soldier his breakfast."

She didn't have to ask twice. Marieka welcomed any opportunity to see the handsome soldier, even if it meant waiting for her breakfast. When she opened the door, he was slightly hunched over, with a grin pasted on his face.

"*Guten morgen, schone Madchen,*"[12] he said.

"Good morning to you too." Marieka beamed. She would think about him calling her a "beautiful girl" for the rest of the day. "It is good to see you are . . . um . . . trying to sit up. I've brought you some breakfast. It's scrambled eggs with a glass of milk. Mama wasn't sure if you were up to solids yet. If not, she said she'd fix you some broth."

"This is good," the young soldier said in a heavy German accent.

"Papa and Bastiaan have been working on a hiding place. We already had one German inspection. If there is another, you will be discovered. Papa said he will move you tonight after dark, and after you eat your breakfast, you are to have a shave and another bath."

"Bath? You, *Madchen*, have given me a bath?" Jorg squirmed, his face turning multiple shades of red.

"Well, not a bath bath. A sponge bath. When we first brought you here, I washed you with a sponge, dried you, and then tried to scrape a few whiskers from your chin." Marieka giggled, watching his discomfort. "I brought you a toothbrush, comb, and a straight edged razor. You can take care of that stuff today, if you're able," Marieka said.

"And this sponge bath, was I . . . uh . . . kept . . . modest?"

"Bastiaan helped with the man stuff."

"Oh," he said, letting out a sigh of relief. "That is good."

Marieka giggled as she placed the tray with scrambled eggs on his lap and put a fork in his hand. His hand trembled as he lifted the fork to his mouth. The eggs tumbled down his front, leaving a tiny piece on his fork. "I am not so good at feeding myself with my left hand," he said, smiling.

Marieka scooped up a forkful of eggs. Her hand shook as she held it to his mouth. The eggs fell down his front again. They looked at each other and laughed.

"Don't make me laugh, *Madchen*. It hurts to laugh."

"At least you are feeling well enough to almost laugh."

"Are you going to help me eat or are you going to watch me waste away right before your eyes?" he asked.

---

12. *Good morning, beautiful girl*

"All right, I will try again, but you must hold still this time. I can't hit a moving target."

"*Madchen,* I was not the problem. You can't hit a target in front of your nose."

Marieka laughed. "Well, we shall see. You know it is not wise to bite the hand that feeds you!"

"Never would I bite such a lovely hand."

Marieka blushed.

"I have never tasted better food," Jorg said after he finished the eggs.

"You would lie to your nurse, Heir Jorg?"

"*Nein, nein.* I speak the truth. It tasted wonderful after so many days of not eating."

"Well, that is good. Now be still. I have to change your bandage," Marieka said as she unwound the gauze from his shoulder. "The swelling and redness have gone. I think you are on the mend!" Her face turned to his. "Now you're going to get out of bed and walk. Your legs need the exercise."

"*Nein, nein, Madchen*! I am too weak."

Ignoring his protests, Marieka threw back the sheet and blanket, put her hand under his feet, and moved them to the floor. She grabbed his hand and pulled gently, putting her arm around his waist. "I will help you if you will help me, but I can't hold all your weight."

"Madchen, I cannot do this. It will hurt too much."

"Oh, nonsense. Be brave. On the count of three. Now." She heaved. "Jorg, you have to help," she said as he leaned heavily on her, almost toppling both of them to the floor. "Stand on your feet."

Jorg swayed.

"You can do this. Stand for a few moments and then we'll try to walk."

Jorg closed his eyes and opened them again.

"Now put one foot in front of the other."

Jorg stifled a groan, gritted his teeth, and shuffled across the room with the gusto of a slug.

"That's good!" Marieka said as she helped him back into bed. "You may rest now. Tonight Papa and Bastiaan will move you to the hideout."

"Hideout? You have a place for me to hide?"

"It was made in World War I. Papa said my grandfather built it to help escaped prisoners. It should be fixed up now and stocked with supplies. You may get bored, but at least you'll have Abram to entertain you."

"Abram? Who is Abram?"

"A Jew."

Jorg gasped. "You are hiding a Jew? That is grounds for immediate arrest. You may be sent to prison or even executed."

"And what is it for hiding a German deserter?"

"I guess it is the same," he said sheepishly.

"Will you be all right with a Jew? Or will you try to kill him?"

Jorg jerked back. His eyes were a dark flinty blue as he looked at her. "I will not harm him. I have nothing against Jews. I am not a Nazi," he said, his tone flat.

"Hold on there. I didn't mean to offend you," Marieka said, lifting the tray.

Jorg continued, determined to make her understand. "I do not believe as they do with their hatred for Jews. I believe all men are equal and God loves us all no matter what race or religion a person is," he said, a little too forcefully. At the same instant, he realized his tartness, and his cheeks burned bright red.

Marieka didn't seem to notice his rudeness but instead was fascinated with the idea of a religious German. "A religious German! Well, I've never heard of that. It's almost like the myth of the unicorn . . . nonexistent." She laughed.

Jorg sunk back into the pillow, pulling the blanket up over his chin, and grinned. "I was maybe a little too strong?"

"It's wonderful to find a good German, even if he gets a little soap-boxy about it. Here, I saved this book for you. I thought it might be something important," Marieka said, holding out the brown leather book. "What is it? German propaganda?"

Jorg's face lit up. "*Nein*. Just the opposite. It is called the Book of Mormon."

"What is that? I've never heard of such a book." Marieka watched as he held it to his chest.

"It is called Another Testament of Jesus Christ, scriptures translated by Joseph Smith over a hundred years ago."

Marieka heard her mother call her to breakfast. "Maybe some time you can tell me more about it. I have to go now. I'll check on you later."

Now and then Jorg could hear the family's conversations: Hendrick's deep voice asking for lunch; Bastiaan's adolescent voice joking about how Papa had put on a few pounds and should skip lunch; Marieka chiding Bastiaan because Papa was as skinny as ever; and Anna humming to herself while working in the kitchen.

A knock sounded at Jorg's door, and Marieka poked her head in. "You awake? I brought some supper." She bounded into the room. "When you're finished eating, Papa and Bastiaan will move you to the shelter with Abram. I hope you will try to behave yourselves and not party too much. It might alert a passing German and he'll want to join in the fun," she teased. "There's lots of food, water, and blankets, and even a change of clothes down there. I also found a few books, but they're not written in German. Maybe Abram could read them to you. I left a deck of cards, paper, and a pen to keep a journal. It isn't the fanciest, but it's better than the alternative. Besides, for a stowaway hideout, it's pretty good. Do you have any questions?"

"Uh . . . *nein*."

"One of us will check on you at least once a day. If we do not come, stay quiet, and do not try to contact us or get out. We will always come, but if we don't, then there is a pretty good reason why we haven't," she said as she flitted around the room.

"*Danke*," Jorg said, unable to get another word in.

"I'll help feed you the stew if you'd like, but either you'll have to learn to eat with your left hand or let Abram feed you," she said, grinning.

"I think I will learn to eat with my left hand. Abram definitely doesn't smell as good as you and certainly isn't as pretty!" Jorg said with a lopsided smile.

"Do you think you can flatter me, Heir Jorg?" Marieka asked. She leaned over to spoon a large piece of meat into his mouth.

"Yes. Is it working?" He smiled, touching a curl of her hair.

"Maybe," Marieka said.

"You sure are all businesslike today, *Madchen*."

"My good sir! It's a serious business keeping all of us safe." Marieka spooned a carrot into his mouth with a pouty look on her face.

Jorg smiled and obediently ate the stew, feigning helplessness. He liked her attention, and if he could keep her distracted long enough, it would postpone being stuck in that dark hole with a total stranger.

"You need to drink lots of water. I brought up some grape juice from the cellar. It's supposed to build your blood," she said as sternly as an old schoolmarm.

"*Danke, Madchen.* Very conscientious of you." Jorg rolled his eyes as Marieka leaned over to wipe the grape juice from his chin. At the sound of footsteps coming up the stairs, she jumped, almost spilling the entire glass of juice in Jorg's lap.

Jorg smiled at Marieka's discomfort. "Ah, *Madchen,* you have been caught tenderly caring for a wounded enemy."

Marieka sat the glass down. "You, my German sir, have an inflated sense of self."

"Ah, *Madchen,* you wound me to my heart!" He laughed before Bastiaan and Hendrick pushed the door open.

"Hello, Papa . . . I was just . . . uh . . . feeding Jorg," Marieka jumped, took the tray, and set it on the chair.

Papa smiled and said, "I can see that. How are you doing with such fine care, Heir Jorg?"

Jorg stuttered and dipped his head. "Uh . . . fine, sir."

Papa reached behind Jorg's back and gently lifted him off the pillow, sitting him upright.

Jorg gritted his teeth as they stood him up. "Okay, sir," Jorg said through clenched teeth. "Let's get this over with."

After the laborious task of getting him to the barn, Marieka lit a lantern and hung it next to Nye's stall.

"Abram, you and Bastiaan move the feeder," Papa instructed.

Abram grabbed one end of the feeder and Bastiaan the other and slid the heavy trough to one side. Bastiaan stepped to the trap door and lifted it, revealing a dark hole.

"Oh, I see. You are going to bury us alive in this tomb, like they buried the Pharaohs of Egypt," Abram whined.

"Calm down, Abram. As usual, your mouth is running faster than your brain," Bastiaan chided.

Marieka picked up the lantern and climbed down the ladder first.

Abram watched Marieka. He took a deep breath and said, "Here I go. Hope it isn't a bottomless pit." Bastiaan followed next.

Hendrick gently lowered Jorg, holding him securely around the chest. Bastiaan and Abram slipped their arms around his back and carried him to the bed nearest them.

Abram looked around. "There's a lot of stuff in here. Look, we have a wooden box for a nightstand and a candle, dishes, and enough blankets to keep an Eskimo warm." Abram laughed.

Jorg groaned as he lay back on the feather pillow.

"You will have two meals a day," Marieka said. "Papa has fixed an air shaft to let the food down to you. There is no heat down here, and it's too dangerous to light a fire, but as Abram already told you, there are plenty of blankets. Let's just hope we can move you out of Holland before winter sets in."

"Jorg, this is your roommate, Abram. He'll keep you entertained," Hendrick said, looking at Abram. "Right?"

"Oh, sure, Mr. Coevorden. I'll enjoy entertaining a German."

Jorg looked at Abram, gave him a halfhearted smile, and winced at a spasm of pain. "This will be good," Jorg said, and he clenched his teeth as Marieka pulled the bedding around him.

"There is water in a jug next to your bed, a flashlight, and your book. If you get hungry, there are apples and nuts on the shelf."

"If you hear anything unusual," Hendrick said, "stay quiet, but you are both smart enough to figure that out. Good night."

Marieka lingered next to Jorg. She set the pill bottle on the crate. "Don't forget to take these twice a day until they are gone."

"Okay. *Danke, Madchen.*"

When the others left and all was quiet, Abram leaned against the table and faced Jorg grinning. "I'm Abram . . . a Jew. We are roommates . . . I guess . . . what do you think of that?"

"Fine."

"Fine? That's okay with you? You don't hate being stuck here with a Jew?"

"*Nein*. Why should I?" Jorg looked at him, raising an eyebrow.

"Because you are a German and Germans hate Jews," Abram said, tugging at his ear.

Jorg tried to sit straighter so he could look at Abram squarely. "I don't see a Jew; I see a person. A person who is the same as all the rest of God's children."

"Wow, a German who believes in God and doesn't hate Jews. You must be as rare as the Hope Diamond." Abram laughed, leaning back and crossing one leg over the other.

"There are a lot of good Germans who don't believe in Hitler, and I am one of them. They are being forced into this war of insanity where he sends millions of good German men to their deaths."

"And Jewish!"

"His evil has spread throughout Europe, and I will not fight for such evil."

Abram stepped away from the table. "Finally I meet a decent German!"

Jorg let out a short laugh. "Yeah, and it looks like we're stuck here together for a while. Glad to meet ya. At least I'll have someone to talk to so I won't get so bored."

"Yeah, I never thought of that," Abram said. "I'm mighty glad to have you as a roommate. Let the games begin!" Abram walked over to Jorg and shook his hand.

chapter TEN

September 1940

The crisp fall air turned the trees into a kaleidoscope of color, yet the afternoon sun still warmed the fields. Hendrick hitched Bet to the plow to steer it down the rows in the potato field, turning the potatoes to the top. In years past, Hendrick enlisted the help of his neighbors with the potato harvest, and in turn, he helped them. But with the war and a shortage of manpower, his family was his only help. Anna, Marieka, and Bastiaan followed along behind the plow, picking potatoes, putting them in baskets, and then dumping them into burlap sacks. Bastiaan sewed the sacks shut with twine and loaded them onto the wagon. They kept a year's supply and sold the rest to Mr. Heingle.

By late afternoon Bastiaan was grateful to see the sun dip behind the hills. Hunched with fatigue, he dragged himself into the small kitchen and dropped on the chair next to the table. He rested his cheek on his palm and shoveled in a cold supper.

"Hey, bud!" Abram hollered just as Bastiaan finished his meal.

"Why don't you just shoot me now and put me out of my misery," Bastiaan groaned. "What are you doing here? You're like trying to keep a butterfly caged. You flit in and out whenever you please. One of these days, you might be caught in the German's spiderweb if you're not careful. How'd you get out of the shelter?"

"Marieka came to check on Jorg. I sneaked out when she wasn't looking."

"I'm sure that wasn't hard," Bastiaan grumbled under his breath. "Well, some of us have to work for a living and not just lounge around all day. Go away."

"But that old hideout doesn't offer much excitement, and I'm stuck down there with a German. What were you thinking? He looks at me as if he is ready to have me as his main course."

"Abram, you know that's not true. He is as much as a prisoner as you are. He wouldn't hurt a flea. Besides, he's not strong enough even if he wanted to."

"I know. He's just not the sort I want to hang around with."

"The only sort you want to hang around with is girls, and he definitely doesn't fit that criterion."

"Oh, if only I could sneak into the village and hold a girl's hand just for a moment."

"That's crazy, Abram. You know you have a bull's-eye on your back. The Germans would shoot you on sight. And as for the girls, you don't know who is friend or foe these days. I hear there are traitors among our own Dutch people who'd turn their own grandmother in for a loaf of bread. You had better be happy you're alive. Now get back to the shelter. I'll go with you and replace the feeder and yell at Marieka for not watching you closer."

Abram reluctantly followed Bastiaan. "Stay put this time," Bastiaan said. "Invent a game or something to keep yourself busy or you'll get us all killed."

Inspired by Abram's will to visit his old friends, Bastiaan ran across the fields to Ede instead of returning to the house. He made his way across the village until he found Adrie's house, but he wasn't certain which window was hers. He lightly tapped on a small window in the back. No response. He tapped again louder. He was about to leave when he saw Adrie's face. She lifted the window and hung over the windowsill.

"Bastiaan? What are you doing here? It's not safe. It's after curfew."

"I had to see you. I've been worried about you since the dance."

"Why? No one bothered us on the way home that night. I have been working with Mama or with Mrs. Diggs a the boarding house. I'm doing okay."

Bastiaan tenderly pushed Adrie's long hair away from her face and gently put his hand on her cheek while trying to hide a bashful grin.

Adrie put her hand over his.

"Will you go for a walk with me?" Bastiaan whispered.

"Now?"

"Is there a better time?"

"What if the Germans see us? We'll be arrested."

"I won't let them catch us, trust me. I know a place in the forest we can go where no one will find us."

Adrie's hands shook as she fastened a shawl around her shoulders, her eyes darting behind Bastiaan as he helped her down from the window.

"I haven't done this since I was eight years old," she whispered. "I used to climb out at night to go see Mrs. Halvestrom's horse until Mama caught me."

Bastiaan smiled and his hands lingered on her waist. He felt his face go hot and quickly dropped his hands. "Come with me."

Bastiaan led her along a narrow path next to a shallow stream in the forest until they came upon a small clearing. The moonlight reflected on the water like a silver dollar at midday. "I used to come here to fish as a kid. My dad and I happened on this one day when we were chasing that stubborn old mule Dottery. She was the meanest mule you ever saw. When she ran away, we'd have to chase after her, and when we caught her, we'd try to lead her home, but she'd plant her feet."

Adrie laughed. "I can just imagine you trying to sweet-talk an old mule into going home with you."

"Would you like to sit a while? It is kind of cool."

"Sure." Adrie smiled.

The moon's reflection disappeared as it moved across the sky while the young couple sat whispering to each other.

"We should probably go," Bastiaan finally said, standing up. He reached for Adrie's hand to help her up and then stood for a moment looking into her eyes. Bastiaan softly rubbed his thumb across her cheek and then bent down, gently kissing her lips. The beating of his heart filled his entire being and drowned out his good sense. He wanted to linger with her forever.

Adrie swallowed and giggled. "Uh, we really should go now." She looked up at Bastiaan, but he wasn't listening.

Then he opened his eyes and looked down at her. "I'm glad your Mama decided you should meet boys," he said softly in her ear.

They walked hand in hand to Adrie's home. Bastiaan helped her in the window, leaned over the windowsill, and kissed her gently. He slowly walked away, wrestling with his emotions, and heard, "Bastiaan, when will I see you again?"

"Soon, I hope."

Adrie stood with her hands on the windowsill. "Please be careful."

"I will," he said and turned to leave.

It was three o'clock in the morning when he finally climbed into bed. He let out a contented sigh despite his aching body and fell asleep.

THEY WERE MAKING good time, or so Twig thought, but the sound of German voices seemed to keep up with them.

"They're following our trail," Twig whispered. "If we keep going, we'll lead them straight to Anton, and to Rapier's hideout."

"Why can't we lose them?" Daan asked. "It's almost as if they know where we're headed."

"That's it! They're not following our trail. They already know where Rapier's hideout is. Someone is guiding them. We've got to warn Rapier."

"Or stop them," Daan said.

"I don't think we have enough ammo between the two of us to take out the patrol." Twig paused. "Follow me."

"Where you going?" Daan called to his tall, slender partner. Twig had sprinted into the brush as if he ran daily marathons through them while Dann huffed behind on his pudgy legs.

"I remember when we came this way before," Twig said as he slowed down. "There's a rock shelf protruding over the edge of the hill. If we can blow it up, it will crush most of the patrol and slow the rest down. Then we should be able to gain some ground and warn Anton in time."

"I hope the traitor is the first one killed," Daan scoffed.

Twig climbed the hill, sidestepping boulders and bushes before Daan stepped onto the hillside. Twig placed several grenades under the rocks and hid behind a large boulder to the far side.

"If I can lob a grenade under that shelf, it will set off the whole side. Shine this mirror at me when you see them coming, and take cover," Twig ordered.

"Okay," Daan mumbled. He found shelter behind a tree and watched for the patrol. "How come you get all the fun blowing stuff up and I get stuck looking at myself in a mirror?" he grumbled under his breath. Finally the patrol came into view, and he froze. In front, leading the patrol, was his younger brother. "Kerstan?" he whispered. "Is he the traitor? How can I give the signal that will kill my younger brother? If I give the signal,

Kerstan will die. If I don't, hundreds of innocent men will lose their lives because I was too weak to kill a traitor. Forgive me, little brother," Daan whispered, and flashed the mirror at Twig.

First one explosion, then another, and then the whole hillside was an avalanche of rock, raining down on the patrol. Daan blinked and saw rock where his brother had been. He wiped away a tear, took a breath, and grabbed his gear.

As Daan and Twig watched from a distance, they could hear shouting from the confused survivors. The lieutenant in the rear walked past the wounded and dying as if they didn't exist. He stopped to retrieve a shortwave radio from a man under a pile of rubble and called in the coordinates of Rapier's hide out for an air raid, having recently received a note telling him where it was.

"We need to go," Twig said urgently, grabbing Daan's elbow. He slowed down to fall in step with Daan. "Hey what happened back there? You hesitated."

"We won't have to worry about the traitor anymore," Dann mumbled.

"You saw the traitor? Who was he?"

Daan took a deep breath and gulped in hopes that his voice wouldn't betray him. "Kerstan."

"Your brother?" Twig stopped to faced Daan. "How . . . ?"

"The last time I saw him, the Germans came to our home in DeHoven, but I escaped. He hated the Germans as much as I do." Daan hung his head. "He was the traitor and now he's gone."

"I'm so sorry."

"I did what I had to do. But we need to keep moving."

UNDER THE CANOPY of trees, the vegetation was starting to go dormant in the fall air. Twig and Daan followed a shortcut through the denser part of the forest, kicking up the shallow carpet of leaves. They came to a shallow ravine where several fallen logs crisscrossed over it.

"This looks like it's the only way to the other side." Twig pointed at the logs. "Secure your rifle, and watch your footing," Twig instructed, leading the way. "These rotting logs are soft and your foot could go right through them."

As Daan jumped off the end of a decaying log, it shattered under his weight, and he twisted his ankle. He grabbed it and groaned.

Twig crouched beside him and felt his ankle. He slowly tried to help Daan to his feet, but he crumbled to the ground. "Let's hope it's just a bad sprain," Daan said. "Go on without me and warn Anton. When the patrol shows up, maybe I can pick a few of them off."

Twig helped Daan to a shelter under some large bushes at the bottom of the ravine. "I'll be back for you. Take care, and stay out of sight," he said and then disappeared.

Dann soon heard voices. "They went this way!" shouted a German soldier.

Daan listened to the shuffle of men as they started across the log bridge. A soldier fell and landed with a vicious thump, hitting his head and shattering his leg.

The blond lieutenant called down to the soldier, "Are you severely injured?"

"My leg, I think it is broken!"

The lieutenant stepped forward, shot the soldier, and then went on. Daan jumped as the shot went off.

Twig doubled his pace, jogging through the trees and sprinting the open areas. Ahead he caught a glimpse of Anton's men disappearing around a cluster of bushes. Twig was tempted to yell but whistled instead, hoping the man in the rear would hear.

The man stopped and dropped in the bushes, waiting to spring on whomever or whatever was coming behind him.

"Wait, don't shoot!" Twig called out quietly. "It's Twig."

When Holtz heard the familiar voice, he put down his weapon and greeted him.

"I've got a message for Anton. Where is he?"

Holtz sent a man ahead for Anton while Twig collapsed against a tree.

"Twig?" came Anton's voice. "We were afraid you walked into the German patrol. Where's Daan?"

"He sprained his ankle. He's hiding a ways back. You must warn Rapier," Twig said, gasping. "There is a traitor among the men. The Germans know where his hideout is. We overheard the lieutenant calling in the coordinates to Rapier's hideout for an air raid."

Anton's eyes narrowed. "I'll send a messenger on to warn Rapier and we'll stay back and attack the German patrol." Anton motioned for a tall lanky boy to come forward. "I heard you were a good runner before the war."

"Yes, sir."

"I need you to run faster than you've ever run before."

"Yes, sir. Where?

"To Rapier's hideout to warn him to get his men out now! Twig, how far is it from here?"

"A few kilometers, sir. We're not too far from it, but he'll need a white flag. They're nervous about intruders."

"Twig, you tell him exactly how to get there, and, Trevier, get him a white rag."

The runner, Olfeson, dropped his pack and rifle, grabbed the white rag and a note from Anton, and disappeared into the trees.

"The Germans are approaching," Anton warned the men. "I want each of you to make yourself invisible, shoot, and disappear. Cause confusion. I want them running around like ants on log, trying to figure out where the shots are coming from." His men grabbed their weapons and disappeared.

Olfeson slowed as he approached the edge of the clearing to Rapier's camp. He held the white rag high over his head as he stepped into the clearing. A guard appeared, pointing a gun at him.

"Don't shoot! I've got a message from Anton!" he shouted. The guard slowly stepped closer and searched him.

"Please," he said as he tried to catch his breath. "It is most urgent that I deliver this message to Rapier now."

The guard nudged him with his rifle. "Walk," he ordered, pushing him toward the cave. The guard called to a man close to him. "Get Rapier. This guy claims he has an important message we might want to hear."

A medium-height man came from the shadows with two heavily armed guards at his side. Olfeson trembled as he looked at them.

The man in front was Rapier, he presumed.

Rapier did not smile or greet Olfeson but walked up to him and said, "You have thirty seconds to convince my men not to kill you."

"Anton sent me. He's not far from here. A German patrol is on his tail."

"And the idiot is leading them here?" Rapier spat.

"No! He and his men are waiting to ambush them as we speak. I'm here to warn you that a spy has disclosed the coordinates of your hideout.

A German lieutenant has ordered an air strike. You have about fifteen minutes to get your men out of here." Olfeson reached into his pocket. "Anton gave me a note to verify what I have said with his mark."

Rapier took the note, scanned it, and turned to his men. "Grab whatever you can and get out, now! A German air strike is on its way."

Rapier turned to the messenger. "Thanks, but now you're on your own." Rapier ran back toward the cave as Olfeson disappeared in the forest.

Rapier grabbed his gear and disappeared around the side of the mountain just as the roar of the engines and the whistle of bombs could be heard overhead.

Ten weary German soldiers walked past the skeletal remains of a charred boxcar as they headed toward Colonel Boere's office. Lieutenant Schmidt lit a cigarette, took a few quick angry puffs, and crushed it out as he looked at yet another reminder of their defeat with the infernal Dutch resistance. Schmidt had been tracking the leader, Anton, with the help of his informant and a paid tracker from the Ukraine but did not catch them.

"How did they know?" Lieutenant Schmidt spat angrily. "Not even a piece of paper left behind."

The lieutenant was startled from his brooding when he spotted Marieka heading toward the bakery. He looked at his watch and noted that her arrival was an hour earlier than usual. Lieutenant Schmidt dismissed the patrol, passed the headquarters, and headed toward the alley. He saw her enter the back door, and he hid around the corner and waited.

The door opened, and Marieka hurried to her bike. When she touched the handlebars, a large hand closed over hers. She screamed and dropped the bike.

"Fräulein, you are earlier than usual today. Is there something you would like to tell me?"

"No, sir," she breathed. "I had a special order for Mr. Buskirk. A large order for the German officers today."

"I know nothing of a special order for the officers, Fräulein."

Marieka remained silent, looking at her hands.

"You will come with me."

She tried to pull away. "I don't know anything!"

Lieutenant Schmidt grabbed her by the wrist and pushed the door open. Mr. Buskirk's head snapped up at the intrusion, and his face paled when he saw Marieka.

"The Fräulein has fabricated a story as to why she is here so early. Now we'll see if her story and yours match," snarled Lieutenant Schmidt.

Mr. Buskirk turned the mixer off and faced the officer. Marieka had come early that morning with a message from Mr. Fiske for Dr. Bijl and had delivered butter and eggs earlier than usual to Mr. Buskirk. The message stated that Rapier had received information that the French spy Sphynx had been discovered and a trap was being prepared for him. The resistance was to warn and make arrangements to get him out of Holland as soon as possible. The spy was the same one who had warned Jully of the bombing of the communication network. Jully had lost his life protecting the spy's identity.

Mr. Buskirk heard the commotion in the alley after the girl had left and quickly wrote an order for a large amount of pastries.

"The Fräulein says she delivered butter early for an important order! I want to see such an order!" the lieutenant barked.

Mr. Buskirk wiped his floured hands on his apron and stepped over to the wall where the orders hung. He thumbed through the slips of paper, but the officer grabbed them out of his hand. He found the baker's fake order for one hundred pastries at 8:00 that morning for a Mr. Heingle.

"You have lied to me, Fräulein. I do not see an order for the German officers."

"I asked her to come an hour early for a large order but did not feel it important to tell her who it was for. She probably assumed it was for the German officers since they are the only ones who have parties these days. However, Mr. Heingle is throwing a celebration for Mr. Veltman and Mr. Husselman because they have been playing checkers in his store for fifty years today."

"You lie! Who would care about two old farmers playing a game of checkers? And to have a celebration over such a thing is ridiculous. Do you think I am a fool to believe such an outrageous story? What is the real reason she was here? Is she helping the resistance?"

"I do not know of any resistance," Mr. Buskirk stated flatly. "And they would be murderers to enlist an innocent girl to do their bidding."

The lieutenant glared at them. "If I find you have lied, I will shoot you where you stand."

The officer yanked the door open and left.

Reaching for the boot at the side of his bed, Jorg grabbed the rim and threw it at the cot next to the wall. It landed with a thud. Abram sat up, rubbing his eyes. "What happened?"

"You sound like the Luftwaffe with the rumbling of a thousand engines. Your snoring bites into my sleep!"

"I don't snore. You are dreaming."

"Trust me, you snore. You're louder than a tank stuck in the mud."

"Now is that any way to get along with your new roommate?"

"I'm trying too, but I can't stand the racket! If you snored consistently, it wouldn't be so bad. But you snort, then you gasp, and then you let out a long loud rumbling sound, then you whistle, then you growl, and then start the whole process over again!"

Abram laughed. "That's hilarious!"

"It would be if one had the presence of mind to think so. Can you roll over and put your head under the pillow or something?"

"Don't let me laugh.[13] I would suffocate! Are you trying to kill me? You really do hate Jews and are trying to find a way to do me in. Very clever, if I do say so myself. If I do away with myself, then you are free from conscience."

"Oh, *das ist banane*,"[14] Jorg said. "I just want to get some sleep. Could you sleep on your stomach or side then? Maybe that will help."

"All right." Abram turned to his side. "Hey, why are you here anyway? You're German . . . one of the superior race?"

"I don't believe in Hitler and his war," Jorg said, looking at the ceiling. "I have a mother and a little sister to take care of. When the train exploded, I saw an opportunity to get away."

"I did have a family," Abram said quietly, "but the Germans took them away, and now I don't know if they're alive or dead." They lay for a moment in silence. "If you're German, why don't you believe the way they do?"

"Many of us don't. Most are just good people who want to raise their

---

13. Dutch saying for "that's ridiculous."

14. That's crazy.

families and make a living. I was taught to love everyone. I can't hate you just because you're different."

"Wow, that's amazing. I'm afraid the Jews look at it differently. The Jewish people think that anyone who is not Jewish is a pagan." Abram laughed.

"Yeah, I know. I think that is one of the reasons that got your people in trouble in the first place," Jorg said.

"Yeah, but me, I just like everyone, especially girls," Abram returned.

Jorg laughed. "They're easy to like . . . well, most of them. Do you have feelings for Bastiaan's sister?"

"Marieka? Nah, she's like a little sister to me. She's always just been there, like an obnoxious kid. But I have noticed lately that she's turning out to be downright pretty!"

"Pretty? She's beautiful!"

"I guess so. I never thought of her like that. I always thought she was rather a spunky little sort. If I'd pull her braid or flip her with my fingers, she'd come at me with the glaring eyes and the vengeance of a sharp-toothed dragon. I'd back off out of fear for my life!" Abram chuckled.

"Ah, she's so beautiful, she could capture any man's heart."

"Man, you've been bitten by cupid and bad!"

"Please don't tell her!"

"Don't tell her? That's asking for trouble. Besides, I don't have to. Any blind fool can see it written all over your face! I wouldn't count on her swaying over to your side though! Partly because she's too young still and partially because she has it in her head that there is a perfect prince out there, a Mr. 'I'll make you happy for the rest of your life,' and she's saving herself for him. She'll do it too. She's headstrong, that one!"

"I'll keep that in mind. Now can we get some sleep? Maybe you could put a clothes pin on your lips or nose?"

"Anything for you, my new friend!" Abram said.

chapter ELEVEN

October 1940

The large orange sun slowly sank behind the hills of Ede, creating a pallet of pinks, oranges, and yellows. Marieka strolled toward the house as small puddles budded along the path. She heard clanging in the kitchen and knew Mama was up. Mama gave her a sense of well-being, the only reality she knew.

The evening meal for Jorg and Abram was on the counter covered with a dish towel. Marieka quickly set the milk bucket down, washed her hands, and picked up the plates. She waited a few moments until the sun disappeared behind the hills. All day she had looked forward to seeing the handsome German. He was always grateful, unlike Abram, who was always complaining he was bored or sick of being cooped up. He continually asked how much longer he had to stay there. *Sometimes I feel like putting a gag on him,* Marieka thought.

Marieka put the food in the air shaft and sent it down on the dumbwaiter, a wooden shelf hidden under a utility shelf to carry objects down to the guests. It was set up with a pulley and rope that lifted things up and down, like a small elevator. Tonight she had to check on Jorg's shoulder. Dr. Bijl had given her instructions to keep him exercising it so it wouldn't stiffen up and become useless. She was determined to see if he was doing them, and if not, he would receive a stiff talking to. Her heart skipped a beat as she moved the feeder and slowly climbed down the ladder.

Abram was unloading the dumbwaiter while Jorg was seated at the wooden table watching him. Marieka flitted into the hideout but stopped when she saw Jorg's arm in a sling. "You think your shoulder will heal in that cradle? You're not obeying the doctor's orders. You're supposed to be using your arm, not babying it in a sling!"

Jorg jumped at the voice behind him. "You ought to wear bells around your neck. You could cause one so weak to have heart failure."

"One so weak? Nonsense! I should be so weak. Now let me have that sling."

"Wait! I've been exercising! As a matter of fact I just finished. My arm was sore, so I had to put it in this sling to protect it."

"You're lying, you kraut-eating, silver-tongued devil!"

"Now, now, *Madchen*. Where's your compassion? I exercised. Ask Abram."

Marieka glared at Abram, daring him to cover for the German con artist.

"Uh . . . um . . . yes, he exercised . . . well, sort of," he said and coughed into his hand.

"Just as I thought. You will not enjoy one morsel of that meal until you have done the four sets of exercises Dr. Bijl gave you. Then I will know you have exercised, and you will clear your name."

"You're a hard woman, Miss Marieka Coevorden," Jorg said with a wink.

"It won't work! Give me that sling!" she scolded and reached for it.

"*Nein*! *Nein*! I'll do it!" Jorg carefully slipped the sling over his head and handed it to her. As she reached to take it, he snatched it away quickly.

"Jorg, you give that to me this instant. I'm going to burn it so you won't be tempted to use it anymore and won't be tempted to lie."

Marieka lunged across Jorg to snatch the sling, and he pulled her close. "Ah, *Madchen*, I have you where I want you!"

Marieka pushed against his chest, feigning anger but secretly enjoying the parody.

"You're just like all the rest of your countrymen, thinking you can reach out and take whatever you want!"

"That's not such a bad idea," Jorg teased. "Maybe I had better think again about rejoining the Nazi Party."

"You cretin," Marieka said as she pushed away, brushing wisps of hair from her face. Jorg laughed, and Abram smothered a snicker.

"Abram, if you know what's good for you, you'll stay out of this!"

"Yes, ma'am," Abram said skulking behind the table.

"Okay, you stubborn German. Let's see your arm!"

"Be gentle, *Madchen*."

Jorg gritted his teeth as Marieka took his hand and slowly moved it up and down, then side to side. She could see beads of sweat on his face. He held his breath as she exercised his arm. It did not pop or crack, a sign of proper healing.

"Your arm is moving well. You'll be able to use it like the other soon enough."

Jorg swore between gritted teeth.

"I'm sorry," Marieka teased. "Did you say you are excited to exercise again? I couldn't understand you."

"I said, *Madchen*, how can it work as well as the other arm if you insist on pulling it out of its socket?"

"It's just a little exercise. Stop whining."

"May I have something to eat, now that you are satisfied with the torture you have administered?"

Marieka could see she had pushed him too far this time and immediately felt sorry. She placed the plate before him and asked if he needed help.

"No, I think I have had enough of your assistance for one evening."

Marieka folded the sling and placed it on the table beside him. She crossed the shelter and put her foot on the ladder's rung but ran back and kissed him on the cheek. "You have been brave, my sweet German soldier," she whispered. Jorg dropped the fork and stared after her as climbed out of the room.

Mr. Alto Rotminson rang the bell on a century-old, three-story, red brick house, asking for sanctuary. The Gestapo was after him, and he needed a place to hide. A white-haired, gentle, old man opened the door and said, "Please, come in."

Four black Gestapo sedans and one troop truck surrounded the house. A highly polished, black, Mercedes Benz with a nickel-plated oak crest emblem slammed on its brakes, crashing through the picket fence, and it came to a screeching halt inches from the door.

The old man, Mr. Mesner, gasped as several Gestapo agents rushed past him into the large main entrance.

"Where are the Jews?" Lieutenant Schmidt shouted.

"I don't know what you are talking about," the old man replied as Mr. Rotminson stood quietly off to the side.

The lieutenant struck him across his cheek, knocking him to the floor. "Search every inch of the house!" he ordered. "How many Jews are you hiding, old man?"

Mrs. Mesner stood at a table near the door of the old manor and pushed an unseen button, warning the Jews in the cellar that Germans had broken into their home, and then ran to her husband and gently placed his head in her lap.

A frightened group of people stood huddled in the cellar. "Please let my wife go first," Aviv, the young rabbi, pled. "She is with child! Please, save Hannah and our firstborn child!"

The elderly Jewish rabbi motioned for the young woman to come forward. With apprehension, she stepped in front of the others and climbed into the freshly dug tunnel. She crawled on her hands and knees as quickly as her robust figure would allow. The remainder of the Jews did not protest as the men helped the other women and children go next. A loud crash jolted the Jews when the soldiers broke through the cellar door. "Halt! Move away from the wall."

The remainder of the Jews stepped away from the tunnel entrance. One soldier moved in front of it and unloaded his rifle. Three Jewish women and two children lay dead. Hannah, though not hit, lay motionless.

Lieutenant Schmidt pushed through the room as if he was royalty making an entrance. He strolled to the opening of the tunnel and looked inside. "Fill it in. It is their grave now. Get the rest of this Jewish rubbish loaded in the truck."

The soldiers pushed them, shouting, "Get moving, *Juden schwein*."[15]

The Jews were loaded into the open truck-bed that had four iron rails supporting the sides. Some were able to sit on the benches that surrounded the bed while the others were crowded into the center. Lieutenant Schmidt arrested Mr. Mesner and his wife. "You'll be interrogated for information about the network that sent the Jews to your home," he said as he closed the tailgate. "You will be shot for helping the Jews. There is no mercy for Jewish sympathizers. Hiding Jews is an automatic death sentence."

Mr. Mesner looked up at the lieutenant. "You may take my life for

---

15. Jewish pig

saving Jews, but I would do it again. I will not turn any man away in need. When I meet God, I would not be able to look Him in the eye if I did."

"How much does your God care for you now?" Lieutenant Schmidt sneered as he slammed the tailgate.

Watching from the curb, Alto Rotminson looked on in silence. Lieutenant Schmidt walked over to him and dropped twenty Dutch guilders into his hand. "Leave, you piece of traitorous scum! You are lower than the Jewish pigs we just arrested. A man that is not loyal to anything has no soul."

Hannah, the Jewish woman, inhaled a long slow breath as she watched the tunnel entrance filled in. "It is now a crypt," she cried. The tepid, black air squeezed her body like the coils of a giant snake, suffocating and crushing with no mercy, no escape, only its ominous grip. She had been swallowed alive. Her heart pounded as fear consumed her. She waited. But for what? She didn't know, and she prayed.

"Hannah, you must get up. You must find your way out. Hannah, wake up!" She heard the familiar voice, the voice of her long deceased mother.

"Mama? Where are you?" She crawled through the dirt of the tunnel. Her knees felt like they were being pummeled with a butcher's mallet. Forever crawling, she finally came to the black end of the tunnel. She pushed against it. Again and again, her arms felt as though they were made of rubber. She willed them strength. She kept prodding and pushing until the sod covering finally moved slightly to the side.

Hannah filled her lungs with the fresh crisp air, sucking the life-giving oxygen into her exhausted body. She peeked into the night. The village was darkened. She crawled from the tunnel and collapsed. Had she fallen asleep? How long had she been there? The stars were still out, and she knew she had to leave before the sun came up. She carefully covered the entrance with the sod and ran toward a field, away from the village. Tired, hungry, and scared she crossed the field and came upon a dirt road along the dike and followed it until it forked toward a darkened house. It appeared to be abandoned, but she didn't enter. Spent, she clutched her stomach. "Are you okay, my little one?" She inhaled deeply and crawled under the wooden porch and fell asleep.

Hannah was awakened by the footsteps above. The sunlight streamed through the cracks on the porch. She was afraid it was a German or Dutch collaborator, but hunger and thirst drove her to speak.

"Please, *meener*,"[16] she softly whispered.

The small yard was strewn with clutter, the result of the ravaging of the Germans. Hendrick Coevorden looked around to see where the voice had come from. He had gone to Miss Remi's home to board it up for the winter and heard the frightened whisper. He stopped, and listened, but saw no one. When he heard it again, he peered through the wooden slats of the porch and saw a tattered young woman. Her face was covered with dirt, her dress grimy, and her hair was matted mud and grass. She looked as if she hadn't had a bath in months, and he wondered when she had eaten last.

"Who are you? Why are you here?" he asked, facing the door so no one could see he was talking to someone.

"My name is Hannah. I was hiding in Mister Mesner's cellar until the Germans found us. I escaped through a tunnel. I was the only one to escape. I ran through the night. I didn't know if anyone lived here or if they were German sympathizers. I have been here for two days and two nights. Please, do you have water or something to eat?"

Hendrick dropped a canvas bag of water. "Do not reach for it until I have gone. I will be back after dark." He dropped a piece of cheese from his lunch. "This will tide you over until then."

"Bedanken, meener."[17]

Hendrick opened the door to Miss Remi's house and checked the kitchen for items he could use. He found candles, a few bars of soap, and a jar of salt. He locked the door and left.

The silence in the kitchen was unusual. "Anna?" Hendrick called.

Anna replied from the back of the house. "Marieka and I are in the sewing room."

Hendrick found Anna sitting in the wooden rocking chair, thread and needle in hand, patching an old pair of Bastiaan pants while Marieka was reading.

"Anna, why are you patching that old pair of pants?"

---

16. Mister

17. Thank you, mister.

"Because Abram is wearing a hole in his. I also sewed buttons and patches on some of Bastiaan old shirts, but I'm hoping we can move Abram out of here soon. Have you heard anything about how to contact the underground?"

"Working on it. The underground is in hiding because the Germans are on high alert since the bombing of the troop train. We'll have to be patient. Anna, I have found another guest," he said, looking down at his feet. "She needs help. She is thirsty, hungry, and scared."

"She? Oh, Hendrick, not another one. Where did she come from? With each stowaway, it brings more danger."

"She is a young Jewish woman with child. She is hiding under Miss Remi's porch. She looked so pathetic, and I couldn't ignore her.

"With child? Oh, Hendrick, what have you done now? And what are we going to do with three of them?"

"Feed them and care for them until we can get them safely out of Holland as the good Lord would want us to do."

"Ouch," Anna cried as she poked herself. "Marieka, put your book away and help with dinner. We will have one more mouth to feed tonight."

Hendrick stepped carefully in the dark, while Bastiaan followed, dragging a homemade litter. He thought the girl would be in no shape to walk after being cramped under that porch for two days. When they arrived, Hendrick crept up to the porch and called to the girl. The girl whimpered.

"Hannah, it's me, Hendrick. I've come for you as promised. Can you crawl out of there?"

"I can't move my legs," Hannah cried.

"This is my son, Bastiaan. He is going to crawl under there and get you."

The girl shrank against the wall as Bastiaan crawled under the porch. "I am here to help you. Give me your hand." Hannah's hand trembled as she stretched it toward Bastiaan. "Are you able to move your legs at all?"

"No," she said.

"Then you will have to climb on my back while I 'belly-crawl' out of here." Hannah put her arms around his neck and climbed on his back. He moved slowly. She cried out once when her leg hit the porch.

"Quiet!" Bastiaan whispered.

"I know! Forgive me."

Bastiaan climbed out from under the porch and then Hendrick gently lifted her and put her onto the small litter. "Our farm is down the road, not too far."

It was midnight before Hendrick and Bastiaan opened the kitchen door. Anna was pacing back and forth, wringing her hands, waiting for them.

"Okay, Hannah. We're going to lift you. Put your arms around our necks while we carry you into the kitchen." Hannah bit her lip as she tried to unfold her legs but did not cry out.

Anna had filled a round metal tub with warm water in the kitchen. Hendrick sat Hannah on a kitchen chair next to the tub and began to massage her legs from her feet to her knees, stretching and working the muscles. Hannah clutched the chair like she was choking a chicken but after a few minutes she visibly began to relax and was able to move her toes.

Anna walked up behind Bastiaan and swatted his behind. "Out you two!" she ordered. "The girl needs a bath. Come, young lady, let's get you out of those filthy clothes," Anna said, lifting her slowly. She supported her while she slowly put one foot and then the other into the warm water, and sat down. The warmth seeped into her aching body, and the water pinked her skin. She let out a contented sigh while Anna took a soapy sponge and gently washed her back and arms and then handed it to Hannah.

Hannah took it but was in no hurry. Anna gently poured water on her hair and lathered it with shampoo. When the water cooled, Anna helped her out and dried her off. Hannah wrapped in the towel, and Anna noticed a rather pretty girl standing before her. She gave the girl an old nightgown that probably could have fit Bet and helped her climb the stairs to Marieka's room.

"Good night, Hannah. I hope you and your baby finally get a good night's rest," Anna said as she turned out the light and shut the door.

"How ARE WE going to get her big belly through the trap door? She'll get stuck!" Anna challenged.

"Oh, Anna, she is not that big and the door is not that small. Have faith!"

"Faith can't make a door bigger than it is. You have a fool's faith, and if I didn't have good sense, we wouldn't get anything done."

"Now, Anna, your sharp tongue can cut a man to his heart."

"Oh, phooey," Anna said as she stormed out of the barn.

"I guess the four of us should be able to figure this out," Papa said. "Marieka, is there enough bedding for her?"

"Yes, Papa! You've asked me that twenty times now."

Hendrick helped Hannah to the trap door. "Maybe if you do a quarter turn, so you stomach faces the corner, it will give you a couple of inches. Marieka get down there and guide her feet."

Hannah looked at Hendrick as if he had lost his mind. "How am I going to put this big round belly of mine in that little square hole?"

Hendrick laughed. "Have faith, little one. It'll only be for a few days. I hope so, anyway. There's got to be a way to contact the underground."

"Oh, there is, Papa!" Marieka shouted up. "I know a way."

"You do? How would you know such a thing?"

"I just do. Don't ask."

Hannah finally made it into the shelter, and her eyes widened when she looked around. There were four beds in the tidy, little room. Two had been pushed together and piled high with blankets.

Marieka pointed to the two men sitting at a table. "Hannah, let me introduce you to the cellar rats. This is Abram and Jorg. They are stowaways like you. Jorg is German but a good German. I know, if there is such a thing, but he's okay," she said, smiling. "Abram is a Jew. You don't need to be afraid of them. You might even bring a little sunshine to their ho-hum life."

Jorg stood and respectfully greeted the girl. Abram, like always, didn't miss an opportunity to impress the girl.

"A woman," Abram beamed. "And a pretty one at that!"

"And married, and with child if you hadn't noticed. Your flattery, flirting, and wily charm won't work on her!" Marieka said.

"You know I would never do such a thing." Abram grinned.

"*Ja*, sure!"

After Marieka left, Hannah started to cry. Abram sat beside her and put his around her. "It's all right. I'm here."

Hannah looked up at him and cried even harder. "You're not my husband. I'm afraid that I will never see him again. The Germans have killed him."

"You don't know that. They may have taken him to a work camp. That's where the young men usually go. Don't think he isn't going to come back unless you know for sure. In the meantime, you have his son to think about. You have to live for him. Now get some rest and don't be afraid. The Coevordens will protect you. I trust them with my life."

She excused herself for personal needs. The powder room was at the top of the stairs to the right. Eikman's office was on the left. She had about five minutes. She would have to get in and out in four.

She listened intently to the officer's conversation at the dining table at Chateau de Canisy about a secret mission, code name "Lobster."[18] A Lieutenant Konig was overindulging and the more he drank, the looser his tongue became. Colonel Warner sat next to the loud-mouthed lieutenant and huffed indignantly at his vocal outbursts. The room was filled with high-ranking officers from the Wehrmacht, SS, and Luftwaffe, including Colonel Boere and Lieutenant Klaus Schmidt. It was a meeting of the utmost secrecy of the highest-ranking officers, informing them of the new secret operations.

Colonel Warner was a stocky, medium-height man, with thinning gray hair clipped neatly at the nape of his neck. His head was too small for his shoulders and his arms were too long for the uniform. The cuffs of his white shirt extended under his uniform, showing off expensive gold cuff links. His dress was impeccable from the shiny brass buttons on his uniform to shoes that shone like polished black metal reflecting tiny cursors of light with each movement. He was dedicated to the Fatherland and sworn to Hitler.

He had just about enough of this so-called nephew of Rommel's. He didn't care who he was. The boy needed to be silenced before the whole country read about the new operation in the newspaper. Colonel Warner politely asked him if he would like to look at the art collection in the library.

"Why, Colonel Warner," he slurred, "it'd be a pleasure to see the collection with you. Which way?" As soon as the colonel closed the door, he slugged the lieutenant in his drunken glass jaw. He fell to the floor, hitting his head with a thud.

Colonel Warner stepped over him and returned to the dining room with a satisfied smirk on his face.

"Colonel Warner," Felicity, the beautiful companion of Colonel Boere, said, "you seem to have returned alone. Where is the lieutenant?"

---

18. German operation to put spies in England and Ireland

"Oh, he decided to dream about the beauty of the art," he said.

"Yes, of course. Would you excuse me please? I need to powder my nose."

"Of course," Colonel Warner said as he rose to help her with her chair.

Felicity closed the door quietly. "Where would the papers be?" she whispered softly as she crossed the room to the large mahogany desk.

This was Felicity's first time at the chateau. Colonel Boere invited her to accompany him to the officer's dinner party. She assumed it would be just that—a dinner party—and would not have to play the role of a spy tonight. However, when she learned about "Operation Lobster" from the exuberant lieutenant, she had to get a copy of the original orders to pass along to England. The drunken lieutenant did not discuss the details of the operation but mentioned something about German agents to be placed in Ireland and England. Her heart beat faster as she searched for the official document.

She retrieved a tiny flashlight from her handbag and quickly shuffled through the papers on the desk. "The plans won't be in plain sight, you idiot," she chided herself. "They're secret. Look in the drawers or behind the picture on the wall for a safe." She pulled open the first drawer. It contained an ink blotter and pens. The second drawer had a couple of Nazi propaganda books, and the third held an attaché case. She opened it and shuffled through the papers until she found the one with the official Nazi emblem and the words, "Operation Lobster." She couldn't steal the paper outright, they'd be on to her for sure, so she took a small camera from her purse and snapped pictures of the document.

She heard voices coming from the hall and froze, and a hand closed over her mouth pulling her back.

She heard a raspy hoarse whisper, "Will you be quiet if I remove my hand?"

She nodded.

The stranger released his hand over her mouth but held her tightly. "You're a bit clumsy at this spy work," he whispered.

She started to retort but heard "Shhh" next to her ear. The stranger dragged her through an open door that hadn't been there a moment ago as the door to the office opened.

Tiny shafts were the only source of light in the hidden corridor. The stranger seemed to know his way through the dark halls. When they came to a staircase, he stopped and whispered, "Put your hand against the wall. There's a rail to guide you." The air cooled as they descended several flights until they stepped onto a rock floor at the bottom.

There Felicity refused to move.

"We can't stop yet," the voice whispered. "We must get you out of here,"

"Not until you tell me who you are. What's going on, and how did you know I was in the general's office?"

"It wasn't hard to figure out. I watched you as the lieutenant was mouthing off. Your head perked up and your eyes widened as you pretended not to listen. Then your sudden urge to use the ladies room was an obvious giveaway."

"I am—"

"Let me continue. This was a trap set for you. Lieutenant Konig wasn't drunk. I watched him all evening. He pretended to overindulge but randomly spilled more than he drank."

"How did you know? Who are you?"

"My name is Adof Hemmerman. I am a double agent for the British. I was born in Frankfurt, Germany. My father is a German, and my mother is English." He gently urged her ahead. "In the early 1930s when Hitler rose to power, my father recognized the warning signs and moved us to England. I was twelve. Be careful. We are at another set of stairs. There's a handrail on the right.

"I speak both English and German fluently without an accent. I later joined the SOE[19] and they sent me back to Germany with the assignment to infiltrate the high government," he said, leading her down the dark stairs by her hand. "I joined the German army and moved up quickly in rank. My contact with the SOE is rare. I only send them messages when something big is to be reported such as an invasion or secret operation, to maintain my cover. When I saw you fall for their trap, I knew you were being played, so I intervened." His voice changed to a taunting lilt. "I know what they do to people like you. I didn't want to see your pretty face altered and your body broken. Besides, I received a message from Rapier in the resistance that the German informant's position had been compromised."

"I've been compromised? How did he know?"

"He has his ways."

"Where are we going?"

"To get you out of Europe. Your informant days are over. They're on to you. They have enough evidence to put a noose around your neck. They

19. Special Operations Executive formed to conduct espionage, sabotage, reconnaissance in occupied Europe against the Axes powers with the aid of the resistance.

will have your face plastered on wanted posters all over France and the Netherlands within twenty-four hours."

Felicity's self-confidence disappeared as the information sank in. She hadn't been aware she was being watched. She had walked among the high-ranking German officials for months now.

Colonel Boere asked her to be his companion to these events before and after he had been assigned to Ede. He found her in the streets of Paris, a beggar hiding in an alley. He felt sorry for the little urchin, took her home, cleaned her up, and gave her a job as a maid. When the British bombed his villa, killing his wife and half his staff, he asked her to be a companion to go with him to the German parties and socials. She was young, but he did not look at her as a courtesan but more like a daughter. She was beautiful, and it gave him pleasure to have her as a companion. Many young officers asked if they might have an evening with her, but Colonel Boere refused. He knew their intentions and protected her like a father.

chapter TWELVE

An hour before dawn, a small reconnaissance plane lost altitude. A black trail of smoke followed the plane as it dipped dangerously close to the trees. The pilot ejected, his parachute reflecting the moonlight as he floated down.

It was 4:00 a.m. when Dedriek, Anton's younger brother, let Bess out of the barn, the second cow he'd milked that morning. He spotted the parachute falling over the forest.

He sprinted across the field toward the downed pilot. Dedriek figured the man wouldn't be far and hoped the German patrols hadn't spotted the parachute. He spotted the man tangled in a large pine tree, struggling to undo the straps.

When the pilot saw Dedriek, he grinned and called out, "Blimey, old chap! Will you help me get out of this bloody tree?"

Dedriek climbed the tree with a knife clenched between his teeth and cut the offending strap. The pilot fell to the ground with a crash and landed on his backside with a yelp.

"Blimey, that could have been done better."

Dedriek laughed at the man's jovial good nature. "You do know where you are sir, right?"

"Yes! I was on my way back to England when a German patrol spotted me. One bloody shot was all! It took the old boy one shot. Got me in the in the tail section. A very lucky shot, I'd say. I had some interesting tidbits to report to the British Command. My good lad, do you have a shortwave radio?"

"No, sir. I'm just a farm boy."

"Then will you direct me to someone who does?"

"Sir, you are in occupied territory behind the German lines. No one has radios. The Germans confiscated them. The only ones who may have a radio, other than the Germans, is the resistance."

"Jolly good, old boy. Then take me to those resistance chaps."

Dedriek laughed. "You don't just knock on a door and the underground just happens to answer."

"I know, old chap. But it's a start. Always have to think positive, you know."

"Well, mister, you need to come down out of the clouds, and realize the danger you're in behind enemy lines. We need to get you out of here, now."

Dedriek helped the pilot stand. He brushed himself off, straightened his jacket, slapped his hat on his knees, put it on, and marched off in the wrong direction.

"They'll see the parachute and will be searching the area. This place will be crawling with Germans within the hour. Let's get out of here. I'll try to contact the resistance later."

"Oh? So you do know how to get in touch with the resistance?"

"Well, I used to."

"If you did at one time, I'm sure you can do it again. Let's be off." He marched off.

"Hey, mister, you're going the wrong way. Follow me. And don't think you're the officer in charge either because you're not."

"Jolly good, old man. Lead the way."

Dedriek threaded his way through the brush and came to the edge of his farm. "We've got to be careful in case German patrols or collaborators are around. You wait here and don't move your royal hind-end."

"How did you know, old chap, that I am royalty? Does it show?"

"Like a bull's-eye on the back end of a mule," Dedriek said as he disappeared into the trees. All seemed quiet. He crept back to the pilot and led him across the field to the barn where he put him in a stall and told him to stay put.

Dedriek found his father letting the cows into the pasture.

"Where have you been, son? Trying to be a hero by joining the underground again? I finished your chores so you don't have to worry about the cows getting milk fever."

"It's not like that, Papa. I saw a British airman's plane go down, and I went to find him before the Germans got to him first. He's some kind of royalty from England. The man is so naïve, he'd tell them everything he knows over a cup of tea."

"Royalty?"

"That's what he says. I've got to find Anton to move him out of Holland."

"If you find Anton, he'll probably shoot you on sight. He was pretty mad at you when he left several weeks ago."

"I know, but this is different."

"Do you even know where to begin looking for him?"

"All I know is they were headed north to Rapier's hideout. I'll head north and see if I can pick up a trail or find someone who has seen him."

"And if the Germans capture you? Anton will again put his life in danger to rescue you. No, you are not going." He paused and looked at his son. "I am."

"Papa, that's insane! We both know it would be better if I go. I'll stay hidden, I won't go on the open roads, and I'll travel mostly at night."

"I don't like it."

"I know. But we can't keep a British airman. If he is discovered, he'll be arrested and we'll be shot."

Dedriek's mama wiped away a tear as she handed him a lunch. Dedriek knew the forest well. It had been his playground since he was a child.

Dedriek followed a path made by small animals and traveled through the night. The clouds hung low, with very little light so he used a small flashlight, but the beam was so dim he could barely see two feet in front of him.

About an hour before sunrise, he decided it might be a good idea to get a couple hours of sleep. He spotted an opening in a hedge that had been hollowed out by a small animal. He climbed inside and laid his head against the foliage and fell asleep.

The sun was high overhead when the wind picked up, and the rustle of leaves woke him. He hadn't planned to travel by day but decided he could catch up with Anton faster if he did. He opened his pack, ate a piece of cheese, and a slice of the wheat bread, drank from a cork-stopped wooden jar and set out again.

Just about the time he decided he wasn't going to find Anton's trail and would have to ask someone if they'd seen him, he came upon a low lying riverbank. The trees masked his movement as he crept closer. He saw the heavily guarded Waalbrug Bridge.

Dedriek crouched behind the bank, peering at the bridge and the swift river current. He crept behind a tree and sat down, clenching his jaw as if he were chewing on a piece of rubber while his mind raced. He countered each new thought with unforeseen consequences and discarded it.

Dedriek watched the Germans for most of the day trying to discover a weak spot. He heard a rumble of trucks—troop trucks—and foot soldiers walking along side, Tiger tanks, Panzer tanks, and open cars with officers.

Dedriek crept behind a small camp where a lone sentry was casually smoking a cigarette. He crawled behind the sentry, hit him on the head with his pistol, and dragged him into the bushes, returning a few moments later and tucking in an oversized German uniform. Then he ran to one of the trucks, threw in the stolen rifle, and jumped on the tailgate. He waved and smiled to the other soldiers, but they ignored him for one of the "Flak-Helfers"[20] who had been left behind. Sitting with his back to them, they crossed the bridge. He rode for a quarter of a mile, picked up the gun, grinned at the troops, and jumped off the truck. There were so many soldiers nobody paid attention to him. He walked alongside the truck until he came to a heavy cluster of trees. Edging over to the side, he looked around and slipped between two heavily limbed trees and disappeared into the forest. When he was sure he was out of sight of the column, he shed the disgusting German uniform and headed north again.

It wasn't long before he came to a hill where a camp had been set up. He found cigarette butts and flattened brush where they had bedded down. There wasn't much left but a few discarded supplies, which told him it was a poor group with limited means. But he found a Russian cigarette in the rubble, which the Germans often smoked.

"I wonder if this was Anton's camp. But why the Russian cigarette?" Dedriek pondered. "Or was it just a German camp? Or both? And if so, had they picked up Anton's trail? And if so, they either have an excellent tracker or someone with them who knows the area."

Traveling a bit further and following a more obvious trail, he came upon a hillside where an explosion had blown half of it away. Several dead German soldiers lay strewn among the rubble.

Dedriek headed through the trees but slowed when he came upon a dead German soldier. He bent over to see if he could find papers that

20. Underage troops

would tell him of their orders and where they were headed but found nothing except three Russian cigarettes in his pocket. Dedriek took his rifle and ammo and continued on.

He came upon another body and heard "*Wasser.*"[21] He learned over the body and saw a young German boy's pale face looking at him. He gave the boy a few sips of water from his canteen and then asked in broken German, "What happened here?"

"We didn't see them," the boy coughed. "We saw our comrades go down one by one. We got scared and ran, then the lieutenant started shooting everything. The snipers were already gone, but he shot me. He kept shooting his own men until they begged for mercy."

"I'll find help for you. I wouldn't go back to the German army. That lieutenant will probably shoot you to cover up what he has done here."

"*Danke,*" the young soldier said.

Dedriek gave him the canteen and put a German pack under his head, and ran on. Anton was good; he hadn't left a visible trail, but Dedriek had been trained by Anton. He taught him the art of tracking: how to interpret signs, a bent twig, disturbance in the lichen, or signs of footprints, such as scuff marks on a rock, dust on a leaf, or seeds of the surrounding foliage scattered in places where they shouldn't be. He also taught him how to hide his trail. He knew Anton's ways of hiding his trail, brushed over tracks erased with a bushy branch in several different directions, and then scattered with leaves. He scanned the area and discovered that they weren't going north, as was the original plan, but west.

Colonel Boere began to worry when Felicity did not return. He excused himself and went upstairs, asking a servant to check on the young woman in the powder room.

"The restroom is empty," the woman said when she returned.

"What?" Colonel Boere asked. He pushed in the door to the lounge and searched for her. "She's petite, dark haired, in a green sequined gown," he said, asking all the servants but no one had seen her. The dinner party had gathered in the den for casual conversation and drinks. Colonel Warner and Lieutenant Konig excused themselves from the men and interrupted Colonel Boere. "I would like a word with you in Eikman's office, please, sir."

Colonel Warner closed the dark oak door behind them and turned

21. *Water*

to face Colonel Boere. "It seems your little companion, the Mademoiselle Felicity, is a spy for the British SOE. We've had her under surveillance for weeks. She has been giving top-secret information to the French underground, who in turn, have sent it on to England. One of our agents in the BND22 intercepted a dispatch from persons in the underground. It was signed by one with the code name 'Sphynx.' After several interrogations, we found the identity of the Sphynx, your little Miss Felicity."

"That cannot be true," Colonel Boere said softly, sweat beading on his forehead.

"We set a trap for her tonight, but it seems she has eluded us. She's a sly one, but we'll pick her up. Her face will be on wanted posters all over France and the Netherlands by morning."

Colonel Boere sat on the sofa and put his head in his hands. "This cannot be. How could she?"

"The French are never to be trusted. What have you told her, Colonel?"

"I . . . I have told her nothing, sir. I don't know how she obtained the information."

"Come now, Colonel Boere. We aren't accusing you of anything, but maybe you let a few things slip over breakfast or after a romantic interlude."

"There were no romantic interludes, Colonel. She's not that type of girl. She's been like a daughter to me."

"Obviously you don't know what type of girl she is."

"Obviously," Colonel Boere said sadly.

"We have set up a watch on your residence in case she happens to show up there. If she does, you will arrest her and notify us immediately. Is that clear, Colonel Boere?"

"Yes, sir."

FELICITY FOLLOWED THE mysterious stranger through the cave, uncomfortable with the fact that her life was in the hands of a man who could speak fluent German. She squinted into the blackness, grasping the rail as if it was the only lifeline in a world lacking perception. The darkness robbed her senses of reality and replaced it with a bone-chilling fear. She trembled every time she put her foot out to step on the invisible stairs.

The steps were rotting and slick with moss, and Felicity pictured the

---

22. Federal Intelligence Service—foreign intelligence

walls of an ancient cave. The handrail was mounted to the cave wall with large rusty iron spikes, driven through rusted mounts. The stranger held a small flashlight but the darkness seemed to swallow the tiny light. Why was this stranger helping her at the risk of his own cover?

She finally felt the cool air on her face and let out a heavy sigh. Adof stopped abruptly, putting a finger to his lip. He whispered, "Stay put," and then disappeared.

Felicity shivered, feeling stranded and alone. She could feel her heart race, then pound, and then the thunder in her ears shattered her lonely silence as if in mockery. She clung to the rock wall as if it too would disappear. The pinpoint rays of the flashlight danced disembodied in the blackness, blinding her. She heard the vaguely familiar voice of the "sixty-second" spy whisper, "Two men from the resistance are waiting to take you to a safe house. You will remain there until they can move you out of Holland to England. There you will be debriefed and placed in security where you will sit out the rest of the war."

"Maybe I don't want to sit out the rest of the war in England. The French are not too keen on the English, you know. Besides there are German double agents all over England that would love to get their hands on me."

"You'll be safe. Trust me."

"I guess I'm in no position not to trust you, am I?"

"No, mademoiselle, you are not."

Felicity followed Adof to the cave opening, hidden behind two large perpendicular boulders overgrown with black hawthorn. They slid through the opening and crouched below thorns that tore at their flesh. On the road next to the hedge was a van with two men looking under the hood. A few cars drove by, but didn't stop, as the couple walked casually across the street.

"This is Peter and Cleg," Adof introduced Felicity. "They will take you to a safe house in DeHoven, and then you will later be moved to the coast to board the fishing boat and head north. When the captain is satisfied the Germans have not followed him, he will turn south to England. There, he will drop you in Yorkshire where you will be picked up by someone from the SOE and taken to London for de-briefing. If all goes as planned, you will be in London day after tomorrow."

"Well, that's a neat little plan, all tied up in a lovely package. And what if things don't go according to plan? Is there a plan B?"

"Plan B? Yea, run like the hounds of Hades are after you and pray you don't get caught." He grinned.

Felicity shook her head and suppressed a response as he moved into the moonlight. She finally got a glimpse of his handsome face. "I didn't see you at the party. Who are you, really? And why are you helping me?"

"One day, mademoiselle, when we meet again I will explain everything. But for now, all you need to know is that your safety is in jeopardy. Peter and Cleg will take good care of you. There is a change of clothes in the back. It would look rather strange if you were to be stopped and found in that gown."

"Thank you, Heir Hemmerman. Until we meet again."

Adof kissed her hand. "Until then." He turned back to the cave.

chapter THIRTEEN

Abram grabbed the underground newspaper from the breakfast tray and began reading while Hannah put the food on the table. "It's kind of nice having a woman around," Abram said as Hannah poured milk into the tin cups.

"Oh, poo. Now be still and say *brashot.*"[23]

After Abram said, "ah-men," Jorg snatched the paper from him.

"Give that back," Abram said as he lunged at the paper.

"Hey, Abram, what does this word mean?" Jorg asked.

"Jorg, you are learning Dutch too quickly."

"Well, I have to. I'm surrounded with people who don't speak the pure language so I have to learn their pagan one!" He laughed.

Abram grabbed the paper and wrestled for it. "If you're such a pure-blood, you don't need to know what is in our pagan paper!"

Hannah giggled and set the food out. "You two act as if you are brothers, not enemies."

HANNAH FOUND SHE enjoyed talking to Abram about Jewish life and reciting Jewish prayers. It kept her mind occupied so she didn't constantly worry about her husband and baby. Abram quit grumbling about being in the shelter and began to enjoy his new friendships. Jorg looked forward to Marieka's visits every evening, he liked to watch her eyes light up when she

23. *A prayer on the food.*

entered. He also kept an accounting of the days in the cellar, while Abram didn't seem to care, carefree as always.

Bastiaan would occasionally accompany Marieka to the shelter to visit Abram.

Abram and Bastiaan huddled in the corner and rehashed old memories. "Remember when you stole old Mrs. Finches sheets off her clothesline and stuffed them in the water barrel next to her house?" Bastiaan laughed. "She sure was mad!"

"*Ja*, my parents made me hang clothes on her line for three weeks after. It was worth it just to see that old lady dancing around to get her sheets dry before bedtime," Abram said, laughing.

"Abram, you've got the devil in you for sure!"

"Yeah, you were always scared and stood by while I did all the dirty work, and most of the time it was your idea!" Abram laughed

"I can't help it if I have a gullible friend."

"*MADCHEN*," JORG SAID, relieved when Marieka finally appeared with dinner the next night. "You are late tonight. Were you delayed in the village?"

"Mama and I went to see Dr. Bijl's wife. She had a stroke today. She's awake and talking, but she cannot move her left side. We took them dinner. So your dinner was not so fine tonight."

"My dinner is always 'fine,' *Madchen*. And it's always 'fine' to see you."

"You have a silver tongue, Jorg. But I'll not be believing you because I have you held captive, what else are you to say?"

"It is not because I am your prisoner. It's because you are a 'fine' person in whom I enjoy."

Marieka laughed. "Oh, silver-tongued one. Please do continue. Then I shall follow you where'er you shall travel."

Jorg took her hand and held it to his cheek. "Little *Madchen*, I would take you where'er I go. I should like to be with you forever."

Marieka moved forward and whispered in his ear, "My sweet German soldier, you have stolen my heart." She pulled away, with a nervous grin. "I fear we are drawing the attention of your roommates. I must go. I've lingered far too long, but you will be in my dreams."

Jorg smiled and held on to her hand. Marieka kissed his cheek and reluctantly stepped to the ladder, trying not to notice Abram's teasing smile behind Jorg.

She walked to the house with a spring in her step. At the kitchen door, she turned toward the barn and whispered, "I love you, my sweet German soldier."

The small sliver of the moon cast an ominous gray light on the austere old manor of Madam Prinns. Her involvement with the Dutch underground started by accident late one evening when she heard a frantic pounding at her door. She opened the door to a terrified young woman, her hair windswept and face streaked with tears. She whispered rapidly as she glanced back over her shoulder. "Please, I need help. The Gestapo is close behind me."

Madam Prinns gasped at the brisk air on the windy evening as she stepped forward, reached for the girl's hand, and pulled her inside. Without a word, she led the girl into the study where she pushed a button under the bookcase. It swung open to reveal a small closet. "Get in," she ordered.

A few moments later, she heard fierce pounding on the front door. She ambled to the door but did not open it. "Who's there?"

The Gestapo's officer ordered her to open the door. She calmly opened the door as he barged in.

"What can I do for you this evening, officer?"

"A young woman with dark hair and brown skirt was seen coming this way. We think she has taken refuge with someone. Have you seen her?"

"I am having tea in the parlor and do not allow anyone to disturb me until tea time is over, except you, of course."

The officer stared at her darkly. "Search the house!" he yelled to the soldiers.

The soldiers ransacked the manor and returned to report they had found nothing out of the ordinary and that no one else was in the house.

"I would suggest, madam, if you should see the young woman, that you report it to the Gestapo immediately."

"Sir, if I do happen to see such a person, perhaps I shall, but I won't, because I do not open my door to strangers. Would you be so kind as to put my door in order before you leave?"

The officer snorted. "Good evening, madam. I hope you are telling the truth. Hiding fugitives have grave consequences."

"I shall keep that in mind, captain. Good night." Madam Prinns turned toward the great room, dismissing him. She walked slowly back to the sofa and sat down, calmly sipping her tea.

When she felt the Gestapo had left the vicinity, she pushed the button on the bookcase. It swung open, and the girl fell sobbing into her arms. "Oh, thank you! I will always be grateful to you."

"Why is the Gestapo after you, young lady?"

"I am sort of a messenger."

"What kind of messenger?"

"It would be better for you if I didn't say."

"You work with the Dutch resistance?"

"You've heard of them?"

"Yes, I've heard of the trouble they've been causing the Germans. *Blenkesims.*[24] All I can say is they're welcome in my home anytime. I have a cellar under my garage, an attic, and this secret closet. Maybe I could be of some assistance, if it is possible for an old woman to be a member of the resistance. We could set up a two-way radio in the attic to pass along messages."

"Thank you for your help. I must go. I will report to my superiors your willingness to help."

"The officer said they are looking for a young woman in a brown skirt with long dark hair. You can tuck your hair under this old hat and wear one of my skirts. I could drive you since they aren't looking for two women."

"That's an excellent idea," the girl said.

"Where am I driving you?"

"Down by the river. I am to meet my contact at midnight."

The message was delivered to London and the young lady reported to Rapier of Madam Prinns willingness to help the underground.

Cleg kept looking over his shoulder as he approached the manor. Felicity and Peter were hidden behind a large hedge several houses away.

"Something doesn't feel right. Why would anyone set a beautiful bouquet of roses out on a cold evening like this?" Cleg looked up and down the street again, and over the premises but saw nothing suspicious but still felt something was amiss. He crept across the lawn to the west side of the manor where a lone light shone through a large bay window. He inched noiselessly forward and peeked around the bush next to the window. He saw Madam Prinns in the middle of the room, her hands tied behind her back. She slumped to one side, with three Gestapo agents next to her.

Cleg slowly moved away from the window alerting a guard. "Halt!" a

24. Mild curse word—bolts of lightning

sentry yelled from across the lawn. Cleg tensed, then sprinted through the bushes, but the soldier shot several rounds into his back.

Peter and Felicity heard the shots. Felicity put her hands over her mouth and gasped.

"Shhh!" Peter scolded. He grabbed her hand and circled wide to the house across the street. "See those flowers on the front porch?" he pointed. "It's a warning that something is wrong and to stay away. Cleg must not have known the signal. Let's get out of here." He pulled Felicity's hand and fled through the backyards of the once stately manors.

"What are we going to do now?" Felicity trembled.

"Get in touch with my contact in Ede. He's our only chance."

Peter sat on the bank of the river, muscles taut as a violin string, his nerves ready to snap, yet outwardly he appeared calm as he watched the windmill slowly rotate in the predawn breeze. He crept toward the barn, hauling the depleted Felicity behind, her shaky legs ready to collapse.

"Mr. Fiske," Peter whispered hoarsely.

Mr. Fiske, whose head was against the belly of a Holstein, jolted at the sudden appearance of the apparition who just as quickly disappeared from his peripheral view. Teetering on his T-shaped stool, Mr. Fiske put his hand on the cow's hind leg before turning to face the visitor.

"What are you doing here?"

"I have the German spy, code name Sphynx," Peter said edgily. "Things weren't supposed to happen this way. I was supposed to get her to a contact."

"Peter, are you crazy bringing a German spy here?"

"Madam Prinns is dead. The Gestapo was there. I didn't know where else to take her with Rapier and Anton on the run." Peter's eyes darted into the blackness behind him.

"I know of a place," Mr. Fiske said hesitantly. He hated to put the family in such a perilous situation but knew no other alternative. "If they'll take her in."

"She's all yours," Peter said, relieved, and disappeared.

Mr. Fiske peeked around the door. He motioned to the girl. "Come with me. We've got to get there before sun up. Are you up to running?"

"That's all I've been doing for the last forty-five minutes. I'm exhausted, but I'll manage," Felicity said with a wry smile.

In deep concentration, Marieka jerked her head up when she heard the harsh whisper. She was unable to move, and her hand tightened around the cow's udder. The formidable old cow took it as a cue to lift her leg, and she spilled the contents of the bucket. Marieka grabbed the bucket, looked toward the sound, and considered grabbing a pitchfork to spear the intruder.

Mr. Fiske didn't wait for an invitation. He slipped into the stall, and Marieka jumped. The disagreeable old cow stomped in agitation. "Miss Marieka, I know you have helped many people in need. I'm asking for your help once again."

"Oh?" Marieka queried as she swung around to face Mr. Fiske, picking up the partially filled bucket.

"I have a young lady in my company, who, if captured, would be a great loss to the war effort. Will you hide her until the underground is up and running again?"

"My mama and papa will want to know who she is and why she's here."

"Tell them you can't say and it's best they didn't know anyway."

"Mr. Fiske, you are asking a lot."

"Yes," Mr. Fiske acknowledged and smiled soberly. "But there is nowhere else for her to go." He left the barn and returned a few moments later with the slender, dark-haired girl wearing oversized pants and a shabby wool shirt. He didn't introduce them nor did he wait for Marieka to give an answer. He left as mysteriously as he came.

Marieka turned to the girl. "My name is Marieka and you are?"

"My name is Felicity," she said in a heavy French accent.

"You are French?"

"*Oui.*"

"How'd you get here?"

"It is a long story."

"I can well imagine. Have a seat on that bale of hay. I'm almost finished milking." A few moments later with her shallow bucket of milk in tow, Marieka said, "Follow me."

Marieka shoved Nyes to one side of the stall and pushed the feeder over to reveal the trap door.

Felicity leaned over the trap door and blinked in disbelief at the deception of the old barn. She looked around one last time, closing her eyes and taking a calming breath. She descended into the dark hole.

Jorg scrambled to his feet. "You're early, *Madchen,* like twelve hours early. I see you have brought us a new cellar rat," he said, looking behind her at the slender legs coming down the ladder.

Marieka placed the lantern on the table. "This is Felicity. She'll be here for a while."

"What is this place?"

"Well, it isn't the 'Regent Berlin,' but it's safe," Jorg said. "It's well hidden from prying eyes."

"You are German," Felicity said, stepping back.

"But a good German," Abram piped in. "He isn't a Nazi."

"And you are a Jew?" She looked at him wide-eyed.

"Yes, we're a ragtag group, hiding for our lives. The same as you, I presume." Abram grinned.

"But a German? You could be an infiltrator who will report us to the Gestapo."

Abram laughed. "No! No, he's a deserter. He'd get shot on sight."

"A German soldier who is a deserter? But why?"

"Long story," Jorg said. "You have nothing to fear from me." Jorg looked at Abram, who had a big, dumb grin plastered on his face, nodding in agreement. "And you? Why are you here?"

"Long story also," Felicity said. "Let's just say I danced with too many high-ranking Germans and opened my mouth once too often to someone I shouldn't have."

"A spy!" Abram whispered. "Holy smokes! We're in with the big guys now. Wow! Would I ever like to pick your brain!"

"Let her alone," Jorg said. "I'm sure she has had quite an ordeal tonight."

"Yes, I was rescued and wasn't even aware I needed rescuing. They were onto me, and I didn't know it, but someone in the resistance did."

"You're either awfully brave or awfully stupid," Abram said. "I would be scared to death to do that kind of work."

"Actually it does, or did scare me. Every time I had to search a desk or file, I was terrified someone would walk in on me."

"Did you carry a camera and a gun and a poison capsule?"

"Oh, for heaven's sake, Abram," Jorg said. "You sound like a little kid with a new spy set."

Felicity laughed. "It's okay. I guess I am just as curious about all of you."

Bastiaan peeked from behind the church at the guard with the German shepherd at his side, and at the other guard who walked in the opposite direction, passing each other occasionally. He was a block away, but the dog sensed something. Its ears pointed and a low guttural growl resonated in its throat.

A dim light flickered in front of the former police station, currently the German headquarters. Bastiaan waited impatiently, hoping the guards would walk the other way and give him a chance to cross the churchyard to Mr. Heimer's shed. When the guards stopped to chat, Bastiaan made a run for it and dove behind the shed. He crawled to the corner and peeked out to see if the guards had seen him, but all was quiet. He ran and ducked behind several houses until he came to Adrie's. He rapped on the window like before, but this time Adrie immediately opened it.

"Bastiaan," she whispered, "you shouldn't have come. It's too dangerous!"

"I had to see you," he said as he kissed her through the open window. "Come."

Lieutenant Schmidt stood on the porch, calmly puffing a cigarette. He couldn't sleep, as usual, so he stepped out to enjoy the night air. He noticed a movement down by the church. He looked to see if the guards were alerted, but they seemed to be more interested in smoking and talking rather than guard duty. He crushed the cigarette and stepped back into the shadows when he saw the movement again, certain it was someone running toward a house next to the church.

Lieutenant Schmidt quietly stole through the street and caught up with the figure but kept his distance. He followed him to a stone house. He crept beside the house and watched as the young man helped a girl climb out the window, and run hand in hand to the forest and disappeared.

The officer climbed into the neighbor's 1927 Model T Ford across the street and waited for them to return, enjoying his cigarettes through the open window. For over an hour, he watched and waited, wondering whether to arrest them immediately or follow them to see if they would lead him to a loftier prize.

When he saw the couple emerge from the forest, he decided he wanted the bigger prize and watched with interest as the boy helped the girl back through the window and kiss her good night. He followed behind the boy to the edge of the village and watched him disappear into the fields until he came to the Coevorden farm. "Ah, he is Hendrick Coevorden's son. He will make a nice addition to the munitions factory in Berlin," he said.

The herbal tea finally calmed his stomach. Colonel Boere rinsed the teacup and sat it on the counter next to the sink under the small window. He looked out on the dark street and saw the tall golden-haired lieutenant dart across the street toward the church.

"Lieutenant Schmidt!" He didn't like the lieutenant or his ruthless ways and his flippant disregard for authority. Colonel Boere decided to follow him and see what he was up to. He saw a dark form ahead of the lieutenant running through the fields and realized Lieutenant Schmidt was following someone. Curious, he followed them to the Coevorden farm. Colonel Boere hid behind the barn and observed the lieutenant step into the shadows and light a cigarette as he casually watched the house.

After a few moments, Lieutenant Schmidt ground out the cigarette and headed toward the road. Colonel Boere watched until he strolled out of sight. He leaned against the barn, enjoying the cool evening air. Then he heard a muffled scream. He held his breath and stood motionless but heard nothing. He decided it must have been his imagination and turned to leave, and then he heard it again.

He crept cautiously around the barn to the double doors in back. Pushing open the one door, he peeked in, but couldn't see anything. He heard the horses nicker in their stalls as he entered, and then the sound coming from the corner.

Curious, he blindly crossed the barn and stepped on a corncob, twisting his ankle. He felt like it was on fire as he dropped to one knee. Again he heard the sound to his right. He turned toward it but couldn't see anything. Then it was behind him. He fumbled in the dark as his fingers slid along the rough board of the stall, unaware of the post in front of him and smacked his head. He swore as he reached up to see if it was cut. He took a match out of his pocket and lit it. This time he saw two green eyes staring at him out of the dark.

Colonel Boere yelped and backed away, shaking out the match. He tried to focus on the eyes, and then they were gone. The hackles on his neck stood up. He limped toward the door, when from out of the dark something hurled at his head. He screeched as he grabbed the assailant and threw it. A feline yowl filled the barn.

"Bedeviled cat!" he cursed. The horses stomped and whinnied as the intruder turned to leave. He dug another match out of his pocket, lit it on the stall, and looked around. The tiny flame revealed a tidy barn with the exception of the wayward corncob. Colonel Boere shook out the match and hobbled to the door.

chapter FOURTEEN

Bastiaan sat in the dark kitchen eating a cookie and gulping down a glass of milk when he heard the animals stir. "Wonder what's gotten into them?" He slipped out the kitchen door, quietly sneaked to the side of the barn, and saw the trespasser go in.

Bastiaan crept around to the back, hoping to surprise the culprit. He reached for the bucket on the post and watched as the intruder hobbled toward the door, holding his head, and mumbling in German.

This is just great, a German. What's he doing here? Bastiaan thought.

When the man opened the door, Bastiaan swung the bucket at his head and watched as he crumpled to the ground.

Colonel Boere woke up, lying on a sofa with a cool cloth on his head, and Hendrick Coevorden leaning over him, smiling.

"What happened?" Colonel Boere asked. "Where am I?"

"It seems you had lost your way. My son thought you were an intruder up to no good and hit you in the head with a bucket. My apologies, colonel. It was an accident of mistaken identity. Bastiaan has hitched the wagon to take you home. I hope you will forgive him."

Colonel Boere looked into the kind face of Hendrick. "My head will feel better in a couple of days."

"We were wondering what you were doing here at such a late hour. Were you looking for something or someone, colonel? Or were you disoriented and lost your way?"

"Couldn't sleep, went for a walk, heard a noise, went to investigate, and got a headache," Colonel Boere stammered.

Hendrick smiled. "Bastiaan will take you home. I hope you'll be able to sleep now."

The earth quaked as the rebels ran through smoke and debris while bombs whistled behind them. Rapier was the last to leave the hideout after seeing that the maps and important papers were destroyed. He gave instructions to his men to split up and rendezvous in a week at the resistance hideout in Goorsteeg. In the meantime, he made plans to do a bit of spying on his own.

His anger spurred him on. He wanted to find the traitor and personally put a bullet in his head. He'd handpicked his men and had been with most of them since childhood. He knew the Germans were putting Nazi infiltrators in other resistance groups or using local people by either bribing them or pressuring them with threats to their loved ones. Still, he didn't have pity or sympathy for a traitor, no matter the reason.

"Sven, I want you to go to DeHoven. Hang around the pub, and be a wretched drunk. Learn if anyone has suddenly had good fortune, new clothes, food, living better than usual, or if a family that was under surveillance is now left alone.

"Dirk, go to Ede to the postmaster. Question him about new men coming into the Resistance. Ask if there have been any strange letters or packages, and if so, ask where they were sent. Track them down and report to me in three days at the fish market in DeHoven. Any questions?"

"Yeah. Where you going?"

"To follow a hunch. See you in three days."

"Phew! Anton, you smell like the underside of toe scum that was just pulled out of a rotten boot." Trevier sniffed as he hit Anton in the shoulder.

"Well, you smell about as fresh as sauerkraut curing in a sewer, and I think the whole lot of them smell just as bad as we do." Anton laughed, looking back at his men.

"We better find a place with a bed and bath before these men are mistaken for walking dead men," Trevier said.

They walked up a small knoll to the other side. Anton halted the men. "We'll make camp here. Hopefully it will be our last time sleeping on the cold ground and smelling each other for a couple of days. Rapier's message said that there is a Madam Prinns who lives in DeHoven. She is our contact and will help us. Get a good night's rest, and keep a cold camp. Trevier and I are going into town to scout out this Madam Prinns. If all goes well, we'll be back before morning."

Anton left his men two miles outside the town of DeHoven. The directions to Madam Prinns were brief, indicating only that she lived on the north side of town, in the high society section, in a white-framed old manor.

Anton and Trevier found the street she lived on and circled wide to the back, so they didn't see the warning of the red roses on the front porch. They crept through a once lavish garden. Anton speculated that in its former days it must have been used for exclusive parties.

They crouched low as they ran behind the garage. All was quiet. They peeked around the corner and scanned the street for any unusual activity but saw nothing out of the ordinary. Creeping to the garage door, they gave three loud raps and two soft ones, along with the password "Jigsaw."

They heard a shuffling on the other side, and the lock jiggled. "Oh dear, these silly locks," they heard a woman's voice say, but she gave no return password.

"Something doesn't add up," Anton said, turning to Trevier. "Let's get out of here," he said as the door flew open. A revolver stared him in the face with a Gestapo agent grinning at him from the other end of it.

"Welcome, we have been waiting for you. Although I fear Madam Prinns will not be the usual gracious hostess. She has gone to another appointment. Won't you come in and have a bite to eat? I'm sure you will need your strength for the interrogation later."

"Ah, Lieutenant Austerlitz," the Gestapo agent said, looking behind Anton to Trevier with a twisted grin. "It is so nice to see you again. You brought him in as promised!"

Anton felt an icy chill run down his spine. He felt sick to his stomach when he looked over at Trevier. The agent's high-pitched, unearthly laugh shattered his defenses. "I see you played your part well, Trevier. He did not suspect you."

Anton clenched his fists in an effort to control his rage.

Trevier spoke in German to the officer. "He is one of the leaders of the resistance." Then turning to Anton, he spoke in Dutch, "His men are camped two miles outside of town. They are weary and have been walking for two days. I hardly think they will put up much of a fight."

Anton's jaw tightened. His fist struck Trevier's face with the pent-up rage of a caged bull. Before Anton's hand dropped to his side, the guard struck him in the head, and everything went black.

When Anton awoke, he was tied to a kitchen chair. Madam Prinns sat across from him. Her face was a swollen mass of purple, streaked with dried blood. He knew she was dead and was thankful her pain was over.

"Do I get the same treatment?"

"Only if you do not cooperate."

Anton spat at the officer's face.

"I see you choose the hard way."

Anton turned to face Trevier. "You traitorous slime! I will put a bullet in your head!" he ground through clenched teeth.

Sadness flitted across Trevier's face, replaced instantly with a charming smile. "It saddens me, Anton, to have to arrest you and saddens me more to hear you talk this way. We have been good friends. But I do what is necessary for the Third Riech and will not betray Hitler. Perhaps I could persuade you to come over to the Nazi Party."

Although restrained, Anton tried to lunge at him.

"I do hope you forgive me, my friend," Trevier said in a flat tone.

Anton scoffed. "Where you are going, there is no forgiveness."

Trevier laughed. "My dear friend Anton, then I'm afraid we shall be there together, for I did not order the train explosion."

Anton held his tongue, thinking of all the times he had put his life in Trevier's hands. The confidence he had placed in him, and the secrets. Then he thought of the mysterious arrests at the safe houses, the priest and nuns at the church in Edenbrook. Now it all made sense. He'd heard of German infiltrators in other resistance groups, but it was difficult to identify them because they blended in so well. They were actors, liars with good memories and could think fast, spies spinning their tales of lies and deceit.

Anton retorted, "You think you have won, but you are only a pitiful pawn in the hands of the Gestapo, the same as I. How much did they pay you to betray your own people? Was it worth it?"

Trevier spat at Anton, curled his lip into a sneer, and walked ahead.

Rapier had a hunch. He knew none of his men was the traitor, no matter the pressure put on them by the Germans, but wondered about a couple of Anton's men. Most of Anton's men had been with him since the beginning, but Anton had recruited several men in the past few months. Rapier ran through the list of Anton's men in his head. He discarded one after another for one reason or another but one in particular stood out in his mind: Trevier. He knew very little about the man. He did know that he was born in Holland and lived his early years of his childhood here but at an early age his parents moved away. He returned to Holland several months before the war at the age of nineteen, telling everyone he had been living in France with a grandmother. *But what if he'd moved to Germany instead?*

Rapier could finger an infiltrator almost immediately by a look, a word out of place, or an inflection in his voice. Although he had never met Trevier, it all added up. How was it that heavily armed German troops seemed to show up at the munitions depot on the night of a surprise attack? Then the communications network was overrun with Gestapo when the resistance tried to destroy the main transformer, and what about the transport train in Ede? Anton was ambushed, but rescued by his brother, but his brother was captured. How'd they know? He'd heard that Trevier seldom left Anton's side when he received correspondence from the BBC. He was known to look over his shoulder and read the secret information that was only meant for Anton. He kept an unusual accounting of the chain of safe houses and the British airmen at each. Some of Anton's men took note of the strange behavior and complained to Anton. But Anton refused to believe them because Trevier was like a brother to him. So they reported the odd behavior to Rapier's men.

Rapier blended into the shadows of the domestic pine tree and squatted on a carpet of brown pine needles as he patiently watched the manor across the street. All was quiet. He figured Anton should be arriving soon because of the note with the instructions he'd given to Twig. After the bombing of his hideout, Rapier cut across the countryside on a short cut to DeHoven, hoping to intercept Anton and warn him of his suspicions about Trevier.

He could see the red color of the flowers on the front porch, though wilted, and he knew it was a warning from Madam Prinns to stay away. He watched as a shadowy figure crossed the reflected light on the grass at the side of the house. When he saw more than one shadow, he sat at full attention. He pulled the binoculars from its cover and watched the shadows intermingle. He wasn't able to find a position to see directly into the window but kept a vigilant watch on the manor for the next half hour. Then the light was extinguished. He heard the groan of a motor as the garage opened, revealing a black Mercedes sedan. Two men and a woman sat in the front with three men in back. The car drove slowly to the corner and turned toward the center of town. Rapier remained squatting underneath the pine tree and watched for any further activity.

When he felt it was safe, he ran across the street to the old manor. He stumbled over a man's body next to the window, bent down, looked at him, and recognized him as one of Anton's men. He looked into the window and saw the chaos and blood splatters in the small room. Two chairs sat opposite of each other. Rapier cringed as he imagined what took place.

The morning after Lieutenant Schmidt's visit to the Coevorden farm, Gestapo whistles blew in Ede. Colonel Boere stood on the steps of the police station, held the official Nazi document high in front of his face, and read, "All available men ages fifteen to forty-two are called to work for the German war effort. They will be shipped to Berlin immediately. This Declaration from the Führer requires all to sacrifice for the benefit of the Fatherland."

The air was filled with hysteria. Wives clinging to husbands like rust on steel and had to be pried away. Mothers grabbed their sons, trying to shield them from the German soldiers that were herding them to the transport trucks, while other armed guards tried to maintain order.

Behind Mrs. Digby's hotel, Adrie was hanging sheets on the clothesline when three German soldiers slammed their rifles into Mr. Vandenberg's door, next door. Adrie heard a commotion.

When Mrs. Vandenberg heard the voice of a German officer, she ran to the outer room and found he was demanding to know where their sons were.

"Why do you want to know?" Mr. Vandenberg asked amiably.

"They are ordered by the Führer to work in the factories in Germany for the war effort."

Adrie overheard the order. "Bastiaan!" She gulped, her shoulders sagging. She started to pick up the basket when a young private intercepted her flight.

"Fräulein, you have a brother, eh?" he said in broken Dutch, grinning.

Adrie screamed,and pushed away from him. Her nostrils flared, as she shook her head. "*Nein*, you German pig!" she yelled in a strangled voice. "Get away from me."

The soldier's laughter rang with ridicule as he watched her stumble backward and fall over the laundry basket. She crawled a few feet, then stood, and ran wildly toward the Coevorden farm.

She inhaled deep ragged breaths as she ran into the yard, willing her panic-stricken voice to shout for Bastiaan, but it only croaked as she collapsed.

The aroma of the stew stirred Anna's senses as she put the lid back on the kettle. Glancing out the window, she saw the panic-stricken girl run into the yard as she stumbled and fell. Anna fumbled with the ties of her apron, cast it aside, and ran outside. Anna bent over the clearly shaken girl and wondered if she was another Jew in trouble.

"What is it, young lady?" Anna asked as she helped the girl to an upright position.

Adrie gasped. "Where is Bastiaan?" she wheezed.

"He's in the barn doing chores."

"Please, Mrs. Coevorden, you've got to hide him now. The Germans are taking all the men to work in their factories for their war effort."

Anna cried in disbelief at this latest grave announcement and ran to the barn, yelling for Hendrick.

Hendrick dropped a bucket of grain when he heard Anna's frantic voice. Bastiaan also heard her distraught voice, dropped the pitchfork, and ran to see what the problem was.

Adrie burst into tears when she saw Bastiaan.

"What happened?" Bastiaan asked, his face paled.

"This morning in town square, the German colonel read a decree from Adolf Hitler that all eligible men were to be deported to Germany to work in factories for the war effort."

Hendrick's face looked grave, and his mind worked feverishly for answers. "Well," he said. "It seems Bastiaan will be joining the other cellar rats now."

Adrie looked at Hendrick strangely.

"Don't worry," Hendrick said. "It seems Bastiaan will have to disappear for a while."

"But when will I see you again?" Adrie cried, looking at Bastiaan.

Bastiaan piped in more cheerfully than he felt. "You will see me often enough."

"I'm afraid not, son," Hendrick said softly. "It might not be until after the war."

Attempting to keep her voice light, Adrie said, "Where will he go, out of the country?"

"I hope that isn't the case," Hendrick said, looking at her tenderly. "But for now, he's going into hiding."

Marieka returned from her deliveries and heard voices coming from the barn. Her mind ran wild. Something had happened to the cellar rats. She threw open the barn door and ran blindly toward Nye's stall, failing to see her papa standing next to the post.

"Hold it!" Papa chided. "What's the hurry?"

"Has something happened to Jorg and the rest of them?"

Hendrick hid a smile. "No. It seems Bastiaan is going to join the cellar rats for a time. The Germans are picking up young men."

"I know. I saw the hysteria in town. I hurried home to warn you." Tears ran down her face as she described the chaos in town. "They were so vicious. They were hitting, shoving, pushing people, and knocking them to the ground. The Germans told them that the Fatherland was more important than their own families. They'll be coming here next."

Hendrick pushed the feeder over and opened the trap door.

Bastiaan's voice was husky. "Don't worry, Papa. I'll be okay. Abram needed someone to play cards with anyway."

Bastiaan turned to Adrie and kissed her on the cheek, squeezed her hand, and climbed into the shelter. Hendrick replaced the trap door and started to move the feeder back when he heard the roar of a truck outside. They heard the running of feet moving toward the house and barn.

Hendrick quickly finished pushing the feeder over and kicked the straw around. He told Marieka to take Adrie to the chicken coop and gather eggs, then bent over Nye's hoof, and resumed scraping it. Anna grabbed the ladle from the bucket of water and held it out to Hendrick, just as the tall German lieutenant entered the barn.

"We have come for your son! Where is he?"

"Our son left here months ago," Hendrick lied.

The blond lieutenant struck him across the face. "I followed him here last night. Now, where is he?"

"He is gone. When he heard of the roundup in Ede this morning, he took off."

"Who warned him?"

Hendrick remained silent.

A tic in the officer's right eye moved like a crack in ice down the disciplined face, the first indicator of his loss of control. Lieutenant Schmidt clenched his jaw and then opened his mouth to shout at Hendrick but stopped abruptly as a new thought came to mind. "Where is the young Fräulein?" Lieutenant Schmidt demanded.

Hendrick again remained silent.

Lieutenant Schmidt hit him across his jaw again and knocked him against the stall. "Answer me!"

"Your little Fräulein will pay for her wagging tongue. She has interfered once too often. Search the house!" he yelled to his men. "As for your son, I will track him down!" He spun around, walked back to the truck, and waited for his man to report.

"Sir," the sergeant said, returning after the search. He saluted. "There is no one in the house."

"I will be back." Lieutenant Schmidt's lip curled. "If I don't find him, you will go in his stead."

chapter FIFTEEN

The next morning after she finished her deliveries, Marieka hung around the bakery to help Mr. Buskirk. She rolled out the Danish dough, cut it, and filled it with raspberry and apple filling. Marieka liked learning things in the bakery. She learned to make a delicate pie crust and butter cream to ice the cakes. She especially liked learning how to decorate a cake. It was getting late. Marieka washed her hands in the big sink that was already overflowing with dirty pans, wiped them on a well-worn towel, and grabbed the empty egg container. She ran to Mr. Buskirk's side, kissed him on the cheek, and, hurrying to the door, she said, "See you tomorrow."

"And good day to you too, young lady," Mr. Buskirk said with flushed cheeks.

THE FOUR GERMAN soldiers were at their usual table in the corner. Lieutenant Schmidt sat brooding as he watched the girl helping Mr. Buskirk. Colonel Boere noticed his dangerous looks toward the girl but said nothing. Lieutenant Schmidt threw some coins on the table and left quickly, moments after Marieka. Colonel Boere watched him curiously and decided to follow him. He paid for his breakfast and left. At the side of the bakery, he discovered Marieka's bike. The fender was dented, and the basket twisted, but no sight of Marieka or the lieutenant.

The sun's pink and orange rays lit the morning sky enough to make his search easier. He looked both ways before stepping into the alley. At the far end, he heard a muffled cry and saw the tip of Marieka's foot kicking frantically before disappearing between two old warehouses.

Colonel Boere ran down the alley and turned up the driveway of the nearest warehouse, frantically searching for any sign of Lieutenant Schmidt. Then he crossed the alley to the larger warehouse, which had an old storage bay in the back. When he opened the door, he heard Marieka screaming. He crept quietly through the dust-begrimed shop and stopped outside the door at the storage bay.

"Go ahead. Scream. It won't do you any good. This warehouse has been abandoned since World War I."

Colonel Boere nosed cautiously around the corner and saw the lieutenant knock the girl to the ground, grab the top of her dress, and tear it open. The buttons flew to the far corners of the room. Marieka screamed, grabbed the torn fabric, and pulled it together. The lieutenant slapped her face with an open hand, and then bent over and covered her mouth with his as his hands began to roam.

Marieka bit his lip and screamed, kicking and pummeling his chest with all her strength.

Then she brought up her knee but he deflected it.

He snarled, clenching his fist, and hit her on her side as she twisted. "If you try something like that again, I will plan the placement of my fist to a more vulnerable spot next time."

Colonel Boere aimed his pistol at the lieutenant's head and yelled, "Get away from her!"

"Colonel Boere," Lieutenant Schmidt said, standing over the girl with a leering smile. "I was just having a little fun with the Fräulein. No harm done."

"Get back or I will shoot you and pry your dead body off her."

"Calm down, colonel. It was only some harmless fun. Look, she's free to go!"

"Marieka doesn't look like she was having fun," Colonel Boere derided.

Marieka scrambled to her feet and clutched her dress as Lieutenant Schmidt stepped back.

"Lieutenant Schmidt, take off your undershirt!" Colonel Boere ordered.

"What for?"

"Do it now!" Colonel Boere shouted as he cocked the pistol.

Lieutenant Schmidt looked at him with a wry smile and slowly took off his shirt and undergarment.

"Now give it to the girl," Colonel Boere ordered.

Lieutenant Schmidt shrugged and flippantly threw the undershirt at the girl.

"Put it on, child, and get out of here," Col Boere ordered.

Marieka held her dress as she bent over to pick up the shirt. She trembled as she pulled it over her waist, and then looked at Colonel Boere and at Lieutenant Schmidt.

"Get out of here!" Colonel Boere shouted again. Without hesitation, Marieka ran out of the warehouse.

"You are under arrest, Lieutenant Schmidt," Colonel Boere said as he stepped toward him.

"For what? Having a little fun with a Dutch tramp?"

"For disobeying a direct order."

"What order? To leave the Dutch girl be? The Gestapo would laugh you out of their headquarters."

Colonel Boere motioned for Lieutenant Schmidt to go ahead of him but knew Lieutenant Schmidt was right. Colonel Boere had no grounds for arrest, but he could see to it that Lieutenant Schmidt was transferred to the front. Colonel Boere lowered his gun and shouted, "Get back to duty."

Lieutenant Schmidt smiled as he stepped past Colonel Boere. "Yes, sir." He saluted and knocked his heels together in mockery.

Sobbing, Marieka ran back through the alley, found her bike, and pulled out the dented fender, climbed on, and headed for home. The bike wobbled dangerously, as tears clouded her vision. When she turned into the yard, her mother wasn't outside as usual, watching for her. She steered the bike to the back door, dropped it, and ran in.

"Mama! Where are you? Please, Mama, be home," Marieka pled hysterically. "Mama!" She collapsed to the floor, sobbing.

"Marieka! What happened?" Hendrick shouted, running in the back door. "What happened to your dress? Why are you wearing a man's undershirt?" Hendrick bent down and lifted her into his arms.

"Where's Mama?" Marieka sobbed, her head against his chest.

"She went to check on Mrs. Bijl."

"Oh, Papa. I need Mama."

"It was that lieutenant, wasn't it?" Hendrick bellowed.

Marieka jumped in fear and knew he knew. She dropped her head and whispered in shame, "Yes."

"I am going to kill him for this," Hendrick said through clenched teeth.

Anna ran into the kitchen when she heard Hendrick's loud voice. She cried out when she saw Marieka.

"He didn't harm me, Mama!" Marieka cried as she ran into her arms. "Colonel Boere stopped him. He told the lieutenant to take his shirt off and give it to me because he had torn my dress." She sobbed.

"Oh, Hendrick! We must not let her go into the village anymore."

"But I have to, Mama. Colonel Boere will protect me," Marieka said. shaking.

Dedriek seldom went anywhere without his faithful pair of binoculars. Anton had given them to him for his twelfth birthday and showed him how to adjust the dual settings to maintain sharpness at distances, how to spot movement, and to pinpoint with exactness an object far away.

Dedriek crested a small rise and dropped to his stomach like he'd been shot. He grabbed the binoculars and watched as the Germans soldiers surrounded and arrested the surprised rebels without a firing a shot. He searched for Anton and Trevier, but they were not among them.

The Germans loaded the men into a tarp-covered truck and drove away. Dedriek crept down the slope into the cold camp. Their packs were scattered in the small area. He searched for clues, which would have been sloppy on Anton's part and highly unlikely, but he was grasping for anything.

He found nothing out of the ordinary. Scattered candy wrappers, canteens, and personal items like soap and toothbrushes were left behind. The Germans had taken their guns, of course. He did find a couple of knives under some discarded packs. And at the outer edge of the camp, he found some interesting scratches in the dirt. "P . . . r . . . i . . . n . . . n . . . s? Prinns?" Dedriek read aloud. Grabbing some of the scattered supplies and shoving them into his bag, Dedriek headed for DeHoven.

He sprinted up the curvy dirt road, and within the hour approached the abandoned outskirts of the city. It was colder than usual for the season, and his frozen breath hung in the air. He watched for a few moments before he crept behind the paper-thin shacks behind the train depot. The shattered windows gaped at him like broken teeth. The roofs were bowed and stooped almost as if ashamed of their hoary appearance. The scabbed layers of paint on the outside wooden planks looked like hideous pockmarks. The shack closest to him appeared to be the most damaged.

Dedriek crept behind to the windows in the back. One window had a large hole stuffed with a greasy rag. The other was covered with a black cloth, he assumed because of the blackout. He looked in the broken window and was surprised to see an elderly man sitting in a broken rocking chair. He sat in front of a pint-sized wood burning stove, rubbing his bony hands together. Two pitiful-looking logs sat next to the stove. If Dedriek hadn't seen the movement of the old man's hands, he would have wondered if he was alive. His face was pale with generous black circles under the hollow eyes.

Creeping around to the side, he found a broken door held by a rusty bent hinge. He cautiously pushed against the splintered wood and stepped into the tiny kitchen. A rusted cast-iron stove was against the outside wall. The smokestack was knocked over and a ring of soot blackened the ceiling overhead. A tired yellowed icebox stood in the corner, long ago emptied of its contents.

The kitchen appeared to be void of food except for a crumpled brown paper sack of rotten potatoes in a corner and one shriveled, yellowed onion next to it. He moved down the narrow hall, stopped at the first door, and pushed it open with his fingertips. The raspy creak of the door sounded like an ailing tortured spirit. In spite of the pillaging, Dedriek could see it had once been a small bedroom. A tarnished brass bed was covered with a threadbare, stained mattress and years of dust. He cautiously looked out into the hall and headed toward the old man.

Dedriek stopped when he entered the arched opening into the small living room. The ruin and deprivation the old man was living in sickened him. The watermarked wallpaper was peeling away from gaping holes that let in the frigid air. Rotted holes in the wood floors were a bustling subway for rats and mice.

Overwhelming sympathy filled Dedriek's chest as he watched the old man stare into the hypotonic flame.

"Are you okay, *minser?*"[25]

The old man's head slowly turned toward Dedriek. He looked at him with hollow, unblinking eyes. Dedriek could see starvation had ravaged his body. He wanted to help the poor old man, make his pain go away,

---

25. *Mister*

but he knew there was little he could do. He was in the last stages of starvation.

Bending down to look directly in the man's eyes, he asked, "Do you know where the Germans have their headquarters and is there any part of town that isn't occupied by the Germans?"

The old man's eyes fixed on a point beyond Dedriek's face. His voice sounded as if he had a throat full of sawdust, and he seized his chest as a raspy cough shook his body. "They are on Balieu Street. They took over the Catholic Cathedral. It is the largest building in the city. They set up their headquarters on the first level and the bottom floors they've turned into a prison. They killed the priests and hung their bodies from the pinnacles of the Cathedral," he said, choking back another cough.

"They killed my wife," the dying voice continued. "She ran screaming at them when they forced their way into our home. An evil-looking SS officer wasn't going to put up with a woman assaulting him. He pushed her back, grabbed his pistol, and shot her." His voice trembled as tears ran down his paper-thin cheeks.

"Is there a street or pub or something by the name of Prinns?"

The old man sat for a time, still staring at the imaginary point behind Dedriek's head. "I don't know of anything called 'Prinns,'" he finally said. "But there was a mayor several years ago by that name. He's dead now, died long before the Germans came."

"Thanks," Dedriek said. He gave him a piece of cheese and a slice of hard bread.

The man's hands shook as he reached for the gift. Tears spilled down his face as he cradled it in his hand. "God bless you."

"And God be with you, old man," Dedriek said as he gently patted his shoulder and left. Before heading toward town, he turned back for one last look. The old man was slumped over, his head lolled to one side, his hand in his lap, the bread had slipped through his fingers. Dedriek knew the old man was gone. *I know you are at peace now,* Dedriek thought, wiping away a tear.

Dedriek headed toward town, hoping to find someone that could tell him where the Prinns' residence was. He walked down a street to an open market. Nazi flags were above every street corner, the vendors displayed pitiful wares. People seldom stopped, disgusted at the modicum. He noticed a dusty pickup full of chicken crates, the farmer nowhere in sight. He took one of the crates and using it for a prop, carried it past two

German soldiers on the corner. He stopped an old woman pushing a rubbish cart and asked her which way to the more affluent section of town.

The old woman cackled. "You're wanting to rub shoulders with the snobbish gents and ladies on the upper side, eh?" She grunted in disgust, sniffed, and pointed north, pushing her cart past him in a huff.

Dedriek stopped her and handed her the small cage containing the rooster. "Maybe you aren't one of those highfalutin gents, after all," she cackled and grabbed the crate greedily.

He walked several blocks before he found the section of town he was looking for. Modest medium-sized homes were amid the tree-lined street. The farther north he traveled, the bigger and more elaborate the houses became. Black sedans were parked in front of several of the elegant homes. The Nazi and Gestapo officers had claimed the manors for themselves.

He walked casually along the street, looking at the addresses and names on each of the homes. He stopped an elderly woman clutching a loaf of bread with one hand and her coat with the other to ask her if she knew of a residence by the name of Prinns.

"On the west side, over several blocks."

He nodded his thanks and headed across the street. The homes in this section of town were older but still magnificent. Black sedans and Nazi flags did not claim these homes as they did the others.

Finally he came to the end of the street to a large white manor. He could see that at one time it was a luxurious home, but the years had left its mark. The shingles were in need of repair, the shutters were paint chipped, and the siding was in desperate need of a new coat of paint. He drew closer and noticed a bouquet of wilted red flowers sitting on the front porch. He looked around, climbed the steps, and rang the bell.

No one answered. He walked around to the side of the house. Dedriek noticed the grass covered in blood. He looked in the window and saw the kitchen in shambles. Two chairs were in the middle of the room, one with a white cord and blood splatters under it. He knew he'd found the right place.

chapter SIXTEEN

In three days Rapier was to meet with his two bodyguards. In a week he was to meet up with the rest of his men at Goorsteg, Rapier's rendezvous hideout. By then Anton would be dead. There wasn't time to go to Ede for Dirk, but he could still find Sven. He needed help getting Anton out of the Gestapo headquarters.

The pub was called the Mortgriest Vissor. It was on the sleazy end of town by the river. Riffraff often frequented the bar and anyone who valued his life didn't dare go there alone. Rapier entered the pub about 4:00 p.m., early enough that the regulars weren't drunk and disorderly yet. The Nazis usually didn't harass the bar because it was good for a drink and entertainment when off duty.

Rapier saw Sven in a corner, his head bent over a glass of amber-colored liquid and a half bottle of whiskey in front of him. Rapier casually walked up to the bar and loudly ordered a beer. Sven didn't look up but peered through the greasy strands of hair that fell over his face.

The bartender served Rapier and then turned his back to him, drying the small shot glasses while keeping his eye on him in the big mirror on the wall. Rapier slowly finished his beer, threw a coin on the counter, and asked the bartender for the directions to Portsmith.

The bartender eyed Rapier suspiciously and leaned on his elbow. "Follow the river for twenty miles. You'll run right into it."

Rapier thanked him and left.

The bartender motioned for the man at the end of the bar. He could be described as a midget, but he was four feet, nine inches tall, so he didn't think of himself as one. His pants, shirt, and hat were stained with fish oil and grease. His left eye was cockeyed, and when he curled his upper lip into a smile, it revealed repulsive black teeth. He hadn't had a date with a razor for months, which allowed the scraggly suet-covered beard to grow in wisps down his chin, making his appearance more loathsome.

As Rapier left the bar, he noticed the contemptible man following him. He casually walked down the pier and disappeared into a small fisherman's shop. The man followed him in. Rapier was waiting for him and hit him as he came through the door. Rapier grinned as he walked past the proprietor. "He doesn't like me dating his wife."

He circled around to find an inconspicuous spot to watch the front of the tavern. A few minutes later, the little man appeared holding his head and swaying. Rapier grinned. "I wish I could hear the yarn he is about to spin to the bartender."

Rapier kept an eye on the pub's door. Sven appeared a short time later, staggering with the bottle of whiskey in his hand. He slovenly bumped the shoulder of a man going into the pub. "Oh, p . . . pa . . . pardon . . . me . . . ," he slurred and let out a hiccup.

"Watch where you are going, you drunken fool!" the other man said as he brushed his lapel.

Sven put his hand up to his forehead and saluted the man. "Aye, aye, your highness." The man gave him a disgruntled snort and pushed past him.

Sven staggered down the street and walked past the old fisherman's shop. Rapier reached out and hauled him into the alley.

"What are you doing here?" Sven objected. "I thought I wasn't supposed to see you for two more days. Boy, I sure was getting tired of drinking this stuff. It makes me pee too much, and it's only watered down apple cider," Sven said as he lifted the bottle toward Rapier. "I was beginning to pick up on some details, German collaborators, spies and such. I think the bartender is one. He's been gathering information and sending it on. I've seen a couple of messages passed between him and customers." Sven ran his fingers through his greasy hair.

"Good work, Sven, but we'll have to put it on hold for now."

"Well, it'll look mighty suspicious if I don't show up for a few days and then show up again," Sven said, trying to control the edginess of his voice.

"We'll worry about that later," Rapier said, ignoring Sven's displeasure. "I think Anton has been arrested and is being held at Gestapo headquarters in the cathedral. We've got to get him out of there."

"Have you gone mad? No one gets out of there alive." Sven glared at him.

"It won't be easy, but if we plan this, maybe we'll be the first. We need to find someone who knows the layout of the cathedral. I've heard that the priests in the crusades had secret passages. Just hearsay, but I wonder if there is some truth to it."

"That's a mighty tall order. How can we trust anybody? There are collaborators everywhere who'd turn you in for a swig of whiskey."

"We'll have to trust our instincts," Rapier stated flatly.

Sven looked at Rapier and blurted, "You're a little young to be losing your mind."

Rapier smiled. Sven grabbed his greasy hair and tied it in a ponytail, then threw the bottle in the corner of the alley. He unbuttoned the shabby wool shirt and shoved it in a garbage can and dumped another can's contents on top of it. He licked his finger and rubbed at the grime on his face. "Let's check it out," he said as he walked away tucking his shirt in.

They could see the pillars of the majestic cathedral several blocks way. Sven stopped for a moment and looked at the cathedral with his mouth open. "The filthy Nazis took over a place of worship for their evil stronghold. They'll be squealing like creatures of the underworld when they meet up with God at Judgment Day."

They approached from the back wall. Sven pushed on the gate, but it was locked. "Guess we'll have to try the front entrance. Now that ought to be a trick." He snorted derisively.

They walked up the side street to the cathedral and climbed the steps to the portico that were supported by two granite pillars in front of the double entry doors. Several people were kneeling on the steps praying because they weren't allowed inside.

Rapier noticed a bent gray-haired man wearing a soiled tan shirt and saggy brown pants, sweeping the steps. An oil soaked rag hung out of one pocket and a feather duster out of the other.

"A custodian," Rapier whispered to Sven and nodded toward the man.

Rapier climbed the steps and knelt next to the custodian. He crossed his chest, put his hands together, and bowed his head. The German guard glared at the insolent parishioner. Rapier motioned with his eyes for him to come close. The man continued sweeping toward Rapier.

"Are you the custodian here?" Rapier whispered.

"One of them," he grunted.

"Have you been here long?"

"For a few years," he muttered.

"Do you know your way around the cathedral?"

"Better than anyone. I've cleaned every crevice and corner for forty years."

"Are you a Nazi sympathizer?" Rapier asked.

The old man swept dirt in his face. "No! I'd just as soon see them all in purgatory."

"But you work with them every day."

"I have to eat," the man hissed. "Just because I have to work with them doesn't mean I like them."

"Did you see two special prisoners arrive in a black Mercedes yesterday, escorted by three Gestapo men?"

"No, but I did see one prisoner escorted by two Gestapo men and a man dressed like the prisoner, holding a gun on him."

"The one with the gun, what did he look like?"

A German guard marched over to the old man and told him to stop dawdling and looked at Rapier. "Leave, no praying is allowed."

Rapier moved down the steps and knelt down again, ignoring the guard. The guard scowled and stalked off.

The old man slowly worked his way to Rapier again. "Get off the steps, you fool!" he shouted. "You are in my way!" Then he whispered without looking at Rapier, "I'll talk to you later, when I get off work, around six o'clock. Meet you at the back gate."

"God will curse you for this!" Rapier shouted at the old man, shaking his fist, and walked off mumbling.

"Ohhhh!" Hannah trembled as she clutched her stomach and sat on the bed gasping.

"What is it?" Jorg asked. He struck a match to light a candle. "Did you have another bad dream?"

"Jorg!" she wailed. "I think the baby is coming!"

"That's crazy!" Jorg shrieked. "It can't be coming! You can't have a baby down here. We're not doctors! And what if the Germans were to come again, how would you keep it quiet?" Jorg said, trying to control his hysteria.

Hannah's face pinched as another pain hit her.

Felicity sat up. Abram turned in his bed half asleep. "Are you trying to get us killed?" he moaned. "Why are you shouting and why is a candle lit?"

Jorg pointed at Hannah and stammered, "She says the baby is coming."

Felicity ran to her and put her arm around her. "It's okay. You'll be just fine. Ignore Jorg; he's just a man." Felicity turned to Bastiaan, "Can we get out of the cellar?"

"The only way to get out is to move the feeder, but we can't from down here."

"Well, you can try, can't you?"

Bastiaan climbed the ladder and pushed against the trapdoor, but it wouldn't budge. Jorg climbed up beside him. Both of them pushed, but it remained steadfast.

"We need clean water, rags, and a blanket to wrap the baby in," Felicity said, her voice rising to hysteria.

"We can always hope she doesn't have the baby until morning when Marieka delivers breakfast," Abram offered.

"I doubt that's going to happen." Felicity's face furrowed.

"Hey, that's it!" Bastiaan said.

"What's it?" Abram asked.

"The air shaft!"

"What about the air shaft?" Abram asked.

"Someone can go up the air shaft and get Mama."

"Oh yeah, like maybe I can fit my head in there."

"Not you, big dumb goon. Felicity. She's half the size as the rest of us. It'll be tight, but I'm sure she can do it."

Felicity was now the one to give the "have you lost your mind" look.

"It'll work! Come on, Felicity. We've at least got to try."

Hannah sat on the edge of the bed with one hand on her stomach and the other gripping the pillow in a viselike grip. Jorg was at her side. The other three were arguing if Felicity was going to fit in the air shaft.

Jorg put his arm around Hannah's back. "Maybe you'd better lie down." He put a cool cloth on her forehead, and then dipped a tin cup in the bucket of water and gave her a sip. "You'll probably get awfully thirsty before this is over. I remember my mama helped a neighbor with birthing once. She was gone half the night and most of the next day. The doctor had been called but didn't show up until she had been screaming for three hours. I was sure glad when that baby was born." Jorg looked at Hannah. "I probably shouldn't have told you about the screaming part, huh?"

Hannah managed a weak smile and nodded.

"When you get to the top, you have to push hard against the shelf," Bastiaan said, looking into Felcitity's skeptical face. "It has tools and stuff on it, so it'll be kind of heavy but don't get discouraged. Push until it moves. After you get out of there, go to the kitchen. A key is above the door. Mama's room is the first door on the right at the top of the stairs. She'll know what to do after you explain everything."

Felicity climbed into the air shaft, grabbed the rope, put her back against the one side and her feet on the other, and slowly climbed up. At the top, Felicity pushed on the underside of the shelf but it wouldn't budge. "It won't move!" she called. "I'm not strong enough."

"Yes, you are!" Bastiaan yelled. "Put your back into it, and push like you are pushing out a baby."

Felicity glowered down at him. "It's not me having the baby. Can you think of another analogy?"

"Uh, like you're Hercules?" Bastiaan said sheepishly.

Felicity gritted and heaved against the shelf. It finally moved enough so that she could stick her arm out. While balancing the shelf on her head, she knocked the stuff off, and then it moved with ease. Next she unpeeled one leg, wriggled her body out, and then the other leg and climbed out. "I'm out!" she cried triumphantly.

"Great," Bastiaan called back. "Be careful, and watch out for Germans."

Felicity rolled her eyes and looked heavenward and then into the night. All was quiet, so she ran to the kitchen door. Reaching up to the doorframe, she wiped her hand over the molding and found the key.

Fumbling with the key, she managed to push the door open and enter the dark kitchen. She took two steps, knocked over a kitchen chair, and bruised her shin. "Oh, for Pete's sake," she whispered. "Spying on the Germans wasn't this hard."

The moon cast enough light through the window to see her way to the top of the stairs. Felicity found Anna's door and rapped gently, but heard no response. She knocked again. The door flew open to a barrel of a gun pointed between her eyes.

"Mr. Coevorden, it's me, Felicity," she said in a strangled tone.

"Felicity? How'd you get out of the cellar? And more important, why? German patrols are going up and down the road all the time now!"

"It's Hannah, Mr. Coevorden. She's having her baby. I've come to get Mrs. Coevorden."

Hendrick stood with the gun still pointed at Felicity, a blank expression on his face. Anna pushed past him and Felicity, leaving them in her wake to stare at one another.

"Have you ever delivered a baby before?" Felicity quizzed Anna when she caught up to her.

"One or two, when the doctor didn't show up in time."

"Is it hard?"

"Not if the baby cooperates like he's supposed to. Hendrick, put some water on to boil," Anna ordered. "Felicity, carry these sheets and towels. I'll get my sewing kit."

"Sewing kit?" Felicity queried. "What for?"

"It has scissors, needles, thread, string—everything I am going to need. Come." Anna hurried past Felicity.

Felicity turned in circles trying to anticipate Anna's next move. She didn't know whether to stay out of her way or be available for the next pile of stuff thrown at her. Anna kept running from the bathroom back to her room. From her cedar chest, she grabbed baby clothes, flannel, and blankets, and threw them on top of Felicity's pile.

Marieka bolted upright when she heard the clamor. Fearing something awful had happened, she ran into her parents' room. When she saw Mama frantically running around, piling blankets and cloth on Felicity's outstretched arms, she cried, "Mama, what is it? Is someone hurt? Did the Germans find the hideout?"

"Marieka, everyone is fine. Hannah is going to have her baby. Come with me. I'm going to need your help."

"My help? With what?" Marieka halted.

Anna hurried down the stairs and stopped in front of the cupboards in the kitchen, grabbed a small brown can with white lettering, and topped off Felicity's pile. She hurried across the yard to the barn, not noticing if the two girls were following. Hendrick had moved the feeder and was opening the trap door when they arrived. He lit the lantern and carried down the items Felicity had.

Hannah was in the corner, breathing fast, clutching her stomach, and holding Abram's hand.

"How far apart are the contractions?"

"Huh?" Abram looked at her with a blank expression on his face.

"How far apart are the pains?"

Abram's face lit up as if he'd received an epiphany. "She squeezes my hand off the Richter-scale every five minutes!"

"That will do," Anna said. "Abram, you, Jorg, and Bastiaan, get out."

"What? You want us to get out of the cellar? But what if a German patrol passes by?" Abram balked.

"I didn't say stand out in the road! I just said get out—sit outside the door."

Hannah clutched Abram's hand. "Please let him stay," she pled, casting a yearning look toward Anna.

"Are you sure? Sometimes men can be more trouble than the actual birthing."

Abram looked at Hannah, wide-eyed. "Have you gone nuts?"

"You are as kind as my husband. If he can't be here, then I want you to be in his place."

Abram grimaced. "Me? What can I do?"

"You can hold her hand and give her moral support, but make darn sure you stay out of my way," Anna said. "I have a small piece of work to do."

"No problem, Mrs. Coevorden. You don't have to tell me twice." Abram choked out a flimsy whimper and shrank into the corner.

"Let's see if we can tell what the baby is doing," Anna said as she got to work. "You're about halfway there."

"Only half way? Can't this baby just come now?"

Anna laughed. "It usually doesn't work that way. Sometimes they can take a long time. Only mother nature gets to decide."

Anna mixed a cup of tea and gave it to Hannah. "Sip on this. It'll ease the pain." Anna sat on a chair next to the bed and asked Hannah questions about her life to keep both their minds occupied.

Abram sat quietly, feeling as conspicuous as a worm in a chicken house.

Hannah jabbered, until the pain cut off her words, and then she'd clench her teeth and put a viselike grip on Abram's hand. Anna talked in soothing tones, telling her to relax and take deep breaths. "Fighting the pain will only make it worse."

Anna put extra blankets under Hannah's legs. Abram's face went as white as the fluff on the backside of a scared rabbit. His eyes rolled back in his head, and he swayed like a drunken sailor.

Felicity caught Abram's shoulder before he fell. "Hold on, big guy. Take a deep breath."

"Wonder who needs attending to first, Hannah or Abram?" Marieka laughed. "Haven't you ever seen a calf or a foal born before?"

"Nope! And I don't want to either." Abram clutched his stomach with one hand and cupped his mouth with the other. "I don't feel so well."

Anna didn't look up but instructed Felicity to put a cool cloth on Abram's forehead and sit him in a chair next to the bed.

"And a blindfold too," Marieka said.

Hannah relaxed for a moment until another pain like a thousand knives ripped through her. She wanted to scream but bit her lip instead and wrung Abram's hand.

"It's a girl!" Anna announced as the baby cried with quick, angry breaths. "Oh, she is a feisty one." She smiled as she sponged the baby with warm soapy water and wrapped a piece of torn flannel around her bottom for a diaper. Next she put a tiny shirt over her soft matt of dark hair, wrapped her tightly in a flannel blanket, and handed her to her mama. Hannah's eyes filled with tears as she looked at the beautiful baby, who was already chewing on her fists.

"Abram, you can go now," Anna said.

"Yes, Mrs. Coevorden. Happy to."

Anna smiled as Hannah began to feed her baby. "She knows her mama all ready. What are you going to name her?"

"Arabella, after my husband's mother."

"I think that is a very nice name," Anna said softly. "Marieka, I need your help to clean up and get out of here. Boys, you'd better get back in here now."

Hendrick was the first to come down the ladder, then Bastiaan, Jorg, and the pale-faced Abram. Hendrick looked at the baby as if he was a proud grandpa. "Cute little thing, isn't she?"

Jorg, Bastiaan, and Abram crowded around as if they'd never seen a baby before.

"Uh, people," Felicity said behind them. "There is a war on, remember? We've got to close the trap door now before we have some unwanted visitors."

Anna folded several of the torn pieces of flannel for diapers and left them with Hannah. "Try to keep the baby quiet as possible," she said as she turned to leave.

Hendrick replace the feeder, and Marieka picked up the bucket to do her chores. "This new addition will be dangerous," Hendrick said. "We'll have to get in touch with the resistance and soon, before they are discovered."

The black Mercedes turned south and headed slowly toward the Gestapo headquarters. Colonel Warner sat smugly in the back seat, one hand on the armrest, the other holding a Lugar P08 pistol pointed at the prize who would earn him the recognition and forgiveness of General Eikman.

Colonel Warner met Lieutenant Austerlitz in Germany years before the war, at the Deutsche's Jungvolk School for boys, later changed to the Hitler Youth Academy. Trevier was tall for his age, handsome, blond, and blue-eyed, the top of his class and a natural-born leader. Colonel Warner saw potential in him and took him under his wing.

The school indoctrinated the youth in Nazi propaganda, aimed at producing obedient, self-sacrificing Germans who would be willing to die for the Führer and the Fatherland. Colonel Warner, a teacher in this program, taught Trevier about the honors and ranks he could obtain someday if he proved himself.

In December 1939, a few months after the invasion of Poland, Colonel Warner approached Trevier. "I have known you for several years now. I'm as proud of you as if you were my own son. The war will spread throughout Europe, and the Third Reich needs intelligent people that will make a difference. Would you be willing to serve on a special assignment?"

Trevier looked at Colonel Warner with questioning eyes. "What kind of special assignment, sir?"

"Work with the Abwehr, the German military intelligence as a field agent."

"You mean a spy?"

"That's exactly what I mean. Do you think you can do it? It's extremely dangerous, but the benefits could be unlimited. There is potential to rise in rank in the German army quickly. I will give you a few days to think about it."

Trevier joined the Nazi party at the age of eighteen and then was sent to special training for spies. His assignment—his homeland, Holland.

"There shouldn't be any questions about one of their own returning," Colonel Warner said, briefing him.

Trevier smiled. "I certainly don't have any endearing ties to Holland, not after the way my family had to leave."

"Your assignment is to collect information, search for political conspiracies, and if possible, infiltrate the resistance. You will report to one person."

"Yes, sir, and who is this contact I am to report to?"

"His name is Scallion. You will meet him every Saturday night at midnight under the train trestle between DeHoven and Ede. You will give him this password phrase. Memorize and destroy it."

Look like an innocent flower but be the serpent under it, Trevier read. "That's unusual. What does it mean?"

"It's Shakespeare. Just memorize it. You will give him a return phrase, 'Tis within ourselves that we are thus or thus.'"

chapter SEVENTEEN

The wall around the Cathedral could be misconstrued as a stockade or a fortress. It was made of rock and decaying mortar, built during the crusades. The portcullis, however, had been replaced with a wrought iron gate. Rapier and Sven combed the alley. It appeared to be empty except for a couple of alley cats snarling in a fight for dominance. Although the alley was clear, Rapier didn't relax, always on a perpetual alertness.

Sven looking seriously into Rapier's eyes said, "I hope the old guy didn't set us up."

Sven could see the muscles tense in Rapier's face. He was always vigilante, always on the lookout. Rapier could smell if a person was German, Jew, or Dutch by the soap they used or the food they ate. He could sense the danger of a trap or spot a spy in a crowd. He hadn't sensed that the old man would betray them.

Without warning, Rapier whipped around, scaring Sven. He put his finger to his lips, motioning Sven to be quiet and stay put. He slid noiselessly along the wall to where he had seen a movement. A dark shadow climbed a stack of wooden crates next to the wall. Rapier silently crept behind him, covered his mouth with his left hand, put a knife at his throat with the other, and dragged him off the crates. In a deadly tone, he asked, "Who are you and what are you doing here? Now I am going to take my hand away from your mouth, if you call out, it will be the last thing you ever do. Do you understand?"

The man's eyes widened, and he nodded. His voice quivered, "I'm Dedriek Gansen."

"And what are you doing here?"

"Might I ask you the same?" Dedriek shot back.

Rapier tightened his grip on the knife, pushing it deeper against his throat. "You can stop your smart-aleck replies, or I'll give you another air hole, which might take the sass out of you."

Dedriek replied, "I have come to rescue my brother from the Gestapo."

"And who is this brother that you want to commit suicide for?"

"Anton."

"And how were you going to do that? Have you got a secret army hidden away I'm not aware of? Or are you foolish enough to think you can take on the Gestapo alone?"

Dedriek ignored the quip. "He was picked up yesterday by the Gestapo."

"How do you know that?"

"I saw his men arrested and loaded into a Gestapo truck," Dedriek spouted off. "How do I know you're not a German and will kill my brother and me?"

"You don't! It looks to me like you're just going to get yourself killed." Rapier put the knife back in the sheath. "I'm Rapier. I've come for the same reason—to get your brother and his men out of the prison if possible."

"Do you have a plan?"

"Working on it."

"How many men do you have?"

"One."

"One?"

"Yes, meet Sven," Rapier said as they walked back to where Sven was waiting for the old man. "Sven, this is Anton's younger brother, Dedriek, who has come to rescue his brother."

"But where are all your men?" Dedriek asked. "Did the Germans arrest them too?"

"No, our hideout was bombed."

"They're dead?"

"We were warned and were able to escape in time, but now they're spread all over Holland. Sven and I are the only ones together. We were to rendezvous with them in a week, but by then it will be too late for your brother and his men. So I am here to figure a way to get them out without getting them and us killed."

They heard the scraping of metal on metal. The three men instinctively reached for their weapons and turned to face the intruder. The old man dropped the key and reached his arms into the air. "*Goedertierenheid*!"[26]

Rapier recognized the old man and motioned for them to back off. He peered behind him. "Did you come alone?"

The old man dropped his hands and snarled, "Yes, I am alone. The Germans know I usually go through the courtyard on my way home. They don't bother me." He bent over and retrieved the key, twisting it in the rusty lock and locking the gate behind him. "Follow me."

"Wait," Rapier said. "I don't work with anyone unless I know his name."

"Wilhelm Beins." He hurried across the alley and disappeared in the shadows of the abandoned building. He waited for them to catch up and then ducked into the recessed doorway of an old leather shop. He took a tarnished key out of his pocket and opened the aged wood door. Mr. Beins stepped past the dust-covered workbench and headed for a door on the opposite wall. He retrieved another key and opened the door.

They entered a dark passage. "We have just been lured into a black widow's lair," Rapier whispered. "Not a fly-speck of light is anywhere."

The old man chuckled. "Stay close behind me. We're going down a flight of stairs."

Dedriek grabbed Sven's shirttail, who grabbed Rapier's. Rapier didn't grab Mr. Beins shirt but kept close enough to feel his presence. On the small landing they could see a dim shaft of light. Mr. Beins lifted the bolt on a large oak door and pushed. They entered a room the size of a small cell with a tiny dust-covered casement window on the west wall. Even though the light was dim, they still squinted, having just exited a black sarcophagus. The room was empty except for one table and chair, and on the south wall, was a recessed bookcase, void of books. The middle shelf held a lone candle. Next to it was a cone-shaped piece of metal with a tarnished brass ball on top. The room, like the leather shop, had layers of dust and cobwebs and appeared as if it hadn't been disturbed for centuries. It was a simple cell possibly used for a priest in solitary meditation, or perhaps a prisoner.

Mr. Beins closed the door, and for the first time since they entered the building, turned and addressed the men. "There is a way into the prison. The cathedral has a network of tunnels and passages under it, built during the Crusades for holy men to escape. They are as secret as the Knights Templar."

---

26. Mercy

"Are you saying we can get the prisoners out without the Germans even knowing?" Dedriek asked.

"I think it will be a miracle, but if you get them out without alerting the Germans, it is possible."

Mr. Beins took the cone, put the cone end in the hole under the candle, and turned it. The wall swung open, revealing steps descending into the oppressive blackness again. They followed the downward winding steps. The blackness chilled them to the bone.

"We're under the cathedral now, just short of the depths of Hades," the old man said. The stairs finally ended at yet another large door. This time Mr. Beins took the butt of his pistol and broke off the rusted bolt, and then all four pushed against the door. It swung open into a large dark void. Mr. Beins retrieved a flashlight and turned it on, revealing a room big enough for a small castle to fit inside. He lit a torch on the wall by the door and several others around the room.

The high ceiling was crisscrossed by huge arched wood beams that connected to four columns in the corners. The room looked like a vault. It was cluttered with broken statues of Mother Mary and other Saints. Boxes and crates were filled with chalices, crucifixes, sterling silver monstrance, and a variety of Catholic artifacts. In the center was a large rectangular table with twelve dusty wood and velveteen chairs.

"This looks like a stockpile of stuff from centuries," Dedriek said as he stared in wonder around the room. "I wonder if any of this stuff is worth anything. Maybe it's worth a fortune."

The light from the torches swirled the darkness and created distorted shadows on the faces of the liberators. Dedriek stopped in midsentence when he noticed Rapier's face turn into a menacing mask of ugly.

"We are not here as treasure hunters," Rapier said. "We are here to save lives. I would suggest you keep that as your main focus or men will die. We will work together with one goal, to rescue as many men as we can, thereby saving not only their lives, but hundreds of others whose identities may be discovered from their tortured lips."

Mr. Beins took a roll of paper out of a derelict wine barrel, spread it across the table, and shined a flashlight on it. "These are the architectural plans of the underground tunnels and passages. They show the passages connected to each room and the tunnels connected into them. These rooms are where the prisoners are kept. In the middle is the torture chamber with an attached room where they hold the more important prisoners in isolation. I suspect your friend is being held there. The Germans like the other prisoners to hear the tortured screams of those being interrogated, to break them psychologically. Most usually succumb and talk. Of course, some die before they talk because they are too old or weak."

Mr. Beins pointed to a series of blue lines. "These are networks of air shafts. The plumbing and electrical work was added centuries later. I would suggest going between midnight and 4:00 a.m. The guards are the only ones here, and they usually don't keep a close of an eye on things."

"You ever been in these tunnels before?" Rapier asked.

"Dozens of times but more in the past few months since the Germans moved in."

"We'll see you back in the alley at midnight then," Rapier said, putting his hand out to shake his.

"*Ja,* see you then." Mr. Beins turned and led them back to the leather shop.

Marieka found Mr. Fiske in the shed next to the barn, his feet planted in front of a three-wheeled wagon, swinging a ball-peen hammer against the fourth wheel.

"Hello, Mr. Fiske," Marieka said as she walked up behind him. He turned sharply, his gentle old eyes narrowed to a beady hard glint as he swung the hammer at the uninvited guest. His face dissolved into surprise mixed with fear when he saw Marieka. His face blanched white, and his hand shook as he pulled the hammer back to his side.

"Marieka," he scolded. "What are you doing here? You shouldn't sneak up on me like that."

Marieka's eyes widened. "I'm sorry, Mr. Fisk, but I wasn't sneaking. I thought you heard me push the door aside."

Trying to calm his shattered nerves, Mr. Fiske angrily retorted, "You shouldn't come here. It isn't safe for you or me. The Germans will think we have connections."

"I've come to ask if you have had any contact with the underground or resistance lately."

Mr. Fiske sat the hammer on the hay wagon, leaned against it, and inhaled deeply. He wiped his brow with a yellowed handkerchief he'd pulled out of his back pocket. "No, Marieka. It isn't possible. There is still too much danger. The Germans are on the very highest state of alert."

Marieka's jaw jutted out as she persisted. "Please, there are those we have taken in whose lives are in danger, as well as our own."

Mr. Fiske shook his head and sighed deeply. "I have not seen Peter, my usual contact from Rapier in over a week. It worries me. I try not to dwell on the things that could happen to him."

Marieka's gaze was unrelenting. "But, Mr. Fiske, we are hiding a Jewish girl who just had a baby. We can't keep a baby in the cellar. I know the area is full of German activity, but we're desperate."

"I'll see what I can do," Mr. Fiske said, shaking his head. "I'll set the signal out, but I'm not sure Peter is around."

"Thank you."

"I'll contact you when I hear something. Now you must go. If the patrols are around, duck in the thick goose grass until they pass. Be safe little one." His warm voice was laced with concern.

Marieka ran along the canal. She heard the roar of a German truck coming toward her. Fear paralyzed her, as if a deadly snake coiled around her, tightening her throat with each breath. But she had to fight the fear like an imaginary foe, and determined to beat it, she began to pray. She felt peace wash over her and knew everything would be okay. She watched as the German truck turned onto the farm.

Lieutenant Schmidt slid his long legs through the side door of the vehicle, his eyes fastened smugly on his newest gambit as he strolled over to Hendrick Coevorden. "It is time to give up your son, Herr Coevorden, or take his place."

"You may search, but you won't find him," Hendrick said, staring into his eyes.

Lieutenant Schmidt signaled to his men to split up and search the area. Marieka's breath caught as she watched the men begin their search. She prayed Mama hadn't left any evidence of the night before.

The soldiers had scattered throughout the yard and were waiting for orders. Lieutenant Schmidt walked into the house ordering some of the men to follow. It was neat and tidy as he had anticipated. At the top of the stairs were three bedrooms and a bathroom. In the bedroom furthest to the back was the boy's room. The bed hadn't been slept in and the drawers and closets were partially empty. He looked at the personal items on the chiffonier: a tarnished ring with a topaz stone, a picture of a pretty girl, coins, a chain, some letters, and a Bible. He stuck the letters in his pocket and picked up the Bible, thumbing through it before he dropped it with disgust.

His men threw the bedding, turned the mattress over, and threw items out of the closet and drawers. He checked the back of the closet but found nothing. Lieutenant Schmidt went back to the small kitchen. There he noticed a lot of dishes in the sink for just three people.

He checked the barn, but nothing seemed out of the ordinary. Two large workhorses munched hay, a calf was in a stall next to them, and the milking area had just been cleaned after the evening's chores.

He walked over to Hendrick, Anna, and Marieka. "Your home and farm are in impeccable order. My compliments, Herr Coevorden. You'll make a very nice addition to the work crews in the factories."

Anna gasped and grabbed Hendrick. "No!" she screamed. Lieutenant Schmidt signaled for his men to take him. Anna held on, crying. A guard hit her and knocked her to the ground. Marieka let out a sob, ran to her, and whispered, "Don't worry, Mama. I know people who can get him back."

The orange sun, like the beacon from a lighthouse, peeked over the horizon, its rays opened into a rainbow of color, blazing the fruit trees as if they were giant flower vases stippling the hillsides. The valley unfolded into a luxuriant carpet of emerald, dotted with variegated wild flowers in a showy display, but the crowning glory of Tevier's homeland was the tulips. Vast fields of tulips in prismatic color were the hallmark of the Netherlands, representing the heart of the Dutch. Their blooms were in every aspect of the valley.

Trevier's emotions boiled as he looked on his former homeland for the first time in twelve years, and he wrestled with his feelings for his former roots. Carried away into another time, he remembered a loving home with a devoted mother and father. With his face close to the train window, he looked in awe at the sun-painted rows of red-brick cottages, their soft pink glow, and butterfly-shaped roofs, painted golden in the early light. The morning mist melted off the swept cobblestone streets, reminding him of playing ball with his papa on the weekend. His gaze focused on the giant windmills lined in a row along the handmade canals. With subdued yearning, he thought he'd finally came home. Then his eyes narrowed into polluted dark slits as he remembered the real reason for being here.

Months before, he had contacted his aunt and uncle, Betje and Hankan Boedekur to inform them he wanted to return to Holland and ask if he might stay with them until he could find a place of his own.

chapter EIGHTEEN

The Mercedes seemed to purr as it wove through the streets toward the Gestapo headquarters. "You have done a great service to the Third Reich," Colonel Warner said. "You single-handedly brought in the leader of the resistance."

Trevier's smile broadened. "I am honored to be of service."

Anton twisted to face Trevier, his nostrils flared in disgust. "You are intoxicated with the nectar of poisonous serpents, you filthy traitor."

Trevier's smile tightened like thin rubber stretched over waxed teeth and choked down the rage that rose in his throat.

Anton remained silent for the duration of the journey, seething. *How could I have been so blind as to not see my closest associate was a traitor?* He could barely see the dark streets and the few people that were out. They passed old manors of the once wealthy, but as they drove closer to town, he saw small businesses huddled on the cobblestone streets. A Jewish bookstore had streaks of blackened soot snaking up the white paint. The windows were broken, the insides gutted. It loomed like a desolate tomb next to the other buildings.

They turned onto the main street and headed toward the center of town where the white stone Cathedral hovered like a giant caretaker over the city. The Mercedes stopped in front, and the driver opened the doors for the three in the back. Anton counted the steps that led to the large carved double doors behind two granite columns, tucking it away in his mind.

Colonel Warner led them into the large vaulted room. Two crystal chandeliers were all that remained of the once grand room, except maybe the worn plush carpets. Two paint-chipped desks were next to the entrance, where two secretaries worked on manual typewriters.

Colonel Warner stopped at the first desk and demanded that Anton give the secretary his full name.

Anton didn't respond. Trevier shouted, "Answer the man!"

Anton grunted, refusing to look at her.

Colonel Warner looked at the secretary. "Put him in cell one, next to the interrogation room. Is Deiter here?"

"No, he has gone for the day," the secretary replied without looking up.

"Well, get him back here. He has work to do," Warner ordered impatiently.

"But, sir," she said, nervously glancing at him, "when he leaves here he goes to the tavern. He'll be drunk by now."

"All the better. He won't remember it in the morning. Do you know which tavern?"

"Yes, sir," she said as she picked up the phone and dialed the number.

The young woman hung up and reported that the bartender would have a couple of men bring him over. "He's not totally drunk but made a good attempt at it for the short time he has been there," she said drily and went back to typing the form for the new prisoner. When it was completed she handed it to Colonel Warner to sign.

Trevier led Anton across the foyer to the door that led to the lower levels.

A large, hunched, middle-aged sergeant sat next to the door and jerked to attention. His nose was flat, his forehead furrowed and slanted. That gave him a gorilla-like appearance. He took one look at the newest arrival and shoved him toward the stairs. Anton noted his defeated look. His eyes had no color. His lips were turned down, not in a frown but as if they had no blood or life in them, like he wasn't alive inside.

The stocky man stopped in front of a metal door with a small Judas peephole at the top. From his belt buckle, he retrieved a large metal key ring that jingled like a tiny symphony. He opened the door and shoved Anton roughly inside, locking it behind him.

Anton looked around. A rope cot was in one corner, covered with a stained mattress that had the stuffing hanging out of mouse-eaten holes. A threadbare blanket was thrown at the bottom. In another corner was a half-filled swill bucket. Above him, a single light bulb hung on a short black cord, emitting a small pan of the dull yellow light. The wall next to the bed was spattered with dried blood. As he looked closer at the cot, he found it filthy with excretion stains, blood, and vomit.

He knelt and prayed. "God, please give me the strength to resist their brutality and keep the confidences I have been entrusted with."

The door swung wide. Colonel Warner stepped in followed by Trevier. "You think God will rescue you?" Colonel Warner shouted. "Many in here have prayed for His help and were not saved. They died alone. I am the only god you will know here. I am the only one who has the power to deliver you. If you give me what I want, you can forego the interrogations and maybe meet death as a whole man. This is the only power you have over your fate."

Unaffected by his threats, Anton raised his eyes to Colonel Warner's and stood erect. Trevier lunged at him, hitting him in the small of his back. Anton faltered but did not fall. Trevier pushed Anton toward the door and led him to the interrogation room, or the torture chamber.

In the center of the room was a raised platform with a worn, barbershop type chair. Bloodstained leather straps were sewn securely to the underside. Another set of straps were positioned at the top on the headrest, at the chest, and at the bottom. Overhead, pendulous electrical wires dangled, and mounted on the wall behind them was an electrical box with a large handle protruding from the side. In a corner was a steel basket containing wooden clubs and metal bars, and on the table was a filthy tray with dental and medical instruments.

A large, cockeyed, bare-chested man with bloodshot eyes, stood next to the chair. His mouth partially opened to reveal a broken tooth as bloody spittle drooled down his lip. He sniffed and wiped the back of his hand across his face, swaying from the effects of his drinking. He reeked of cheap beer.

Colonel Warner warned him, "I want him conscious. Do not hit him in the head because it will make him forgetful and slur his words. Do you understand, you drunken lunatic?"

Dieter nodded. Trevier pushed Anton in the chair, and Deiter put his wide square hands on Anton's shoulders, holding him steadfast as Trevier fastened the straps. When Trevier backed away, Deiter lunged at Anton, hitting him in the stomach. Anton's head fell forward as he expelled a large rush of air.

"No, you idiot! Stand back!" Colonel Warner screamed.

Colonel Warner fixed his eyes on Anton. "You will tell me the names of every resistance member, and every safe house, and I want to know who the man code-named Rapier is and how to find him."

Anton spit in his face.

Colonel Warner hit Anton in the face with a closed fist, ignoring his own orders. He collected himself as quickly as he had lost his temper. "Now, Anton," he cooed. "You do not want to anger me. It may have disastrous consequences. I will be disappointed if I lose my head and kill you prematurely."

Anton's eyes bore into Colonel Warner's as if daring him to do just that.

Colonel Warner laughed. "Oh no, Anton. You will not win that easily. I have plans for you before I kill you."

The colonel blindfolded Anton's defiant eyes. They unnerved him. He asked again for the names of the resistance members, but Anton held his tongue. He nodded to Dieter. Dieter swung the club and connected with the side of Anton's head. "Not his head, you imbecile!" Colonel Warner yelled. "I want him to be able to talk."

Dieter put his head down as if he were a reprimanded child. Spittle blew from Colonel Warner's lips as his anger got out of control, but he tried to calm down as he walked behind Anton. "You will tell me what I want to know. My sources have informed me your family has been arrested and is at the German headquarters in Ede," he lied. "If you cooperate, they will be released unharmed. If you don't, you will have the honor of seeing your family brutalized in front of you. It is up to you if they experience freedom or agony."

The chair twisted around. The hit to the side of his head had loosened the blindfold Anton faced the antagonist and readied for the battle. Then an idea popped into his mind, to change his tactics. If he could convince Colonel Warner he was weak and afraid, maybe Warner would feel an upsurge of superiority and pride. Then he would become careless, and make mistakes, exposing his vulnerability like the underside of a porcupine's belly. If he could get Colonel Warner to bite at his game of wits, maybe he could buy some time. *I hope this is a trial run, and I will be sent back to my cell; then I may have time to formulate a plan.* His mind raced as he geared up for the brutality.

"I see you have a will of iron. You won't be so high and mighty after a few more hours," the colonel said. He nodded at Dieter, but this time he swung the club at his knee. Anton writhed in agony.

"The name," Colonel Warner demanded.

"The names who will make thee a fool," Anton quoted, "is written in the sacred books of Yamanue."[27]

Colonel Warner's displeasure showed in his lack of self-control as his fist exploded on Anton's cheek.

"You do try my patience, Anton!"

At that moment the door swung open and a messenger came in. "General Eikman has just arrived and is demanding a meeting immediately."

Colonel Warner swore. "I'll continue this tomorrow. Get a good night's rest, Anton. Tomorrow may be a long day."

A few minutes before midnight, Rapier and his companions crouched in the alley between two vacant buildings. Rapier looked up at the sky. "No moon or stars to give us away," he whispered. "A good omen."

Mr. Beins hadn't arrived yet. Rapier paced nervously. Waiting was always a dangerous time, a most vulnerable time. A time when a person gets fidgety, uptight, and careless, and it could mean a set up or a trap.

Rapier gripped the pistol in his hand, slowed his breathing, and listened to the sounds of the night for the familiar and the unfamiliar. He listened with his body, to jittery feelings, prickling on the back of his neck, or a hum in his head. This was his sixth sense, and it had saved his life many times.

The church bell rang, signaling the top of the hour. Rapier cursed the noise drowning out the silence. When the reverberations stopped, Mr. Beins materialized in the shadows. Rapier looked behind him for a tail.

"I like your thoroughness," the old man whispered.

"It's kept me alive."

Mr. Beins motioned for them to follow. In the chamber room, the old man lit the torches and walked over to the table where he'd left the blueprints. His arthritic finger pointed to the long corridors outlined with black. "These are the tunnels and passages." He pointed to two rooms in the center. "The small one is connected to the larger room by a short hall. This is where you'll find your friend. Let's just hope Dieter didn't get carried away again. Sometimes he enjoys it so much, he doesn't stop until the victim is dead."

---

27. Hebrew for "hidden one"

Dedriek cringed, struggling to push the picture out of his head.

"It will be difficult to get your friend through the air shafts if his injuries are too serious," the old man continued. "Your friend's men are on the opposite side of the prison, several in each cell. Getting thirty men out of here without alerting the whole German army is going to be a miracle, but this is a place of miracles."

When he finished explaining the map, he looked up into three skeptical faces. "You look as if you don't believe this can be done."

"Yeah, we get the men out of the prison and then what?" Dedriek mumbled. "They'll be spotted when we take them back through the alley. Then they'll be recaptured and shot."

Mr. Beins looked at the boy. "Young man," he said. "Your job is to lead the men out of here after we rescue them." He walked over to the steps leading to the white stone fireplace. His hand disappeared underneath the mantle and the fireplace swung open, revealing a dark passage. "This tunnel leads to the outskirts of the city to the wharves. It was used by the monks to escape in the 1600s."

Dedriek's mouth dropped, his face flushed.

With his back still turned to them, Mr. Beins continued, "I've arranged for a fishing boat to take all of you up river. It's a rusty, tarnished barnacle, but it's the perfect cover. The skipper's name is Jarius. He's a good man. The Germans search his boat from time and time but never find anything, so they usually leave him alone. He goes out to fish every day. When he comes back, he nods at the Germans as he passes. He'll take you down river to the south side, where two resistance members will meet you.

"Rapier, you and Sven will come with me. Your friend will need assistance. I don't think the Germans have interrogated his men yet. They're more interested in catching bigger fish . . . you. They would be humiliated to know that the man called Rapier has walked into their headquarters right under their noses." Mr. Beins laughed. "Let's go. The tunnels are dark and confusing, follow closely."

The brick tunnel was about two shoulders' width wide. The subterranean air was stale, as if it hadn't felt a fresh breath of air in centuries. A moldy smell intermingled with the stale, causing Sven to feel claustrophobic. He dragged in deep breaths, as if a casket was being closed on him.

"Get hold of yourself," Mr. Beins said. "Take a couple of long slow breaths and relax. The air shafts are up ahead. You'll feel better soon."

The rock floors were damp and covered in places with slippery mold. Occasionally, small yellow eyes reflected in the beam of the flashlights. The clicking of their claws reverberated against the walls as the creatures disappeared into tiny crevices.

"Networks of these tunnels run under the cathedral," Mr. Beins said over his shoulder. "There are other tunnels under this prison level also. They open at a farmhouse to the north. The monks had two different directions from which to escape, depending on which direction the enemy was coming."

They moved noiselessly through the tunnel, arriving at the iron grate-covered air shaft just before Sven was about to pass out. Mr. Beins took a wrench from his pocket and loosened the bolts. "This is the main air shaft. A separate tunnel runs from it to your friend's cell. The room is small and has a heavy metal door with a Judas peephole at the top. The guards check on the prisoners every thirty minutes."

Rapier crawled into the stone air shaft first, his stomach churning. When they reached the grate over the cell, he looked in. In the pale light he could see a person curled up on a cot in the corner.

Rapier lowered himself into the dimly lit cell. He heard the guards coming toward the door and ducked in the opposite corner, barely dodging the swill bucket. The guard flicked his flashlight through the peephole to the cot, glanced at it with indifference, and moved on. Rapier then moved to the cot's side.

"Anton, my friend," he whispered. There was no response. He shook his shoulder. Anton rolled over, letting out an injured cry. He looked up with a puffy, bloodshot eye. In the dim light, Rapier could see the left side of his face was disfigured, his left eye was swollen shut, and over his right eye was a red gash. His upper lip looked as if a swarm of bees had attacked it. It was so swollen it cut off one side of his nose.

"Anton, its Rapier." Rapier watched as Anton tried to focus. He managed a weak smile, coughed, clutched his side, and croaked something indecipherable.

"I've come to get you out of here. We better go before the guard comes back and finds the two of us."

"Have you heard anything about my men?" Anton slurred in a whisper.

"*Ja*, they were arrested yesterday."

"They're in here?"

"On the other side of the prison. We hope to get them out too."

"How?"

"We're working on it. Can you walk?"

"My left knee is badly bruised, but I can hobble on my right leg."

"Yeah, like a man in a one-legged race, right?"

Rapier helped him to the air shaft and lifted him to Sven's outstretched arms. Anton winced as Sven grabbed his right arm. His brow beaded as he dragged himself into the air shaft where he collapsed.

Rapier took off his jacket and put it under the threadbare blanket on the cot, hoping to buy some time. The cot's odor smelled like mercaptan spray from a skunk. The putrid smell ripped through his stomach with the savageness of the Typhoid Mary. His eyes blurred as he crossed the tiny cell to Sven's waiting arm.

"You look a little peaked, boss. You feeling okay?"

"Just give me a moment. This place reeks worse than the inside of death's lair." Sven placed the grate back and tightened the bolts. He could hear the guards in the hall as they drew near, but they didn't check the cell.

Sven took off his jacket, laid it on the floor, and helped Anton onto it. "Hold on while we drag you out of here."

Mr. Beins kept rubbing his neck and wringing his hands as he paced back and forth. Finally, he heard scraping in the tunnel and shined his flashlight inside. His voice deepened with emotion. "I was beginning to worry the Germans had captured you." He helped Sven pull the makeshift litter out of the passage followed by Rapier. He looked at Anton. "Dieter must have had quite an evening. We've got to hurry. If it takes as much time to rescue each man as it did for your friend, we'll be here until tomorrow night," Mr. Beins said, spreading a gap between Rapier and Sven. "Your friend can wait here."

The grate covering the air shaft was rusted over from a constant drip of water. It led to the quarters where Anton's men were being held.

"I don't think there's any way to break through that rust unless we blow it," Rapier said.

"We can't blow it," said Mr. Beins. "That would alert the Germans."

Sven looked at him. "Got a file in that pocket of yours?"

"Just a screwdriver and a wrench."

"That'll do." Sven took the tools from him, tore a piece from the bottom of his shirt, and placed the screwdriver under the bolt. He dug around the edge, scraped off the iron oxide, placed the shirttail over the end of the screwdriver, and then struck the screwdriver with the wrench. He positioned the claw of the wrench around the bolt and twisted. Rapier placed his hand over Sven's, and they pulled until the bolt finally loosened. "One down and five to go," Sven said breathless.

"In this block there are ten cells, and an air shaft goes to each," Mr. Beins said. "Start with the closest and then go to the next. You have forty-five minutes before the guards check this area again. When you get the first few men out, I'll take them and Anton back to the chamber, and then I'll be back for the rest of you."

Rapier and Sven crawled to the first cell. Rapier put his face on the grate and looked in. Three men were sleeping on the floor, huddled in fetal positions without coat or blanket. The weathered door looked as if was from an old barn. It had a swill bucket in the corner but no cots. The men appeared to be uninjured.

Sven dropped into the room and looked down at a young pimpled-faced boy in the dim light. He nudged him with his foot and the kid came up swinging. "Hold on, young man," he whispered as he grabbed his swinging fist. "I'm here to rescue you."

The boy rubbed his eyes and blinked. "Who . . . who are you?"

"Shhh, I'm one of Rapier's men. I've come to get you out of here."

"But how?"

"With a little prayer and a whole lot of luck. Now get over to that air shaft. I'll give you a boost up." Sven helped the men through the opening and followed after them.

After Sven replaced the grate and tightened the screws, Rapier sent the men back to Mr. Beins while he and Sven crawled to the next opening. It was the same scenario with each cell. The men seemed shocked, yet trusting, and held their silence as they crawled along the passage to where Mr. Beins was waiting.

When the first group of men got back to where Mr. Beins was waiting, the pimple-faced boy saw his leader and friend, and his eyes lit up. He reached out to help Anton. "Can you walk?"

"With your help," he slurred, "Thanks, Twig."

chapter NINETEEN

Dedriek paced back and forth, his eyes flecked with anger at being left behind. "They treat me as if I am a little kid not capable of handling dangerous assignments."

He heard the ancient door creak and twisted around to face the incomers but stopped as if he was about to step on a trip wire. Crouching behind the large oak table, he aimed the bead of his gun at the door. Mr. Beins entered first, followed by Anton, supported by Twig.

Dedriek put his hand over his mouth to quell his excitement. He closed the space to Anton. "Little brother," Anton rasped in surprise. "I'll see to it that you get a whipping for disobeying me! But not yet. I'm afraid I couldn't beat the fluff off a dandelion right now. You'll have to wait. I suppose you probably had something to do with this?"

A lopsided grin appeared on Dedriek's face. "*Ja*, I probably would have gotten myself killed barging in here like a bumbling hero. Thank goodness I met up with Rapier. He's more level-headed than I am."

"Assuredly," Anton said.

Mr. Beins climbed the steps to the fireplace and opened it. He handed Dedriek a key and a couple of flashlights for the men. "Your contact is Jarius, an old fisherman. Give him the signal of three short flashes. He'll give you two in return," Mr. Beins instructed. "Go with God."

Dedriek led the men into the inky tunnel. He squinted, trying to focus on any unseen obstacles. He felt it was his duty to get the men to safety, and for once, he felt important.

Twig let Anton lean against him, his hip cushioning the jarring movements. "You are some kind of a hero keeping your mouth shut to protect the lives of others."

"For a while I was beginning to wonder if I could hold out," Anton said. "But as if by some miracle, Colonel Warner was called away. I wasn't so sure if I could face the next day. Slugging bruises from the previous night's ordeal would have been doubly painful. I sure was glad to see you guys."

"Where's Trevier? Did he get the same treatment?" Twig asked.

Anton snorted. "I wish!"

"What?"

Anton tilted his head slightly to peek at Twig through his good eye. He spat. "Trevier is a traitor." Through painfully swollen lips, he told of Trevier's deceit.

Twig watched Anton to see if he was joking, but his face held a look of gravity.

Anton continued, "During Trevier's time away, he evidently lived in Germany under the tutelage of Colonel Warner. At eighteen he was asked to join a special spy unit. Thereafter he was sent to Holland to infiltrate the resistance."

"*Heilig Kak!*[28] He sure skunked us! I never suspected him."

"He fooled us all," Anton admitted. "Except Rapier. He knew something was fishy about him from the beginning. I wish I had his gut instinct."

Dedriek forged ahead of the group. The tunnel seemed endless, as if he were walking in a dream through a dark abyss, never going anywhere. He scouted ahead for any obstructions or danger, but amazingly, the tunnel was intact and had little or no decay. Occasionally he'd slow down to check on Twig and Anton, asking if they needed to stop and rest. But Anton always refused. "We've got to meet up with Jarius. Keep going."

The tunnel began to slope, and the air cooled and became more humid. Dedriek came to a large renaissance door with a crossbar in the middle. He lifted the bar and examined the door. The door-pull, made of iron, was on the left and on the plate under the doorknob was a keyhole.

Without waiting for the others, Dedriek took the key Mr. Beins had given him and opened the door. The gray morning light seeped through the cracks of the faded clapboard in front of it. It couldn't have been more welcoming to him than a priest's smile at absolution.

"It looks like they built something in front of the entrance," Dedriek announced.

---

28. Holy crap

Gottfreid was the rear sentry. He was tall and lanky. His shoulders reminded Dedriek of a scarecrow with a broomstick shoved through the shirtsleeves. His shirt hung limp and looked as if it could out-flap any flag on a windy day, hiding his V-shaped form. When he saw the wall behind the door, he hurried to the front of the group and lamented, "You've got to be kidding! There's nothing here but another wall!"

Dedriek narrowed his eyes at the assault. "All you have to do is think about it. They're not going to leave the door out in the open for all to see." He turned and kicked the boards in like matchsticks, and they collapsed into an old fishing cannery. The fetid fish odor, though weak, caused a gag reaction in the men. Dedriek shined the flashlight around the dingy room. A warped table was on one side with two aged wooden barrels on one end of it. Empty beer bottles were in one corner along with a broken chair and a crooked rack of rusty knives hung over the table. The door to the cannery was made of thin planks hurriedly nailed together, and they did nothing to keep the weather out.

When Dedriek opened the door, it groaned like a drunken sailor with a hangover. He peeked into the gray morning, and it seemed quiet. Gottfreid set a chair upright and fitted it snugly against the wall so Twig could sit Anton down. Then Twig ran to catch up with Dedriek to scout the docks.

The old fishing boat was at the lower dock as promised. "I'll give the signal, and after the return signal you go back for the others," Dedriek whispered. He flashed the signal and within moments a reply was seen.

Twig backtracked to the shack and motioned for the others to follow. He helped Anton to his feet and hiked him against his hip again. They crept along the decaying warehouses that lined the water's edge to the fish-bucket boat. The old man looked like he was out of the sixteenth century. He reminded Dedriek of an old pirate, with a murderous glare, who couldn't be trusted. His long gray hair fused with his beard in a matted snarl, and he smelled like rotting fish mixed with rum. It looked as if it took great effort to finagle his upper lip into a crooked smile, and his right eye was blind and milky blue, which added to his swashbuckler guise.

"Welcome aboard," he said, stretching his hand out. The men boarded the boat, keeping an eye out for Germans. The old captain put some of the men in the cabin; the rest he hid in the hull and covered them with tarps. Then he started the engine and sputtered out onto the river. For a moment, Anton felt relief, but Rapier and most of his men were still in the cathedral. He hoped he hadn't traded one resistance leader for another.

chapter TWENTY

Rapier took the grate off the sixth cell. They had been able to rescue fifteen men. Things had gone smoothly, but the hair on the back of his neck stood up. "Sven, I have a bad feeling about this one. I think we should get out of here."

"But what about the rest of the men?"

"I feel bad about them. They'll pay a heavy price for the others getting away, but my instincts tell me our luck has run out."

"We've got this grate off. Let's rescue these men first, and then we'll get out," Sven said.

"You have thirty seconds," Rapier replied reluctantly.

Sven dropped quietly into the cell. *This one is different from the others,* he thought. It's larger, cleaner, contains cots, and the smell isn't as overpowering as the others. The door was a Dutch-style: the bottom half was wood, and the top half was open and barred.

Sven crept to the first man, whom he assumed was asleep. He could see he was about half the size of the other men and wondered if he was a child. His biscuit-colored curls added to his youthful appearance.

He crept behind him. The man jumped up with his hands in front of his face, as if expecting to be shot. He started to say something when Sven's fist came up and hit him under the chin. He fell to the floor.

"Shut up! You'll alert the whole German army," Sven said in a raspy whisper.

"Who are you?" the short man whispered, looking up. He leaned on one elbow as he rubbed his chin.

The commotion woke up the other two men. "It's a Kraut!" the short man choked. "It's a trick. He's going to lead us into a trap."

"*Wateen onzin*!"[29] his roommate snarled. "You moron. We are already arrested! Shut up."

Sven pointed to the air duct and motioned for the men to climb up. While he lifted the short man, Sven stepped into the swill bucket. He gagged, trying to maintain his balance, but stumbled backward, hitting his head. He sagged to the floor and the bucket, free from his foot, clattered across the room.

The guard standing against the wall, slouched in a dreamlike state, jerked awake. Startled, he knocked his hat to the floor and bent over to pick it up, thinking he'd just been caught sleeping on duty. He looked up and saw the guard at the other end of the hall rush to the cell. He ran to the cell and shined his flashlight in the window just as a man disappeared through the air shaft in the ceiling.

"Halt!" he yelled, fumbling for the key. He threw open the door. Sven was halfway through the opening when the guard fired. The shot hit him in the leg, and Sven fell to the floor.

Rapier put the grate back and ordered the men to get out, but he didn't have time to put the bolts on. The guards ran into the cell. One kept his rifle on Sven while the other climbed through the hole. He shouted for the men to halt and opened fired. Rapier flattened to the floor as the others kept going. The guard shot and killed the three men. Rapier waited for the guard to stop firing before he rose up and put three rounds into his chest. He crawled past the dead men to where Mr. Beins was waiting.

"I sent the others on ahead," he said. "I gave them directions and instructions to wait in the abandoned cannery." Mr. Beins raised his eyebrow. "Your friend?"

Rapier shook his head. "Let's get out of here."

---

29. Utter nonsense

In the chamber room, Rapier followed the men to the fireplace and turned back to Mr. Beins. "Come on."

"No, I won't be going with you," Mr. Beins said. "My work is done here. The Germans will not know I was the one who helped you. Besides, I have to close the fireplace and destroy the maps. My duty is to the other prisoners now."

There was no time to argue. Rapier ran back to the heavy outer door, helped Mr. Beins push it shut, and moved the rusted bolt in place.

Mr. Beins went to the table, gathered up the maps, and shut the fireplace behind Rapier. In the leather shop, he dumped the maps into a small barrel and lit them, and then disappeared into the alley.

Whistles of the Gestapo sounded throughout the streets, but they hadn't made it to the back alley. Mr. Beins hurried around the corner and disappeared on a backstreet.

Rapier led the men through the tunnel, hoping to catch up with Dedriek before the fishing boat left. When they came to the renaissance door, he signaled the men to stop and then went on alone. He peeked into the cannery and found it was empty. He crossed to the outside door, looked out, switched off the flashlight, and walked into the night.

He heard the distant hum of an engine headed down the river and silently cursed. He backtracked to the cannery and signaled the men to follow. "Our ride is heading down river. We have to find another way out of here. Zaan, come with me. The rest of you stay here until we get back."

Rapier and Zaan crept under the eaves of the dock down to the jetty, trying to find a boat to hijack. There were two small open boats and one larger vessel with a three-man crew getting ready to head out to sea.

At the north end of the dock, they saw a tarped army truck being unloaded into a German commerce raider. Rapier motioned for Zaan to follow him back to the men.

"There's a truck at the end of the pier with a small crew unloading it. It is our ride out of here."

The morning light gave Rapier an uneasy feeling. The dreary gray seemed like a foreshadowing of an impending calamity. He sucked in his breath and shook off the chill as he led the men along the dock to the north end of the pier. They paused behind some empty storage containers. Rapier peeked out and watched as two privates unloaded unusually small crates from the rear of a truck. He watched as they pushed a hand truck over the ramp to the ship's deck and unloaded the cargo instead of stowing it below, which usually meant explosives. On the next trip, one private missed the ramp and knocked the cargo over. The sergeant barreled toward him and put his nose an inch away from the private's face. "Are you trying to blow us up?" he yelled.

The commotion gave Rapier the opportunity to run to the truck. He motioned for the men to get in the back. Rapier signaled to Falco, Hamel, and Zaan to take care of the three Germans. Falco and Hamel quickly disposed of the privates, but Zaan was a half second late. He grabbed the sergeant from behind, but the sergeant turned and hit him in the stomach. Hamel flew at the sergeant, stabbed him, and ran toward the moving truck. Hamel leaped aboard easily, but as Zaan was about to jump, German guards shot him.

"The whole German army will be alerted," Rapier said as he pushed the gas pedal to the floor. He didn't like it. It was sloppy, and sloppy could get them killed. He felt safer with his own men who didn't make mistakes—well, not as many. He worried what would happen if the Germans caught up with them. He and the remaining men were basically helpless. They only had a few pistols and some knives to defend themselves.

Rapier heard the roar of a truck behind them. He turned onto a narrow backstreet, shut off the engine, and cut the lights. Once the troop truck went by, Rapier started the truck again and headed toward the forest. The truck bounced violently over the neglected, pot-holed roads in the shabby part of DeHoven.

Truck lights came up behind them again, and someone fired at them. Hamel was hit. "We'll be picked off! We've got to do something!" Falco said. He looked at the cargo. "The crates. Break them open and dump the gunpowder out."

Clete smashed open two boxes with his knife and threw one box onto the road. Then he immediately dumped gunpowder from the second box as bullets whizzed past his head. "Shoot it, Falco!" Clete yelled.

Falco aimed and fired, igniting the gunpowder and exploding the box. The troop truck swerved, rolled, and caught fire. "Yes!" the men cheered.

"Let's get out of here," Rapier said. He was pleased at the ingenuity of the men. He headed to the edge of the forest and unloaded the men. Then he drove the truck to an abandoned granary and parked it.

He crept around the building and saw a filthy old woman rummaging through the putrefied grain. He startled her, and she screamed, dropping the moth-eaten sack of grain she was filling. Rapier put his finger to his lips, but she continued to scream. He had never hit a woman before but if she didn't stop screaming, she'd alert every German in the area. He grimaced, swallowed hard, and hit her across the jaw. She crumpled to the ground next to the precious bag of grain. He stepped over her, hid behind the building, and then peeked out to see the open stretch to the forest. Running straight, he would be an open target. He crouched and ran across the road and then belly-crawled in the open field. He lifted his head and then sprinted to the place he had dropped off the men.

chapter TWENTY-ONE

It was an indecent hour when Colonel Warner marched into the luxurious office and threw his hat and gloves on the glass-top mahogany desk. He had dressed quickly. The third button on his uniform was undone, his tie was wrinkled, his shoes were scuffed, and his face was ten shades of angry.

Earlier he had been awakened to the alarming news of an escape from the heavily guarded Gestapo headquarters—the headquarters under his command. What might have been the best day of his life was quickly becoming the worst.

As he burst into his office, he failed to notice the man sitting in a white satin chair in front of the desk. When he turned toward the guards, he noticed the man and that he was wounded. Blood was dripping from his pant leg onto the floor. Two guards were standing next to him, pointing their rifles at his head.

Colonel Warner looked at the guards and frowned. "He's bleeding on the chair and carpet, you fools! Put something on that!" His nerves were about as taut as a bowstring, and his strides resembled that of an enraged bull bent on crushing every bungling guard in the cathedral.

"Anton is lost and has been replaced with a lowlife who probably doesn't know anything." Colonel Warner took the pistol from his side holster and aimed it at the man's face.

The door swung wide, smacking the wall. General Eikman and his assistant, Adof Hemmerman, entered the office. "I warned you that the next time you bungled things up I would have you arrested and shot! This is the sloppiest security I have ever seen."

"But, general, I was in the middle of interrogating the prisoner last evening when you summoned me. I intended to interrogate him again first thing this morning. I don't know how this could have happened."

"Silence! Why wasn't the cathedral inspected for such escape routes?"

"We have looked at the blueprints, but saw nothing allowing for such an escape."

"You obviously overlooked something!" Eikman yelled.

Eikman turned to the guards, who imperceptibly moved back. Their expressions were a mixture of duty and fear.

"Keep an eye on the prisoner," he said. He turned to Colonel Warner. "Come with me. You, and you also," he said, pointing to Adof and Lieutenant Austerlitz.

THE GROUP CROSSED the foyer and headed for the lower level. Eikman was unprepared for the deterioration that had mutated the once-beautiful second floor into a place that transformed human suffering into important information.

He entered the first cell and examined every detail: from the swill bucket and cot to the bits of filth on the floor. He walked to the back of the cell, looked up, and swept the flashlight over the ceiling, stopping at the air shaft. "Get up there, Lieutenant, and find out how fifteen men could get through this and where it goes."

Lieutenant Austerlitz jumped at the order, and in doing so, kicked the swill bucket. The sounds that came from Eikman were as violent as an erupting volcano.

Lieutenant Austerlitz grabbed a white handkerchief and began a singsong of apologies. Eikman held his hand up and walked out of the cell, slamming the door behind him. Lieutenant Austerlitz stared with his mouth open, the handkerchief dangling from his fingertips, locked in. He quickly banged on the door and another guard opened it, letting him out.

In the next cell, Eikman ordered the guard to climb into the passage.

The guard cleared his throat. "Excuse me, sir, but it is sealed. All of them are sealed, except for the sixth cell, sir."

"Then take us there!" he bellowed.

The sixth cell was like the others. Eikman walked to the air shaft and shined the light in it. "Where does this lead?"

"We checked it after the breakout, sir. It runs into a tunnel system under the cathedral."

Eikman ordered the two guards to climb into the opening and motioned for Warner to lift him up.

At the chamber room, the door had already been blown. Eikman looked around, his eyes glazed over as if looking into a past where all this had happened before. *Were the Germans fighting a Holy War like the ones centuries earlier? Were they building a new Holy Empire to supplant Christianity with the new, more amenable Nazi ideology? Were they building a superior race, ridding the world of Jewish rubbish as had been done in centuries past? Yes,* he thought. *This is the new Golden Age, the New Holy Empire, the future of the world.*

Eikman looked around the room. Prurient desire for the artifacts filled his soul, like coveting a beautiful woman, but he restrained getting lost in the alternate reality and focused on searching the room for the prisoners' escape route.

He saw a large oak door on the other side of the room and ordered the guards to break it down.

The short guard with a pockmarked face crept forward cautiously in case it had been booby-trapped. He climbed the stairs and found it ended at a wall. "What?" he stammered.

"Oh, for the love of country!" Eikman shouted. "They must have gone through here somehow—blow it!"

Eikman was the first to run for cover as the guard pulled the pin and lobbed the grenade against the wall. The blast shook the entire area, and smoke rolled out like a dust storm in the desert. The men mounted the quivering stairs. The blast had blown a large hole in the wall revealing a small room with a massive amount of debris.

Eikman tightened his fist and shook it. He did a remarkable job of yelling through clenched teeth. To Eikman's chagrin he stared at yet another cursed staircase.

Eikman had never been in battle. He always sat safely behind the lines giving orders, and now he inwardly cringed at the thought of going up those stairs.

Although the blast shook the stairs, they were unharmed. The guards crouched, primed to fire at the slightest movement as they entered the abandoned leather shop. The west wall was bare brick, and the outer walls were made of pine, another indication it was a later addition. The room was mostly bare. There were no hidden closets or cupboards for an eager suicidal resistance member to hide in. In the center was a tool-scarred leatherworking table mounted to the floor.

A lingering odor of smoke hung in the room, like a faint scent of perfume. Eikman spied a barrel next to the window with the charred remains of paper. He discovered some unburned corners and placed them on the table.

"This looks like some kind of building plan. Look at the different colored lines," he said. "Do you think these are the blueprints of the secret tunnels? And who put this here? For that many men to escape this way, surely someone would have heard something. Lieutenant Austerlitz!" Eikman yelled. "Order the men to search the alley and surrounding areas, and question the locals. And Warner! Back to your office. Let's see what the prisoner has to say."

Eikman masked his frustration as he walked calmly into the elegant office and sat down at Colonel Warner's desk. Sven still sat in front of the desk, eyes fixed, jaw set, with his leg stretched out, now wrapped in a white cloth.

Eikman settled into the plush Victorian chair, his voice honeyed with concern. "I see your leg is injured."

No response.

"Can I get you something for the pain?" Eikman offered.

The prisoner stared past him and remained silent.

Eikman's nostril flared, and his eyes narrowed to hard flinty slits, but he recovered quickly with a placid smile.

Lieutenant Austerlitz entered the office and overheard Eikman. Ever vigilant in his service to the hierarchy of the German command, he stepped forward. "Um, excuse me, sir, but may I offer my assistance with the interrogation?"

Eikman looked over at the reprehensible lieutenant and scowled. Sven turned slowly toward the voice behind him. He scowled. "You are Trevier, Anton's friend, and a traitor."

Trevier's gaze fell downward.

"You slimy piece of sewage," Sven spat.

Trevier threw his head back and laughed. "He must be one of Rapier's men," he said. "I haven't seen him among Anton's men. I've heard Rapier has two special bodyguards. I'm willing to bet he's one of them."

Eikman's face lit up. "Maybe we do have someone important after all. Is this true? Do you know the man Rapier? Are you one of his closest associates?"

Sven's face was taut.

"Sir, you are an injured prisoner at the headquarters of the Gestapo, surrounded by armed agents and a lunatic interrogator who enjoys his job. To refuse to answer is futile." Eikman walked over, took one of the rifles from a guard, and pummeled Sven's wounded leg.

Sven screamed. He hunched over and threw up on the floor. Beads of sweat puddle on his forehead, but he didn't speak.

Adof Hemmerman stepped forward. "General Eikman, shouldn't we do this in the interrogation room? We still have several resistance prisoners. The sounds of interrogation may loosen their tongues and we may get more information out of them. Besides, we wouldn't want to ruin this office further with blood and vomit. We could have a cup of coffee while he gets settled."

Eikman stepped back, wiped his forehead with a white handkerchief, and called for the secretary to clean up the mess. "Good idea. I'm getting rather tired. Coffee is just what I need."

Eikman ordered the guards to take Sven to the interrogation room on the lower level. "And . . . leave the door open!" he yelled after them.

"Look, the strap isn't fastened tight enough," Adof barked. "He may slide out." The guard hurried to secure the strap for a second time. Adof pulled out his pistol and shot him, and then hurried to the door and shot the two guards in the hall.

Sven looked at him in disbelief. "Who are you and what are doing?"

"Shhh," Adof demanded. "They'll be changing guards in ten minutes, and Eikman, Warner, and that bumbling Austerlitz with that goon Deiter will be here shortly."

Adof unfastened the straps, put his arm around Sven's waist, and helped him to the door. He leaned him against it and grabbed the keys from the guard's belt. Running back to the cell block, he unlocked the remaining cells and signaled for the men to follow.

"Up there," he said, pointing to the air shaft.

Hanns, an older man, stared at Adof warily. "Who are you? Aren't those passages full of Germans like you? You're leading us to our deaths."

"I'm a British spy for SOE. I decided it's time to quit the double life and help the resistance. I'm sure you won't mind. The tunnels were full of Germans earlier, but they've been ordered to search the outlying area. They won't think another escape will take place in the same night." Adof grinned. "Especially using the same escape route."

The prisoner stared at him and looked up at the air shaft. "After the prisoners escaped earlier, the Germans combed the air shafts like maggots on a dead dog, and now you're telling me there's not a single German in there?"

Adof nodded with a smile. "Yes, sir." He ordered two men to help Sven into the air shaft. "I'll cover you and keep an eye out for Eikman and his guards."

Adof heard the cast iron door open at the far end of the corridor and Eikman ranting about the shots fired below.

In every army there is at least one officer whom no one deliberately crosses, and in this army, it was Eikman. Adof had been his right-hand man for months. He knew if Eikman were to catch him, he would see it as a direct affront. Eikman would have a point to prove and Adof would most assuredly suffer. The ignominious death of a traitor would be broadcast all over Germany.

Adof clasped Hanns's forearm firmly and looked steadily into his eyes, "*Danke*," he said as Hanns nodded and lifted him through the hatch.

Eikman was the first to see the two dead night guards. Eikman and the men ran to the interrogation room and saw the empty chair and another dead guard. Turning to Colonel Warner, Eikman yelled, "He's escaped! Find him! And what happened to the rest of the prisoners?"

"All the cells are empty, sir," Warner stammered after he received a report.

Eikman glowered at Colonel Warner. "They escaped the same way twice in one night? And where's Adof?" Eikman roared. "Where is he when I need him?"

"I haven't seen him since he said he was going to the privy, sir," Colonel Warner said and looked at Lieutenant Austerlitz as if it was his duty to keep track of him. "Well, where is he?"

"Silence!" Eikman yelled. "Warner, get a squad into the alley immediately. We'll be waiting for them this time."

Black smoke puffed from crooked stack as the old fishing boat chugged away earlier than usual. The old fisherman, Jarius, waved at the night watchman as usual on his way down the river. He rolled a cigarette, licked it, stuffed it into his mouth, and chewed on it like a candy stick as he steered the boat away from the dock. He sang an old sailor's song so off-key that it made the hair on Dedriek's neck curl. The fisherman hung one arm over the helm and pulled his hat low, exaggerating a drunken sway, all the while keeping his eye on the shore for the covert signal from the resistance.

As he rounded the bend near Johannsen's Cove, Jarius noticed the light in the reeds. He gave the return signal and steered the mussel-encrusted boat to shore.

Dedriek and Twig carried Anton to shore. Anton, though feverish, was alert and watched the two resistance men appear from behind a thicket. The older one looked about sixty. His gray hair curled over his coat collar. His whiskers were trimmed neatly. He looked as if he were a businessman or a man of wealth at one time. He led the group to a small farmhouse where an elderly man and woman lived with their son. The wife gave them stew and bread and then took them to a potato cellar for the night.

"Okay, little brother," Anton said through heavy lidded eyes. "Why is it you can't follow my orders and stay home where you belong?"

"Well, I did until an arrogant British pilot parachuted next to our farm. I had no way of getting him out of Holland, so I came looking for you and the resistance."

chapter
TWENTY-TWO

The flames, like a malignant entity, climbed higher, leaping, whirling, licking energy from the night sky. The boiling display created an inauspicious beauty, enveloping the night in an angst embrace of foreboding. The display captured every eye for miles around, hypnotic as a deadly viper inviting its onlookers into its seductive embrace. The German arsonists looked at the fiery inferno with satisfaction as they loaded into the cars and left.

The unkempt fugitives stepped into the meadow adjacent to Mr. Fiske's farm. The windmill was engulfed in flames, and next to it were four black sedans.

Peter, who delivered messages for Rapier to Mr. Fiske, ran toward the windmill. "No!" he shouted.

Rapier had anticipated the move when he saw the orange glow over the trees. He lunged at Peter, knocking him to the ground and covering his mouth.

"Shut up, man! You can't help them now!" Rapier whispered.

Peter fought against the iron grip until his strength was exhausted. Only then did Rapier let him go.

"Why?" he moaned. "He was just a kind old man. I suppose he didn't even see them coming."

Rapier ordered the men to stay low. He hoped the Germans were so focused on their handiwork they didn't notice them. Then he instructed the men to go through the forest to Ede.

Peter dropped his head, slapped his cap on, and moved silently back into the trees. Olfeson, one of Anton's men, waited for Peter and gently put his hand on his shoulder. He noticed Peter wipe the back of his hand across his face and then looked down to avoid Olfeson's eyes. Olfeson walked by him quietly into the forest.

Rapier crawled through the frost-tipped grass on his elbows, binoculars in tow. He wanted to get a closer look at the men who did this.

He crawled to a tall clump of grass, its silver tips swayed with the night breeze, slapping its icy fingers against his face. He parted it. His warm breath married with the cold night air glazed the binoculars with a translucent veil. He rubbed the lens on his shirt and focused on the men at the fire. The stately arms of the windmill crumbled to the earth like the death of a monarch. Sparks twisted, curled, and floated, ascending to heaven as if taking the spirit of a potentate with them.

He noticed one officer stood above the rest. The reflected red glow of his hair could have mirrored the flames of Hades as its keeper. Guards stared into the fire, smoking cigarettes, and laughed in camaraderie. He could imagine the boasting of the heartless deed done this night. He took note of the car's makes and models. All were black sedans except for one, a Mercedes 260D. He crawled back to the edge of the forest and disappeared.

The men sat guardedly at the edge of the forest outside Ede. Peter heard a soft snap behind him and spun around, lifting his rifle. He aimed it into the dark. Rapier stepped into the faint moonlight between the large cedars. Peter sighed and dropped the gun. "You shouldn't be so loud coming into a man's camp," he said, smiling.

"Are all of you here?" Rapier asked.

"*Ja*, we're all here," Peter replied.

"Good. I need to know where the Germans are positioned. Peter, you and Olfeson check out the police headquarters. See if you can find a black Mercedes 260D. Ike and Norm check out the school on the south end of town. Locate the main German unit. Jacques and Fryer, scout the church, and Hank find a doctor." He'd already sent a messenger back to Anton to tell him to head for Ede but stay in the forest.

The blond German was the one he wanted. He'd seen the work of men like him. They were strong willed, without conscience, and intelligent. They could inflict pain without feeling and would exploit those around them for their own selfish needs. They were ruthless, self-imposed dictators, and if others got in their way, they would crush them.

Rapier gritted his teeth and ground out, "If you find the tall blond, I want him alive. He's mine."

"Oh, *ja*. I know the big Kraut," Dedriek said. "He's the one who was so antsy to get his hands on me after blowing the train, but Anton interrupted his plans. That guy is bad news. I've heard he shot a woman and her child for no reason and didn't even blink."

Rapier continued with the instructions. "The cover of night is to our advantage. Men are slow to respond when jolted out of a deep sleep. They are easily rattled and confused. The first few moments in a surprise attack are the most crucial, so be on your toes."

The first to report back were Olfeson and Peter. They had gone to the police station and found the Mercedes. "Hood's still warm but no lights at the headquarters. The lousy Kraut is probably sleeping like a baby now."

"Good," Rapier replied.

The next to report were Jacques and Fryre. "They've got a bunch of unarmed men in the church. They must think they're not much to worry about because they only have four guards on the place."

Hank came next, dragging in poor old Dr. Bijl at gunpoint.

"You don't have to use force on him, you moron," Dedriek said. "He would have come anyway."

"How am I suppose to know that? Going into a German occupied town, you don't know who's with us or against us."

"He's a doctor, idiot. Think about it. They're the good guys who help people," Dedriek said as he knocked the weapon away. "Sorry, Doc."

Ike and Norm were the last to report. "There are a whole lot of Krauts in the school. Give us some dynamite and wire, and we'll blow them back to Germany."

Rapier sat on his haunches, rolling a cigarette between his thumb and forefinger and digesting the information. He had only a few men and had to use them wisely. The German soldiers in the school he'd rather not disturb unless forced to. The church he'd send four men to kill the guards and lead the captured men into the forest, and he assigned Dedriek to assist the doctor.

"Can't I do anything but babysit?" Dedriek complained.

"Hey, calm down," Rapier said. "The job's got to be done. Anton will be grateful that you have the doctor waiting."

"*Ja, ja,*" Dedriek muttered.

Twig, Gottfreid, and Anton were separated from the other men after leaving the potato cellar. The men came upon a German patrol and a skirmish ensued. Dedriek ran on ahead, hoping to impress Rapier he was capable in combat, leaving instructions for Twig and Gottfreid to take care of Anton.

"Watch out!" Twig yelled. Twig's grip on Anton tore away as he slipped over the wet edge of an escarpment. He rolled down the rocky slope and hit his head on a boulder in the depression below. Twig wasted no time sliding down the slope to Anton.

"He's out cold. He has a gash on his head the size of Holland," he yelled back to Gottfreid. Gottfreid slid down the hill and stopped behind Twig. He tore the bottom of his shirt, wadded it up, and put it over the wound.

"We've got to get him to a doctor and out of these woods. You're from around here. Is there anywhere we can hole up for a while, take care of that wound, and let him rest?" Twig asked.

"There's an old hunter's shack about a mile back. It hasn't been used for years. It was built over fifty years ago and has more holes than a backside of a bear hit with buckshot. My brother and I used to go up there when we were kids and play like we were mighty hunters until a bear chased us down the hill one day."

"We'll have to carry him. I'll take the first stretch," Twig offered.

The old hunter's cabin was a welcome sight for Gottfreid. Anton's dead weight seemed to get heavier with each step. He ignored the pain in his back and legs and focused on making it to the cabin.

The log walls loomed pasty-gray against the dark sky in the moonlight. The overgrown bushes seesawed with the breeze, and the dirt path, filled in with weeds, was barely visible as he carried Anton to the front. At the cabin door, Gottfreid noticed mud-filled gaps in the logs. It looked like the roof had been repaired, and the ground beneath the water pump was wet. Then they noticed a small crack of light under the slats of the door. When they opened it, they walked straight into the barrel of a rifle.

"Turn around and get out," the young woman ordered.

"Who are you?" Gottfreid asked as he shifted Anton's weight on his shoulders.

"Never mind. You're not welcome here."

"Our friend is injured, and we need a place to rest up. We thought this cabin was empty. He's in need of some patching."

"You German?"

"Do we look German?" Gottfreid asked.

"Can't tell. Germans can be disguised. Don't trust any man. Leave! Find another place to stay."

"There isn't another place for miles. What are you doing up here anyway? This isn't a place for a young woman."

"It's none of your business," she said.

Anton groaned.

"Please, he's waking up. He needs attention," Twig pleaded.

The young woman kept the gun pointed at the men. She motioned for Gottfreid to put him on the bed and for them to put their hands up. She kept her eyes on the men and then quickly looked at Anton. The shirt wrapped around his head was soaked with blood. She lifted the makeshift bandage and looked at the wound. Twig calmly reached over and took the rifle out of her hand and sat it at his side.

"We don't want to hurt you, *frau*.[30] We just want to get help for our friend, let him rest, and then we'll be on our way."

She backed away from the men. Her hands shook but she remained silent.

"Will you please help our friend?"

She nodded and walked over to the sink to get first-aid supplies on the shelf above it. She cleaned the wound with antiseptic and wrapped it in clean cloth.

"Would you like some broth and a slice of bread?" she offered. "It isn't much, but it's all I have."

"Thanks, *frau*. That should stop the growling within for a while." Twig smiled. "What are you doing up here all by yourself?"

"Same story as anyone else. The Germans broke into our home and arrested my parents and one of my brothers. The other brother and I escaped. Later I heard they threatened to kill my parents if my younger brother didn't scout for them. I don't know what happened to my older brother. We got split up. I wandered the hills until I happened on this

30. Dutch word for "ma'am"

cabin. I've tried to patch it up a little to keep the cold out. This place is so remote I hoped I would be safe here for the rest of the war."

"Your secret's safe with us," Gottfreid said.

Anton stirred. "Where am I?"

"In a cabin, in the forest, with a beautiful young nurse to care for you," Gottfreid said.

"We've got to get out of here," Anton said and tried to get up. "Dedriek needs . . ."

"Wait a minute. Dedriek is fine. You need to rest. We'll be on our way tomorrow. You took a nasty tumble."

"You can stay the night," the woman said. "There are blankets on the shelf over there. You can sleep on the floor. It gets cold, but I don't light a fire because of the German planes. At least you're out of the wind and rain."

"Thanks, *frau*. My name is Gottfreid and this is Twig."

"My name is Adelein Husleina. I used to live in DeHoven."

"Do you have a brother by the name Daan?" Twig asked.

"*Ja*. How did you know?"

"He's in the resistance with me. He sprained his ankle in the forest a while back. When I was able to, I asked Rapier to send a couple men back for him. Daan will be glad to know his brother wasn't a traitor and that he was forced to scout for the Germans."

"A traitor? What are you talking about?"

"Daan will have to fill you in on that. He saw your brother. He was caught in an explosion," Twig said reluctantly. "I'm sorry for your loss."

Adelein said nothing as she sat in the wooden rocker and gently rocked, crying herself to sleep.

The next morning, Gottfreid and the others got ready to leave. "Thanks again, Adelein. I'll be back to check on you and bring supplies. The boss is anxious to get going," Gottfreid said as he touched his hat in a polite gesture.

"Good-bye," Adelein said. "May God go with you."

ADOF DROPPED TO the ground and motioned for the others to do the same. Sven crawled over to Adof. "What is it?"

"Behind that stand of trees. Don't know if it's four legged or two, friend or foe. Stay here. Hanns and I will investigate." Adof motioned for Hanns to follow him. They skirted to the cover of a large poplar tree. Hanns crept behind Adof and peeked around a leafless bush. They saw two men carrying a wounded man. Adof aimed his rifle. "Halt!"

The three men froze.

"Drop your weapons. Hands in the air!"

The tall boy obeyed and dropped his rifle immediately, but the man let out a snort as his eyes flickered over to a dense group of trees.

"Now!" Adof yelled.

The first boy whispered out the side of his mouth, "Don't do it. You can't outrun a bullet. You'll get us all killed. You'll get a chance later. Drop it."

The second man grunted, dropped the weapon, and put one hand behind his head while supporting the injured man with the other.

"Who are you?" Adof demanded. "And what are you doing out here?"

"Hunting," the tall boy said.

Hanns ran up behind the men and grabbed their weapons. He looked at their faces. "Anton! Am I glad to see you!"

"How'd you get out of prison?" Anton asked, dropping his hand to his side. "I thought you were history."

"It was Adof. He got us out. He took us out the same way as you. The Germans abandoned the underground chamber and tunnels thinking you'd somehow escaped through the alley and that we had gone the same way. I'll bet the Germans are still trying to figure out how all of us got out of that alley without being seen."

"Adof? A German?" Anton scoffed.

"Well, not exactly," Adof said as he approached. "I'm a British double agent. I work for the SOE in Britain. But after the Germans find out what actually happened, I'll be a wanted man all over Europe."

"You got my men out of Gestapo headquarters?" Anton looked at him, puzzled.

"Yes. I couldn't let Eikman and that animal interrogate them. I've seen enough of their methods."

"Thanks. You'll have to fill me in on the details sometime," Anton said.

"Rapier and his men are headed to Ede. We got word from a messenger a couple hours ago that the Germans rounded up all the eligible men and are shipping them to Berlin. Rapier is going to rescue them. We thought maybe he could use some help. You know how unarmed men can be hard to control."

"There's no rest for the good guys." Anton smiled.

"Can we put down our arms now?" Twig asked, rubbing his shoulder.

"Of course," Adof said.

chapter
TWENTY-THREE

They crept to the wall behind the cathedral. Eikman could see the door to the leather shop and ordered his small unit to get out of sight. His eyes narrowed as he contemplated catching every one of those insolent irritating insects, which he intended to dispose of. "I'm tired of these homemade spies," he said. "But I will still need a couple of them alive."

"We haven't picked up Anton's trail yet," Trevier reported.

"There's still two hours until daylight," Eikman said. "If we let the rest of them slip through the alley, maybe they can lead us to Anton. You sure you know all of Anton's men, Lieutenant Austerlitz?"

"*Ja*, I've lived with them for five months. I've smelled their stinking bodies, shared their grub, listened to their resonating snoring, and relieved myself on the same rocks."

"Good," Eikman said. He paused and looked toward the cathedral. "I wonder what happened to Adof? I wonder if he was shot or maybe taken hostage during the escape."

"They must have taken him prisoner," Lieutenant Austerlitz said.

Through the tops of the old merchant buildings, Eikman could see the stars check out of the night sky. He looked at his watch again. "Something doesn't add up. They should have been here by now. Get in the tunnel!" he shouted. "Follow the stairs back down to the chamber."

In the chamber room they found nothing to indicate another way out except to go back past the cells. Eikman threw a statue, shattering it against the stone wall. He kicked over chairs, threw lamps and pictures, and finally threw a wooden box at the fireplace. It hit the upper corner. Eikman's mouth dropped, and he stared incredulously as the fireplace swung open. He stopped in mid bellow, his face fraught with rage as he barreled toward the fireplace. "Colonel, get in there and find out where it goes!"

The men stormed toward the tunnel with the hostility of barbarian warriors, Eikman's rancor being contagious. But they cautiously entered the tunnel, sweeping the passage with flashlights for trip wires. Eikman followed behind. After a time they came upon a large renaissance door that had the lock broken off.

The first man cautiously pushed against the door, gave an all clear, and then the men charged into the empty fish cannery.

"Search every corner of the docks and pier," Eikman ordered. "Find out if anyone has seen them.

A corporal finally reported. "No one noticed anything unusual. Only an old fisherman left the dock as usual, but the boat watchman said he left about three hours ahead of schedule."

"They were on that fishing boat." Eikman ordered the men to search up and down the river.

"They're headed for Ede," Lieutenant Austerlitz said from behind.

"How would you know that?" Eikman turned toward the lieutenant.

"Because Anton is from around there. He's got family there. They rounded up the men in Ede to ship to Berlin. He'll think it's his duty to free them."

Although Adof shed his German uniform, he moved with confidence and authority of one used to being in charge. At midday he ordered the men to rest. Adof walked over to Anton, squatted in front of him, smiled, and offered him a dried German army issue wafer.

"Sure it won't kill me? It's not full of cyanide, is it?"

"*Nein,* Herr Anton. It's only tipped with strychnine. Cyanide is reserved for the more notorious prisoners."

"Jews?"

Adof scoffed. "The Germans do not know what they are doing killing the Lord's chosen people!"

Anton looked at him curiously. "Chosen people?"

"I've read the Bible. Wasn't Jesus a Jew? The Nazis destroy the Lord's people. I'd hoped by living among them and spying I could be an instrument in bringing the war to end faster, but I only witnessed atrocity after atrocity and was powerless to stop it. I've seen grown men cry like babies and tell everything they know, even to the betraying of their own mothers." Adof's eyes misted. "When and if I ever get out of this war, I intend to become a man of the cloth, to put families back together, and to help to repair their broken lives."

Anton's eyes watered as he listened to a man who worked among the top ranking officers of the Third Reich. He'd seen the Germans round up Jews and others but had not witnessed the results. He put his hand out. "I am honored to meet you."

Adof smiled. "I have heard of your reputation. It seems you are a highly prized trophy for the Gestapo. Eikman is probably furious over losing you. Many good men will hang for this," he said sadly.

"I do what I can to be a pain in the Nazis' butts."

Adof laughed. "And that you have done very well with the dents you've made in their operations. You've been added to their most highly prized list."

"I like the fireworks," Anton said as his swollen lip curved to a distorted smile.

Marieka watched from her bedroom window as the flames climbed high to the heavens. "Mr. Fiske!" she screamed but knew it was already too late. The Germans had kidnapped her papa, Bastiaan was in hiding, Miss Remi was gone, her beloved hometown of Ede was occupied by Germans, and now Mr. Fiske had been killed. Anna sat next to her and put her arms around her as they cried together.

"What are we going to do, Mama? How are we going to get Papa back, help Abram, Jorg, Hannah, and Felicity, and protect Bastiaan?" Marieka wailed. "Mr. Fiske is gone. He can't help us now."

Anna looked up at her daughter. "What do you mean Mr. Fiske can't help us? He hasn't been to our farm for years, not since he broke his leg in '38."

"Dr. Bijl! Dr. Bijl. That's it! He can help us!"

"What are you talking about? We're not sick."

Marieka jumped up, ran outside, and grabbed her bicycle. Her mother followed her out the door.

"Marieka, where are you going? It's one o'clock in the morning."

"Don't worry, Mama. I've got to see Dr. Bijl."

"No, Marieka!" Anna ran after her. "You can't go to Ede alone at this time of night!"

"I'll be all right," Marieka called over her shoulder and disappeared down the road.

Anna ran after her until Marieka was out of sight. She ran to the barn, emptied the feeder so she could move it, and threw the trap door open. "Bastiaan! Marieka's headed for Ede!" she cried. "She's in danger. Help her, Bastiaan. Find her!" Anna fell to the floor, crying hysterically.

Bastiaan climbed out of the hideout and threw his arms around Anna. "Don't worry, Mama. I'll find her."

Jorg climbed out behind him. He put his hand on Bastiaan's shoulder. "We'll find her."

"I'm coming too!" Abram added from behind Jorg. "But how are we going to do that with no weapons?"

Bastiaan grinned. "I've got an arsenal hidden in the old cellar by the chicken coop."

"You what? But where did you get it?" Anna stuttered. "How did you get it?"

"Never mind. All you need to know is we have a way of defending ourselves," Bastiaan said. "We'll be back before you know it, Mama. Those Germans won't even know we were there."

"No, it's too dangerous," Anna cried when she realized she could lose Bastiaan too. Felicity and Hannah ran to her side and put their arms around her, trying to calm her.

The sunken door on the cellar broke as Bastiaan lifted it. He threw the broken pieces aside and descended the steps into a small dank room. In the corner was a nook covered with a mouse-eaten tarp. Bastiaan pulled off the tarp and exposed a piece of plywood covering several German army-issue wooden boxes. He lifted a lid on one of the boxes revealing a full box of rifles.

"Wow! Where did you get this stuff?" Abram said, gazing at it. "There's enough here for a small army!"

"Exactly," Bastiaan said. "And we're it."

Jorg took out the weapons and inspected them. There were several

MP40 submachine guns, Mauser C96 semi-automatic pistols, Model 39 hand grenades, and a box of ten Kar98 bolt-action rifles with ammunition. The last three boxes contained ammunition.

"How'd you get this?" Jorg asked.

"A few nightly excursions to the German arsenal."

"The German arsenal? How'd you? You crazy? They'd cut you into chicken feed if they caught you," Jorg said.

"It's easy if you know the back way."

"What back way? That place is a fortress," Jorg said.

"They used the old Karle Brewery." Bastiaan grinned and looked at Abram as if they had a secret between them.

"Oh, *ja*," Abram muttered "I remember. We used to sneak in the air vent under the truck ramp. No one ever caught us. But that's when we were about ten. You're a whole lot bigger now. How'd you get in?"

"It took a bit of finagling with a few Houdini moves, but I managed. Getting out was the tricky part. I had to throw the weapon out first and do the Houdini thing again."

"How come you never mentioned this before?" Abram asked.

"I didn't want anyone else to be in danger. Besides more than one person can draw attention."

"We can be like that American actor James Cagney and shoot the place to smithereens," Abram said excited. "I'd like one of the Mausers, please."

"Do you know how to use it?" Jorg asked.

"Sure! You just point and pull the trigger. Easy."

"Right, and you'll shoot your foot off, or shoot one of us," Jorg said. "Why don't you let me show you how to use it properly?"

"Can I have one of the MP40 machine guns too and some of those egg-shaped things?" Abram asked.

"Do you mean the hand grenades?" Jorg said. He sat down and lectured Abram on the proper use and safe handling of the weapons. Abram sort of listened as his leg bounced impatiently.

"You will keep the safety on until we get into Ede, understand? I wish we had more time to train you on this. I hope you don't shoot me or Bastiaan in the back. Make sure you point that thing at the enemy, not us!"

"I will. Now let's go kill us some Germans! Present company excluded, of course." Abram grinned.

chapter TWENTY-FOUR

The lone bulb in the tiny checkpoint station didn't furnish enough light to reach the corners. The guard, Tilde, leaned over the desk squinting as he concentrated on writing his report. The other guard sat with his feet up, balancing a chair on two legs. His hat lolled to one side, and his mouth dropped while he inhaled deeply in a quiet stupor that he wouldn't call sleep. Two floodlights were fastened to each side of the roof to cast just enough light to create shadows and make one jumpy. A high-powered spotlight situated on top of the desk inside the large window was used for spotting.

Tilde jerked when he heard the limousine approaching. He kicked his companion. "Wake up. We've got company." The second guard scrambled to his feet and stood at attention as the black limousine stopped by the open door.

Tilde stepped out and cleared his throat as he bent down to ask the driver for their papers. The flags identifying the car as Gestapo were missing, but Tilde recognized General Eikman in the back seat. Though his stomach felt like it would lurch, he remained at attention and waited for the papers.

His hands shook as he looked the papers over. He stepped inside, called the German headquarters, and read the identification numbers to the clerk to get official clearance. He handed the papers back to Eikman's driver. "You may go." He saluted and opened the arm on the gate.

The driver took the papers, handed them to Eikman, and then sped away. General Eikman clenched his teeth as a tick appeared at this temple. "Delays! Always delays! Step on it, Corporal. I want to get to Ede before Anton and his men do."

As they drove along the road, Colonel Warner winced at every bump while trying to ignore Trevier in the front, who kept turning around and talking non-stop to Eikman. Colonel Warner watched him for the last half hour and decided he would somehow see to his demise or see him sent to the front. His only desire was to rise in rank and position without regard to others.

Trevier caught Colonel Warner's eye and pulled him into the conversation "Isn't that what was reported to you, sir?"

"Uh . . . er . . . yes, that is correct." Colonel Warner nodded, jolted from his thoughts.

Colonel Warner turned to look at the wrecked cars and trucks pushed to the side of the bridge. They were used in a vain attempt to block the German invasion last spring. He smirked, recalling how easy it had been for the tanks to push the pitiful blockade aside. They arrived at the headquarters at half past three.

The night air was cold, the town quiet. "I hope this is a good sign that Anton's men haven't arrived yet," Eikman said. The limousine skidded to a stop in front of the steps and the corporal jumped out to open the door for Eikman.

The corporal stood at attention as he opened the door. The pale light overhead revealed the shocked faces of the two night guards. When the one guard saluted, he accidently hit the corporal, who was opening Eikman's door, slamming it on his foot. He shuddered as his mind flashed to a picture of him standing erect before a cement wall, eyes blindfolded, hands tied behind his back, yelling, "It was an accident!"

The corporal did not remember what happened next, although he was sure Eikman's face was as befitting as a psychopath, twisted in a murderous rage.

Eikman hobbled from the limousine with his pistol in his hand and aimed it at the guard. The guard's eyes widened as he stepped back. His companion stepped forward and said, "Excuse me, sir. It was my mistake. I bumped my companion by accident and it had a domino effect. My apologies, sir."

"You ignorant fools! You should be shot," Eikman shouted, but holstered the weapon. He wasn't here to bring to justice impertinent guards. He was here to capture the escaped resistance fighters.

"Where is Colonel Boere?" he demanded.

"Home, sir," the guard said. "Asleep, I presume."

"Well, go and wake him!" Eikman yelled.

"Yes, sir. But what about my duty here, sir? I cannot leave my post."

"I am here, you imbecile! Now go!"

The guard almost dropped his rifle as he stumbled off the steps and headed toward Colonel Boere's residence.

Colonel Boere hadn't had a good night's sleep since his wife died. He missed her warm body next to his and didn't like the silence of loneliness. He didn't like the responsibility of being in command of the German affairs in Ede either. He'd just as soon retire to a quiet farm and sit out the rest of the war.

He had watched as Lieutenant Schmidt brought Hendrick Coevorden in earlier. Hendrick Coevorden was a leader of the community; he helped keep the people calm and caused the troublemakers to back down.

"No, I will not let Lieutenant Schmidt deport Hendrick, even if I have to kill the lieutenant myself."

Colonel Boere heard pounding on his door. He reached to turn on the lamp and checked the time. Grumbling, he put his robe on to answer the door.

He opened the door to a young corporal. His rifle strap was slipping off his shoulder and his hat askew. From the boy's expression, he thought the British had overrun them.

"Excuse me, sir. Sorry to wake you, but General Eikman is at your headquarters and has ordered your presence, sir."

"Very well. Tell him I will be there shortly."

The soldier saluted, spun around, and hurried away. Colonel Boere shut the door with a heavy sigh.

Marieka steered the bike along the road she'd ridden many times before. But because of the ruts made by the constant German patrols, the bike veered into the reeds, flattening a tire. She threw the bike down and ran toward Ede. Unable to see because of the impending storm, she wandered into the weeds along the canal, soaking her shoes and stockings. The cold seemed to seep through her, twisting its tendrils of ice around her, generating uncontrollable shaking. She tried to stay calm but remembered stories of people getting lost in a storm only a few feet from their homes. "I am okay. God is with me," she repeated over and over.

She breathed a sigh of relief when she finally saw the familiar village in the distance. It was as quiet and serene as a picture on a calendar. The late fall had turned the shrubs and trees dormant and the tinge of frost added to its tranquility.

Marieka crept through the alleys to the back door to Mr. Buskirk's bakery. It was locked, of course. She quietly slid along the side of the building and looked into the street. Thankful now for the blackout, she crouched and ran across the street toward Dr. Bijl's. She looked around to see if she was being watched and knocked quietly on the door. No one answered.

She went around to the back and rapped softly. Still no answer. She reached for the doorknob to check if it was unlocked, when a hand covered hers and another covered her mouth. Marieka gulped down the panic as the antagonist hauled her across the street to the German headquarters. She kicked at the man as he opened the door and towed her toward General Eikman.

Eikman spun around when he heard the commotion and barked, "What do we have here?"

"I caught this girl at Dr. Bijl's, sneaking around after curfew," the soldier disclosed.

Eikman looked at the young girl and frowned. "Do you know there is a curfew?"

"Yes," she replied.

"What are you doing out so late alone?"

"I was sent to fetch Dr. Bijl because my mama is ill." She choked on the lie.

"You are out after curfew. It is against the law. Throw her in a cell. I'll deal with her later."

chapter

TWENTY-FIVE

The small beam of the flashlight was Bastiaan's guide across the harrowed fields followed by Jorg and Abram. "There's never any Germans out here," Bastiaan whispered over his shoulder. "I come this way all the time. Walking on these giant dirt clods can topple the most sure-footed man. It's just like balancing in a log rolling contest, so be careful."

Abram let out a stifled howl. "Hold up, Bastiaan. Not so fast. We can't see a thing and balancing on these clod-logs is like tiptoeing on humped-backed whales blindfolded. Why didn't you get a few more flashlights in your stockpile when you were doing all this preparing?"

Bastiaan ignored the quip and kept going. "We've got to get there before dawn."

Abram carried a rifle across his shoulder and a pistol stuffed in the back of his pants. His pockets were full of hand grenades. Jorg carried a submachine gun and bandolier across his back, along with a cloth sack of grenades at his side and a pistol in his pocket.

They circled around Ede and hid at the edge of the forest. Jorg whispered, "We've got to plan this. We can't just go in there and shoot up the place. Your mama said Marieka's heading to Dr. Bijl's office. Where's that?"

"In the middle of town, not far from the German headquarters."

"That's not good. Is there a way of getting there without being seen?"

"Not really. We could go through the alley but we'd still have to cross the street to the east at some point."

"Where is your father being held?"

"In the church at the north end of town, not far from the forest."

"We could get your father out first, but that would probably alert the whole town," Jorg said.

"We could circle around Ede, go through the forest, and come out on the east side to Dr. Bijl's first," Abram suggested.

"But what of Marieka? Which way do you think she went? Do you think she could have been spotted by the Germans?" Jorg asked.

"Let's hope not!" Bastiaan said.

The three were engaged in conversation and didn't notice the men sneaking through the brush until they felt the rifle in their backs.

"Slowly drop your weapons," a voice commanded harshly.

Bastiaan turned around to face the culprit without dropping his weapon and was clobbered in the chin.

"Drop 'em," the low threatening voice whispered again.

Jorg and Abram dropped their rifles and slowly raised their hands.

"Who are you?" the voice whispered. "And what are you doing here?"

Jorg didn't speak because of his German accent. He nudged Abram to speak up.

"We've come to rescue Bastiaan's sister and their papa from the church."

"And how did you kids plan on doing that? Circling them and hope they give up?"

"No, we've got guns," Abram said.

The deep voice laughed quietly. "That's very well, but three kids with a couple of guns isn't going to get you in and out of Ede safely."

"Get moving that way and help your friend," the man said.

Jorg kept quiet as he grabbed Bastiaan's arm and Abram took the other. Bastiaan moaned and walked in a daze as they half carried him ahead of the men, getting jabbed occasionally in the back.

"GOT SOME KIDS here," a rebel spoke. "They say they're going to rescue a couple of people from the Germans tonight."

Their leader arched an eyebrow, stood in front of them, and looked into Abram's eyes. "What are you up to?"

"We've come to get his sister and rescue his papa." Abram nodded at Bastiaan.

"Where'd you get those weapons? You German?"

"No, sir. Bastiaan here stole them from the German's arsenal."

"Awfully gutsy of him, if it's true."

"It is."

"How'd he manage that?"

"He knows his way around the factories in this area."

"We could use a couple more men. Do you know how to use those weapons?"

Abram eyes lit up. "Sure do!"

Jorg could hold his peace no longer. "*Nein*!" he said.

As fast as a magician's card trick, the lead rebel leaped to Jorg and stuck a knife at his throat. "What are you kids up to? What's a German doing here? You spying on us for the Germans?"

"No! Heck, can't you see I'm a Jew? He's our friend," Abram said in a high-pitched warble. "Let him go."

Jorg stood on his tiptoes, his neck stretched like a turkey on the chopping block, his chin lifted skyward. "I'm a deserter, sir," he said. "I was wounded and the Coevorden family took me in. I've been hiding there ever since."

"A deserter? What makes you think we'd trust scum like you?" The man's face was an inch away from Jorg's.

"He's a good German, if there is such a thing," Abram said. "He was forced into service. Remember the troop train that was blown up? He was on it. The blast practically blew him up. He just wants to go home and take care of his mother and sister, not fight a war he doesn't believe in."

The leader kept the blade to Jorg's throat as he got a better look at Abram. "You're a Jew?"

Abram nodded.

"And you call a German your friend?"

"Yes," Abram said. "We're like brothers."

"You would ask to save the life of a German?"

"I would give my life for this German," Abram said defiantly.

The man looked into Jorg's eyes. "Is what he says true?"

"Yes," Jorg replied.

He dropped his hand away from Jorg's throat and let him go.

Bastiaan moaned as he came to. When he saw the men with their weapons pointed at him, he jumped up, ready to fight.

"Calm down, Bastiaan," Jorg said. "These men are the good guys."

"Your sister is missing and your papa is in the church?" the leader asked as he squatted down by Bastiaan. "And you have come to rescue them, right?"

"Well, yes, something like that," Bastiaan stuttered.

"How about if my men and I join you? I'm sure the Germans would be delighted if we were to relieve them of the hardship of feeding fifty men for the next few days."

Bastiaan looked at him curiously. "Really? But who are you? Why would you offer to help us?"

"I'm in the Dutch Resistance. We have been giving the Germans a lot of headaches for the past few months. The name's Rapier."

"The resistance?" Bastiaan said in awe. He stumbled to his feet and grabbed Rapier's hand, pumping it vigorously. "Am I glad to meet you. Of course you can join us . . . or . . . er . . . rather . . . we could join you. I was a bit worried how we were going to pull this off anyway."

Although the Germans had ordered a blackout, a few rays of dim light filtered through the boarded up cathedral-style windows of the church. Hendrick Coevorden had lost his quiet benevolence. He was furious. He was angry that the Germans would tear good men from their homes and farms to work in Germany to support their evil war. He knew in the long run they were causing their own demise by destroying their food source. If the farmers and dairyman were unable to raise food and milk, many would go hungry, including their army.

He and fifty other men were locked in the church's chapel. The men slept on the long wooden benches. Hendrick scoured the room for anything that could be used as a weapon. He checked all the windows; they were locked and boarded up. But what if he could pick a lock and knock a couple of the lower boards out? They could climb out and get away before the Germans even woke up.

Father Eisen, in his gentle way, worked around to each of the men, comforting and trying to lift their spirits. Hendrick watched and waited for Father Eisen to finish with a fourteen-year-old boy who was sobbing uncontrollably.

Father Eisen looked up, clearly affected by the boy. "He is too young for the Germans to take him away from his mother. I am a man of peace, but sometimes I wish I could forget my vows and send a few of those Nazis to hell."

Hendrick hid a smile, enjoying the fact that Father Eisen was just as human as the rest of them. "Father Eisen," he said, losing the smile completely. "May I inquire, is there anything, any tools, we could use to break the lock on one of the windows and pry the boards off?"

Father Eisen shook his head thoughtfully. "I don't think so. The Germans have cleared all the sacred items and anything that could be deemed a weapon out of the chapel," he said. "Wait, I remember under the alter is a professional cross and a solid brass candlestick. The Germans didn't think to look there."

"Great! Father, you'll have to forgive me for the desecration of your sacred items but I am going to use them as tools." Hendrick took the professional cross and brass candle stick and went to the window farthest in the back. All of the windows had been padlocked.

"To hammer this off would make too much noise," Hendrick said, discouraged. "Do you have any kind of sharp instrument?" Hendrick asked.

"I think there are some pins for the girls' hair in the restroom."

"Good. Will you get them?"

When Father Eisen returned, Hendrick thanked him. "I've heard this can be done but I've never actually tired it. Pray it works." He stuck one side of the pin in the lock and moved it around. In frustration, he aroused the men. "Is there anyone here who has any knowledge of how to pick a lock?"

No response.

He asked again earnestly, "If we can get this lock open, we may be able to escape. Please, does anyone know how to pick a lock?"

A tall, skinny teenager unwound his lanky legs and slowly raised his hand. "Uh," he croaked. "Maybe I do."

"Well, get back here!"

The boy took the two pins, pulled the protective covering from the ends, and bent them in two opposite directions. He skillfully put both of them into the lock and turned one while he fidgeted with the other. After a few seconds, the lock popped open. The priest and Hendrick stared at him in dual amazement. "Where did you learn how to do that?" they asked simultaneously.

The lad looked down at his hands. "I sort of learned it . . . to steal things."

"Well," Hendrick said, "this is one time I am thankful you have such a skill."

The boy looked up at him, his face flushed. "I guess I learned something that could be used for good after all."

"I know the Lord forgives all your previous transgressions in the use of this skill." Father Eisen winked.

They pulled the lower portion of the window up and were assaulted with blast of cold air. They pushed against the bottom boards but they were nailed solidly.

"It'll take some pounding to get those off. The Germans will surely hear it."

The boy interrupted. "Uh, excuse me, Mr. Coevorden. I . . . uh . . . kinda had some learning in that too."

Hendrick looked at him quizzically. "You do amaze me, young lad." He watched as the boy took the cross and pushed the tip under the nail between the board and the window like a lever. It took two or three tries but soon the nail popped out. He put the tip of the cross into the next nail on the same side and popped that nail off.

Hendrick took the cross and was about to put it under the nail on the other side, but the boy stopped him. "Leave it, sir. If the Germans come by they will see the hole where the boards should be, but if you only open one side, they will think it is still boarded up. The boards can be pushed out for the men to crawl through, and then pushed back when we're done. It may take a while before the Germans figure out how fifty men escaped under their noses."

"Well, Jasper, you do intrigue me," Hendrick said as he slapped the boy heartily on his back. Hendrick turned to the priest. "Wake the men and organize them in groups of five. Jasper, will you go first and be our lookout? I think that would be a fitting job for a talented, trustworthy young man like you. Let us know when it's not safe. Gorge, will you go next and head for the back of the church and knock out the guards?

"Father Eisen, pray this works and we all get out safely."

chapter TWENTY-SIX

Four of Rapier's men approached behind the church from the north. Olfeson motioned to Jacques and Fryer to circle around to the front and dispose of the two guards while he and Peter took out the guard in the back.

Jacques and Fryer ran along the bushes next to the church and crouched at the front corners. The two guards leaned leisurely against the pillars. Fryer looked at his watch and then nodded to Jacques. They crept behind the men, cupped their hands over the guards' mouths, and drug them into the bushes.

When they circled around to the back, Jacques noticed movement in front of him. He motioned for Fryer to stay put and circled around behind the lone figure. Jacques cupped his hand over his mouth and pulled him to the ground.

"Who are you?" Jacques whispered. "What are you doing here?"

The boy stared wide-eyed. Jacques slowly moved his hand and put his finger to his lips. The boy lay still, but his eyes darted toward the church.

Jacques saw a man climb from the back window. "Who are you?" he whispered again. "What's going on here?"

"I climbed out of the church. I'm supposed to watch and give the signal if it isn't safe."

"You're escaping from the church without any help?" Jacques asked, surprised.

"*Ja*, we have to run to the forest."

Jacques smiled at Fryer. "I don't think we're needed here. It seems like they're doing fine on their own."

Jacques looked up and saw another man climb through what he thought was a boarded up window. He pulled the boy to his feet and motioned for Fryer to follow. They stood on each side of the window. Jacques told Fryer to lead the men to the back. "Five men at a time are supposed to escape in five minute intervals. They want to make sure it is safe before they proceed. Well, boy, get in there and tell them to file out. We've got them covered. Tell them to hurry. We don't know if the Germans have check-in times, but the four guards are dead. It will alert the Germans if they don't answer the radio."

The men climbed out faster now. Thirty men escaped in ten minutes.

They heard the roar of a truck skid to a stop in the front of the church. Jacques stuck his head in the window. "You've got about three minutes. German troops out front. Move it!"

When Colonel Boere entered his headquarters, he found an agitated General Eikman and a room full of people. Colonel Boere saluted Eikman and then asked stiffly, "What is going on here?"

Eikman did not like Colonel Boere's attitude. "We captured several men from the resistance in DeHoven, but they've escaped. Our informant here, Lieutenant Austerlitz, an infiltrator in the resistance, says they are headed this way."

"Why would they be headed here?" Colonel Boere asked. "There's nothing here. We are a remote village."

"It seems the leader of the resistance is from here and the lieutenant says he knows him. He says this Anton feels it's his duty to rescue the men who have been rounded up to be shipped to Germany. Where are they being held? We may be able to capture all of them together."

"In the church on the north end of town."

"Then we'll be there waiting for them!" he shouted. "Order your men to the church."

Colonel Boere knew better than to protest, but he did anyway. "But, sir, it is the middle of the night."

"You only fight wars in the daytime, Colonel Boere?" he snapped. "Order your men to the church."

Colonel Boere nodded. He knew it may be a bloodbath, but he gave the order anyway to dispatch the troops.

As one guard went out, Lieutenant Schmidt came in. He walked with a spring in his step, his eyes bright with excitement, as he approached the general and saluted.

Eikman seemed unimpressed and turned his back to him. "Get the car. We'll follow the troop truck to the church."

Lieutenant Schmidt evidently didn't notice the brush-off. When he heard the order, he asked permission to lead the troops. Eikman glanced at him with disinterest, but he wanted Colonel Warner and Lieutenant Austerlitz with him, so in the absence of another suitable officer, he gave him permission. Eikman ordered two soldiers to stay behind and watch the prisoner.

Colonel Boere's head jerked up, his voice inflected with anger. "There's a prisoner?"

"Yes, she was brought in about a half hour ago," Eikman said with an air of dismissal.

"She? Who is she?"

Eikman ignored him, consumed with the plan to recapture the prisoners.

Colonel Boere walked to the back to see who was in the cell, fearing it was someone innocent and arrested on some trumped up charge. "Marieka!" he cried. "What are you doing here?"

Marieka ran to the window and put her face to it. "Please, Colonel Boere, let me go. I was just trying to get Dr. Bijl, but they arrested me for being out after curfew."

"Who arrested you?"

"The general," Marieka replied.

"Oh." He knew he couldn't release Marieka if Eikman had put her there, and he didn't have time to deal with it now. He ordered the guards to keep a close eye on her. "And do NOT let anyone near her. I mean no one! Officer or enlisted man! No one is to see her."

Jacques peeked inside the window. "Hurry up! Troops will be storming the place in minutes." The men climbed on top of each other in their haste to get out. "That way!" Jacques pointed to the forest.

Hendrick and Father Eisen were the last ones in the church. They heard the outside doors crash. They ran to the back of the chapel and rammed the brass candlestick through the door handles. "It'll hold for a few minutes,"

Hendrick said, and ran back to the window. He heard gunfire. Jacques crouched and shot the soldiers that came around the corner.

"You go first," Hendrick ordered Father Eisen.

"No, I'm staying here. My duty is with my church and my people," Father Eisen said as he stepped back.

Hendrick frowned. "Your people just left the church. As I see it, your people are gone and so will your church when the Germans get through with it. You are a fool to stay here. The Germans aren't merciful to any man, man of the cloth or not."

Father Eisen quietly nodded his head. "God be with you."

Hendrick nodded, climbed on the windowsill, and jumped. A soldier fired at the dark figure. A bullet hit his shoulder, and Jacques and Fryer ran to cover Hendrick. Jacques picked him up and ran while Fryer covered them with rapid fire, taking out the soldiers as they came around the side of the church. They heard shots fired in the back. The Germans had circled around behind the church.

Fryer was hit in the side. "Flesh wound," he yelled as he grabbed his side and kept running. Jacques grabbed Hendrick's other side and headed west, away from the church and away from the forest.

Bastiaan stood at the edge of the forest, directing the men. Rapier's men each took three or four of the escapees and disappeared in different directions. Bastiaan watched as each man ran toward him, but his father wasn't among them. He stopped Mr. Barnard and asked if he knew where his papa was.

"The last I saw of him, he was still in the church, helping the other men out," Mr. Barnard said without stopping.

Bastiaan looked back at the church and heard gunfire. He threw the rifle over his shoulder, stepped from the protection of the forest, and headed for the church.

"Don't," Olfeson said, running toward him. "The place is crawling with Germans. You'll just get yourself killed."

"But my papa, where is he?"

"They said everyone got out but the priest. He'll show up. Let's get out of here!"

"I have to find my father!"

Olfeson turned around, grabbed Bastiaan by the front of his jacket, and hauled him back toward the forest. Bastiaan clenched his fist and threw it at Olfeson's face. Olfeson saw it coming and ducked, shoving the butt of his rifle into Bastiaan's stomach. Jorg and Abram were at the edge of the forest, firing rapidly at the Germans running toward them. "Get out of here now!" Olfeson yelled. Jorg and Abram walked backward, firing on the Germans. They turned and ran into the forest, dragging the crumpled Bastiaan with them.

Lieutenant Schmidt ordered the men to break down the chapel doors. He found the chapel empty, except for the arrogant priest standing by the altar; he stood calm as the raging lieutenant ascended upon him.

"Where are the men?" the lieutenant demanded.

"They are gone," Father Eisen answered softly.

"How did they get out, and who helped them?"

"God helped them," the priest said serenely.

Lieutenant Schmidt was not in the mood to put up with the priest's lofty answers and struck him across the face. "Don't be insolent with me. Where have they gone?"

"To follow in God's footsteps, I pray."

Lieutenant Schmidt struck him again. He pulled the pistol from the holster and held it next to his head. "Would you like to change your story?" he said with a disparaging smile.

Father Eisen remained calm. "They are in the Lord's hands now. I don't know where they are."

Lieutenant Schmidt's eyes ignited with anger. He cocked the weapon just as Colonel Boere and General Eikman entered the chapel.

"Lieutenant Schmidt!" Colonel Boere barked. "We need him alive!"

Lieutenant Schmidt stopped abruptly and willed himself to follow the order, but he would have loved to put a piece of cold metal between the arrogant holy man's eyes. He snorted and holstered the weapon. He backed away from the alter, annoyed, and shouted orders to the soldiers, "Take him away! You won't get off so easy, you arrogant hypocrite. I'll deal with you later."

"Search the premises!" Lieutenant Schmidt shouted, ignoring the higher-ranking officers. "Find out how they got out!"

The church was a small country church that could hold a hundred and fifty people. It didn't take long to find where they escaped. "Over here!" a young corporal called. Eikman and Colonel Boere hurried to the window where the soldier stood. The window was shut. An open padlock was on the windowsill, with only the left side of the boards pried open.

"Very clever," Eikman said. "Get outside and pick up their trail. Maybe it was only an inside job."

"Then where did the weapon fire come from?" Lieutenant Schmidt interjected. "The men in here had no weapons and everything else was taken out."

"You're right. They had help . . . from the resistance. We didn't beat them here as I had hoped," Eikman said.

Lieutenant Schmidt walked around the church with a flashlight. A young private yelled from the edge of the forest, "Sir, they went this way." They didn't notice Jacques, Fryer, and Hendrick's trail headed in the opposite direction.

Colonel Boere, Colonel Warner, General Eikman, and Trevier stayed inside. Eikman questioned Father Eisen with as much luck as Lieutenant Schmidt. "You won't be so high and mighty at the prison in France. I would talk now if I were you," Eikman threatened.

Father Eisen looked at him. "God is with me. I do not fear you."

"Your God may be with you, but He won't save you."

"He already has."

chapter
TWENTY-SEVEN

Jacques and Fryer disappeared into the shadows carrying Hendrick, who was on the verge of losing consciousness.

"He's losing a lot of blood," Fryer said. "The doctor is with Rapier. If we can meet up with him somehow, he can patch him up, and me also."

"No," Hendrick said. "To my farm. There is shelter there."

"That's the first place those Krauts are going to look for you."

"Take me there. We'll be safe. Go across the fields."

They stopped at the edge of the field and wrapped Jacques's shirt around Hendrick's shoulder. Hendrick pointed the way and muttered, "It's about a mile."

"If what you said is right, I think we're about there. Hang in there, Mr. Coevorden."

Fryer saw men coming toward them. "Is that Rapier?" Jacques whispered as the men drew near.

"Maybe it's Germans. Take cover." They dropped to their stomachs. The men filed by. "They don't look like Gerries to me," Fryer whispered. "The injured man looks like Anton, doesn't he? *Ja,* I remember him from the meeting with Rapier months ago."

"How can you tell? There isn't enough light to see facial features," Jacques whispered.

They flattened against the ground. The one in front stopped and put his hand up for the others to halt. He listened for a few moments. "Must have been a rodent," he said calmly and motioned for the men to keep going. He walked past Fryer and then in an instant he turned and pointed his rifle at the men in the grass.

"Get up!" he ordered.

Jacques was the first to rise with his hands in the air, then Fryer. "Our friend is wounded. He's in and out of delirium at the moment."

Adof didn't know the men of the resistance, but Anton did.

"Jacques, Fryer? You're Rapier's men, aren't you? Why aren't you with Rapier's group? What happened?"

"The Germans attacked the church when we were rescuing the local men. We were the last to leave. We headed in the opposite direction as Rapier, across town, but the Germans didn't notice. Mr. Coevorden says he has a safe place on his farm, and that's where we're headed. He needs a doctor. He's got a bullet in his shoulder."

"Who's with you and where are you headed?" Jacques asked.

"To Ede to rescue the men rounded up and held in the church, but it looks like we are too late."

"Anton," Jacques said, "your little brother is with Rapier. They sort of kidnapped the doctor in Ede because they said you were wounded."

Adof looked at them. "If your friend has a secret place, it might do well to put you both there until we can find the doctor. How far is it?" he asked.

"Not far. Just another field over."

Adof ordered the men to stay put. He crept to the barn, eased around the corner, and cautiously inched along the plank wall until he was directly across from the back door of the house. He looked up at the gathering clouds and felt a few drops of rain on his face. "We better find safe shelter and soon before this storm gets ugly. I hope we're not walking into a trap."

The door was open and the place deserted, but according to Hendrick, his family should be around somewhere. Adof didn't have a good feeling about this. He darted across the yard and flattened against the house, listened, and stepped quietly inside. He searched it thoroughly but found nothing.

He went back to his men and knelt beside Hendrick. "You have to wake up. You're the only one who knows where this hideout is," he said, talking to the unconscious man. "There is a storm coming and we've got to get you out of this weather." He gently shook Hendrick and softly slapped his cheeks. "Come on, wake up!"

Hendrick moaned but didn't wake.

Adof turned to the men. "Does anybody have some spirits?"

No answer.

"Come on, I know one of you must be carrying some. Hand it over."

Jacques sheepishly stepped forward, took a flask from the inside of his jacket, and handed it to Adof. "It's only used for medicinal purposes, sir," he said, grinning.

"Of course. What else would you use it for?"

Adof opened the flask, leaned over, and passed it under Hendrick's nose. Hendrick jerked away from the offensive odor. Adof lifted Hendrick's head forward, tipped the flask, and poured a small amount of alcohol into his mouth. Hendrick coughed and sputtered, opened his eyes, and cried out, "What are you doing, trying kill to me?" He tried to focus on the man in front of him but couldn't. "Who are you?"

"Adof at your service, sir. I ran into you and these two men in the fields. They told me you have a formidable hideout here. Now, I need you to tell me where it is before we get drenched and have unwanted company."

"In the barn," Hendrick whispered hoarsely.

"Well, let's take a look. You and Anton need shelter."

"Anton?" Hendrick asked puzzled. "Anton Gansen, the little kid at the Gansen farm? What's he doing here?"

"The same as you. He's wounded and needs patching up and shelter. The Germans seem to want him very badly."

The barn was dark except for a light coming from under the feeder in the stall. "There shouldn't be a light there," Hendrick stammered as he tried to wrench from the men's grip. They carried Hendrick toward the feeder. "Move the feeder and lift the hatch."

Jacques pulled on the circular rope and lifted the hatch, revealing a small room. Adof leaned over and stared in disbelief. The room contained several beds with wooden crates between them. The walls and floors were covered with new plywood. A lamp was on a small table in the center where three women were seated, one clutching a baby.

Adof sat next to the opening and looked back at Jacques. "I want you to hand Hendrick to me and keep your eyes peeled for trouble. There are three women down there, and I want to know what's going on."

Hendrick stifled a scream and gritted his teeth as he was slowly let down into Adof's arms. As Adof was helping him to a bed, the eldest of the three women ran to them. Adof put his hand up to deflect the assault, almost knocking the woman back.

"Hendrick!" she cried.

"Anna? What are you doing down here?" Hendrick slurred. "Where are Bastiaan and Marieka?"

Anna gasped when she saw the bloody wrap on his shoulder. "Hendrick, you are wounded," she cried. "You need a doctor. I must go for Dr. Bijl."

"No," Adof interrupted. "Ede is in turmoil. The Germans are searching for the escaped men and desperate to recover them and the men who helped them escape. I am told that Dr. Bijl is with the resistance. They kidnapped him so he could help Anton, who got separated from them."

Adof directed Jacques to let Anton down and then Sven.

The tiny room buzzed with activity as the other two women sat quietly at the table, watching the men with interest. Felicity couldn't get a good look at the man in charge, but there was something strangely familiar about him. The way he moved, his voice. "I know that voice," she said. "You're a German officer." Her eyes widened.

Adof stopped, his face hidden in the shadows. He put up his hand for the others to be quiet. "It's you! I thought you would have been long gone by now. What are you doing here? You should be living in luxury, sitting out the war in England."

Felicity let out a squeal, ran to Adof, and threw her arms around him. "The resistance men were good to care for me, but one of them was killed and the other brought me here until I could be moved out of Holland. They say the resistance is on the run and can't help me, so I sit here."

"Yes, they have been very busy," he said.

"But what are you doing here?" Felicity asked.

"Well, things were starting to get uncomfortable for me also. I decided it was time to end my spying days and get out while I still could. I helped the rest of Anton's men escape from the prison in DeHoven. If I am caught, Eikman will use me as an example, so I have to get out of Holland as soon as possible. I'll be heading to England for debriefing and a desk job, but there are still a few things to tie up here." He turned to leave but stopped. "Is there another way out of here except the trap door?"

"No," replied Mrs. Coevorden as she hurried past him and up the ladder to get more bandages.

"Good, you'll be safe here until I get back."

Felicity stopped Adof. "Let me go with you. I can shoot."

"It's too dangerous. We'll track this man, Rapier, who has the doctor with him and bring him here. Then I'll work on getting us out of Holland."

Marieka heard the key turn. She stepped into the shadows at the rear of the cell and shuddered. Her skin prickled as if a feather was drawn over it. She felt the malignant shiver of panic rise in her throat as she stood motionless in the corner.

The door opened. An outline of a tall man appeared in the jaundiced light, pushing someone ahead of him. Marieka saw Lieutenant Schmidt and Father Eisen step into the halo of light. Her breath stopped. She prayed he wouldn't notice her and flattened in the shadows.

"Step forward!" Lieutenant Schmidt shouted.

Marieka stood frozen. Lieutenant Schmidt took three long strides across the room, grabbed the girl's arm, and pulled her into the light.

"Ah, Fräulein," he said, his eyes gleaming. "It is a pleasure to see you again. How convenient."

"Do not touch the girl. You shall not defile her!" Father Eisen ordered.

"Hold your tongue, you pious hypocrite. I'll deal with you later."

"God will strike you if you harm this girl."

Lieutenant Schmidt laughed. "And I would like to see this God do such a thing."

Father Eisen stepped into the room and hit the lieutenant's hands away from the girl. In an instant, Lieutenant Schmidt pulled his pistol and shot the priest.

Marieka screamed. Lieutenant Schmidt grabbed her arm and headed for the door.

"Our orders are not to let anyone near the girl," a guard yelled, bursting through the door.

"Well, I am the superior officer here and I am giving you a new order. You will stand aside."

"You cannot take her!" the private shouted.

"Oh?" Lieutenant Schmidt said, raising his eyebrow. "We shall see." He shot the guard in the same manner as Father Eisen. The other guard appeared, and Lieutenant Schmidt smiled and shot him too.

Marieka screamed. "You're a murderer!"

"Now we go." He grabbed Marieka's arm, pulling her out of the building and into the night.

General Eikman stayed behind to search the church but found nothing. When Eikman and Colonel Boere walked into the headquarters, they found the two dead guards, the priest with a gunshot wound to the head, and an empty cell.

Colonel Boere's face was a mask of rage. "Lieutenant Schmidt did this."

chapter
TWENTY-EIGHT

Most of Anton's men were born and raised around Ede, but the impending storm made the trek through the forest treacherous. Rapier assigned the men to go in different directions, but he was going back to Ede. He had two men missing along with Anton.

"Sir," Olfeson said. "I think it would be better if I went with you."

"No, it's best if I go alone. One man doesn't draw as much attention as two."

Rapier put up his hand before he could retort and left.

Rapier crouched just inside the forest. He heard shouting as the Germans stormed the town.

They'll knock on every door looking for the escaped men, Rapier thought. *They'll drag old men, women, and children from their beds.*

He ducked behind an old car parked next to an abandoned gas station kitty-corner to the German headquarters and waited for an opportunity to get across the street. When he saw the patrol turn down the side street, he saw his chance.

Rapier ran across the street to the side of the building and slid along it to the back. He crouched behind some garbage cans and cautiously checked the area, when he heard a scream. He spied the blond lieutenant dragging a girl down the alley. Forgetting about his original plans, he followed the lieutenant.

In the midst of all the chaos, Rapier's men ran one way while Bastiaan led Jorg and Abram in the other, back to Ede.

"You're going the wrong way!" Abram objected. "We're headed right back into a nest of angry Krauts."

"I still haven't found Papa and Marieka," Bastiaan said, dismissing Abram.

They stopped at the abandoned gas station across from the German headquarters.

"Are you crazy? This is the worst place in the world we can be. Why'd you come here?"

"I figure some German must have seen Marieka and picked her up. This is the only logical place they'd bring her."

"How are we going to get her out of there?"

"Well, we're not going to barge in, that's for sure. We'll watch for a while until we know how many are in there. Then when it's quiet we'll go in there and get her, and hopefully nobody will get hurt."

"If I surrender, it will give them something else to think about and it will get me inside," Jorg volunteered.

"Are you suicidal?" Abram whispered.

"No," Bastiaan said. "You're not going in there, but maybe you could get close and watch for a while."

Jorg slid along the building next to a broken-down car while Bastiaan and Abram hid in a stack of old tires. Four German soldiers came down the street dragging a middle-aged man. "We've found ourselves a Jew!" one of the soldiers boasted.

"Hey, look at that old car over there. It would make an excellent hiding place for Jews," his companion shouted. "Let's have a look." The youngest soldier turned on a flashlight and walked over to the rusted jalopy.

Jorg didn't have time to run, so he slid down the wall and crawled under the car. The soldier shined his light in the front and back windows and saw nothing but torn leather seats. Next he went around to the back, pulled on the trunk handle, bent over, and shined the light in the trunk, putting his face into the small opening. A feral cat hissed and lunged at him, slashing his cheek. He screeched and jumped back, dropping the flashlight. The other soldiers grabbed their rifles and pointed them at him.

"*Nein, nein,*" he said, shaking. "It's only an alley cat." The soldiers laughed and poked fun at him for being so scared of a little cat. He scowled at them as he bent down to pick up the flashlight, but being so shaken, he didn't notice Jorg under the car. At that moment Colonel Boere came running out of the headquarters and shouted to the soldiers. "Lieutenant Schmidt has murdered two guards and the priest. He has also taken the Dutch girl. Find him."

Jorg's face drained. "Someone has taken Marieka." He crept back to Bastiaan and told him what he had heard.

Bastiaan's eyes darkened. "I'll kill that lieutenant," he spat.

"You'll have to get in line," Abram said.

Bastiaan sat quietly for a moment and then smiled. "He's got to be heading toward DeHoven! It's the closest town and has the nearest port. It's the most logical place. And he can't go on the roads, so he'll have to go through the forest by my place. Let's go."

Trevier stood behind the officers as they shouted at each other. He rubbed a hand over his mouth, unable to erase the smile. "Lieutenant Schmidt has deserted and sealed his fate."

"This is the most inept area in the Nazi regime," Eikman ranted. A rabid flush twisted his face. "If we do not get this under control and now, it will send a message to all of Holland that they can resist and we can be defeated."

Outside the headquarters the storm was gathering strength. When Colonel Boere went out, his face was pelted with a torrent of rain. He turned up his collar and pulled his hat low, running for the canvas-covered truck. He wanted to find the lieutenant before the storm got worse.

"Get some rest," Eikman ordered. "We'll get an early start."

"Yes, sir," Colonel Warner said.

"Lieutenant Austerlitz," Eikman said, slapping him on the back, "you'll be an invaluable help tomorrow."

Lieutenant Austerlitz had no intention of going to sleep. He wanted to help Colonel Boere. Hopefully it would impress Eikman and, besides, his old nemesis, Anton, was still out there, and he had a score to settle with him. He crossed the room and slid out the door, eager to catch up with Colonel Boere.

Colonel Boere suspected Lieutenant Schmidt would take the girl through the back alley to stay off the main roads and then head for the nearest port in DeHoven through the forest. The quickest way was through the Coevorden farm.

The storm had abated momentarily. Colonel Boere ordered the truck to stop when he saw a *Kubelwagen*[31] coming fast behind him.

Trevier climbed out of the hijacked *Kubelwagen* and saluted Colonel Boere, saying that Eikman had ordered him to assist him.

Colonel Boere saluted in a dismissive manner and turned his back on him. The arrogant lieutenant reminded him of Lieutenant Schmidt, and he didn't like him.

The plowed fields were frozen, making the trek even more hazardous in the rain, but Lieutenant Schmidt paid no mind as he adeptly maneuvered across them with his long, swift strides, dragging Marieka behind him.

"Your farm is abandoned, is that right?" he asked.

Marieka refused to answer him.

Lieutenant Schmidt turned around and struck her across her face.

"Your farm is abandoned. Am I correct?"

"My mama is there," Marieka cried.

"Good! She will be useful in getting supplies."

"Let me go!" Marieka pled. "I'm slowing you down."

"*Den Mund halten,*"[32] Lieutenant Schmidt ordered.

They came to the farm and made their way to the kitchen door. It was locked. Lieutenant Schmidt snarled and shot the lock off.

"Get your mama, and don't play any tricks. I won't hesitate to shoot you."

Marieka found her mama crying at the top of the stairs. "I was so worried about you. What happened?"

"It's the German lieutenant," Marieka cried.

Lieutenant Schmidt stood at the foot of the stairs, pointing his gun at them. "Enough!" he barked. "Get down here and pack us some provisions."

"He does not intend to let you go?"

"No," Marieka sobbed.

Anna's hands shook as she put bread and jerky in a canvas bag. "I have apples and cheese in the cellar. May I get some? I don't think this is enough. I also have a tin coffee pot for campfires."

Lieutenant Schmidt looked at her suspiciously as he considered the offer. "*Ja*, go. Just remember the longer you're gone, the angrier I get. I will

---

31. *Volkswagen type-82 bucket seat car, resembling the American jeep.*

32. *Shut up*

not hesitate to kill the girl if I think you are after a weapon instead of supplies."

"I'll hurry," Anna said, her voice shaking. "It's at the side of the barn. It'll take at least ten minutes to locate everything, sir."

"You have five."

Anna ran into Nyes's stall and tried to move the feeder, but having just been filled, it was too heavy. She ran to the air shaft and called, "Felicity, a German lieutenant is in my house and has Marieka. I need help."

"Hold on, Mrs. Coevorden." Felicity shimmied up the air shaft.

They tried to move the feeder to let the men out but couldn't. "You better go, Mrs. Coevorden, and do as the lieutenant asks. I'll get Nyes to help me move the feeder."

When Anna returned to the kitchen, the lieutenant was pointing the pistol at Marieka's head.

"Mrs. Coevorden, it is good to see you. You had thirty seconds before I pulled the trigger. Where have you been? May I ask what delayed you? I know where your cellar is. What took you so long?" He sneered and cocked the pistol.

"No!" Anna screamed. "I ran into the barn. I thought the horses—"

"You felt an overpowering need to feed the horses?"

Anna's breath caught in her throat.

"Maybe we should make sure the horses have enough to eat. You may have been in such a hurry that you didn't feed them enough."

Anna quickly covered her surprise. "No, I'm sure the horses aren't hungry."

"Ah, the horses . . . the feed . . . there's something about feed. Are you hiding your son in the hay? Maybe we'd better pay him a visit." Lieutenant Schmidt pushed Marieka ahead of him and followed her and Anna toward the barn.

Colonel Boere felt as if he were reliving the nightmare of World War I. His shoulders slumped, his eyes dull, yet alert. He was weary, and the soldier next to him provoked fear. He was arrogant, foolish, and reckless.

Colonel Boere ordered his men to stop about one hundred yards short of the farm and quietly surround it. If Lieutenant Schmidt was there, he wanted to surprise him.

The wind slackened but the night remained cold. The plowed fields were not as easy for the shorter, slimmer man to straddle as it was for the taller lieutenant. Rapier tried to keep a certain distance behind the lieutenant and the girl, but found he was losing ground. He was unfamiliar with the area and if he lost them, he wouldn't know his way back.

The outline of the white farmhouse thankfully loomed like an apparition against the night sky. Rapier watched as the lieutenant fiercely dragged the girl into the darkened house. His hand tightened on the pistol. He vowed to kill the arrogant German before the night was over.

Rapier crept to the back of the barn and climbed the fence, arousing the old Jersey. He opened the barn door quietly and slid inside. He crept to the corncrib on the right, crouched behind the rail fence, and waited. A few moments later an older woman hurried into the barn from the back. He ducked as she ran to the cupboard at the front, put her head in, and called. If he hadn't known the woman was probably scared out of her mind, he may have thought she was crazy. But to his surprise, a young girl crawled out of the cupboard a moment later.

He watched as the older woman and the girl tried to move the feeder. The older woman cried, "There isn't time, I must go," and ran out the back door.

Rapier stepped into the shadows again as she ran by. He was curious about the girl and wondered what was so important about that feeder. He peeked under the rail. She was trying to put a rope on the horse but didn't know how to do that any more than he knew ballet. Rapier quietly walked up behind her and asked, "Would you like some help?"

The girl spun around, her hands in front of her face, anticipating an attack.

"Calm down. I won't hurt you. I was wondering what two women found so important about this feeder?"

"This feeder . . . ," she replied in a thick French accent. Then she hit him on the head with the bucket hanging on the post nearby and ran to the hayloft.

"Ow," he growled. He put his hand on his forehead and pulled it away. His hand had blood on it. "Why you . . . are you working for the Germans? Because if you're not, you just clobbered the only help you're going to get."

Felicity guardedly came back realizing that the man wasn't a German.

She felt guilty for hitting him. "Mrs. Coevorden says there's a German lieutenant in the house wanting supplies and has kidnapped her daughter. There's a trap door under the feeder that opens into a shelter with three men in it, but they're wounded, so I don't know how much help they'd be."

"Wait, you are French? How'd a French girl end up in a barn in the middle of Holland in this war? And you're telling me there's a hidden shelter under the feeder?"

Ignoring the French remark, Felicity articulated, "Yes, that's what I said." Tears ran down her face as she sat down on the feeder overcome with emotion.

Rapier moved closer and lifted her chin. "Let's see if we can move that feeder. You grab the one side, and I'll grab the other." They pushed on the feeder until it finally slid over.

Anton was sitting on the side of the cot when the trap door opened and Felicity stuck her head in. "A German lieutenant is in the house. He kidnapped Marieka. We need your help." Although Anton's right shoulder was useless, he picked up the pistol from the crate and headed for the ladder. The strain on his shoulder was excruciating and his knee was stiff as he pulled himself up the ladder.

He sat exhausted next to the feeder and watched Sven slowly climb out behind him. He heard voices coming from the front of the barn. He looked up to see two women enter, followed by a German lieutenant, who held a gun on them. He didn't have time to run, nor could he if he wanted to, so he sat and waited to meet his fate. Rapier disappeared into the corncrib again.

chapter TWENTY-NINE

Adof had circled back through the forest when he saw a small set of lights crawling down the rutted road followed by a larger set, bouncing up and down as if it were light painting the sky. He found himself taking the same route he had just used hours before.

"It looks like the Germans are headed to the Coevorden farm, where Mrs. Coevorden is alone. He ordered the men to get back to the farm."

Adof had been full of unrealistic hopes and ideals when he volunteered to be a double agent the year before. He had been foolish enough to believe he could make a difference. If he was just clever enough or a good enough actor, then surely he could outwit the Third Reich. But he soon learned that he made about as much difference as a pebble in a pond. He'd seen many good men die and was powerless to save them. But he could make a difference to the people on the Coevorden farm tonight. He slid the rifle from his shoulder and cocked it and said, "Let's go."

Adof watched as the dancing lights stop some hundred yards away from the barn. "It looks like they're planning to sneak up on poor Mrs. Coevorden. Do they think the escaped men have come here?"

The rain pelted the hooded raincoats of the German soldiers as they fanned out, their weapons cradled across their chests. Adof watched as the dark silhouettes skulked to different positions around the house and barn. He ordered his men not to shoot while he climbed to the top of the storage shed next to the barn and had a clear view of the whole area. Twig was at his side.

Adof sat quietly, rain dripping down his neck as he watched two men, officers he presumed, approach the barn.

Although a torrent of rain assailed the officers, the one didn't try to shield his face but stood erect, as if defiant to the elements. The shorter officer paused, drew his pistol, pushed it through the narrow opening, and threw open the door.

"Drop it, Lieutenant," he said, his voice dripping with malice, "or I'll put a bullet in that arrogant head of yours."

Standing with his back to the door, Lieutenant Schmidt spun around, his hand clutching the girl's throat. A mocking smile crossed his face. "Colonel Boere, we meet again."

"Lieutenant Schmidt, you think you can use the girl as a shield, but she will not protect you from your fate. You've lost your position in the Third Reich and are a hunted man. You can't escape. My men have surrounded the building. Leave the girl be."

Lieutenant Schmidt pressed his lips against the girl's hair. "You always had a soft spot for her. Why? Do you want her for yourself?" His eyes stared fiercely into his.

Colonel Boere moved slowly toward the lieutenant. "She is just an innocent child."

Lieutenant Schmidt scoffed. "She is the most beautiful woman I have ever seen."

Trevier stood to the side of the colonel. He held a P38 pistol in his hand, pointing it at the cocksure lieutenant. He choked down the urge to pounce on the lieutenant, but at the same time he was enjoying the interlude, watching the lieutenant's eyes shift from triumph to fear and back.

The tension in the barn could have choked a chicken. Anton sat on the feeder, his head heavy, and shoulder throbbing, as his mind worked fiercely on a plan. He watched the exchange, surprised at the animosity between the two men, and watched Trevier's undeniable hatred for both and was surprised that Trevier hadn't noticed him. Anton thought he could let the parody of hatred play out. *Maybe they would all do each other in,* he thought.

Marieka screamed and dug her heels into the dirt floor as the lieutenant dragged her toward the back door. "You see, old man, if you don't want this girl's blood on your hands, I suggest you drop your weapon and step aside."

COLONEL BOERE FELT like he had to protect Marieka just as he had Felicity. Trevier, however, did not have the same feelings about the girl, and Colonel Boere could sense it. Colonel Boere dropped his gun and at the same time hit Trevier's weapon out of his hand. Trevier snarled and ducked behind a barrel, grabbing a small pistol from inside his uniform and aimed it at Lieutenant Schmidt.

Lieutenant Schmidt clutched Marieka, backing toward the rear. Inches from the door, he threw her aside, turned, and ran. Trevier shot him, grazing his shoulder.

In all the chaos, Felicity, who was hiding in a stall, crept to the feeder and pulled Anton to his feet and pushed him inside a big pile of hay, covered him, and then dove in after him.

Trevier swung around, his turquoise eyes flecked with fire. He pointed the pistol toward where he thought he saw Anton. But Anton was gone. His muscles tensed, and then he turned his hatred toward Colonel Boere. He knew Colonel Boere would interfere with his climb to the hierarchy of the Nazi government. He was one of those officers who had ideals and would interfere with his plans.

Colonel Boere anticipated his move and ran for cover. He dove behind a barrel as Trevier fired, hitting him in the leg.

Trevier swore under his breath. He pushed a dazed Anna out of his way and headed for the front of the barn. Sven lifted his pistol and fired at Trevier, but missed.

Trevier turned and fired at Sven, hitting him in the chest, and then ran out of the barn

THE FROZEN FURROWS were turning into slippery logs of muck as Bastiaan headed back to the Coevorden farm. Abram, who was cold, drenched, and a bit out of sorts, followed him. "Hey, slow up for those of us who were not blessed with long legs and a constitution for bounding over mountains of slimy mud. We can't keep up."

Bastiaan ignored him and kept going. They were about halfway across the field when they heard gunfire. Bastiaan's heart caught in his throat, and he started to run toward the barn. Jorg ran after him and knocked him to the ground. "What are you doing?

"My family!" he yelled.

"You're going to help your family by walking into the middle of a gunfight?"

"Get off me! I've got to help them."

"You'll help them more with a cool head. Calm down. You don't even know who's doing the shooting."

"Germans obviously. Who else?"

"Is there any way to sneak up on them?" Jorg asked

"Through the hay field. Nobody ever goes that way because of the forest."

The three circled around to the forest and entered the hay field from the west. Bastiaan was impatient with the detour but held his tongue. Bastiaan, Jorg, and Abram crawled under the wagon and saw the German soldiers crouched around the barn. They watched as the men from the resistance sneaked up behind them and demanded their surrender.

A German lieutenant ran from the barn door and headed into the fields. "That Kraut thinks he can get away," Abram said as he crawled from under the wagon.

"Abram!" Bastiaan said in a loud whisper, but he was gone.

Bastiaan crawled out and followed Abram, followed by Jorg. Abram was five strides ahead of them. He ran to the side of the smoke house and peeked around the corner in time to see a figure run into the field. Abram shot and missed.

"He couldn't hit a target if it were six inches in front of his face," Bastiaan said. The dark figure turned and shot at Abram. Bastiaan saw Abram collapse, and he ran to Abram's side. He lifted his head and moaned. "Abram, you big dumb idiot! If you die on me, I'll never forgive you." Bastiaan pulled him to the side of the smokehouse and covered him with his coat. "We'll be back for you shortly. Don't die on me."

Bastiaan and Jorg ran back to the hay wagon and crawled underneath it. "Are those Rapier's men?" Bastiaan whispered, seeing the men surrounding the Germans. "I thought Rapier's men were in the forest with the escaped townsmen. Maybe they brought the men here and the Germans followed them."

"But the Germans are the ones surrounded," replied Jorg.

"Good point."

They watched from under the wagon. Bastiaan noticed a German soldier creep over the top of the barn, his black raincoat reflected tiny snippets of light. He pointed his rifle at the back of a resistance man near the fence. Bastiaan chambered a round into the rifle, aimed, and fired at the sniper.

The man grabbed his abdomen. His knees buckled, and he dropped the rifle and rolled off the barn. The man by the fence spun around when he heard the German fall, and then the gunfire ceased. Bastiaan hung his head. "That is the first time I have ever taken a man's life. Not a good feeling."

Jorg looked at him sadly and nodded his head in agreement. They crept to the side of the barn and peered around the corner. The German soldiers were crowded in the middle of the barnyard with their hands on top of their heads.

After Lieutenant Schmidt ran out of the barn, he dove behind a large pile of rain-soaked, slippery hay that sent him sprawling nose-first into the fence of the coral. He crawled along the fence, keeping his head down and looking over his shoulder. He was proud of himself for his fast thinking and quick getaway, but the old cow announced his presence with her constant mooing. He aimed the small pistol at the cow's head. "Be quiet, beast, or I'll put one between your eyes." He put his polished boot, caked with manure on the fence. It slipped, and his cheek hit the rail and his face planted into a pile of manure.

Rapier watched the absurd display as the lieutenant crawled along the fence, favoring his shoulder. Lieutenant Schmidt flicked his hand, trying to shake the manure off. He grabbed the fence. Rapier stood in front of him and stepped on his hand. He pointed a Sten gun in the lieutenant's face. "I would assume you are out of weapons, but it is wise to never assume."

Lieutenant Schmidt looked up into Rapier's victorious grin.

"My win and your unadulterated defeat," Rapier said.

The lieutenant growled. His left arm swung up, hitting Rapier in the stomach and knocking him back. Lieutenant Schmidt grabbed the top rail, leaped over it, and slammed his boot into the dazed Rapier's stomach. He reached down and pulled his last weapon from his boot, a six-inch blade. Inches out of reach to kill him, he slashed a flesh wound across Rapier's chest.

Rapier hadn't expected the agility or the ferocity of the wounded man but wouldn't underestimate him again. He stepped back momentarily to clear his head. Lieutenant Schmidt raised the blade to strike Rapier again. This time Rapier anticipated the attack. He spun away from the blade and continued to turn, slamming his fists down on top of Lieutenant Schmidt's arm and knocking the knife from his grasp.

Lieutenant Schmidt lunged at Rapier, pushing him backward and sending them both sprawling to the ground. Each scrambled to their feet in a matter of seconds. Lieutenant Schmidt grabbed a nearby feed bucket and swung it at Rapier's head. Rapier ducked, came up under the bucket, and slammed his fist into Lieutenant Schmidt's stomach. The lieutenant gasped and fell to the ground. Spying the knife, he grabbed it, scrambled to his feet, and lunged at Rapier, clutching his stomach with his left arm and slashing the knife at Rapier with his right.

Rapier saw the flash of the blade. It slashed across his upper chest, and he fell. Lieutenant Schmidt stood over him, sneering. "As you can see, the better man wins again." Lieutenant Schmidt raised the knife high overhead and screamed as he plunged the knife toward Rapier's heart. Rapier jerked. He heard a shot. He looked up dazed at Lieutenant Schmidt, standing motionless as blood seeped from the corners of his mouth, and then he fell.

Rapier slowly got to his feet and wearily looked toward the barn. Colonel Boere was leaning against the door, with a P38 pistol in his hand. Rapier didn't have much use for Germans, but tonight he was thankful that one was around. He lifted his hand to his forehead, smiled, and saluted the colonel. The colonel smiled, nodded, raised his hand to his forehead, and saluted in return.

"Where's Anton?" Adof asked Mrs. Coevorden as he entered the barn after the small skirmish with the German soldiers.

"He was here a moment ago."

Adof quickly scanned the barn. He looked over Mr. Coevorden's shoulder and saw Sven crumpled beside the open trap door. He knelt beside him and felt for a pulse. He shook his head. He hadn't known Sven for long, but in the short time he did know him, he had gown to respect the man. He lowered his head and in a quiet voice said, "He's gone."

Rapier entered from the back clutching his upper chest, blood oozing between his fingers. Mrs. Coevorden cried out and ran to him. His eyebrows knit together sadly when he saw Sven. He bowed his head in an effort to calm his emotions and quietly asked, "Where's Dedriek? We need the doctor."

"I haven't seen them since we were on the outskirts of Ede in the forest," Twig replied. "I don't know which way they were headed."

Adof turned to Twig. "You and Gottfreid head into the forest toward Ede. If Dedriek is heading this way through the forest, you may find him. Tell him we have three wounded men who need a doctor."

Felicity crawled from under the hay, scrambled to her feet, and ran to Adof. Anton, trying to surface, swam through the hay, grumbling about getting help out of the wretched rubbish. He clawed at the hay and finally surfaced, exhaling loudly and spitting out pieces of chaff. He swept away the remaining bits from his face and hair.

Colonel Boere limped from the barn, leaning on Marieka for assistance. Adof now stood erect in front of the men and greeted Colonel Boere.

"Colonel Boere, we meet again," Adof said with a respectful nod. "But it seems we are on opposite sides now."

Colonel Boere nodded with a raised eyebrow. "My regrets, sir. We have lost a good man. But maybe we are not so different after all, eh? Lieutenant Schmidt is in the back. He is dead. Austerlitz seems to have disappeared. Were you able to find him among the survivors or the dead?"

Adof shook his head. "No, sir."

"That's too bad," Colonel Boere said solemnly. "We still have a loose end to tie up."

Bastiaan stepped forward. "Could he be the one we saw running through the fields earlier, sir? We didn't get a good look at him. He shot Abram and ran across the fields back toward Ede."

"I would assume that was him." Colonel Boere frowned. He looked directly at Adof and shook his head slowly. "Will you let me go? I've some unfinished business with him. If he gets to Ede before I do, he will spin a tale of lies and see to it that I am court marshaled and shot. His reign of terror will continue unchecked and many good people will die at his hands. After I have dealt with him, I will surrender to you and you can do with me as you wish."

Adof shouted to his men to stand down. "You and your men are free to go, Colonel Boere."

Colonel Boere dipped his head slightly, acknowledging respect. With the help of a private, he climbed into the truck, favoring his leg. The truck roared off, fishtailing over the frozen mud.

"I let Colonel Boere go with the promise that he would find Lieutenant Austerlitz and see to his arrest," Adof told the men.

"Where is Trevier?" Anton asked, limping out of the barn.

"You mean Lieutenant Austerlitz?" Adof corrected. "He escaped. We think he's back in Ede by now, telling a tale of lies about what just happened here with Colonel Boere."

"Austerlitz? That's what the Germans call him? And you sent an injured German to arrest him alone?"

"He has troops," Adof said.

"Troops who are loyal to him or the Third Reich? You may have sent a man to his death," Anton chastised.

"I trust that Colonel Boere is capable of taking care of himself."

"Well, I would trust it a whole lot better if I were there to see to the demise of Trevier."

"You are in no condition to do such a thing."

"May I make a suggestion?" Rapier interrupted. "General Eikman believes you were kidnapped or shot by the resistance, correct?"

"Yes, that is what I have been told."

"What if you were to take a highly sought after prisoner to the German headquarters and tell them that you had escaped from the resistance and captured him as hostage. Then you'd be inside."

"What prisoner would they want enough that they'd be willing to trust me again?"

"Me," Rapier said.

"I think it would be better if Adof had two highly sought after resistance leaders," Anton said.

"You're injured. You would slow us down."

"So are you," Anton said.

"It's just a scratch," Rapier rebutted.

"All right," Adof said. "But I don't like it, hauling two wounded men in. That could get us all killed."

"We've got backup. The boys know the way to the headquarters. They'll watch out for us."

chapter THIRTY

The truck slid around the corner, skidding to a stop inches from the general's Mercedes. Despite his best efforts, the young private failed to get Colonel Boere to the German headquarters before Lieutenant Austerlitz.

Lieutenant Austerlitz was already in Eikman's office, telling him about the ambush and how he barely escaped. He said he overheard Colonel Boere talking with the resistance leader, making some kind of deal with him.

"That traitor. He won't live to carry out his schemes," Eikman vowed.

"I waited outside the barn and overheard their conversation," Lieutenant Austerlitz continued. "I couldn't believe what I was hearing. When the colonel came out of the barn, I stepped in front of him. He tried to deny the deal with the resistance and said that I was making it up and that I was a traitor. I pulled my pistol and shot him in the leg when he tried to run, but he got away. The resistance men followed me and one shot at me, but I managed to escape across the fields."

"I commend you for your loyalty to the Third Reich. I will see Colonel Boere shot for this."

The headquarters had several privates standing on guard when Colonel Boere entered with the brash young driver. He headed for his office and heard Lieutenant Austerlitz and Eikman's voices. Colonel Boere entered the office with one hand held out in front of him and said, "General Eikman, my apologies for being so late."

"Guards!" he shouted. "Arrest this traitor immediately. Confine him to his office until I make arrangements to move him to the Gestapo headquarters."

"General, let me explain. That is not what happened," Colonel Boere started, but Eikman raised his hand and motioned for him to be quiet.

The driver stamped his feet nervously together. Eikman looked at the driver standing behind Colonel Boere. "If you don't want to be considered a traitor along with Colonel Boere, I suggest you leave."

A few moments later, the door of the headquarters crashed open. Eikman heard shouting in the outer foyer. "Get moving, you lowlifes. Anyone here with authority?" Adof shouted. "I have a couple of renegade resistance leaders here."

Eikman recognized the voice and hurried to the outer room. "Adof!" he cried, grabbing his hand and pumping it up and down. "I thought the resistance killed you."

"No, they captured me and wanted to use me as a hostage, but I got the drop on the guard, took his gun, and captured their leaders. Well, it wasn't quite that easy, but you get the gist of it anyway."

"*Wunder*!" Eikman said as he clasped Adof's shoulder.

Adof turned to see a handsome young lieutenant enter the room. Adof watched him casually while secretly keeping a vigilant eye on him. Lieutenant Austerlitz strolled to the counter with his hands in his pockets and leaned against it. Adof saw his eyes dart at him with one raised eyebrow, as if he was curious about him. Adof noticed a begrudging pout that said he wasn't very pleased to see him, but then it disappeared behind a smile. Adof glanced at Eikman and back to the lieutenant, and noticed the lieutenant's face redden when Eikman addressed him.

Stepping away from the counter, he saw Anton. "Anton!" Lieutenant Austerlitz said. "I seemed to have misplaced you at our last encounter. How nice of you to come."

Anton didn't say anything, but Rapier spat at him. "You filthy traitor."

Lieutenant Austerlitz smiled and sauntered over to stand in front of Rapier when Adof turned the pistol on Eikman and shot him and then the guards.

Anton grabbed the pistol hidden in his shirt and aimed it at Trevier, but Trevier obviously anticipated he would be next and was halfway down the hall before Anton fired. The shot hit Trevier in the hip. He dove down the hall and limped into Colonel Boere's office.

The office was colder than usual, so Colonel Boere was wrapped in a blanket. He had retrieved a pistol hidden in a false bottom of a desk drawer and was sitting on the sofa, with his leg propped up. He aimed the pistol at Trevier's head as he came crashing through the door. Trevier put his hands up, a small derringer hanging on his thumb. "Colonel, you don't want to shoot me! I could have killed you back there, but I only wanted to wound you, to fool that arrogant Lieutenant Schmidt."

"Cease your lies!" Colonel Boere yelled. "I've dealt with your kind before. The world will be better off without the likes of you."

"You won't shoot me. You haven't got the guts," Trevier said. Colonel Boere lowered the gun imperceptibly. Austerlitz was right. He couldn't shoot a man in cold blood. It was difficult enough to shoot a man on the battlefield. When Trevier saw the hesitation, he flipped the gun into his hand and shot Colonel Boere, grazing his head. He limped out the door.

Anton sat on a box in front of the door, blocking the exit. He aimed a gun at the hall opening.

Trevier limped into the hall with the derringer and pointed it at Anton.

"I knew you'd be coming this way, you coward," Anton slurred.

"I thought I would get even with you eventually," Trevier said, cocking the derringer.

"Get even for what? I've been your friend for a long time. I do not recall a time when we were at odds with each other. You were five when you left the Netherlands. It couldn't have been before that."

"We had to leave because your father caused mine to lose his farm." Trevier's eyes were black with hatred.

"As I recall, you lived on the other side of Ede on a small rundown farm. How was my father responsible for the loss of your farm?" Anton said, leaning forward.

"Your father bought seed potatoes from my father and never paid him. We weren't able to pay our debts and lost our farm," Trevier spat.

"I was too young to remember that and so were you," Anton said. "That happened years ago. Let it go."

"My papa moved us to France where he worked in a steel factory. The fumes, the hard work, the lack of food—all made him sick. He died when I was eight." Trevier's voice trembled. "With no money, and no way to get any, my mama and I were thrown out into the streets. My mama begged for food to keep us alive, but after a year on the streets, she died." Trevier's eyes misted but his face was like stone. "I was put into an orphanage." His voice raised with intensity. "And after a couple years of hunger and beatings, they found a maternal grandmother in Germany and I was sent to live with her.

"Your papa did this to us. My uncle told me. Your papa will be sorry when he finds out who killed his son and why," Trevier hissed.

"Trevier, your father was a good man," Anton said calmly. "I'm sure he wouldn't want you to seek revenge. I don't know exactly what happened between your father and mine years ago, but I'm sure your father would want you to let it go."

"You don't know anything about my father!" Trevier yelled.

"I know that my father spoke highly of him."

"Highly because he let your father get away without paying the money he owed him?" Trevier asked.

"My father told me about a time your father planted potatoes for him in the spring when he had pneumonia. He said your father wouldn't take any money for it. I didn't know he gave him the potato seed also."

Trevier's hand rose. "Enough!" he yelled. "Lies! All lies!"

Colonel Boere staggered in, aiming his gun at Trevier. "Put the weapon down," he ordered.

Trevier warily turned toward Colonel Boere. He stared at him incredulously. "You are a hard man to kill," he ground out.

"You made a good attempt at it," Colonel Boere slurred. "Now drop the weapon."

Trevier swung the pistol toward Colonel Boere and fired, but the shot went into the ceiling as Anton threw a knife at his arm. Holding his arm, Trevier turned toward Anton, his eyes black. He lunged at him with the knife.

Because of his wounds, Anton knew he couldn't survive a knife fight. He aimed the pistol at Trevier's heart. "Don't!" he shouted. "Trevier, I don't want to kill you. We're friends. One of us doesn't have to die. Let it go. This is your home, your country. We can make it right."

The hatred had been for so long, the brainwashing too ground in, and the scars too deep. Trevier couldn't see anything but the hatred that filled his soul. He rushed toward Anton with the knife held high. Anton fired. Trevier's eyes widened. He tried to utter something as blood spewed from his mouth, and then he fell. Anton struggled to stand and limped over to Trevier. He knelt beside him; he was gone.

Anton looked at Colonel Boere. "Are you okay?"

Colonel Boere nodded.

Adof and Rapier appeared around the corner. "Let's get out of here," Adof said. "The Germans will be crawling all over within minutes." They went out the back door and disappeared through the alley.

The night had turned to chaos; the German leaders had been killed and no one seemed to know how to give orders or how to follow the orders that were given. Sergeant Muller hung up the phone. "New officers will be here in five hours. Meanwhile our orders are to pursue and hunt down the men who did this."

They heard an explosion at the far end of Ede. The munitions building was blown up. All the troops at headquarters ran toward the explosion.

chapter THIRTY-ONE

Bastiaan and Jorg put the unconscious Abram in the shelter. Dr. Bijl showed up with Twig and Gottfreid, and Dr. Bijl was able to remove the bullet from Abram's upper chest. "He's lucky. It didn't hit the anything vital. He'll heal in a week or two with good care." Then he operated on Hendrick's shoulder.

"Keep them both quiet," he told Anna. "Push fluids, change the bandages, give them sulfa pills in case of infection, and pain medicine three times a day."

Hannah watched Dr. Bijl from the corner of the shelter. He walked over to her and smiled at the baby. "He's beautiful."

"He's a she," Hannah stammered.

"She looks like a beautiful, healthy baby," he said.

Hannah looked away, embarrassed. "Dr. Bijl, may I see Abram now?"

"Of course, but he probably won't wake up for an hour or two."

"He's a good man," she said as a tear slid down her cheek. "He's going to live, isn't he?"

"He will mend, young lady. Is he your husband?"

"No, my husband was taken by the Germans. He's just a good friend."

"Well, it looks like he has a good friend too. Take care, young lady."

Bastiaan hovered over his papa about as much as Mama did. "Will there be permanent damage to his shoulder, Dr. Bijl?"

"No. It will be fine and work as good as ever. But it will take some time and exercise to heal."

"Thank you, Dr. Bijl." Bastiaan said. When he learned that his papa would be okay, he gave his mama a kiss on the forehead and turned to leave. "Watch over Papa," he said.

"Where are you going?" Anna asked.

"I'm going out. I'll be okay."

Anna ran to Bastiaan, clutching him. "You can't go out. Germans are everywhere and some of Colonel Boere's men know of the shelter now. We have to get out of Holland as soon as possible."

"I realize that, Mama, but I have to get Adrie. She is coming with me."

"No, Bastiaan! You can't! It's too dangerous!"

"I know a shortcut through the fields and behind the houses. I have to go, Mama. I can't leave her here at the mercy of the Germans. Please, Mama, let me go. I love her just as you love Papa. Would you leave him here?"

"Of course not. That's different."

"How is it different, Mama? We aren't married yet, but we will be. There is no difference. Love is love."

Ede was bustling with German activity, which in a way made it easier to get across town. Bastiaan rapped on the window. Adrie appeared, her face pale.

When Bastiaan looked at her, his heart raced. He knew he would be devoted to her forever. He wanted to wrap his arms around her to comfort her, protect her, and give her the desires of her heart. He didn't want to keep his feelings inside anymore. He wanted to whisper them in her ear all night long while stroking the softness of her neck and kissing her soft lips. The heady scent of her hair infiltrated his senses. He leaned over the windowsill and kissed her, touching her cheek gently to give her assurance.

"What's happening?" she whispered, unable to take her eyes off him. She immediately felt comforted upon seeing Bastiaan. She loved him. She knew she would always love him and wanted to be with him always. But this war worried her. How would that ever happen?

Bastiaan whispered to her, "It looks like Rapier's men blew the munitions building. I came at the right time. In another hour the whole village will be locked down tight, and the Germans will be arresting a lot of innocent people."

"Oh, Bastiaan. What are we going to do?" Adrie cried.

"You're coming with me. The resistance are helping us get out of the country."

"Really? That is so wonderful. We can be together now. But I can't leave Mama."

"We'll take her with us."

Bastiaan heard another explosion. "Come on," he whispered, while pacing back and forth.

Adrie came around the side of the house with her mother. "Where are you?"

Bastiaan hurried to her side. "I'm here, Adrie."

Bastiaan crouched as he made his way across the field. Adrie and her mother were several yards behind, trying to keep up. He dove under the hay wagon, spied one of Anton's men, and signaled him. He ran to the side of the barn to where Dirk was standing in the shadows.

"You're back," Dirk said. "Rapier's in the barn. He sent me to watch for you. We're headed out. Part of the men have left already. We stole a German truck and took some uniforms off a couple of dead Krauts. Some men have already headed for the river to meet up with a fishing boat that will take Abram and Hannah to the north shores of England."

"And my family?" Bastiaan asked.

"We'll call for a plane to pick you up tomorrow night."

"Are you coming with us?" Bastiaan's brow furrowed.

"No, my work is here. There are many who need our help to get out of the country."

"What about Rapier?"

"He won't be going either. We'll disappear. Maybe find a new hideout. We still have a lot of trouble to stir up for the Krauts. Blow up a few trains and communication networks, and just be a royal pain in their butts."

chapter THIRTY-TWO

When Bastiaan came through the door, Anna ran to him and hugged him. "Oh, Bastiaan, I was so afraid I'd never see you again."

"Where's your faith, Mama?" Bastiaan teased, squeezing her hand.

Marieka observed the love between Bastiaan and Mama and was also aware of the tenderness he showed Adrie as they entered. She ran to him and hugged them both. "I was worried about you, you reckless dare-devil," she said. "Maybe in England you could curb some of those wild desires?"

Marieka turned toward Jorg. Her face paled when she thought how utterly stupid it was for him to go back to Germany. *If only he could see that he would be safe in England and we would be together,* she thought. She started to cry and slipped out the front door while everyone was making plans.

THE MEN WERE attentively talking. Jorg didn't notice Marieka leave. After a time he realized she wasn't at his side. He looked around but didn't see her. "Bastiaan, have you seen Marieka?"

"She was here a minute ago. In all the excitement I don't know where she went."

Jorg decided she must have gone outside. He slipped out the barn door and heard sobbing coming from around the corner. He found Marieka sitting on an overturned bucket wiping her eyes with a hanky.

"What are you doing here? It's not safe for you to be out here alone."

Marieka turned away from him. "Go away."

"What's the matter, Marieka? Why are you crying? You should be happy your family is safe."

"As if you didn't know," she said, sniffling.

Jorg's eyebrows furrowed, puzzled at her strange behavior. "Everyone is happy. We're all safe for the time being and sent those Germans packing."

"Oh, you stupid man. Don't you know?" She started crying harder. "Jorg, please. You cannot go back to Germany. Your mama and sister will be okay. I'm sure there are good people who will watch over them. If you go, I will never see you again."

"Marieka, don't worry. I'll be safe. I have contacts that will help me get in and out of Berlin, and then I'll come back for you. Besides, miracles do happen."

"Miracles don't happen anymore." Marieka sniffed and blew her nose loudly.

"That's not true. Why it's a miracle every day we are still alive." Jorg grinned.

"*Ja*, well, I think it is only by chance or luck."

"Have faith, little one. I will be back for you."

"How can you? We'll be in England, remember?" She looked at him and cried harder. She sniffed. "I've heard God watches over fools."

Jorg laughed. "Well, I must be a fool because I know He watches over me."

Marieka peeked up at him and a smile flickered across her face. "How long will you be gone? How will I ever find you again? We'll be in England, and you'll be in Germany."

Jorg took out his leatherbound book and tore a few pages out of it. "Here, read this. It will give you comfort. It always does me. I love you, Marieka. I will be back for you."

Jorg pulled her close and held her. She felt a peace wash over her. "Promise me we will be together again."

"We will. I know there is a way."

The barn seemed to buzz with activity when Adof, Rapier, and Anton came through the back door. Dedriek stood as a look out at the front, eavesdropping on Adof and Felicity.

Adof looked at Felicity and said, "They'll order us back to Britain to the SOE headquarters, we'll be debriefed, and then retired. I wonder if I will be happy sitting in an office in Britain. Espionage is an enticing game. I shall miss it."

"Oh, maybe you won't have time to miss it," Felicity said coyly. "I hear love is as almost as good in London as it is in Paris."

Adof smiled. "I shall enjoy finding out if that is true."

"Anton!" Dedriek shouted as Anton walked in with Rapier "I was afraid I would never see you again."

"What are you still doing here? I'd hoped you'd hightailed it for home by now," Anton said.

"Uh . . . I . . . was hoping to find you first," Dedriek stuttered.

Anton smiled and clasped his brother on the neck. "Well, I'm glad you're here. I probably wouldn't have made it if you had stayed at home like I told you. Thanks, little brother."

"Remember how I told you we have an obnoxious British pilot at home? That is the reason I came searching for you in the first place, to find the resistance and get him out of there," Dedriek said. "He's probably driving Mama and Papa crazy."

"Well, that is one I won't worry about," Anton said, looking at his brother seriously. "Rapier and his men can worry about getting him out of Holland. I'm too tired. Let's head for home."

Dedriek put his arm around Anton's shoulder and helped him as he hobbled to the front of the barn. Anton looked back, waved to the men, breathed deeply, and headed out the door. "It has been quite a difficult experience," he said, "but I would like to just relax for a while, and mend in peace and quiet with Mama as my nurse."

Dedriek seems different, Anton thought. *He seems more cautious, and less rebellious. I think he has grown up a bit.* Anton smiled. *But I'm not going to tell him. It would go to his head, and there's no telling what I would have to deal with then.*

Dedriek helped Anton as they made their way into the countryside, stopping in short intervals to let him rest, lifting him over the rough spots, and making sure he had enough to eat and drink. When they came to a village, people watched them out their windows smiling. Others would stop on the street and nod at them respectfully. "Do you think they know who we are?" Dedriek asked Anton.

"Perhaps, but I think our tattered clothes and wounds are a big hint that we have been doing something to be a pain in the Germans backsides." Anton grinned. "We haven't been too quiet in the past few months." He laughed. He hit Dedriek on the arm pointing toward the dormant tulip fields. "Look, the beautiful tulips are gone. Their stems are dead, their life extinguished by the oppressive winter, just like Holland is bent and beat down with the oppressions of the Germans. But, look, one stem is peeking through the soil against all odds of surviving the winter. Yet it stands straight, as if it were unafraid of the peril it faces, strong, and determined to bloom again. It's like the people of Holland. It is a symbol of hope. And we, like the tulip with an undying spirit, will rise again to bloom in our crowning glory."

ABOUT THE AUTHOR

Lynne Leatham Allen grew up in Othello, Washington. After thirty years as a professional cake decorator, she is retired. She attended Ricks College and married her husband, Ross, in the Idaho Falls Temple in 1970. They have six children and now are empty nesters and live in Wellsville, Utah. She loves writing and sewing. She's an artist of charcoal, pastel, and color pencil portraits; oil landscapes; and acrylic tole painting. She is a self-taught artist and seamstress and has many hobbies ,including cross-stitch, hardanger, crocheting, knitting, candy making, cooking, gardening, and reading. Her writing career began with jingles and then graduated to humorous poems. Three years ago, she wrote her first children's book, *The Sugarplum Fairy's Little Sister,* which was awarded an honorable mention at the LUW writing contest in 2012. *Frogo and Turnip* also received an honorable mention at that time, and *The Courtship of the Ice Queen* received first place. She joined the LUW and has been writing ever since. *The Tulip Resistance* is her first novel. She is working on the sequel, with the tentative title *Operation Tulip.*